# LORD GRAY'S LIST

# LORD GRAY'S LIST

# MAGGIE ROBINSON

BRAVA

KENSINGTON PUBLISHING CORP.

www.kensingtonbooks.com

BRAVA BOOKS are published by

Kensington Publishing Corp.
119 West 40th Street
New York, NY 10018

All Kensington titles, imprints, and distributed lines are available at special quantity discounts for bulk purchases for sales promotions, premiums, fund-raising, educational, or institutional use.

Special book excerpts or customized printings can also be created to fit specific needs. For details, write or phone the office of the Kensington special sales manager: Kensington Publishing Corp., 119 West 40th Street, New York, NY 10018, attn: Special Sales Department; phone 1-800-221-2647.

BRAVA and the B logo are Reg. U.S. Pat. & TM Off.

ISBN-13: 978-0-7582-6909-6
ISBN-10: 0-7582-6909-9

First Kensington Trade Paperback Printing: November 2012

10 9 8 7 6 5 4 3 2 1

Printed in the United States of America

# CHAPTER 1

**December 5, 1820**

"This is the outside of enough." Baron Benton Gray tossed *The London List* on the floor beneath his breakfast table, where the new footman quickly scurried to pick it up.

"Burn it! No, wait. What is the business address of the infernal thing?" He should have paid attention to that two years ago, when the first of the scurrilous stories about him had appeared in print. Ben had assumed the attention would eventually fade away.

He'd assumed wrong.

Callum the footman blanched and smoothed the news-sheet between his spotless white gloves. "I dinna know, my lord. I canna read, my lord."

"Enough of the my lording, if you please. Tell Severson you want some reading lessons after your duties. All men should be allowed to read. Except I devoutly hope they turn the pages of something far more edifying than this rag. Give it over."

"Aye, my lo—" Callum blushed and thrust the wrinkled paper into Lord Gray's large hand. His gloves were now streaked with gray from the cheap ink that was spilling into Ben's life every Tuesday and ruining it.

"I need nothing else; leave me be. Colin, is it?"

"Callum, my lo—Lord Gray."

"Come down recently from Castle Gray, have you?"

"Yes, sir."

"How is the old place?"

This gave the young footman pause. "Old, Lord Gray."

Ben didn't doubt it. His ancestral home in the wilds of Scotland had begun as a humble fortified tower on a rocky promontory overlooking the sea. Centuries of wind and neglect had driven his mother back into the bosom of London society as soon as his bellicose father had the courtesy to meet an early end. Consequently, Ben had not been raised to tramp the hills in a kilt and kick sheep out of the way. No, Baron Benton Gray was a modern, cultured man, prosperous with his investment in Sir Simon Keith's railroad scheme and suitably celebratory. How dare *The London List* make him sound like he was the veriest devil? Veronique had had no objection to—well, Ben reflected, she never objected to anything. She was paid well not to.

Perhaps it was time to give her her conge. Let the talk die down. She'd been his mistress for seven months and that thing she did with her hips was beginning to feel old hat.

Ben scowled. How did his morning decline from smug satisfaction over his bacon to this depressing state? He was not going to give up Veronique!

Unless someone better came along.

*Not* a wife. Ben had avoided the slavering mamas—except for his own—for over a decade. He'd been successful, for the most part. One did not reach the advanced age of thirty entirely unscathed, however. There had been that misunderstanding with the Crittendon chit a few years back, and he didn't allow himself to ever think of Evie.

She must be over thirty now herself. Probably running

and ruining some poor man's life so that he longed for an early death. Ben hadn't heard a thing about her for ages. He'd stopped looking for her dark head in a London crowd once he'd found out she'd gone back to Scotland. Evangeline Ramsey was one reason he enjoyed living in London so much as a confirmed bachelor with as many mistresses as he could handle.

Enough of the sentimental journey. Ben poured himself another cup of coffee and opened up the distasteful newspaper. He skimmed the advertisements, chuckling only briefly when he came upon: *"A young woman from a respectable family, honest, hard-working, country bred, would like to correspond with a city gentleman for amusement and possibly more. Physical attributes are unimportant, though it would be helpful if said gentleman is under forty and in possession of most of his teeth and a modest fortune."*

Ben swiped his tongue over his even, fully intact teeth, dislodging a morsel of toast. He supposed he was a prime candidate, not that he was going to mix himself up with some uncivilized wench who probably had a hairy mole on the end of her chin. He pitied the poor people who were desperate enough to use *The London List* to try to solve their problems.

Blast! Where were their offices located? He began squinting again at the front page of the slender publication, avoiding the prominent article mentioning his recent activities in such lurid detail. He might have all his teeth, but he wondered if he was becoming eligible for reading glasses.

There was nothing the matter with his nose however. His mother was on her way into the dining room, her lily-of-the-valley perfume announcing her arrival quite a bit before she stepped through the door. He hastily shoved the paper underneath his bottom and plastered a smile on his face.

"Benton, darling, good morning!"

Ben angled a smooth-shaven cheek for his mother to kiss. Lady Emily Gray was a well-preserved forty-seven, her nut-brown hair only beginning to silver. She had practically been a child when she married and was brutalized by his father. The fact that Ben was the image of the man—large, tawny-haired, green-eyed—did not seem to stop her from holding her only child in deep affection. Sometimes too deep. She was most anxious to become a grandmother, and never ceased to remind Ben of his duty to his title, such as it was.

Lady Gray's slate blue eyes swept the table. "Where is it?"

"Where is what, Mama?"

"*The London List*. It's Tuesday. For that matter, where is Callum? Though I suppose I'm still capable of fetching my own breakfast."

"Let me get it for you, Mama."

Ben recognized his error immediately. If he rose to get her a plate from the sideboard, she would see the newspaper. For the life of him, he could not see its appeal. But everyone from the loftiest viscount to his valet seemed addicted to the thing. Tuesdays could not come soon enough. There was much speculation in the clubs as to the identities of the blind items, and servants were always seeking greener pastures in the employment columns. Ghastly young poets could pay to have their ghastly poems published, too. Something for everyone, whatever their station in life.

There were plenty of people to write for and write about. Ben was extremely tired of finding himself on the front page week after week. It was almost as if *The List*'s publisher had a particular grudge against him.

He was saved from discovery as his mother waved him

away and attacked the sideboard herself. She was pleasantly plump, convinced that she kept wrinkles at bay with a few extra pounds. Ben watched her pile her plate high with eggs, mushrooms, bacon, and toast, then returned to his own food, which was sadly cold after his perusal of the paper. But if he got up for a fresh helping, he'd be right back in his pickle. Sorry now that he'd dismissed Callum, he took a sip of lukewarm coffee.

"Did *The London List* not come with your post this morning? I knew we should have ordered more subscriptions."

Ben clinked his cup into its saucer. "More? Just how many do we get?"

"Well, Cook insists on her own copy. Severson as well. The maids share theirs, except for my dresser Barnes, who is far too top-lofty to share with anyone. I doubt she'd share with *me*. I believe a copy goes out to the stables. One for the footmen—"

"Callum does not read," Ben interrupted.

"Oh? I'll make sure Severson is apprised of that, although I'm sure he knows. He knows *everything*. He mentioned as I came downstairs that you managed to make the front page again."

*Damn.* So much for keeping his household, especially his mother, in the dark. If he'd counted correctly, he was paying for seven bloody subscriptions to announce his every peccadillo to the world.

"It's all a pack of lies!"

His mother raised a sculpted brow and took a forkful of egg. Once she swallowed, she said, "You are a grown man. How you choose to spend your time is, I suppose, your business. But you will never get a decent woman to marry you unless you curtail your notoriety. As it is, you're verging into desperate widow territory."

"Mama, I don't want a decent woman or a desperate widow. I have no interest in marriage, as well you know."

"Just because your father was a brute does not mean you will follow in his footsteps," his mother said, her tone remarkably mild.

Ben's father had died when he was a child, but not soon enough. He could remember every blow he and his mother had suffered under Laird Gray, and the pervasive feeling of hopelessness and helplessness had never quite gone away. His father's temper had been legendary, which was one reason Ben worked so hard to control his. To cultivate an attitude of laissez-faire. To permit the unpermitted without much fuss or bother. He was the epitome of utter affability. Nothing would ruffle his feathers.

Except for the damned *London List.*

"Perhaps I've not yet met the right woman," Ben parried, his tone equally light. "Maybe I'm not holding out for a desperate widow but a buck-toothed virgin with spots."

"There are plenty of those this year." His mother laid her fork down. "Let us be serious for a moment. I made a mistake in my marriage—or rather my parents made it for me. There were whispers about your father, but they ignored them. The Gray fortune was temptation incarnate."

"It still is."

"I'm not questioning your stewardship, Benton. Everything you touch turns to gold. Which is why if you put your mind to it, I know you could be an adequate husband. And father."

The portion of his breakfast he had eaten turned to a hard lump in his stomach. "I will count that as a compliment, Mama. High praise indeed."

"It is meant to be. I have faith in you."

His poor mama. He supposed all mothers were easily

gulled. Even his paternal grandmother had probably loved his father.

Ben changed the subject. "What are your plans for today?"

"Well, I'll have to cadge a copy of *The London List* from one of the servants. One can't start one's Tuesday morning without it."

With a sigh, Ben shifted in his chair and drew out the crumpled copy.

"Benton Alexander Dunbarton Gray! You devil!"

"I wanted to protect your delicate sensibilities, Mama. The article about me is pure rubbish." *Mostly.*

"My delicate sensibilities have gone the way of your good judgment. Hand it over."

His mother slipped her reading glasses out of a pocket sewn specially for them. For the next five minutes Ben was subjected to his mother's pursed lips and head-shaking. It seemed she needed to read the story about him four times, if following the pattern of her finger was any indication. But she was mercifully silent. Ben was relieved when she turned the page to the paid advertisements.

"If you don't plan to give me a scold, may I be excused from the table?"

His mother looked up, her eyes wavery under the thick lenses. "I'll scold you later. I wonder who is in need of 'a strapping young valet whose hands and teeth can make quick work of neckcloths and falls'?"

"Mother!"

"Oh, do be quiet, Benton. It's not as if I can shock *you*."

A pity she had such a low opinion of him, but she was right. *Mostly.*

Ben left his mother to her gossip and speculation. Braving the kitchen and Cook's opprobrium, he snagged an extra scone and her copy of the newssheet. Over his crumbs he found the offices of the paper buried between advertisements for the improvement of manly vigor and custom reupholstery.

*R. Ramsey, Publisher.* An odd coincidence that the bane of his existence shared the surname of his lost and unlamented love.

He had nothing better to do today but defend his honor and demand satisfaction or retraction. He was *not* going to sit in his club and endure the jibes of his so-called friends as they reminded him that he was the number one topic of conversation in the ton. Bad enough Severson gave him a gimlet eye as he assisted Ben with his coat against the raw December wind.

It would do him good to walk the distance to the newspaper's office. Work up his umbrage and indignation. His calves would get exercise, too. Ben wouldn't let a few nights of dissipation wreck his carefully crafted body. It was damned hard to stay fit in Town, but Ben did by fencing regularly at a private *salle d'armes.* Using his fists was far too reminiscent of his father's proclivities, so he left Gentleman Jackson's to others.

In a matter of half an hour, he had traversed quite a bit of fashionable London and stood before the impeccably scrubbed front window of *The London List.* He could see clear to the back of the rear brick office wall and the hulking black printing press which would be idle for the rest of the week. A young gentleman, his black hair cropped brutally short, shirtsleeves rolled up and jacket discarded, appeared to be tinkering with the source of Ben's choler. If the infernal machine was broken, that would save him the trouble of smashing it himself.

No. Ben had other methods of persuasion. He would make the fellow, or his employer if he had one, an offer no sensible person could refuse.

Ben startled at the tinkle of bells over the door as he entered. The printer turned abruptly to him, his welcoming smile quickly draining away, looking ready to faint onto the wide pine floorboards.

*By God and the saints and all that is holy.* The young gentleman was no gentleman. Ben felt light-headed himself as he stared into Evangeline Ramsey's parchment-pale face.

# CHAPTER 2

Evie supposed she might have seen it coming. Seen *him* coming. One could not expect to goad the ton's louchest libertine without eventual consequences.

At first skewering Ben almost weekly had seemed a fine lark. He made it so easy, he and his string of mistresses and equally ramshackle friends. It was as if he were following a pattern book of bad behavior. Disappearing under some courtesan's skirt in a pitch-black opera box? Tick. Cavorting nearly nude in Lord Egremont's garden fountain with Lord Egremont's wayward daughter and several other improper gentlemen? Tick yet again.

Poor Lord Egremont. Lady Imaculata Egremont had run away again and again, probably to escape the hideous name her parents had imposed upon her. No one should have to live up to being born "without stain." It was tantamount to ensuring that their daughter would seek all manner of staining activities. Evangeline had stopped writing about the family—it gave her no pleasure to air Lady Imaculata's tattered chemise in public any longer. And the truth was, her readership was bored with Lady Imaculata. Unless the girl did something truly spectacular—like take vows to become an Anglican nun—she had overstayed her few minutes of infamy.

Evangeline ran an ink-stained hand through her scandalously short ink-black hair. It was so much more convenient to be shorn like a man. When she had to don wigs to go undercover, as a footman or an actor or an Oxford student, there was much less heat and itch involved. In fact, it suited Evangeline to the ground to masquerade as a male. Made her business life simpler, too. People who braved her shop door rather than sending their adverts by messenger found a conservatively dressed young man who spoke little but lent a sympathetic ear to their predicaments. In her opinion, Evangeline provided a valuable service for society. She was matchmaker, employment agency, and patron of the arts all rolled into one. If it meant burying her useless femininity under a linen shirt and starched cravat, so be it. It was not as if she had much up top to be reckoned or wrestled with anyway.

And men moved around so much more easily in society—these past two years had been liberating to an amazing degree.

"You!"

Ben looked like a thundercloud, if thunderclouds looked like rumpled golden lions. He was, regrettably, more handsome than he was ten years ago when she had fallen so thoroughly in love with him that she had lost her virginity and her wits.

Evangeline decided to see how far she could get and lowered her timbre. "May I help you, sir?"

"Don't 'sir' me! You know perfectly well who I am. What the hell are you playing at?"

Evangeline put on her most vacuous expression, the one that had served her well so many times as she blended into the scenery. "I'm afraid I fail to understand you, Mr.—or is it Lord? I shouldn't like to cause any offense."

"You've caused enough offense for four lifetimes, my girl. I'm not taken in by your breeches. I've seen your bottom before, Evangeline."

It had been too much to hope that he wouldn't recognize her. As he had just so crudely stated, they had known each other *very* well.

Ben waved his arm wildly around her office. "How have you gotten away with all this?"

"Not everyone has seen my bottom, Ben. People see what they expect to see. To most, I am a young man with dirty hands and a printing press that holds the promise of their future. I've done very well with *The List*."

"At my expense! What does your father have to say about this?"

"He—he is not well." And if her poor father ever figured out exactly what she was doing with the failing newspaper he'd won over a hand of cards, likely it would send him to meet his Maker. Robert Ramsey thought the business that kept a roof over their heads and a nursing staff round-the-clock was managed by Evangeline's pressman Frank Hallett. Frank had higher aspirations than spending every Monday cranking out *The List*—he was an actor the rest of the week and had earned a standing ovation from Evangeline every time he reported to her father.

"I should think this career of yours would make him sick! And your hair! You look worse than Caro Lamb."

"I'm sure you didn't come here to discuss my hairstyle, Lord Gray," Evangeline said, her voice frosting. "And whatever the reason for your visit, I'm a busy ma—woman. You can't intimidate me."

Ben took a step forward. "Oh, can't I? What would your subscribers think if they knew the publisher is a woman masquerading as a man? I daresay you might become the scandalous subject of your own front page."

She expected the threat, and was prepared to parry it. "I'll stop writing about you," Evangeline said instantly. "Then you'll have no reason to divulge my identity."

"Too late! You've blackened my name for months. How can you ever make up for the ruination of my good reputation?"

Evangeline gave an unladylike snort. "You haven't had a good reputation since you were in short pants."

"Damn it! That didn't seem to bother you once."

"I was young and foolish. I'm older and wiser now."

"Yes," Ben said, looking down at her with his sea-green eyes. "You're a veritable hag. How old are you now, anyway? Thirty-three?"

"Thirty-two, my lord. Well past the age to be frightened of losing my own reputation. I'm not on the Marriage Mart, nor am I forced to seek employment as someone's demure companion."

"Demure!" Ben sputtered.

Evangeline shrugged. "Well, I was never that, was I? Our *affaire* proved that. The one regret of my life."

"Only one? How can you look at yourself in the mirror after the tripe you print week after week?"

"Very easily. *The List* puts food on my table and pays for very fine mirrors indeed." He didn't need to know the true state of the Ramsey household. Every penny went to her father's care and the repayment of his crushing debts. Evangeline was grateful she didn't need to waste money on all the accoutrements that seemed so necessary to adorn the females of the London species. Gentlemen's clothing was far more affordable. And comfortable. She doubted she'd ever go back to corsets and petticoats once—well, it hurt too much to think of what the future held. She'd have to spend the rest of her life as a withered spinster in some gray sack or other. Posing as a man would eventually prove too troublesome.

But for now, it suited her to the ground. Men like Benton Gray left her alone. Unless their tastes turned to almost-handsome boys—which had happened a time or two. Evangeline had very firmly appeared obtuse to their overtures and that had been that.

She was blessed with inordinate height, angularity, and the substantial Ramsey nose that saved her from true beauty. As a young woman she had been an abysmal failure with everyone. Except, damn his eyes, Baron Benton Gray.

Ben had been a beautiful youth, wild and impossible to resist. For several weeks, at any rate. Then her judgment returned—how could she shackle herself to a reckless compulsive gambler, no matter how lovingly he looked at her?

He was glaring at her now, his eyes stormy as the North Sea that surrounded his castle. Evangeline had seen him a great deal the past few months, although he'd never noticed the bewigged footman who'd passed him drinks— too many—or the youth at his elbow at a cockfight. He'd bumped right into her at the races the day he'd thrust his mistress on the back of his winning horse. Ben led an aimless life, one that should be exposed for all the ton to see. It was a criminal waste that a man of his wealth and instincts should be so dissolute and dissipated.

Dismissive. Disgusting. Disappointing. Evangeline could "dis" him forever, and had quite handily on her front page.

"I will cease and desist," she said, her husky voice made even thicker by nerves. "You've begun to bore me anyway. Your exploits seem increasingly—I don't know. Juvenile? Are you not getting long in the tooth to act like a fractious schoolboy?"

If she was not mistaken, he growled a little at her newly formed opinion. Evangeline thought she'd be assured of many more scandals to disseminate, but alas, self-preservation was key. If Ben dreamed of toppling her modest publishing empire, she'd better compromise. There would always be another foolish lord to write about—they were bred from the cradle to be useless idle creatures.

"Who owns this paper?"

"I do, my lord. That is to say, my family does."

"Which means your father, I suppose. R. Ramsey. Let me guess. He won it in a game of cards, just like he won your Portman Square house all those years ago. He always was a lucky devil."

Evangeline bit her lip. It rather depended what one's definition of lucky was. Her girlhood had been at the mercy of the next house party, the latest card craze, the deepest den of vice. Evangeline had dutifully followed her father, learning to make do or spend madly as the circumstances dictated. There had been no debut, but she'd managed to toss away her virginity to the handsomest boy she'd ever seen—the man who was looking at her right now as though he was undressing her all over again.

"That house is gone now. As you can see, we've come down in the world."

"But still close enough to your victims."

"The paper does a lot of good as well! Just last year we reunited Lord Pennington with his childhood sweetheart."

"If I recall, the poor soul died on his wedding night."

Evangeline showed a few teeth. "But he died happy." The truth of it was Lord and Lady Pennington were married a full week.

"I'm sure Lady Pennington is happy as well living it up on her widow's jointure. She was some sort of dairymaid, wasn't she? If a sexagenarian can be called a maid."

"She was a farmer's widow. A lovely woman." The kind of woman Evangeline wished had been her own mother. Warm, practical. They took tea together every other week at Pennington Place. Lady Pennington never batted an eye when Evangeline turned up in her high shirt points and carefully tied cravat. The woman fed her advice and lemon scones she made herself much to the consternation of her cook.

"I wish to speak to your father."

Evangeline swallowed hard. She should have known she couldn't get rid of Benton Gray so easily. "What for?"

"I can only assume he doesn't know the lengths you've gone to get your 'news.' I'll not reveal your methods, *Mr.* Ramsey, but I'll buy the paper from him. For enough to set you both up comfortably—and purchase you some skirts." He paused, his full lips twitching. "Although those breeches flatter you enormously."

"Stop looking at me like that!" Evangeline cried, feeling a hot blush sweep from her damp forehead to her throat. Benton Gray always unsettled her. To have him looming in her little office was enough to make her sweat. Despite her perspiration, she snatched up her discarded jacket and put it on.

"How the devil have you passed for a man? Your acquaintances must be blind."

"Most of my custom is done through the mails. And you cannot see my father. As I said, he is ill."

"I'm sorry to hear it." Ben reached for her pen and a piece of paper from her neatly arranged desk. Despite her best efforts, she was unable to read his scrawling script upside-down. He sanded his missive and folded it, leaving it in the middle of the desk. "Please give this to your father. It might make him feel better."

"He doesn't want to sell the paper," Evangeline said, stubborn.

"He will. And you should hope he does, for I'll not keep your secret, Evangeline. You must be stopped. At all costs. Fortunately for me, I have money to throw away. You've been watching me do it for two years now, haven't you? That's when I was 'discovered' by your roving reporter. You, I presume."

"You were hard to resist, my lord. So very conspicuous," Evangeline snapped.

"At least I'm not sashaying about London in *skirts,* Evangeline. You—you are unnatural."

"How dare you criticize me? With your penchant for nude frolicking and—necrophilia for all I know."

Ben raised a mocking golden eyebrow so high Evangeline fought her desire to bat it down. "Necrophilia? That's a stretch. One moonlit dance in the churchyard on All Hallow's Eve does not make me a grave robber. I assure you my partners are very much alive. And *satisfied.*"

"Hah!" Evangeline could not seem to manage a more suitable riposte. Even when Ben was a stripling, he'd been a satisfying sort of fellow. His large hands, his gentle mouth, the sweep of his tongue—

But he paid his partners now. All five of them she'd kept count of these past months. The fake Frenchwoman Veronique was just the latest in a long line of expensive courtesans he kept in his little house on Jane Street. She'd lasted longer than the others, though, so there must be some depth there beyond her fluctuating French accent.

No, not depth. He wouldn't appreciate depth. Benton Gray was as shallow as he was genial. Although in truth he didn't look especially genial at the moment.

Evangeline smoothed down the lump of sleeve beneath her padded jacket. While her shoulders were broad for a woman, a little tailoring was necessary to complete her transformation as a young gentleman. In an hour she'd go home for lunch and change into something insipid and muslin and check on her father. She most certainly was not going to upset him with any sort of business transaction with Baron Benton Gray.

Let Ben think her father rejected his offer, whatever it was. No matter how generous. He was not going to waltz in here and destroy her livelihood.

"Well? Will you take it to him?"

Evangeline slipped the folded paper into the inside pocket of her coat. "You are wasting your time."

"Ah, but I do that on a regular basis, don't I? At least according to your featured articles. Let's shake on you delivering that letter to your father. Man-to-man." He extended a well-manicured hand to her, his signet ring flashing in the sunlight streaming in through her window.

With the utmost reluctance, she placed her smudged hand against his. A ripple of awareness coursed through her, stiffening her nipples and causing the hair at the back of her neck to tingle. *Oh dear.* What was it about this dreadful man that caused her body to go on alert? She was an experienced thirty-two-year-old independent woman, not some moony virgin. Grimly she gripped his hand and shook it hard enough to rattle his teeth.

"A gentleman's handshake," Ben said softly. "Don't disappoint me, Evie. I'll be back tomorrow to hear what your father says."

"Suit yourself." But it didn't suit her. At all.

# CHAPTER 3

Ben found it somewhat difficult to hide his bulk as he lurked near *The London List*'s office. He spent an inordinate amount of time in the tobacco shop opposite—he who did not smoke. Smoking was one vice he did not care for at all. But his friends were fond of their after-dinner port and cheroots, so he deliberated with the deferential shopkeeper over flavor and value, all the while keeping an eye on Evie's shadowed form beyond the glass across the busy street. He noted she'd taken off her jacket again and had wiped her brow with a large handkerchief several times. Doubling over, she went back to tinkering with the black behemoth of the press and he lost her from his line of vision for too long. When she popped back up, she'd torn up some papers, stomped around her desk, and thrown a pen clear across her floor.

So, she still had a temper. Ben remembered that temper very well. Evie enraged was a force to be reckoned with— by some other man. Lord Benton Gray worked too hard on his amiability to test it with a termagant.

Just as his stomach informed him it must be lunchtime, Ben saw her slip out her door, rigged out now as a respectable gentleman. A beaver hat covered her black curls—really, what a shame her one true glory was so butchered—and she fielded a walking stick as though she were leading a march through the Alps.

Ben made a great show of drawing out his pocket watch. "Oh! I've just remembered an appointment. Where do you suppose Mr. Ramsey is heading? Off to gather up dirt on an unsuspecting innocent? " Ben asked.

"Regular as clockwork, he is. Visits with his old ailing father from noon until two."

"Wrap these up and send them to this address," Ben said, digging out his card from its embossed silver case and jotting his address.

"Very good, my lord. Thank you for your custom. I hope you enjoy these and that I'll—"

"Yes, yes." Ben dashed out the door and turned the corner. Evie's backside swayed rhythmically as she walked up the street at a brutal pace. In Ben's opinion, no amount of tailoring could hide her womanly form. Marveling again that anyone would be stupid enough to take her for a man, he kept a safe distance behind her until she turned on to a short, shabby street. Ben watched as she let herself into a mustard-colored house with a key, closing the door gently behind her.

What to do? Confront Robert Ramsey while his dragon of a daughter was home? Ben thought not. If the tobacconist was reliable, Evie would be safely back at work by the middle of the afternoon. And then the field would be clear for Ben to inform Ramsey of his intentions.

Satisfied with his plan, Ben strolled back to the better neighborhood of his club. Any hope he had of slipping in, sinking into a chair, and having a quiet whiskey and soda with a bit of beef on the side was dashed almost at once. Ben was immediately hailed by his old friend Jack Stanforth, armed with the latest copy of the bloody newspaper.

"There he is! The—what did they call you?" Stanforth

squinted down at the enormous headline. "The Jane Street Jackanapes! However did you get your Veronique to ride naked on your shoulders in the middle of December? Great sport, what? Courtesan races! A pity your competition withdrew at the last minute."

It had seemed a good idea at the time. Jane Street, home to the most sought-after courtesans in London, was not very long, and Veronique was light as a feather. But some of the girls had put their delicate feet down and refused to let their protectors participate. Ben had felt somewhat foolish jogging down the lane alone—if one didn't count a giggling Veronique—but he had issued the challenge and was required to hold himself to it. His back had not been quite right since.

He was getting old—too old for such silly games. Evie, damn her, was right to mock him.

"That was my farewell fling, Jack. I'm turning over a new leaf. Becoming respectable at long last." If he said it, he'd have to make it true. But in case he had a lapse, that dratted newspaper would not be around to publicize it.

His friend raised a gingery eyebrow. "Not you, Ben. What will we read about on Tuesdays?"

There was no way he was going to confess to Jack that he was going to buy and then shut down the gossip rag. "Some other poor soul will have to be the object of *The London List*'s derision. I'm done."

"I don't believe it. I've known you practically all my life, Ben. Never met a fellow who was more fun. The rest of us poor married sods live through you vicariously. You know I couldn't hoist Mariah on my shoulders—six children tend to ruin a woman's figure, although I tell her I love her just the same. There's just a lot more of her to love."

Mariah Stanforth had been plump when Jack married her. He'd always had a weakness for fleshy women, and in truth was delighted about his wife's *avoirdupois*. Ben, on the other hand, seemed to be attracted to slender, haughty brunettes with large noses and deep voices.

Damn. A few minutes with Evangeline Ramsey and he felt like a stupid schoolboy. She had been his first love— hell, he had wanted to *marry* her until the night she broke his heart. Now it appeared she wanted to break his standing in polite society. He could not let her get away with it any longer. Once he spoke to her father, they could slink back to Scotland and he would be free to live life as he chose to.

But what, exactly, did he want to do? He was thirty years of age. Rich. Handsome, he supposed, although his wavy blond hair had a mind of its own and refused to be tamed. He might supplant Veronique with a heavier girl— maybe a redhead this time. He might even sell the Jane Street house and move back to Castle Gray and learn how to be a mason and count sheep.

*Blast*. He wasn't going to that drafty outpost on the sea. He'd go mad without Town amusements, and by the time he would learn of new investment opportunities, share prices would have tripled. No way was Baron Benton Gray going to isolate himself from where the action of the Empire was. That was London. He may have been half-Scottish—the worse half—but he was a city boy now through and through. Damn Evangeline Ramsey for making him think. Question his life. He was happy, by God, with his whore and his friends and his whiskey.

Ben waved to a passing waiter and ordered some of that whiskey. He spent the next hour listening to Jack brag of the boring exploits of his too-numerous infants, wondering if his friend didn't realize gentlemen came to clubs like this to escape such domestic discussions. When the mantel clock struck two, he excused himself, realizing too late he'd forgotten to order a sandwich for his grumbling stomach. He sauntered slowly back to Evie's home, careful to watch for her long form wending its way on the sidewalks. Screwing up his determination, he rapped upon the mustard-colored house's mud-brown door, thinking the whole place could use a refreshing coat of paint. Ruining his reputation was perhaps not as lucrative as Evie had said.

After Ben spent an interminable time standing on the crumbling front step, the door was finally opened by a frazzled housemaid who looked in need of a good meal and a wash, not necessarily in that order. Ben slipped his card and few shillings in her hand. "Lord Gray to see Mr. Ramsey."

She gawped at him with large blue eyes. She was, he supposed, pretty enough, or would be if the soot were off her nose.

"The Jane Street Jackanapes?"

Ben tamped down a wave of irritation. Of course Evie's servants would have first crack at her paper—everyone in Town seemed to consider it the Tuesday Bible. "The very same."

She made no move to open the door all the way, standing there with her mouth half-open.

"I say, it's chilly out. December, you know. I promise not to snatch you up and run down the street with you. May I come in? I have an important business matter to discuss with Mr. Ramsey."

"He doesn't receive visitors." She began to push the door closed. Ben stuck his large, well-shod foot in the gap.

"I'll give you a pound if you let me in."

"Two," the little maid said quickly.

"Extortion of the first order. Why am I not surprised?" Ben mumbled as he reached into his pocket. He followed the maid up the stairs, noting the lack of decoration in the house and the extreme sway of her hips. Everything appeared scrupulously clean though—except for his extortionist.

"Thanks, love. My name's Patsy in case you want to treat me kindly in the future. I'll let his nurse know you're here. But if he's having a bad turn, you're out of luck."

"I don't suppose I'll get my money back either."

"We've all got to make hay while the sun shines. Wait here, sir."

She knocked softly on the door at the end of the corridor and slipped in the room. The air in the hallway was stale and smelled of too much heat. Ben shrugged his greatcoat off in anticipation of being allowed in to see Evie's father. He rattled the knob of a nearby door and poked his head in. The room was as spare as a monk's cell, but on the dresser was a wig form with a dark curly updo sitting askew atop it. Evie must be in disguise at home as well as out in the world.

"Lord Gray? I'm Mrs. Spencer, Mr. Ramsey's day nurse. How may I help you?"

Ben turned to face a plump matron. He turned on his dependable charming smile. "Good afternoon. I am here to see my old friend. I trust his health will permit a short visit? I have something of great import to discuss with him."

The nurse frowned. "I doubt he'll understand anything you have to say, Lord Gray. His wits are often befuddled. Today is one of his more lucid days, but I don't believe Miss Evangeline would approve of you seeing him."

"Evie? It was she who sent me," Ben lied. "It's to do with—I trust you know about Mr. Ramsey's ownership of *The London List*?"

"If you're here to harangue the poor man about what was written about you, you must know he has nothing whatever to do with the paper. That's all Miss Evangeline and Mr. Hallett."

Another regular reader. Ben didn't have any idea who Mr. Hallett was—no doubt someone who was in league with Evie to besmirch him further. "Yes, I know. And I wish to relieve them of the burden. She is the sole support of this household, is she not?"

"Aye," the woman said, her brows knitting. "And don't judge her. She's done the best she can under the circumstances. Mr. Ramsey got them in a terrible fix. He gambled, you know. And when he lost his memory, he couldn't count his cards. Made foolish wagers he didn't remember. His debts were prohibitive. The only thing he had at the end was that rackety newspaper and a mountain of vowels, and Miss Evangeline is finally settling them and making a go of *The List*."

"At my expense. Surely you would like to be employed in a household not dependent upon scandalmongering."

Mrs. Spencer looked him in the eye. "Miss Evangeline prints only the truth."

"Her version of it," Ben snapped. "I'm here to buy the paper. Settle an exorbitant sum upon Mr. Ramsey so he and Evie—that is to say, Miss Ramsey—can go about the rest of their lives comfortably. In Scotland. Or anywhere they like, as long as they leave London."

"You'd do better talking to Miss Evangeline."

"But she is not the owner of record now, is she? Come, Mrs. Spencer. You've done your guard duty and warned me off. Let me see the man for myself. I promise you, I won't take advantage of him."

The nurse worried her hands in her apron. "I shouldn't."

Ben smiled again at her, turning on his vaunted charm full blast. "But you will. You care about the family, I can see that. And I have the wherewithal to improve everyone's situation here. You must not stand in the way."

"You won't cheat him? He's had enough of that."

"On my honor as a gentleman—and I am a gentleman, despite what Miss Ramsey has written—I intend nothing but the best for the Ramseys."

He waited a tick while the nurse edged over to his point of view, keeping his impatience hidden. It was not often he had to work so hard to get what he wanted. Usually his good humor swayed even the most recalcitrant individuals.

Except for Evie.

But he had been young then, too young according to her. Too unpolished. Well, he had a blinding gleam about himself now.

"Very well. But don't tire him out. I'll be right in the hallway on my chair, trying to hear every word."

"I'll speak up, then, Mrs. Spencer. I've got nothing to hide."

The nurse led him to the end of the hallway, where a plush but worn chair was indeed stationed right outside the door. A basket of mending sat on a rickety side table.

"Mr. Ramsey," Mrs. Spencer said brightly, with that false voice adults sometimes use on children, "look who's come to see you! It's Lord Gray!"

Ben's eyes adjusted to the gloom of the room. The dark curtains were drawn against the thin winter light and draft of cold air coming through the window that managed to circumvent them. There was no smell of sickroom, however, and Evie's father was not abed. He was seated at a small table, shuffling a tattered deck of cards between trembling fingers. He looked up, and Ben could see the intervening years had not been kind to him. His once jet-black hair was white, and the beaky Ramsey nose was more prominent than ever in his gaunt face.

"Ben Gray, is it? My, my. Have you come for my Evangeline at last? I won't hold it against you that you didn't come up to scratch before, y'know. Boys will be boys."

"Good afternoon, Robert. I'm afraid your daughter wouldn't have me then, and surely won't have me now. I believe she holds me in some aversion."

"Ah! That silly paper of hers. I know she helps Frank Hallett with it sometimes. Bookkeeping, editing, that sort of thing. Don't credit anything in it." He waved a hand. "Sit down, my boy, sit down. A hand of piquet, perhaps? A penny a point."

Frank Hallett again, but Ben was fairly sure *The London List* was entirely Evie's domain. He eased himself down in the chair opposite. He imagined Evie sat in it, keeping her father company. Keeping vigil. "I'm afraid I haven't come to play cards, sir, but I have come about the newspaper."

"Can't sue me for defamation. Look around you. The place is a dump. Haven't a turnip to suck blood from. Doctors take it all. The lot of them quacks. Have me chewing bark from some damn tree and drinking the most vile potions. Evie won't let 'em bleed me, thank God. Day nurses, night nurses. Wilfred—you remember Wilfred?— always lurking about to make sure I don't wander off and get lost, too. My mind's shot. Won't bore you with the worst of it, because I can't remember half of it. Hah! Poor Evie." He cracked a smile, revealing the charming old gambler he used to be.

"I don't want to sue you. I'd like to purchase *The London List,* though," Ben said, getting right to the point. If this was one of Robert's more lucid afternoons, he'd better make haste. Ben named a figure, impulsively doubling what he originally thought was fair and had written down for Evie to deliver. He could afford it, and it was clear the Ramseys were in dire straits. The debts must have been crippling for them to come to this pass.

"You're mad. No, that would be me, wouldn't it?" Robert chuckled, though his dark eyes remained bleak.

"Not mad. I hope my faculties are as intact as anyone's. But I am somewhat perturbed to see each and every breath catalogued each and every Tuesday. I take it Evangeline didn't mention my offer when you took lunch together."

"If she did, I simply don't remember," Robert shrugged. "Evie does hold a grudge, but not with me. Don't know why she takes such good care of me. I wasn't much of a father."

Ben silently agreed. Robert Ramsey had dragged his impressionable daughter throughout the British Isles and the rest of Europe in search of an elusive golden jackpot. It had been feast or famine for the Ramseys, probably one reason Evie had been so reluctant to throw her lot in with the youthful, feckless, gambling Ben.

She might have noted in her constant investigation of his activities that the only risks he took currently were on the Exchange. He wagered now in only the most minimal way, as any gentleman did to pass the time and keep boredom at bay. He had never been struck with her father's fever, but at twenty-two—older than he by two long years—Evie had thought she knew everything. She had seen what she had wanted to see—a careless, good-natured youth anxious to rub elbows with more experienced men at the tables. Become a man of the world. She had helped in that effort, and not entirely against her will.

Only her better judgment.

Gad, but there was no point in crying over spilt milk. He'd been better off without Evangeline Ramsey to harass and harangue him in person—bad enough she did it in the poisonous pages of her news rag.

"What say you, Robert? I mean to make my offer

tempting—you could leave this address, perhaps go to Italy to get out of the worst of the winter."

The old man turned up a card. The Jack of Hearts. He slipped it back into the deck and continued to shuffle. "It will be rainy season there. The south of France might be better. A jolly Joyeaux Noel, what? Evie might like that now that Boney's settled."

"Anywhere in the world, Robert," Ben said with patience he did not feel.

The Ace of Spades dropped to the table, and Robert's mouth turned down. "I'll have to talk to Evie. She won't like it that you're here, going behind her back."

"I spoke to her this morning. She knows full well that I intend to buy the paper from you. In fact, I charged her to make my offer."

"She may have . . . but I don't think so. We had toasted cheese, though. My favorite."

Ben could sense the man withdrawing into his private world. Robert's mouth slackened and his eyes slipped from his cards to a corner of the room.

"We can draw up a simple agreement now, right here. I'll get my solicitor to work up something more formal if you wish later. I'll place no stipulations on the sale—you'll have the full amount before the day is done."

Robert was silent for a long while, lining his cards face-down on the table in a concentric circle. When all fifty-two had been placed where he wanted, he nodded his head. "I'll talk to Evie."

"This is in her best interest, Robert." He waited a beat. "Do you know she goes about town dressed as a man?"

To Ben's surprise, the man's eyes lit. "Does she now? She used to do that. When she was a girl. Sometimes the places we were—it wasn't quite safe for her to be a young lady. I'm sorry for that."

Ben played his own last card. "Robert, she's a girl no longer. Imagine the scandal if people discovered her disguise. She'd be shunned. If you sell me *The London List* there will be no need of her to risk her reputation. You'll have enough to provide her with a handsome dowry." Not that any man in his right mind would ever marry Evangeline Ramsey—Ben's offer was more than generous but still not enough to sufficiently bribe some poor soul into losing his heart to that vixen.

"All right, all right. You can have the paper. I don't care anything about it."

"Truly?"

"Aye, I said it, didn't I? Let's shake on it before I forget I did. You say you'll get me the money today?"

Ben breathed an inward sigh of relief as he took the old gentleman's hand. "You have my word."

It would be a scramble, and his banker wouldn't like it, but Baron Benton Gray was not a man to be argued with. In haste, Ben opened up the small leather-bound notebook he always carried and sketched out the terms of their agreement with a pen he found on the dresser. He signed it with a bold flourish, then tore the page from the book. "If you will sign it yourself, now, I'll get to the City this afternoon to make the arrangements."

"Get me my spectacles, boy."

Ben's honor made him oblige, and he sat for a few uncomfortable minutes while Robert seemed to be committing his words to memory. A white eyebrow raised. "We're to leave London?"

"I think it for the best."

"Evie won't like that either. I think, on the whole, I'd better cross that part out and you can initial it."

Ben bit his tongue. What difference did it make where Evie was, as long as she wasn't sneaking around after him at night and writing about him in the morning? Her platform would be closed, locked up, the balky printing press sold or destroyed. Ben would rent the space to some other business and that would be that.

Before he left, he shook Robert's palsied hand again, nearly wanting to spin the old gambler around and kiss him. Ben's life was about to get back to normal at last.

# CHAPTER 4

"You bloody bastard!"

Ben ducked from the whoosh of what he thought was a walking stick, though it was too dark to see. The youth who wielded it as a weapon was no youth, however, but Evangeline Ramsey, rigged out in evening clothes. Her top hat flew off with the force of her sweep and rolled into the gutter in front of his townhouse.

"Good evening, Evie," he said genially. "Come to thank me?"

"You arrogant son of a bitch! How dare you go to my father? He—he's not in full possession of his faculties!"

"He seemed quite well to me this afternoon. He reminded me a bit of my great-uncle Mackenzie. As Uncle Hal aged, he became forgetful at times, but other days he was as sharp as a tack. Even Mrs. Spencer said this was one of your father's good days."

In the flickering gaslight, Evie's face was as white as the silk scarf she wore wrapped around her throat. "I don't care what she said! You had no right to go to the house today. I told you I would discuss the sale of the paper with him."

"But you didn't."

"I would have! I didn't have the opportunity."

"Shush. You'll wake the household. Why don't you come in with me and we can discuss this like . . . gentlemen."

Evie expelled a breath, her huff a white cloud in the frigid air. How long had she been lurking in front of his house? The woman was mad—this might be Mayfair, but footpads were known to strike with impunity throughout London. And the air was damp with moisture. Judging from the ring around the moon, it might even snow before dawn.

"You must be freezing."

Her tone certainly was, icicles dripping from each syllable. "I am perfectly fine."

Ben doubted it. She didn't have an ounce of fat on her—she probably didn't even have to bind her breasts for this ridiculous masculine masquerade. She was not wearing a greatcoat, and impulsively he slipped out of his and tossed it across the pavement to her.

"Here. Put this on before you sicken yourself and have no one to care for your father."

"You—you—*bastard*."

"Now you're repeating yourself. I thought you had a famous way with words, Evie. Even I have to admit that 'The Jane Street Jackanapes' does have a certain ring to it."

"As if you didn't deserve it! I've only printed the truth. And now you've cheated me out of the paper!"

"Cheated? Did your father disclose what I paid for the damned thing? You can hardly object, Miss Ramsey. You might even attract a fortune hunter so you might know wedded bliss."

"I'll never marry. Not after—" She stopped herself. "Oh, this is useless. I should have kept better rein on my temper—you're not worth the effort." She turned away, but Ben's arm shot out and stopped her.

"Come inside. I'll arrange for my carriage to bring you home. It's not safe for you to wander about the city at night."

Evie struggled beneath his gloved hand. "I'll be fine. I'm always fine."

"So you say. You look tired, my girl. And snow's in the air." As if on cue, a tiny flake swirled and settled on Evie's crisp black hair. Ben had an unaccountable longing to brush it off, but he kept hold of her elbow as she continued to pull back with a fair degree of determination.

An imp whispered in his ear, and he released her as she tugged away, causing her to stumble and fall flat on her backside at his feet. She looked up, her great dark eyes glittering with fury. Praise God for the invention of lamplight—she was as beautiful as she would ever get in its glow. Really rather magnificent. Ben looked away.

"You—you—"

"I believe we've established the word you're looking for is *bastard,* although I assure you my parents were married, more's the pity." Deciding quickly, he bent over and scooped her and her hat up as if she didn't weigh even a stone. She was too light in his arms. All her braggadocio about the paper's profits didn't seem to spell an extra éclair for her. "Come, Evie. Let's cry truce. You must want to do something else with your life besides follow me around and advertise my indiscretions."

She wriggled in his arms, causing a frisson that could have been assuaged by his visit with Veronique tonight but had not been. "Where are you taking me?"

"I told you. I'm going to deposit you in my library—"

"You read?" she asked scornfully.

"Of course not. The books are hollow, all for show," he snapped. "Certainly I read. I'm not the stupid boy you knew a decade ago. For your information, there are even *two* libraries in this house. We will have a brandy, and I will see you home."

"I don't drink."

"You used to," he said, a cruel reminder of what went wrong—or right—between them.

Before he had a chance to mount the steps with her, the front door opened. Callum stood in nervous anticipation, the hall light glowing behind him.

"Where's Severson?"

"Gone to bed, my lord, with a touch of the gout. He begs your pardon most sin—sincerely."

"And Lady Gray?"

"She sent word that she is staying the night at Lady Applegate's. Her friend is also unwell."

Lady Applegate was, in fact, dying a little bit every day. His mama was a mainstay in the Applegate household, and had probably spent the day reading *The London List* out loud to amuse the invalid. Ben would go himself in the morning and see what he could do to assist her and the family.

There was no further need for a bleary Callum to prop himself up in the hall chair. Ben kept a generous supply of brandy on the shelf along with various improving tomes in his private library.

"Go to bed, laddie."

"Is this gentleman unwell also?" Callum blurted.

Ben realized Evie was still crushed to his chest, no matter how she writhed in his grip.

"Dead drunk." He was rewarded for this prognostication by a sharp elbow to his ribs.

"Shall I make coffee to sober him up, my lord? My mam taught me how."

"Nay, Callum. I've my own method in dealing with inebriation. Dinna fash yourself," Ben said, breaking out his limited Scots brogue. "Go on to bed now. I'll deal with Mr. Rams—Montague." It would not do for the household to cotton to the fact that the ex-publisher of *The London List* was trapped in his arms.

"I hope Mr. Rams-Montague improves, my lord. Shall I wake up Lizzie to make up one of the guest rooms?"

"I don't believe that will be necessary." When would this stripling leave them alone? Callum's earnest ambition was beginning to grate, and Evie's elbow was like a knife to his gut.

"Verra good then, my lord. Good night to you, my lord, Mr. Rams-Montague." With an absurd bow, Callum left them standing in the pool of light. Ben blew out the candle in the sconce and marched to the rear of the house, where he had turned what had been intended as a housekeeper's office into his small library. There was a larger room upstairs, with leather-bound and gilt books, maps and charts and all the other accoutrements of a civilized English gentleman, but this little room was his simple bolthole.

"Put me down at once or I'll scream," Evie gritted against his shoulder.

"No, you won't, Mr. Rams-Montague. You'll frighten that boy to death. And gentlemen don't scream." He set her down in a leather chair, his coat still wrapped around her too-slender frame, and set about coaxing a fire out of the languishing coals in the grate.

He'd spent time in here earlier this evening before he'd seen Veronique, planning what he was going to say. She had taken it remarkably well, perhaps because she was as tired of courtesan contests as he was, and even offered a farewell fuck, which he had politely declined. Ben had assured her she could remain on Jane Street until she could find a new protector. Hell, he'd even offered to find one for her—he might dispose of his mistress and the charming little house all in one fell swoop. It was time he sold the Jane Street property and did the unthinkable.

Damn Evangeline Ramsey for putting him on the path to boring respectability. His mama would be happy even if he felt the noose tighten around his neck. In response to his mental dread, he loosened his neckcloth and went to the shelf. What had come over him today, all this talk of turning over new leaves and dismissing mistresses? Perhaps he'd wake up tomorrow, moderately wicked again and glad of it.

"Brandy, port, or Madeira? Or perhaps some good Scottish whiskey?"

"Nothing, thank you."

"Oh, don't be stubborn, Evie. You're as cold as a block of ice." He poured them both a healthy tot of brandy and stood before her with the glass. She refused to meet his eyes, but took the glass from him with stiff gloved fingers.

Impulsively he took it back and set both glasses down. "Let's get your hands warm." He stripped the kidskin from her hands and tugged her over to the fire before she had a chance to curse him. Evie's long fingers seemed frozen, as was the rest of her as she stood like a statue in front of the flames. Ben rubbed her skin, feeling unladylike calluses on each fingertip. Bookkeeping and editing indeed. If he wasn't mistaken, Evangeline Ramsey was a mechanic. She probably scaled fences to trespass and spy and delivered bundles of newspapers herself to his neighborhood, too.

"Who is Frank Hallett?"

She startled at his question, still making no attempt to escape his attentions. "My pressman. I'd appreciate it if you kept him on. He needs the work."

"Keep him on?"

"Yes. He knows what he's about, most of the time."

Ben dropped her hands. "I'm afraid you don't understand. I'm shuttering *The London List*. I'll have no need of a pressman."

Evie looked up at him now, her lovely mouth falling open. "I beg your pardon?"

"Did you think I bought the bloody business to dabble

in destructive gossip? I have no quarrel with society, Evie, and people can go back to using reputable employment agencies for their servants. I don't imagine they've been best pleased that you've stolen their fees from them."

"I haven't stolen anything! Those agencies take money from both the employers' and the employees' pockets, and don't really care where they place people as long as they get their money. My advertising rate is most affordable. If you don't wish to write about your idiot friends, I quite understand. But the rest of the paper—"

"Will be done. People can wrap their fish in something else."

Evie's cold hands were clenched. Ben sincerely hoped she wouldn't spring forward and punch him, as she looked very ready to do. "But people depend upon *The List*!"

"They'll find some other amusement. This is London, after all."

"You bastard!"

Ben hid his annoyance with a smile. "Yes, yes. We've already established your appellation for me, inaccurate as it is. I suppose there's no point in sitting down and drinking our brandy. I'll see you home."

To his surprise, Evie marched to the table, tipped her head back, and downed her glass in one long swallow. Her neckcloth had wilted, and he was able to see the white of her throat. No wonder her shirtpoints were so high—they concealed the Adam's apple she did not have. Ben's own mouth dropped open as she picked up his glass and gave it the same treatment.

"I thought you said you didn't drink," he needled.

"This occasion calls for it. You have singlehandedly destroyed all that I've spent two years of my life building up, and ruined the lives of countless others."

"Ruined the lives?" Ben asked, incredulous. "Because they can't read rubbishy poetry and exchange love notes?"

"You may mock, but for some, *The London List* has been their lifeline. You try being buried in the country with no prospects. A harmless flirtation through the personal ads may result in a lifetime of happiness."

"If you're referring to the marital state, surely you jest."

Her lip curled. "What would *you* know of marriage?"

"What would *you,* unless you've already killed off some other poor idiot foolish enough to ask you to marry him?"

"I've had offers besides yours. I'm particular. I have standards." Quite at odds with her words, she collapsed in a chair, her legs sprawling. This masquerade of hers had engendered very bad habits.

Ben snorted and poured himself another drink, pointedly leaving her glass empty. He took a punishing sip. "Look, Evie, I'm sure you see yourself as a regular Joan of Arc, come to save England. But somehow we're all going to manage without *The London List.* I know *I* am. I cannot wait to wake up next Tuesday to a breakfast devoid of speculation and scandal, not to mention the knowing smirk from my butler."

Ben turned to her, the smirk on his own face dissolving as he watched silver tears slither down Evie's pale cheeks. "You can't be crying! You have no reason to cry. Think of the money I settled on your father." A blasted fortune for a building in an indifferent neighborhood and a business he knew nothing and wanted to know nothing about. His banker had complained, his man of business *would* complain, and here Evie sat in misery as if he'd killed a basket of puppies. Her hands trembled as badly as her father's as she wiped the tears away, her thick black lashes clumping.

"Here. Stop this now," Ben said, handing her a snow-white handkerchief.

"I cannot stop just because you want me to. I'm not your mistress ready to take your every direction." Evie hiccupped and blew her nose in a significant blast. Veronique would never have made such a noise, but then her nose was much smaller than Evangeline Ramsey's.

No point to thinking about Veronique. He was done with that aspect of his life. He supposed he'd have to go to Almack's when it opened and look for a buck-toothed virgin.

WIFE WANTED: One reasonably attractive young lady of pleasant disposition and some wit to spend the next three or four decades with a reformed rake in marital harmony if not bliss. Childbearing hips preferred to silence the imprecations of his mama.

Good grief. He was not still tied to his mother's apron strings. He wouldn't marry because of his *mother*. Why, just this morning, marriage was the furthest thing from his mind. How had it come to pass that he had dismissed his mistress and was now constructing a personal ad for a publication that he was definitely, definitively removing from breakfast tables across the country?

Ben couldn't spare the time to think about his life-changing decision now, for Evie was quaking as if she sat on top of a volcano. Her sobs were altogether alarming, far surpassing the dead puppy level. He hated to see a woman cry—it reminded him of all the nights he lay huddled with his mother after one of his father's rages. Emily Gray had been a brave young woman, but even she had her limits, and was sometimes unable to conceal her marital un-bliss.

"Please don't cry anymore," he begged.

Somehow he took Evie up from the chair and in his arms again. She quivered like a willow in the wind. He rocked her as she sniffed and snorted and spread nasal mucus on his second-best jacket. He didn't care. The press of her fragrant body against his robbed him of all thought.

She was wearing a man's cologne which he found unusually stimulating—sandalwood and spice and something else which filled his senses and made him do a very rash thing.

He cupped one wet cheek and kissed her, tasting salty tears and the lingering taste of cheroot and brandy. By God, she'd been out doing who knows what before she lay in wait to ambush him—smoking, certainly. A filthy habit. She couldn't keep parading about as a man—his hands told him that she was very much a woman as he brushed down the curve of her back to her pert derriere and held her close.

At first her mouth opened merely in surprise, but soon she returned the parry of his tongue with a tentative riposte of her own. The years dissolved and Ben was once again a twenty-year-old youth, lost in the flush of first lust. His erection warred with the plackets of two pairs of breeches, and the fire became unbearably hot. Wool and linen fell away to their feet, aided by two pairs of scrambling hands, the kiss never breaking but deepening. Ben ignored the feeble warning bell that sounded just beyond sanity. He had kissed dozens of women in the past decade, but none were Evangeline Ramsey. None had touched him, tormented him like she did. None had broken his heart as she had.

*Rubbish.* He had no heart to break.

But his desire—now that was a tricky thing. He lifted her shirt—she still wore her cravat, for God's sake—and skimmed Evie's white skin. She was chilled again, her flesh speckled with goose bumps. Ben himself was an inferno of heat, the blood rushing to the surface and fairly lifting the golden hair on his arms. Evie's inky fingers were now entwined with the hair on his head, and he wished she would move them lower. He took a step toward the hearthstone rug and stumbled, hampered as he was by crumpled small-clothes and trousers at his ankles. If Callum came in now, he'd expire of shock. Or laugh—there was no doubt Ben was a semi-naked fool.

But still the kiss went on, a desperate affair now as their bodies slid against each other like raw silk. Ben tugged down the wrapping Evie wore to conceal her feminine charms. Her nipples were diamond-hard from cold. Ben drew a slight breast into his palm, thumbing the pebbled point until she shuddered against him, their unbroken kiss absorbing her sound of pleasure. If they both didn't topple over amid tangled clothing, he intended to maneuver her to the floor and fuck her senseless. It seemed she had stopped crying, and there was no scruple stopping him from finishing what they had started.

Floors were good. Floors were fine. Floors had been their friend ten years ago, and walls as well. There had been no time for finesse or feather mattresses, or even un-dressing. He had taken her on a piano bench once as he recalled, with Evie riding him as his elbows rested on the keys and his hands gripped her slender waist. The music they'd made had been jarring, but there had been no ser-vants present to complain of the cacophony. Evie had been unchaperoned, a daring, dangerous girl to a twenty-year-old Ben. Irresistible. Insatiable. Until that last night.

No, he would not think of her bitter, cutting remarks, not while she was soft in his arms, her tongue tangling with his, the tip of her proud nose pressed into his cheek. He angled her face so she wouldn't suffocate and slowly dropped them both to the floor. Somehow she wound up atop him, her damp curls taunting his flesh. He plunged his fingers up into her center to find the evidence of her desire, a flow of nectar caused by one hopeless, heartfelt kiss. A drunken kiss, but Ben wasn't particular tonight, not when a decade's worth of longing was about to be resolved. The taste of brandy and tobacco and yearning coursed through him, sweeter than anything he'd consumed in years. The fact that Evie's long fingers gripped his shaft to guide it home was only icing on the sensual cake.

Every cell awakened, leaped into the flame. She was so tight. It was nearly painful for him to forge into her, but she must not have minded, as she pushed down against him, ever efficient. He was swallowed up in one fierce plunge, surrounded by hot wet honey. He opened his eyes to see hers—feral, black as printer's ink—staring straight back at him, too close for comfort, their lips still engaged in the dance. He broke away reluctantly, feeling an absurd need to say something—anything—to her. To stop this madness if he had to, although he was perilously close to spilling himself already. Shaking her head, she placed a trembling finger across his mouth and rose above him, her curls lit like polished ebony in the firelight.

He felt blinded by her beauty, though she was nothing like his recent conquests. He had sought comfort with softer, easier, more pliable women—pillowy women who were paid to keep their tongue, or use it to wicked effect. Wanton women so very unlike Evangeline Ramsey that Ben was nearly bludgeoned by his own stupidity.

He felt something for her still, and had sought escape from that inconvenient emotion for a third of his life. Calf-love, never grown, a great moo-y mess of need and want. Impossible. Insupportable.

But an indisputable fact. And what would happen when Evie sobered up?

But she wasn't so far gone—two glasses of brandy couldn't bewitch her into losing all her good sense. She'd not seemed inebriated when she sought to assault him at his front steps. She moved above him now with deliberate grace, twisting and turning until he stopped worrying about their future altogether and concentrated on their present. He was buried deep in the woman he both hated and loved and would not want to be anywhere else but on his hearth rug, tangled up in evening clothes and Evie.

# CHAPTER 5

What was she doing? The obvious answer—riding Benton Gray's cock like a Jane Street whore. She had come tonight to murder him—oh, not with her cane but her words. To tell him she hated him for going behind her back and taking advantage of her poor father, for living a wastrel's life and robbing her of her own accomplishments. And had anything she'd said stopped her from falling disastrously into his arms again?

She could not blame it on the brandy—she'd drunk far more of the stuff trying to loosen an informant's tongue on many other occasions. She would blame it on her traitorous tears instead—men never could resist them, which was why she never, ever gave in and let herself weep no matter how many reasons she had to cry. She didn't need anyone's pity. Evangeline had taken care of herself her entire life and was good at it. Damned good.

With a few exceptions. Well, one. She'd been unable to guard her heart from a reckless, smiling boy, a boy who played deeper than her father and was therefore a terrible risk. A risk she could not afford then and could not afford now. Ben had done nothing this past decade to indicate that he'd changed one unruly hair on his golden head.

She shut her eyes so she could not see his satisfied smirk

as she bounced atop him. No, smirk was not right—he wasn't smiling as if he'd gotten his just deserts. In fact, she saw as she cracked one eye he wasn't really smiling at all, but looking as if he was in absolute bliss. Ridiculous. True enough, their coupling did feel good. Extraordinarily good. Evie realized with a start that any gentleman she'd taken to her bed in the last ten years—all two of them—had never managed to breach the chill around her soul like this stupid man beneath her. Whatever one could say about Baron Benton Gray, he was not mechanical or miserly in his attentions.

And he'd only gotten better, judging from that elegant twist that made her flex helplessly around him. He had no further need to hold her in place—his cock did that completely—so his hands moved up to her aching breasts beneath her shirt. Evangeline shivered as he circled and swooped, his fingers causing a flush of swollen pink heat to spread across her skin. She stared down to where their bodies joined, dark curls to golden, an inch or two of his cock exposed each time she lifted—no, flew—up. Higher and higher and faster and faster until she cried out his name and tumbled across his broad chest.

She realized her mistake at once—she'd given him no time to withdraw before she clamped down and milked him. His seed was still spurting within her as he thrashed below, gripping her tight. She was too exhausted to panic now. She'd panic tomorrow. Or later today, as midnight had long since come and gone.

This evening was the worst night of her life. She'd gotten nothing that she'd come for—not job security for Frank or opportunities for the countless desperate people whose letters arrived on her desk daily. Her recent life's work was in ruins, as was her resolve. She was at the mercy of a useless lord, a typical female who'd fallen for a pretty face and pulsing cock, heedless of the consequences.

Evangeline felt like punching someone—herself, really, although Ben's firm chin was so very tempting.

They lay in silence, covered in sweat and the scent of sex, the only sound the crackling fire. His arms did not relax but instead held her firmly against him. He was still seated within her, still hard, still hot. Another frustrated tear escaped from Evangeline's eye and dripped onto his shoulder, lost in the slick sea between them.

She couldn't blame him. It had been she who kissed him back. It had not occurred to her to draw away and slap his face or stomp his foot. Her fingers had fumbled with his cravat and his falls and the two of them had been so precipitous their limbs were still partially strangled by their garments. She still wore her stockings, for goodness' sake.

And one evening shoe.

Evangeline had had an appointment this evening with the reclusive, stammering Lord Maxwell. She had gone to his modest home to assure him that his quest for the next Lady Maxwell was fully in train despite the fact that her ownership of *The London List* was now in question. She had given her word—her *gentleman's* word—over a Spanish cigar that the poor man would be married by Christmas. The terms of his great-aunt's will were quite specific—it was either marriage for him to inherit or continue on as a bachelor in less-than-genteel poverty. He was in such despair he had not noticed when her voice had faltered and became more feminine. If he had, no doubt he would have turned scarlet and bungled his words.

Lord Maxwell was not at ease with the fairer sex. Unaccountably, he became so tongue-tied that a complete, comprehensible sentence was impossible for him. When Evangeline finally got him married off—and she would no matter what Benton Gray had to say about it—she planned to reveal to him he had been negotiating his future with a female all along.

Maxwell deserved his chance at happiness, unlike the vexing man beneath her. Benton Gray had squandered any right he had, fornicating his way through society and frittering away his income. *Courtesan races.* Contemptible.

Ben seemed unaware of her current scorn. His shaggy tawny hair haloed his too-handsome face, gleaming against the dark threads of the carpet. His eyes were closed in repose, thick fringes of eyelash shadowing his skin, the quirk of his lips proof that he was satisfied indeed. The man didn't have a care in the world now, did he? Spent, satiated, smug in his mastery of her. Damn him to everlasting hell.

Evangeline elbowed him. "Let me up, you brute."

His arm did not relax even fractionally. "Not yet. Don't spoil this, Evie."

"Spoil it! This whole evening is rotten to its core."

"Yes, you did try to kill me. Or at least incapacitate me in some way." He didn't sound the least troubled by her earlier assault upon him.

"You deserve death, not that I wish to hang for removing a feckless boil upon society such as yourself."

One clear green eye opened. "Feckless boil? What a wordsmith you are, Evie. Surely that's something of an exaggeration."

"Is it? What have you done to earn respect from anyone who's not a libertine? Your drinking, your gambling, your whoring—why, you're legendary."

Ben shifted underneath her but still did not let her go. "And you and your silly paper have made me so. There's not a literate soul in London who doesn't think they know everything about me, but they don't. *You* don't know me at all, Evangeline. You never did."

"Don't know you?" Evangeline sputtered. "I only wish I didn't! I can't believe—" She broke off, too disgusted with herself and her current situation. To her dismay, Ben gave one more thrust to remind her exactly where she was and whom she was with.

"Now, no regrets, sweetheart. You wanted this as much as I did."

"You flatter yourself. I was drunk."

Ben raised an infuriating golden eyebrow. "On two glasses of brandy?"

"I—I had been drinking before I got here," she admitted.

"Smoking, too, I'm sorry to note."

She felt her cheeks grow warm. She'd had a few sympathetic tots of Lord Maxwell's inferior brandy and a fairly vile cheroot when the idea came to her to confront Ben. And then she'd been forced to take a nip or two from a small flask of equally tepid stuff to keep herself warm on the frigid December night as she waited for him to come home. Who knew what licentious activity he'd been participating in? She thought she'd fall asleep on her feet on the street.

"So, your inebriation explains your clumsy aim. At least you'll have no more excuse for your unnatural adaptation of a man's worst habits. Lovely as you look in breeches, Evie, it's skirts you'll be wearing from now on."

"How dare you tell me what I may or may not do!" Truly furious now, she struggled in his arms, but he effortlessly flipped her onto her back and nuzzled her throat. His weight was not quite crushing, but she was pinned beneath him. She slapped his back with all her might, which only drove him deeper.

"Your movements are having the exact opposite effect of what you seek, my dear. You're not going anywhere, and neither am I."

"You would rape me? I'll scream the house down!"

"No one said anything about rape. Don't lie and say I

forced you." The breath of his words buzzed against her neck, and she shivered.

No, he had not forced her. She had been completely complicit.

"Please stop."

"I admit I do not want to." He raised himself and looked into her face. "There is still something between us, Evie. I don't like it any more than you do."

He was so very beautiful. Too beautiful. Even more handsome now that he'd grown into his height and breadth. He'd been rangy and a bit gangly at twenty when she'd let him seduce her.

No, she'd seduced him, more fool she.

"How very flattering. At least we can agree on something. We hate each other."

"I don't hate you, Evie," he said with sad softness. "I make it a practice not to hate—it drains one so. Think of the last two years you've wasted hating me in print."

"You made it too easy, my lord," she snapped. And he had—she'd almost pushed him out of her mind until she'd returned to London to man the paper her father had won. But there was Baron Benton Gray, the ultimate libertine, cutting a sexual swath through the ton with cheerful, heedless grace. His antics had infuriated her and roused a need for some sort of retaliation. He seemed to be managing his life quite nicely without her, even after his pledge of enduring love. Rubbish. She'd known the emptiness of his words then, and knew it now.

"I've done nothing more than what most men of my acquaintance do. Could you not have been seeking some other kind of amusement rather than vengeance? A vengeance I didn't deserve, by the way. It was *you* who rejected *me*." As if to take the sting out of his words, he tapped her nose with a forefinger. Ben looked completely at ease hovering over her, untroubled by the heat and scent between them.

"My stories had nothing to do with our misbegotten past. I need to get home," she ground out. "My father . . . I never know how his nights will be."

"So how then have you managed to spy on me? I hate to think I've kept you from being a dutiful daughter."

"Some things are worth doing." Pointedly, she turned her head and counted the crammed shelves that lined one side of the little room. Most of the books had not been covered in tooled leather and gilt, and showed obvious sign of wear. Of someone reading them many times over. Benton Gray? The idea seemed absurd. When would he have time when his every waking moment was spent in debauchery?

"Whose books are these?" she asked.

"Mine. I told you that. And if you want to be seriously impressed, I could escort you upstairs to the true library in the house, but then we'd have to get dressed." He nibbled all too casually at her earlobe. For once Evangeline wished she had all her hair back so she could cover that sensitive spot. Most of the time she did not miss the snarling mass of coarse black hair that had defied taming, but right now she wished she could veil her face with it and shut herself off from Ben.

He still pressed her into the soft carpet, the quality of the weave so high she could not complain it was making her bare bottom itch. Ben seemed enamored now with the spot just under her ear and was giving it altogether unwelcome attention. Evangeline swallowed a cry and sank her fingernails into his shoulders. "Get off me."

He lifted with lightning-like speed, withdrawing his cock from her passage with ruthless efficiency. Her damp skin puckered with the loss of his body heat as she struggled to sit up. He remained on his back, staring at the pattern the fire left on the ceiling.

"This must not ever happen again, Ben. I cannot imagine why I was so foolish to let myself be taken in by you." Her voice wavered, diminishing the intensity of anger she surely felt, mostly at herself. She might even be pregnant, and then her life would be ruined for sure.

"Whatever you say, my dear."

His drawling words infuriated her further. "You could be pox-ridden for all I know." She tugged up for the crumpled strip of cloth she used to bind her breasts, not that she needed it.

His hand stayed hers. "Evangeline, I urge you to examine me," he said, each word dripping ice.

Her eyes darted to his cock, curled now in its nest of golden hair. There were no blemishes to be seen, but that meant nothing. She was about to tell him so, but he squeezed her hand, causing her considerable discomfort.

"Do you really think I would bring you to harm if I were diseased? What kind of man do you think I am?"

"I know what kind of man you are! You—you—"

He pulled her down so they were virtually nose to nose. "I have had my share of fun, but have been very careful. Careful with my person as well as preventing any unwanted issue."

"You forgot yourself tonight!" she snapped.

"Yes, I did. And for that I am sorry. Sorrier than you know. Imagining being tied to you for the rest of my life is enough to make me long for a quick death. The pox would be too slow."

Evangeline could feel the color leach from her face. "Perhaps you can step in front of a brewer's wagon then, or induce one of your fake French mistresses to murder you. If the unthinkable happens, I would never ask you for a single penny to support a child. I would certainly never marry you!"

"I haven't asked. Recently," he said, his lips a flat, angry line.

Evangeline was dizzy from the shift of their physical bliss to emotional warfare. Ben radiated fury that was almost touchable, his hand still fastened on hers like a cockle. She had made a dreadful mistake coming here.

"This is a ridiculous conversation. Let's just forget this night ever happened."

"Drunk, were you? So in your cups you consented to fuck me?"

"Yes, exactly! What was your excuse?"

Ben dropped her hand and she pulled back, trembling from cold and temper.

"I was not drunk, Evie, or in any way addled. Except, perhaps, by you."

Evangeline grabbed up the clothes within her reach and mashed them to her chest. She didn't think she could stand quite yet. "What do you mean?"

"I don't know. When I held you, I forgot the reasons why I shouldn't."

"They are legion."

"Yes. You've tried to ruin me with your poison pen, Evie, and for that I should not forgive you."

"D-don't then." She shivered despite the cozy rumble of the fire.

He raised himself up on an elbow, his sweat-slicked skin glowing in the flickering light. "I don't have enemies. No one except you, that is. What have I ever done to make you hold me in such contempt? I admit I didn't know what I was doing with you when I was twenty, but surely you cannot hold me responsible for failing to satisfy you all those years ago."

Oh, he had satisfied her. Ruined *her* for other men. Why that was, when he was just an aimless, brainless—

There were all those books now, so perhaps he wasn't the dim creature she thought him. But he was not a serious man. He was a rake and a gambler.

And a man too lovely for her own good.

"You have nothing more to worry about. You own the paper, and I cannot bother you again."

He actually *chuckled*. "Your very existence bothers me, Evie."

"Do I need to fear that you'll murder me in my bed?"

"That's not precisely what I'd like to do in your bed, God help me. Let's part as friends."

His chiseled lips were turned up, as though he hadn't a care in the world and they hadn't just said the most dreadful, cutting things to each other. What was wrong with him?

"I'll get dressed and then we can shake hands if you think that will mean anything."

"As one gentleman to another? I've got something else in mind. Something far better than a handshake for you to remember me by."

Evangeline was never quite sure how the rest of it happened, but her clothes were forgotten in a jumble as he kissed her. Everywhere. And she, God help *her,* followed suit, tasting the salty come on his cock until he spilled again as she came apart beneath his tongue. He was wicked and evil, and his concept of friendship was entirely foreign.

After, he woke his sleepy driver and nearly had to carry her to his carriage, her legs were so weak. But Ben sent her off alone, which was a blessing. Her mind was as useless as her legs.

# CHAPTER 6

*December 12, 1820*

Ben was dreaming. He was vaguely aware it was probably his own hand on his rock-hard cock, but he preferred to think he was inside Evangeline Ramsey, her long sinuous body brushing against him instead of the linen sheet. The dream was taking a particularly poignant turn when he woke to the sight of his mother standing over him, brandishing a clutch of newspapers in her hand. When they came down upon his head, he hastily removed his hand and tucked a pillow over the tented bedsheet.

*Damn it.* He felt like an errant schoolboy. What on earth was his mother doing monitoring his self-pleasuring? He was thirty years old—he'd not had a woman in a week. Evangeline. And it was, by God, barely light outside. What the hell time was it?

"Mama! Is something wrong?"

"You tell me! What is the meaning of this, Benton?"

Ben could feel himself turning red. "Now, Mama, men have urges, you know. And I believe I was asleep. You cannot hold me responsible for my nocturnal—"

"Not that, you stupid boy! This!" She shook the papers again and he rolled away from further abuse.

His mother was rarely angry. Since the death of her husband, she emanated nothing more heated than a strong sense of relief. Even when Bad Ben had been at his worst—which was often—his mother had been remarkably calm. She was not calm now, quivering in indignation, and still in her dressing gown.

"I'm afraid I have no idea what you are talking about."

"You have put *The London List* out of business!"

"I have. I should think you'd be pleased. You'll be much more able to digest your breakfast on Tuesday mornings."

Wait. Today was Tuesday. There should be absolutely nothing in his mother's plump hand, but it looked very much to Ben in the dim light that his mother had a raft of newspapers there. How many? Seven? Wasn't that the number he'd been paying for so that his entire staff could mock him weekly?

Ben's jaw twitched. "What's that you've got there, Mama?"

"The last edition ever of *The London List,* according to the publisher, a young gentleman named"—she squinted at the print—"Mr. Ramsey. He says you lied and cheated him out of the paper so that you could continue your wicked ways and keep your indiscretions to yourself. Fat chance of that! You are a byword, Benton Gray, of loose morals and louche behavior and I don't know what else. And now you've taken advantage of a poor old man. I'm disappointed in you, Ben."

Ben did not know which of his mother's sentences to address first. Clearly he had underestimated Evie. Should he have sent her flowers after that unbelievable night last week? Locked up the newspaper office? Taken a pickaxe to the press? He'd given the business barely a thought as he'd tried to reform himself.

Well, fuck reformation. His own mother thought he was beyond salvation.

"I am sorry you hold me in such low esteem, Mother,"

Ben said, his tone as frosty as the white haze on the windowpane.

"Oh, don't go all haughty baron on me, Ben. I'm sure there's more to this story than is printed on the page. Why don't you tell it to me?"

Ben lifted his chin and folded his arms, remembering his father in just such a pose before the apoplexy took him to warmer climes. "As you can see, I am not dressed. If you will give me the courtesy of a few minutes, I shall meet you downstairs in the dining room."

His mother bit a lip. "Very well. Severson seemed most anxious to talk to me about something when we met on the stairs. The man is agitated, and that's not like him. Don't be long. Here, perhaps you should prepare your defense." She tossed a single copy of the newspaper on his bed.

He was not going to pick it up and read Evie's lies. He may have deserved some skewering before, but he had done nothing now but ensure that she and her father could live in the lap of luxury for the rest of their days. He'd even found that fop Frank Hallett at the theatre and paid him more than a year's wages of severance pay.

But nothing was ever enough for Evangeline Ramsey.

He could have her prosecuted for trespassing. For surely she had entered *his* building and used *his* ink, *his* paper and *his* machinery to produce this latest calumny. Damn the black-haired witch.

Ben conveniently forgot just what his dream black-haired witch had been doing to him not a quarter of an hour ago. His ardor was definitely depressed now—finding one's mother hovering over one when one was at the *non plus ultra* was a withering experience.

He splashed some chilly water on his face, not bothering to ring for his valet. There was no point to shaving—he'd go right back to bed once he'd dealt firmly with his mother, but he did manage to get into fresh clothing. A glance in the mirror told him his golden stubble and disordered hair only added to the dangerous look he was trying to cultivate. He was not about to be called on the carpet by his mother—if she didn't care for the life he was living, she could go back to Scotland and be damned.

This was all Evie's fault. Even in his sleep she was a distraction. Ben had hoped that one night would get her out of his system for good, but apparently that was too much to hope for.

He didn't take the stairs in his usual bounding pace, but one could delay the inevitable but for only so long. When he got downstairs, there seemed to be some disturbance outside on the street, but he walked resolutely into the dining room to get this over with.

His mother was not there. Lord, if she was decking herself out for the day, he might be alone until luncheon. Callum was nowhere to be seen either. Ben wondered how the reading lessons were going, and debated if he should take a hand in them himself. He had more than enough time now that he was trying to give up his wicked ways.

He lifted silver lids and started putting food on his plate, not that he was remotely hungry. As he sat, there was very audible banging at the front door below, most unseemly for a neighborhood such as his. And it was devilish early for guests. Perhaps poor Lady Applegate had taken a turn for the worse.

Ben swallowed a mouthful of hot coffee and was just about to cut into a thick slice of steak when the dining room door burst open. Six or seven strangers in varying stages of dishabille and obvious disgruntlement stared at him from the doorway, a red-faced Severson elbowing his way through the throng. After some shoving and curses from all quarters, the butler quelled the motley crowd with his perfected *froideur* and turned to his employer.

"I am sorry, my lord, but I was unable to prevent these—*persons* from entering. Callum has the door barred from the rest of them."

Ben put his knife down, although perhaps that was unwise. He picked it up again. "The *rest* of them?"

"Aye. Easily a dozen more, sir."

There was more pounding. And a rather distinctive shriek.

He knew that shriek. He'd heard a version of it a week ago when Evangeline Ramsey had come apart in his arms. But he doubted his ex-lover was fornicating on his front steps. He rose.

"Severson, would you please admit Miss or Mr. Ramsey as the case may be. Now, ladies and gentlemen, what may I do for you before I call the watch?"

"Oi, there's no need of that, guv. We've come to talk some sense into you." This from a rather large man in workman's boots and a threadbare cap. The others nodded in agreement.

"Indeed. And in what way am I deficient in sense, my good man?"

"You've shut down *The London List,* my lord," said a diminutive, spinsterish looking woman. She, at least, was dressed like a lady, unlike the rabble that had accompanied her. She was garbed in plain and neat brown from head to toe, but seemed fully at peace with her comrades-in-arms.

"Yes, I have. And if you wait a minute, Miss or Mr. Ramsey—depending—will be able to provide proof that I am not the monster she—he—painted me out to be." The group stared at him as if he'd lost his mind, and he was afraid he might be in the process of doing so.

"You robbed a poor old man," said a freckled youth, who looked much too young to read a newspaper.

Ben gritted his teeth. "I did no such thing. He was well-compensated for the sale of his enterprise. Ah, E—

'ere 'e is. At last. Would you kindly retract the fiction you printed in this morning's paper?"

Evie was flanked by Severson on one side and a rather oily-looking fellow on the other. She was in trousers, a tartan scarf wrapped practically up to her nose. She had the grace to look ashamed, as well she should be.

"I tried to stop them," she mumbled through the wool.

"Not very successfully. I thought we had an agreement, *Mr.* Ramsey."

"You never said I couldn't publish a farewell edition."

"I never said you *could*. I suppose you have another key to the building." Ben held out his hand. He wasn't quite sure where his was, having had no interest in setting foot in the premises last week, or ever again, for that matter.

"I—I need to get back in to get the last of my things." Her voice was not as husky as it might have been, and the oily fellow shot her a suspicious look.

"Then I'll have the distinct pleasure of escorting you. The key, please. I seem to have misplaced mine. How convenient there's another. You've saved me the trouble and expense of hiring a locksmith for *my* building."

Evie dug into a pocket and handed over the heavy metal key with reluctance.

"See here, Ramsey. Don't let him bully you."

"It's all right, Lord Fitzhugh. He's fully within his rights."

*Fitzhugh.* Ben had heard the name before, although the face was not familiar. Evie's champion was slender, dark-haired, and had a neatly trimmed moustache over rather damp lips. His clothes were exquisite, and Ben had an urge to knock him into the sideboard and cover him with shirred eggs.

Fitzhugh spoke up, his voice plummy. "You are right. 'He who fights and runs away will live to fight another day.' With my backing, you won't need this barbarian.

We'll establish an entirely new newspaper, something that will eclipse *The London List* and set all these good peoples' grievances to rights."

There was a murmur of approval from the little clot of people in the doorway. Even Severson looked pleased, damn him.

Ben felt an unaccustomed wave of something that felt a lot like fury. "Let me get this straight. You plan on founding another scandal sheet?"

Evie looked him in the eye, a martial gleam in hers. "Only if you refuse to resurrect *The List*. You don't have to report on the gossip, but these people deserve an outlet for their needs."

"Their needs? Just what might they be?" Ben asked, his voice arctic.

"I have been corresponding with a Mr. Jefferson through a box at the paper each week," the little brown spinster said. "If there is no paper, there is no Mr. Jefferson. He has no way to find me, as I naturally did not use my real name in my correspondence. I'd like to get married, my lord." She opened up her reticule, pulled out a scrap of well-worn newsprint, and began to read. " 'A respectable mature bachelor, intelligent and sober, is desirous of immediately marrying some neat, plain, economical woman, between the ages of thirty and fifty. Reply to Mr. Thaddeus Jefferson, Box 81.' He seems like a most amiable gentleman, and I was just about to arrange to meet him at the British Museum. We share an interest in antiquities."

Ben suppressed a snort. This Mr. Jefferson was probably an antiquity himself.

"I'd watch out, dearie," said a vulgarly dressed woman in the back. "He probably wants to tie you up and cane you or some such thing. And when a man claims to be sober, you can bet he drinks like a fish every chance he gets."

The spinster colored. "Well, I'll never find out, will I? Lord Gray has ruined my life!"

"And mine," said the freckle-faced boy. "I was this close to being hired by Lord Meacham. He's got the best stable in Dorset. He was to tell me where to meet him when he came to Town, but now I'll never know."

"And I'm looking for my Bertha," the workman said. "She left home two months ago. I'll take her back, no questions asked."

"Oh, you're the one who wrote those affecting couplets," the spinster said. " 'Please come home, my sweet Bertha. Life without you has no mirth-a.' "

*Mother of God.* These people had to get out of his house. He didn't begin to want to know why the whore was here.

"Very interesting, all of it. Perhaps you all will allow me to discuss this over breakfast with E—Mr. Ramsey. If you would kindly disperse, sh—he will notify you of our decision."

"You heard his lordship. Move along now," Severson said severely, probably trying to earn back Ben's trust. Not for a minute did Ben think the butler had legitimately been bamboozled by this unprepossessing group.

"Yes. I promise to meet you all in front of the newspaper office in"—Evie looked at Ben for help—"two hours?"

"I certainly think that will give us time to discuss these pressing press matters," Ben quipped.

"I shall stay," Fitzhugh said.

"You shall not," Ben retorted, irritated. What was Evie doing with this overly familiar man? He was far too beautiful for his own good. In fact, he seemed the sort to prefer his own sex—

And then Ben smiled. Poor Fitzhugh, tricked by Evie's snug breeches.

"It's all right, Lord Fitzhugh. I'm not afraid of Lord Gray."

*You should be,* thought Ben, as he firmly closed the dining room door.

# CHAPTER 7

Ben pulled a chair out for her and Evangeline sat down glumly. This morning had been unexpectedly atrocious. She'd never dreamed that a crowd would begin to mill around *The London List* office before dawn, apprised of the regime change early by her crew of fleet-footed delivery boys. By eight o'clock the uproar and unrest was out of control. Worried what they might do, Evangeline had accompanied the group—which forcibly reminded her of torch and pitchfork-bearing Luddites, although their intent was not to destroy machinery but ensure its continued use. But she didn't want harm to befall Ben, not really, so she'd tried to calm them down as best she could. When that glacial butler wouldn't let her in with the self-appointed "representatives," she'd howled in frustration.

"I'll ring for fresh coffee."

"Don't bother. I—I *am* sorry, Ben. I didn't anticipate this reaction. But now that you've seen what the newspaper means to people, perhaps you will change your mind about discontinuing it."

Ben leaned back in his chair, looking like a delicious, disheveled large cat. His jaw was sprinkled with gilt stubble, and his fair hair curled in poet-like disarray. He was quite a contrast to Lord Fitzhugh, who fancied himself an actual poet. Fitzhugh's offer to sponsor another newspaper had come as a shock, but Evangeline had jumped on it. Perhaps if Ben felt a bit threatened, he'd relent and let her run *The London List* for him. She'd put out the last issue entirely on her own, as that coward Frank Hallett had refused to help her. Ben had bribed him all too generously, Evangeline thought in disgust.

She stared down at her hands, black with ink. She hadn't had a chance to grab her gloves before the lynch mob had decided to storm Baron Gray's castle. Her warm greatcoat was still hanging on its hook, too. All she really wanted to do was crawl back into bed—she'd been up the whole night through gentling her recalcitrant press to produce its final edition.

But perhaps not. Evangeline widened her dark eyes, then let her lashes drop, fluttering a bit at the end.

Any hope that she had harbored to somehow brazenly seduce the bastard over breakfast was dashed by a rapid knock at the door and the entrance of a plump, handsome older woman.

"I see the coast is relatively clear. I thought it best to remove myself from the fray, Benton. Is this young gentleman the previous owner of *The London List*? If so, I'm pleased to meet you, sir. You've given me an enormous amount of pleasure, even when you pilloried my poor son. Were it not for you, he might just be coming home from a misadventure on Jane Street." Lady Gray extended a hand, and Evangeline wondered whether she was expected to kiss it. She had been forced in the past to perform such acts of politesse, but somehow she couldn't bring herself to do it. Reluctantly, Evangeline grasped the woman's soft hand and shook it with more manly force than was necessary.

"Good heavens!" Emily Gray's blue eyes narrowed. She dropped Evangeline's hand as if it scorched her. "Benton Gray, what is going on?"

"I'm being blackmailed by Ramsey here. I expect he's going to organize a mob to parade in front of our house all day unless I put that damned newspaper back in business."

"R-Ramsey?" Lady Gray stared at her with acute focus. Evangeline wanted to disappear down into her scarf, but instead examined a three-tined fork on the table before her. She felt the rough wool of her trousers chafe her thighs, and suddenly wished to be far, far away from Lady Emily Gray.

The woman looked as if she wanted to say something, but instead she dropped to a chair gracefully and turned to her son. "Benton, would you fetch me a muffin from the sideboard? All this excitement has depressed my appetite, but one has to eat to keep body and soul together."

"Certainly, Mama." Ben rose and selected a toasted muffin, then poured his mother a cup of coffee. Evangeline's throat was suddenly dry, but she'd already refused his offer of sustenance. But coffee—she'd been up all night and was dead on her feet. Well, dead on her arse as she came under the speculative gaze of Ben's mother.

"Ben, dear, fetch Mr. Ramsey some coffee, will you? He looks peaked."

An understatement. Evangeline nodded gratefully and soon had a fragrant cup in front of her. She took a cautious sip, but the pot had cooled while the rabble roused. It was still warm, though, and tasted like ambrosia. Her stomach rumbled, but eggs were out of the question. The sooner she got away—

"So, what are we going to do?" Lady Gray asked brightly.

"*We?* Don't trouble yourself, Mama. Mr. Ramsey and I will come to some sort of accommodation, I'm sure."

"I do hope so. Severson's nerves are quite overset." Lady Gray took a delicate bite of muffin.

"Severson's a damned traitor."

"Now, Ben. I advised him to allow a few of the petitioners in. They were attracting a great deal of curiosity from the neighbors, and it's very cold out this morning besides. Do you think it might snow later, Mr. Ramsey?"

Evangeline was not even up to a sensible discussion of the weather. "I'm sure I couldn't say," she murmured.

"I do—did—enjoy your weekly weather predictions. So often inaccurate, but then we live in England and must be prepared for anything." Lady Gray folded her napkin. "I shall leave you two to hammer out the details of the newspaper's disposition. I don't for a moment believe my son cheated your family, although you do write eloquently. It's a gift. I'd put it to better use if I were you."

Lady Gray stood. Ben did also, and Evangeline scrambled up to join him. Sometimes it was difficult to remember that she was impersonating a man—there were ever so many ridiculous rules and requirements. She still had not learned to spit properly.

When they were alone, Ben looked at her with the same sharp expression that his mother had trained upon her. "You've really done it now, Evie. What the hell are we to do?"

She straightened in her chair. "It's obvious, Ben. Keep the newspaper running, at least until you can sell it to someone else. Lord Fitzhugh might be interested."

"That's not the only thing he's interested in. I believe you have an admirer, Evie."

"Nonsense. I'm quite sure he doesn't know I'm really a woman. And he only likes me because I've published his execrable poetry without batting an eye. Any writer is a slave to praise, no matter how faint it is."

Ben barked a laugh. "My mother's right, you know. You do write well, even when you are accusing me of all sorts of things."

"Not accusing! Just stating the facts."

"Too persuasively. And not at all in a fair and balanced way." He sighed heavily. "Water under the bridge. I thought we were done tormenting each other after last week. Why did you publish this last issue?"

"I had a responsibility to my readers. As you heard, if you yank the paper away, they'll have nowhere to find their husbands and jobs and runaway wives."

"One of the other papers in the city can step up. I'm surprised they haven't been in competition with you already."

Evangeline had worked very hard to ensure she had a loyal readership. Her advertising rates were the lowest— too low, sometimes even free if circumstances warranted it. So many of her readers did not have a penny to spare. It was the ton's subscriptions that had kept *The London List* afloat, the greedy thirst of the aristocracy for the latest *on dit* and scandal broth that was never quite quenched. Ben might not know it, but articles about his escapades had provided most of the funds for Evangeline's charitable impulses. There was a great deal to the newspaper that few suspected.

She shook her head. "There's nothing like *The List*."

"Yes, most papers have standards. Am I never to have peace? I've told you I'm reforming. I am going to a bloody Christmas ball with my *mother* tomorrow evening, curse it. Why can't the Capshaws keep an abstemious Advent like good Christians?"

"This isn't about you anymore, Ben. You were the marquee performance, but countless other people have a stake in this enterprise. Please reconsider your decision."

"Because if I don't, you'll get that gang outside to make my life a daily misery!" Ben snapped.

Evangeline suppressed a grin. That was a very attractive thought, although the idea of standing around in the cold street all day long had little appeal. "Please think about it. I'll go back to the office and let the people know you might change your mind. And I wonder if I might have my key back. My coat and gloves are inside."

"I told you I'd go with you."

"You'll only become more aggravated when you don't tell them what they want to hear and they pounce on you."

Ben grimaced. "I'm sure I can hold my own if anyone dares to lay a finger on me."

Evangeline didn't doubt it. Ben's strong, sinewed body was perfection, and she would never see it again. She pushed the little pang of regret away and pulled her scarf tighter.

"You can't go out like that—you'll freeze your cold heart. Let me get you one of my coats."

"Really, I'm perfectly all right."

"Just for once, Evie, show some sense and do as I ask. You've always been a little fool."

"I am neither little nor a fool, my lord," Evangeline said, struggling to keep her temper. "You can't go ordering me about. You have no right. You're not my husband. If you recall, I turned you down."

"And praise God for it—if you were my wife I'd have been shipped off to Australia years ago for your murder."

"As I said just days ago, I would never marry you under any circumstances." Her courses had come, thank heavens, so there was no need to worry about finding herself with Ben's bastard child.

"Too right you'll never marry me, because I'll never ask again. But I am offering you a coat, because, you silly chit, look out the window. It is snowing! You may think me a blackguard, but I don't want your death on my hands unless I can get some actual enjoyment out of it."

"I don't want your bloody coat!"

"Severson!" For good measure, Ben yanked the bellpull from the wall.

The butler arrived immediately. Evangeline hoped he had not had one hairy ear pressed against the door. "You rang, my lord?"

"Get Mr. Ramsey one of my warmer coats and then show him out. Gloves and a hat, too. And I am not to be disturbed again for any reason today, damn it, no matter who comes to the door—orphans looking for their parents, dukes looking for dominatrixes. Am I understood?"

The butler's face remained impassive. "Yes, my lord. Absolutely, my lord. This way, Mr. Ramsey."

Evangeline shot Ben a look of loathing. "I'll expect your answer by tomorrow morning, else I'll have to take matters in my own hands. *Capable* hands."

"Filthy hands, you baggage. Now get out!" He threw her key at her and she caught it with one filthy hand.

"With the greatest of pleasure." Lifting her imposing nose in the air, Evangeline left the blasted baron to stew in his own juices and found herself standing in his hallway closet. She had every confidence that he would see the error of his ways and be forced to deal with her, or she and her newly found minions would make his life hell.

Severson gave her a good long look, then pulled a soft gray wool coat from a hook and helped her into it. Evangeline couldn't help but take an experimental sniff. Ben was not one to drown his body in expensive scent, but wearing his coat was like being in his arms, a trace of spicy masculinity lingering in the fabric. Despite her great height, Ben was so much larger everywhere, so the sleeves of the garment were too long. She stood obediently as Severson rolled up the cuffs. He clearly disapproved of the state of her hands and fished through a basket for a pair of fur-lined gloves. A high-crowned beaver hat finished off her ensemble, although it had a regrettable tendency to droop over her left eye. Ben's head was bigger, too, not that he was so damned smart.

Perhaps she wasn't being fair. Or balanced, she thought ruefully, stepping out into the snow-swirled street after refusing Severson's offer to procure a hackney for her. Ben had books in his little library, after all. Lots of them. And he'd told her there was an even larger depository of books upstairs. Just because he preferred the company of whores and opera dancers did not mean that he was ignorant, just immature.

He was simply drifting through life, with no particular purpose. If he decided to become the publisher of *The London List,* he'd become aware of the inequities she saw every day.

Evangeline had a republican streak, not that she wanted to haul out Madame Guillotine. She truly did believe the pen was mightier than the sword. Every time she had written about Ben or some other rakehell, she had hoped to shame them into reform and responsibility.

And it had worked with Ben, for the most part. He was going to a ball with his *mother.*

Evangeline brushed a snowflake from her nose, breathing in leather and Ben. The closest she'd come to having him touch her again was wearing his clothes against her skin. She would not feel his hand on the small of her back, guiding her in a waltz in a glittering ballroom, not see his green eyes glint gold with admiration, not feel the press of his warm lips as they stole a kiss in a winter-frosted garden. But she *could* work for him if he discovered his conscience.

If he could work with *her.* He didn't know the first thing about putting the paper to bed.

Her lips twitched. Here at least, was one aspect of bedding where she had the upper hand.

★   ★   ★

Going back to bed was futile, but Ben did lock himself in his bedchamber. His valet Timms shaved him and then left him alone in his bath, Ben's rusty temper as heated as the scorching water he preferred. His room faced the back garden, but he knew without a doubt that people were tramping up and down his front steps to complain that he was altering the very face of British civilization by shuttering *The London List*'s doors.

By now he had read Evie's article, every scurrilous word imprinted on his brain.

> It is with great regret and sadness that I announce the discontinuation of the newspaper you are holding in your hand. For two years, it has been my privilege to report on the vagaries of human nature, restore lost souls (and pets!) to the bosom of their families, and match wives to husbands and employees to employers.
>
> But a certain Baron G, who has oft been the subject of your well-deserved righteous indignation for his profligate ways and puerile stunts, has in his dubious wisdom decided to discontinue this publication. The dastardly Baron G has made the publisher, an elderly, fragile gentleman, an offer which he was unable to refuse in consideration of his desperately poor health and his beloved family. In taking advantage of such a situation, Baron G has proven to the world that he has stooped to the lowest level of despicable conduct. It matters not to him whether E.P. reunites with the mustachioed major who spoke to her so kindly at Hatchards, or who can supply T.C. with a first-quality Spanish leather whip, or if J.K can share expenses to a secluded villa in Italy. Certainly Baron G cares only about himself and continuing his debauched depravity in secret from society. But we will never forget.
>
> —E. Ramsey, *Editor*

Bloody hell. She had made him sound like the veriest monster. Perhaps he should print his own edition next Tuesday and turn the tables on her.

It is with great regret and sadness that I announce that Editor E. Ramsey is not an Edward or an Erastus or an Ethelbert but an Evangeline, who was lately lying on my library floor after she had her way with me. So much for depravity and debauchery—Miss Ramsey is the most infuriating, insulting—Incomparable.

Ben threw his sponge to the carpet. How he could still find her so attractive after all she'd done to him was a mystery. And now she really had his ballocks in a vise—either he had to publish the damn paper or be hunted down at his own home by irate readers. Or worse, be front-page fodder for a brand-new rag. This Fitzhugh had more money than sense or talent—Ben had read the poem he wrote, *Ode to an Oracle's End,* bemoaning the sale of the paper, and had not been impressed. Byron he was not.

Ben had until tomorrow to meet Evie's ultimatum. Hauling himself out of the tub and dripping across the carpet, he picked up the "collector's edition" of *The London List.* He would read the advertisements this afternoon and weigh his options. And tell Thomas Crowe he might have the perfect whip for him in the attics.

# CHAPTER 8

*December 13, 1820*

Evangeline sat in her shabby parlor, a book upside-down in her lap. She had not bothered with her wig—her father had had a bad spell last night and was mercifully sleeping the morning away, so he couldn't see the shocking state of her hair. How women of the last century had endured their outrageous powdered creations she had no idea—every time she donned the wig she itched and sweat something fierce.

And anyway, quite a few ladies of the ton had chopped off all their curls—fast ladies, to be sure, but Evangeline supposed she qualified. Lurking around the stalls at Tattersall's and betting on cockfights were hardly ladylike pursuits.

When she thought of it, it was quite amazing that no one had recognized her in London, but ten years had passed and she was not the awkward girl she'd been. Plus, people saw what they expected to see, and why would one suppose that beneath the figured waistcoat and brass watch fobs was a young woman of relatively gentle birth?

Her father had of course squandered what there was of the Ramsey fortune, thus necessitating a career in cards. He'd lost every piece of property he'd ever owned save for the disintegrating family seat in Argyll. The huge manor house was uninhabitable, and too far from the doctors he was now dependent on. Their return to London to this mean little house went unnoticed by the ton two years ago, and Evangeline had been relieved to hide behind her newspaperman's façade as she struggled to turn a profit on her father's last unlucky winnings.

*The London List* had been an extremely unsuccessful publication, fit only to start fires or wrap produce. Evangeline had singlehandedly made it so vital to London—indeed to the entire countryside—that the closing of it had sparked a near-riot yesterday. Even more readers had greeted her upon her return to its office to fetch her belongings, expecting her to be their champion with the wicked Baron Gray.

She presumed Ben would come here to give her his decision, and had taken more than unusual care with her toilette. She could do nothing about her hair except let the ringlets spring, but she was wearing a rather pretty white dress trimmed with carmine ribbons. Evangeline had found a dried-up rouge pot and dabbed a bit on her cheeks and lips to make her look less dead—the night had been a trial for her and her father's man Wilfred.

So now she waited, her mind spinning possible scenarios. If Ben chose to keep the paper up and running, she would offer her services—at a fair wage, for no matter how much money he had given her father, she would not work for nothing. He could stay away to live his frivolous life and leave everything in her hands, for surely a wastrel such as he would have no interest in the day-to-day tedium of reading letters and setting type.

If he sold the paper to Lord Fitzhugh, she was certain he'd need her, too—the man had no head for anything except badly rhymed quatrains.

If Ben closed it down for good—well, she had a cadre

of unhappy people at her fingertips, many of whom were unemployed and had time to march in front of Lord Gray's home. A few days of that, and Ben would have to bend.

Whichever way Ben decided, she had an interesting future ahead of her.

Ben's topcoat, hat, and gloves were laid neatly on the tattered parlor sofa. She could smell them from across the room, Ben's distinctive fresh scent as pervasive as cooked cabbage in a tenement. If he didn't come today, she'd send Wilfred with the clothing—she did not need the fragrant reminder of the one man she seemed unable to get out of her system.

A quick knock at the door, and Evangeline straightened, setting her book to rights. Her frowsy maid Patsy curtseyed ungracefully but with enthusiasm. "Lord Gray to see you, Miss Evangeline."

Evangeline's heart skipped a beat, but this was what she was waiting for, wasn't it? "Thank you, Patsy. Send him in."

In seconds Ben appeared in the doorway, bringing the full force of his odor and rugged handsomeness. Evangeline fixed him a cold look. "Well, my lord?"

"Hmm. Not even a 'How pleased I am to see you again in one piece' after setting your jackals on me. My mother—and my butler, which is even worse—are in distress, their last nerve shredded by the rude individuals that have been camped out in front of my townhouse for over twenty-four hours. My mother has gone to stay with her ailing friend—apparently the company of a dying woman is more congenial than that of her beleaguered son. She's not speaking to me now, you know. Closing *The London List* has hit her very hard." He sat down next to his coat and the sofa screamed at his weight.

Evangeline tried hard not to smile at Ben's peevish tone. It served him right to feel the consequences of his highhanded action.

"I take it you are sticking to your original plan then."

"How can I? Everyone but me seems to think the damn rag is the very life's blood of society. I was cut at my club, Evie—*cut* by that cur Winkler."

She nodded. "Yes, he collects naughty snuffboxes. He's paid for an ad right through the next quarter. It's amazing how many people have them tucked away in a drawer. Lord Winkler pays top price, I understand. His collection is legendary."

Ben snorted in disgust. "You should not know such things even exist, Evie."

"Well, I do, and there's no taking back knowledge. I know a great deal about your friends and acquaintances, Ben. Sometimes I've permitted myself to accept a bribe *not* to publish certain things."

"Corruption coming from such a crusader as you? Is that all it would have taken? A few pounds from me and I wouldn't be saddled with the damn paper?"

"No. No amount from *you* could have kept me silent. And I've used whatever extra I received to help people in true need," she said primly.

Ben's mouth curled. "You are a regular Robin Hood and Joan of Arc combined. Blast it, Evie, you set out to ruin me and you've succeeded. No matter what I do, I'm cursed."

"Not really. I'm proposing a compromise for you. I'll edit the paper and take care of all the details—leaving you out of it entirely, both in the back room and the front page. We can continue to do good, and you can repair your reputation at your leisure."

Ben looked a little like a fish out of water, his mouth flapping a bit before he sputtered, "You expect me to work with you?"

"Not at all," she said serenely. "I just said I'd do all the work. All the writing. You need do nothing but collect whatever profits there are. Unless, of course, you decide to sell the paper. I could stay on as it transitioned to new ownership. I think," she reflected, "that should be a condition of any sale."

Ben's green eyes sparked. "And let me guess—I'd have the honor of paying you a salary."

"Why, certainly. That would only be fair. The paper takes a great deal of effort. Hours and hours a week."

"Fair!" Ben barked. "You are a madwoman. Your continued association with the publication is at an end. I can get someone else to do it—even that actor Frank Hallett."

"Ah. You gave him so much money I doubt he needs to return. And my understanding is that he's going to Italy for the winter. He may have already left." She shut her unread book with a snap. "Face it, Ben. You need me. You'd never make heads or tails of my advertising system, and without it you'd probably be matching innocent governesses to gouty satyrs. At least keep me on for a few weeks until you get your footing."

Ben looked ready to growl. "I'll sell, then."

Evangeline shrugged. "Suit yourself. Know that Lord Fitzhugh holds you in very little affection—for some reason he finds you unsettling. You're apt to find yourself on display again."

"Not if there's nothing to report! And believe me, Evie, my life has been dull as ditch water this week. And anyway, Fitzhugh's not the only one in London with money."

"Ben," Evangeline said gently, "don't you think I tried to sell the paper myself? Despite all the advances I've made, I was unable to interest anyone, even as an investor. It's a daunting undertaking putting out a quality product week after week." There had been times in the beginning when she'd wanted nothing else but to divest herself of the responsibility. She might have welcomed a sale once—but not with Ben as the buyer.

"Quality. That's your word for it," Ben sneered.

"You saw yesterday that some folks rely upon it. I'd call that quality."

"I'd call it insanity! How can one find one's wife on the pages of a newspaper?"

"How can one find one's wife in the crush of a ballroom? Or at the whim of one's parent? Don't tell me that society's rules make any sense at all."

"I suppose we can agree on that. What's the point of following them when they're so damned boring?"

For a moment, Evangeline was reminded of a young Ben, the boy who was ready to be dared and diverted from propriety. The very qualities she'd found so attractive at first had led her to reject him. For how could she cast her lot with a man who might turn out to be her father all over again?

She'd wanted security. Well, she had a form of it, with her loyal, ragtag advertisers, people who were desperate to find happiness and looked to her to help. Shockingly, Evangeline had even been entrusted with finding a gentleman willing to help ensure the continuance of an old family name. She had saved every letter of thanks—some tear-stained—had gone to every local wedding and the resulting christenings. She'd even found the motherly Lady Pennington through *The List,* and had the oddest desire to curl up in the woman's lap for comfort right this minute.

Instead she sat across from a man who made her uncomfortable—a rake, a libertine, and quite the most astonishing lover she could imagine.

Not that she'd had much experience. The two other men she had been with had been . . . not Ben.

He'd used the word *insanity,* and she must be insane to think that she could work for him. But it might be only for a little while. Perhaps a buyer could be found—after all, she performed miracles every week.

She experimented with a smile, feeling suddenly exhausted. "I'm prepared to be completely professional, Ben. I'll even call you Lord Gray. And if you want to feel useful, you could take over the accounts for me. I always seem to transpose numbers." The truth of it was, totting up a column of numbers made her sleepy, although they were rather key in turning a profit.

"Professional." The way he said the word sounded as if he were tasting it upon his tongue and found it sour. "Just how do you expect us to be *professional*, Evie, when we are at each other's throats all the time?"

"Simple. Let me go about my business with no interference. You needn't even see me."

For a moment his face was frozen, and then he laughed. Watching Benton Gray laugh did something to her insides—his eyes crinkled, his mouth opened wide to reveal his excellent teeth, and his large form shook from top to toe. He was so completely swept away by the humor of his predicament that she felt a stab of envy. Evangeline couldn't remember the last time she'd had a reason to feel genuine amusement. Watching Ben's bafflement yesterday had come close, but that was more smug satisfaction than joy.

And still he rumbled. She tapped an impatient foot on the ancient carpet.

Ben wiped away what appeared to be a tear. "This is priceless. Evie—*Mr. Ramsey*—I salute you. You have me tied up in a devil of a knot. But I'm afraid I cannot accede to your wish of noninterference. You wanted me to make something of myself, remember? What did you say three—or was it four—weeks ago? *'Lord G, for all his faults, has a fine mind that is wasted with each passing week. Would that he only find an outlet for his energy besides frolic and fornication.'* An exact quote, if I recollect correctly. I was impressed by the alliteration. I believe I've found my outlet as publisher of *The London List*. I've nothing better to do, as you have so frequently pointed out. You seem to think I've never done an honest day's work in my life, but that's about to change."

He rose from the sofa, incurring another groan from its springs, and scooped up his belongings. "I will meet you at the office tomorrow at ten—no, make that nine. Begin as you mean to go on, eh? The early bird catches the worm and all that. You'll instruct me in the art of the newspaper business. What with my fine mind and all, I'm sure it won't take long. Good day to you, and give my regards to your father."

He was gone. The book slid from Evangeline's lap to the floor. What monster had she created? *This* was not how she'd hoped to spend her winter.

For a moment she wished she was off to Italy with Frank Hallett, but that would be the coward's way out. There were people dependent on her, and she could endure most anything, even working shoulder to shoulder with Baron Benton Gray.

# *C*HAPTER 9

*December 14, 1820*

When Evangeline got to the office of *The London List* at half eight, she was shocked to see Ben with his feet propped up on her desk, sipping from a flask that smelled very much like coffee. He grinned and looked at his watch.

"Ah. Definitely an early bird."

"And you must be the worm," she snapped.

"Or it could be the other way around. I was here first, you know."

"How did you get in? I thought you lost your key."

"Picked the lock. Just one of my many talents, my dear. Comes in handy for entering locked houses at night to ravish jaded countesses and such. I climb up trellises, too. Like a monkey."

He looked inordinately proud of himself. She would *not* smile. "An overgrown ape, more like. I can't imagine such structures holding your weight." She unwound her muffler and hung it on a hook by the door—*hers* was already taken by his gray topcoat. He had fired up the coal stove, but perversely she kept her brown plaid greatcoat on. She didn't like the gleam in his eye when he looked at her so boldly, no matter what she was wearing.

"Alas. I've filled out a bit since my youth. But then you know that from a week ago. You can't have forgotten so soon."

Evangeline felt the blush coming on. "I thought we agreed we would never mention that night—or any of our nights—"

"And days," Ben interrupted. "We were quite shocking ten years ago."

"Well, I am not shocking now! I've tried to lead a respectable life."

Ben raised a golden eyebrow. "In those breeches? Tell me, must you continue to prance around in menswear?"

"Yes, if our working together is to go unremarked. The shopkeepers in the neighborhood gossip like magpies. They are frequently excellent sources for me." She held her greatcoat closer.

Ben took a sip of coffee and her stomach rumbled. She'd dashed out so early to beat him here she'd not bothered with breakfast. Ben gestured toward a basket by his feet, which were still atop her desk. He hadn't stood when she entered, and made no effort now to treat her with excessive civility, as a gentleman might do with a lady, she realized. Good. That would help to keep up the appearance that they were simply two colleagues.

"Do you care for a roll? They might still be warm."

Evangeline warred with herself—this charming, casual, *twinkling* Ben was just who she did not want to spend time with. It was one thing when they were sparring, but with him looking so comfortable and offering her food—

"No. Thank you, my lord."

He shrugged and dug into the basket. "Suit yourself. I'm famished." He bit into the roll and her traitorous stomach betrayed her yet again. She looked away as he licked the flaky crumbs from his fingers, remembering what that tongue had done to her just last week.

This was not going to work. For once in her life, Evangeline questioned her judgment—she should *never* have put out that last issue of the paper naming Ben as the destroyer of *The London List*. She could have just shuttered up the shop and slipped away to care for her poor addled father, instead of trying to get in the last skewering word. Now she was stuck with trying to avoid the unwelcome knowledge that she still—despite everything—had feelings for the man. Feelings—not all positive to be sure—that disrupted her sleep and waking hours.

Ben raised the flask toward her. "If you don't mind drinking after me, do you care for some coffee instead? I'm afraid I didn't think to pack any cups."

Evangeline moved swiftly to the little cupboard in the corner where she kept tea, a loaf of sugar, and a tin of biscuits to get her through the grueling, dirty days when she set type at deadline. She snatched up a delicate gilt-edged cup without its matching saucer, a leftover from a period of time when her father had been winning. Her hands shook a little as she poured the steaming liquid into her precious relic, then she took a scorching sip. She must remember to take the cup with her when she left.

"Now then." Ben uncrossed his ankles and set his expensively shod feet on the wooden floor. "There's quite a batch of mail already. I've pulled out what seem to be tradesmen's bills, but I imagine the rest are from your constituents. Suppose we start with those."

Ben was all business. Well, she could be, too. She set the cup down and dragged a chair to a corner of the desk. Brisk. She would be brisk and forthright. If he couldn't follow, that was his loss.

"Every letter is opened, read, and placed in the appropriate stack. Lonely hearts in one pile, employment ads in another, for example. Replies to the numbered boxes are placed in the correct mail slot to be picked up or forwarded."

"That seems simple enough."

"One would think so. But sometimes one must read between the lines." She picked up a smudged missive and opened the seal. A coin rolled out of the paper and Evie set it aside, ticking a checkmark at the top of the note with a pencil.

" 'Dear Mr. Ramsey, I do hope you can assist me again, although truthfully your previous assistance with my employment does not have much to recommend it. I am enclosing the cost for one week's worth of advertising and the accompanying postbox. It is all I can afford since I was dismissed from my current position. I was lately the Basingstokes' governess—not for very long, fortunately or unfortunately as the case may be. I am afraid I cannot get a reference, either, for Lord Basingstoke has not been not able to write since I slammed his hand in my bedroom door and in any event would not have been predisposed to sing my praises since I refused to become his mistress. I know winter is upon us, but I would very much like to be settled in a proper Christian home before Christmas. Thank you for your attention to this matter. I remain most sincerely, Elizabeth Amelia Sturgess'—"

"Good Lord! You're not going to print that as is, are you? Basingstoke will have us charged with libel."

"I'm not going to print it at all, nor am I going to take this poor child's money. This is where the job gets tricky, Ben." She laid a hand on the unopened mail. "I can hope that somewhere in these letters is Elizabeth's next situation. If I printed every request, the paper would be five times its size, and I'd have to order newsprint by the forest." Evangeline stood, went to a wooden cabinet, and pulled open a drawer. "I may have something that didn't come in time to make the classified section last week. Let's pull out both the matrimonial and governess files."

"Matrimonial!"

"Yes, Ben," she said patiently. "I met Elizabeth Amelia Sturgess the last time she sought a position—she came here to the office. She's a sweet, gentle girl, loves children, and is very pretty. If it's not Lord Basingstoke, it will be some other father or oldest son who has designs upon the new governess. Best to get her suitably married before her immortal soul is imperiled. Wait a moment! I may in fact already have the perfect candidate for her." Of course— Lord Maxwell needed a wife immediately. And here was Lizzie, who might be just the balm that would ease him out of his shyness. The girl was wholesome and natural, very unlike the usual society miss that so terrified him. Evangeline smiled, imaging Lord Maxwell saying, "I d-d-d-do."

Ben stared at her as if she'd grown an extra head.

"I told you I had an unusual advertising system."

"You have no sensible system at all! This is madness. We could be at this *forever*."

"I agree. And you thought all I did was spy on you. Pass me the ink and pen, Ben." She wrote as she spoke, her elegant handwriting rapidly covering a sheet of paper. "I'm writing to Miss Sturgess to see if she'd like her request fulfilled in a slightly alternate manner. I'm afraid after you bought the paper I dismissed my usual errand and delivery boys, so I hope you won't mind going round to her lodgings yourself to deliver this. If she's amenable, bring her back here at once. Make sure she's suitably dressed to meet a viscount. In the meantime, I'll go through the rest of the correspondence."

"A viscount. Why am I not surprised?" Ben mumbled. "I'm the publisher, Evie, and a stranger. Should you not be the one to deliver the tidings that Miss Sturgess is about to come up in the world?"

"Look at the mess on my desk, Ben. *Our* desk. The sooner I can work through all this, the better. You don't want to be here with me until midnight, do you? And more mail will come in later. *And* tomorrow and the next day—you'll have plenty of time to learn the ropes."

Ben put his hat on his golden head. "I feel like I'm swinging from one already."

Miss Sturgess was just as Evie said—very pretty, with shining light brown curls and darker eyes. And also as unhinged as Evie, since she read the letter, nodded, disappeared for an unconscionable amount of time while Ben paced the foyer of her boardinghouse, and emerged down the stairs dressed in the first stare of fashion. For a girl who earned her living educating sticky-fingered urchins, the dress was a surprise.

Miss Sturgess must have caught his look of admiration, for she said, "Lady Basingstoke gave me a few old dresses out of guilt, as if bribery would make me hold my tongue. Her husband is a beast. Shall we go?" He helped with a serviceable cloak that did not match the elegant finery underneath.

Ben extended an arm. The girl did not come up to the middle of his chest. He thought her a plucky little thing— he knew Basingstoke, though not well. The man was overfond of drinking and dining, and looked it, rather like a bloated Vauxhall Gardens balloon. It seemed he had sexual excesses as well if he was interfering with his staff. No doubt Lady Basingstoke would be widowed in short order, perhaps at her own instigation.

"Are you acquainted with the gentleman I am to marry?" Miss Sturgess asked, a stray curl blowing out from underneath her bonnet across her faintly freckled nose.

"You really are considering it?"

The girl nodded calmly, as if proposals fell in her lap on a daily basis.

"I know absolutely nothing about your potential groom—or much of anything, I'm afraid," Ben replied, helping her into his carriage. "I'm rather new at this publishing business. Ev—Mr. Ramsey is somewhat unorthodox, I'm finding."

"He is a very helpful man," Miss Sturgess said, settling herself against the squabs. "Although placing me with the Basingstokes was a bit of a misfire. I'm sure this new scheme will be better."

Ben hardly knew what to say to that, so he sat back, letting the hot bricks do their best against the frigid December air. Yes, becoming a viscountess was likely better than becoming a governess or unwilling mistress, and he could see this little bird making someone a happy husband.

He was soon robbed of his silent meditation. "Forgive me for being blunt, but you are the infamous Jane Street Jackanapes, are you not? I thought you were closing the press down."

"The road to damnation is paved with good intentions," Ben said wryly. "My plans have altered."

"I'm so glad! When I read the last edition Tuesday, I feared all was lost. A young woman without a respectable background and references has very little opportunity, you know. I have no family to fall back on—I have no idea who my parents are, actually—and limited skills. I cannot, for example, trim a hat—my feathers droop instantly. My needlework is atrocious—" She leaned forward, her cheeks pinking. "I shouldn't tell you, but I've altered this dress with pins and they are presently sticking quite uncomfortably in places I'm loath to discuss. But I had a good education at the foundling home. The matrons let me stay on to teach the little ones until their benefactor died and they had to close. Such a shame, as there are always so many more orphans than money."

This artless speech touched Ben's heart and made his head spin a little. He'd never given much thought to foundling homes, other than to make sure none of his mistresses was required to place a by-blow in one. He thought the fine-boned Miss Sturgess the likely result of a society gentleman and some unlucky lady, and wondered if this might be a fly in the ointment of Evie's plans to elevate the girl to the peerage. But Evie exuded confidence and had been at this mad business much longer than he had.

Miss Sturgess chattered happily all the way to the office as Ben rapidly reevaluated his understanding of exactly what services *The London List* provided. And then it hit him.

Evangeline Ramsey was a *romantic*. A modern-day Don Quixote tilting at the windmills of British life, organizing everyone into the little cubbies he'd seen on the wall, turning Miss Sturgess into Cinderella with the stroke of a pen. For all Evie's viciousness with him, she was a Fairy Godmother—or, in their minds, Fairy God*father*—to the rest of the world.

But who was going to make *her* wishes come true?

# CHAPTER 10

*December 16, 1820*

Somehow word had spread that the paper was back in business, and the volume of correspondence seemed to quadruple. Ben's eyes had crossed trying to make sense of the misspelled letters, and his hand was numb from turning three-page pleas into ads of under twenty-five words. Evie had actually praised him on three occasions for his brevity and wit, and he'd been as pleased as a pup with a good ear-scratching.

He didn't know how Evie had done all this by herself and still had time to infiltrate the ton to sweep up its dirt and write about it. He was exhausted after one full day of it. But they were both to get a reprieve from the endless tedium this morning. Viscount Jeremiah Maxwell was marrying his bride by special license that Ben himself had gone to considerable trouble to acquire and pay for in a private ceremony at St. George's. Ben and Evie were the only guests, with Ben serving as the best man to the apparently friendless Maxwell, and Evie standing up for Lizzie Sturgess. Ben had been present when Evie not only introduced his future wife to the viscount but revealed that she was in fact a woman. Maxwell had fainted to the floor, which Ben did not think was a particularly good omen for the success of his marriage.

"We still need a feature article for the front page," Evie said as she climbed into his carriage. Beneath her cape she was in the dress with the red ribbons again, and looked pretty enough to be a bride herself. Her hair was covered by a smart velvet bonnet trimmed with a bunch of cherries and lace, and her cheeks were flushed with the cold.

"You're not going to write about me."

"Of course not! I told you I would not, and I keep my word. I suppose I could do an article on Lord Maxwell and Lizzie's wedding. It's like a fairy tale come true, isn't it?"

"I suppose. Poor Maxwell. The fellow's absolutely rigid with fear around the fairer sex, isn't he? Can't get out three words in a row. I bet he's still a virgin."

Evie swatted his arm. "Well, so I should hope is Lizzie, so they'll teach each other. And she talks enough for both of them. She's very patient and cheerful—I think it's a perfect match!"

Ben was not so sure, but at least the man would get his great-aunt's money upon his marriage, and in his experience money went a long way to easing one's problems. He'd been fortunate in his investments himself, rich enough to buy the newspaper with the intention of tossing it away. The best-laid plans . . .

If he was honest with himself, he'd enjoyed the last few days even if he wasn't sleeping much. Evie's work ethic was alarming, and he had no wish for her to think him a slacker. He'd been almost too busy to pay much attention to the curve of her arse in her trousers, or the way the masculine scent of sandalwood did not entirely mask an underlying feminine allure.

But she smelled of roses today—she was all woman. Ben shifted in his seat, willing himself to think of something other than bedding her.

They were getting along far too well. He actually missed her in the middle of the day when she went home for lunch with her father. After his arm-twisting visit to Doctors' Commons, he'd tried to eat at his club yesterday, but had been swamped by people who wanted to know what was happening with *The London List*. After three bites of roast beef, he'd given up and gone back to tackle the books.

Truth was, he didn't know what he was going to do with the paper. Now that he knew the work it entailed— and they had yet to actually print the damn thing—he could not imagine spending the rest of his life at it just to prove a point to Evie. Right now, he didn't even remember what that point had been.

To convince her he could be a serious man? To annoy her? To have a legitimate reason to spend more time with her after they had parted for all time? He swallowed back a sigh.

Opposite, Evie was composed, obviously not having a family of demented squirrels playing leapfrog—or would it be leap-squirrel?—in her mind. She radiated a happiness that he'd not ever seen in her. Weddings tended to do that to women, even for an unconventional woman like Evangeline Ramsey.

For a man, they were usually the mark of doom.

At least he didn't have to worry about finding a wife right now—he was far too busy, and so he had told his mother. She was still spending most of her time at Lady Applegate's, which was just as well—she had been perceptive enough to be suspicious of "Mr." Ramsey when she met him, and had quizzed Ben unceasingly when he went to tell her of his change of heart about the paper.

He was now partners with the one person who had come perilously close to ruining him.

Perhaps she already had.

But now he and Evie were on the way to a wedding, after which Evie would begin to show him how to set type. In two days' time, they'd be slaving over machinery, hand-cranking the press until it spit out sheets of black-and-white hope.

"What a lovely day," Evie said, interrupting his squirrels.

"Rubbish. It's arctic outside, and looks as if it might snow again."

"Nonsense. And if it does, London will be all the prettier for it. A dusting of snow covers up its less savory aspects."

"Evie, I can't believe we're talking about the *weather*."

"Don't be such a gruff old bear. I thought it was a safe enough topic. You seem preoccupied."

Yes, he was. Wondering what to do with his life and the woman who sat opposite.

"I'm tired."

"Oh. Did you have a late night off dazzling one of your lightskirts with your mighty . . . sword?"

"Don't be vulgar." He'd fallen into bed just after he came home from the office, tiny numbers and letters imprinted on his eyelids. He'd dreamed of schoolmasters seeking new situations and jewelers advertising their gems. And Evie, standing just out of reach, the sandalwood lingering in the air between them. She was wearing neither her dress or her trousers and had bedeviled him all through the night.

"Well, if anyone could spot vulgarity, it would be you."

"Yes, yes. I'm the darkest sinner. Do you never get tired of totting up my faults?"

Evie cocked her head as if she were thinking deeply. "No, I don't believe so."

"You've kept me so busy these last two days I've no time for sin. That should give you satisfaction."

"It might." She stuck her tongue out at him.

He wanted that tongue to do something altogether different from taunting him—perhaps something that it had done on the floor of his study the week before last. She had licked him clean and quite out of his mind in the wee hours of the morning. He had been, in fact, so witless that he'd agreed to never touch her again once she had finished him off. For really, they could bring each other nothing but trouble, wasn't that so?

And he could have kept his vow had she not plastered his purchase of the paper on the front page, causing him no end of headache with the rabble at his door. Even his own mother had refused to speak to him when she thought he intended to shut down her premium source of gossip. What else was he to do but hobble along with the paper until he found a buyer to take it—and Evangeline Ramsey—off his hands?

He might even lose it in a card game. That would be a fitting punishment for her.

"Tell me more about Maxwell. I've not seen him about."

"Well, he'd never darken the door of *your* favorite haunts," Evie said with some scorn. "He's far too honorable. And shy. He was brought up in the back of beyond somewhere by his dragonish great-aunt, who was awfully anxious that he marry. I told you the terms of the will."

"Aye. What would the dragon say to him marrying an impoverished governess who's most likely a bastard?"

"I daresay she wouldn't like it, but she's dead. There were no caveats as to the legitimacy of the bride, just that Lord Maxwell marry before Christmas of this year. We've cut it a bit close, but here we are, on the way to the wedding."

"How long have you been trying to matchmake?"

"He came to me at the end of the summer in a panic, right after the old woman died. I'm afraid I had difficulty finding suitable candidates for him."

"Don't tell me you couldn't find a whole ballroom of

mamas who wanted their daughters to become a viscountess."

"I won't tell you then. But the Season was over, and the
Little Season's crop of eligible young ladies was disappointing. Lord Maxwell was picky."

"Fainted a lot, did he?"

Evie grinned. "The poor man is absolutely terrified of
women—he literally cannot speak coherently. Even the
chance to become a viscountess was dimmed for the three
girls I thought somewhat worthy of the title when they
met him. It will take someone with a backbone to draw
him out."

"And any girl who breaks Lord Basingstoke's fingers between the door and the jamb qualifies."

"Lizzie is very remarkable in her own way. She's never
had a proper home, and will be grateful to him all her life."

"Grateful. Somehow that does not strike me as what a
man needs to hear."

"Oh, *men*." Evie waved a gloved hand. "Men don't
know what they want until a woman tells them."

"Indeed? That's a novel thought." And a bit disquieting.
Ben did not care to think he'd been manipulated by the
women in his life to making his choices. He was pretty
sure he'd done any number of things no decent woman
would approve of, but then he'd not been especially interested in decent women's approval of late.

"Of course the key is to make the man think that *he*
thought of whatever it is first," Evie continued. "With
some skill, any woman can make a man eat from the palm
of her hand."

"You know this from experience, do you? Have a damp
hand and cadre of conquests to prove your assertion?"

Evie blushed primly. "A lady does not disclose such
things."

"This is the most absurd conversation. You cannot

make me eat from the palm of your hand or anywhere else on your body." Delectable as it was. Ben imagined a strawberry placed *just so* and a muscle in his cheek twitched. A veritable banquet.

"I wouldn't bother trying! You are not the sort of man I'd even try to convert. It would be a hopeless, thankless task."

"Beyond the Pale, am I?"

"Entirely."

"Irredeemable? Bound for hell in a handwoven handbasket?"

"That's between the Lord and yourself. I wouldn't presume to judge."

"Ah, but you've judged me for most of two years. Did you expect me to just roll over so you could continue your onslaught?" His fist hit the seat, a cloud of dust billowing up. "Wait a minute! Did you *intend* for me to buy *The London List* in some sort of elaborate, expensive hand-eating? Is that part of your diabolical master plan to punish me?"

Evie was as white now as the snow that had just begun to fall. "I never dreamed you would go to such lengths, as you well know! It's not to my advantage at all to be saddled with you!"

"Who is saddled with who?" Or was it whom—Ben was too angry to care. "You are in my employ, Miss— Mr.—whoever you are Ramsey."

"Fine! Fire me and then see how you muddle through till Tuesday. It brings me no joy to have to spend day after day, hour after hour, minute after minute with you. One second is too long to find myself in your company."

"For once we agree on something." Ben's lips snapped shut. All the squirrels were in an uproar in his head, urging him to have the last, final, *killing* word, but he wanted to see what other absurdity Evie would lob back at him.

But she sat silent, as frosty as an ice maiden in her white gown.

And continued to do so until his carriage stopped in front of the church. Without waiting for his driver to descend, collapse the step, and open the door, Ben pushed it open into the wind and jumped down, leaving Evie to fend for herself in the carriage.

He strode into the vestibule and down the aisle, appreciating the irony of being in a rare towering rage in an alleged place of peace. The interior of the church was dim and cold, the altar flower-less, presided over by a large painting of Christ and his disciples lying around on couches at the Last Supper. They looked a good deal more comfortable than Ben felt. There was no sign of either the bride or bridegroom.

The heavy church door slammed behind him, and he turned. Evie did not meet his eye, but marched toward him, clutching her ratty fur-trimmed cloak to her breast.

"We should have picked up Lizzie," she said to a carved box pew.

He studied the stone squares beneath his feet as if they were quite the most fascinating thing he'd ever seen. "I thought Maxwell was going to fetch her."

"Yes, but what if he got cold feet and didn't? And it's unlucky to see the bride before the ceremony. Where is the blasted vicar?"

"How the devil do I know? I'm not even sure why I'm here."

"You are here to shore up Maxwell. And catch him if he faints again before he dashes his brains on the stone floor." She muttered something under her breath, and Ben was certain she cast aspersions on his own brains. He was nearly in agreement with her—he had lost his mind as well as his temper.

He *never* lost his temper. He'd made an effort all his life to be affable and equable. However, several days of close propinquity to the most irritating woman on earth was enough to try the patience of a saint, and Ben was no saint. He wondered if, now that he was here, he should light a candle and pray for deliverance from Evie.

Suddenly a man emerged from the vestry, rubbing his hands to warm them up.

"Ah," he said, beaming. "The happy couple! I'll be right with you."

"No!" both Evie and Ben said at the same time, sounding horrified. Or at least *she* did, as if becoming his baroness was akin to being eaten alive by rats. As for himself, he'd prefer something larger, like wolves, who could devour her faster and put him out of his misery sooner.

"We are merely the witnesses." Ben stepped forward and shook the priest's hand. "Benton Gray, at your service."

The man's tufted white brows knit. "The Jane Street Jack—I mean, how honored I am to meet you, my lord. I am Mr. Constantine. And this charming young woman is?"

Good Lord. Everyone *did* read the damned paper, even the clergy. "A friend of the bride's, Miss Ramsey. There's been no sign of Lord Maxwell and Miss Sturgess?"

"Not as yet. But I've been busy in the back getting ready for the ceremony. If you will just take a seat, I'm sure they'll be along at any moment. I'll go get my prayer book."

Ben held the pew door open and Evie sailed by, nose in the air. She pointedly sat as far away from him as she could without vaulting over into the next pew.

Thank heavens they didn't have to wait long. Maxwell and a blushing Lizzie Sturgess entered in a swirl of snow. There was no wedding march as she tugged him up the aisle, and Ben was almost tempted to hum a few bars of Bach's *Jesu, Joy of Man's Desiring* just for the hell of it. She stopped in front of Ben and Evie, beaming, Maxwell lurching by her side.

Her bridegroom did not radiate equal happiness. Maxwell's face matched Lizzie's serviceable gray cloak. She looked up at her betrothed expectantly, but he seemed to find the floor as interesting as Ben had.

"That's all right, my lord, I'll just remove my cloak myself, although it's dreadfully cold in here, is it not? But what a delightful surprise! A romantic snowstorm!" Her gloved fingers fumbled with the hooks, and she laid the garment over the pew. The dress she had chosen for her wedding looked very governessy—she must have decided against wearing Lady Basingstoke's castoffs to begin her new life. Ben noted her neat figure and cheerful demeanor, and hoped Maxwell might one day see her as she was—a little jewel who glittered with hopeful trust.

Evie brushed by him to hug the bride, and Ben felt obliged to shake Maxwell's hand.

"Well, old chap, here we are."

"Um."

"It won't be too bad. Miss Sturgess is a fine young woman. You've done well."

Maxwell gave him a hunted look but nodded.

Ben took him aside and leaned down to whisper in his ear. "If you have any questions about the wedding night, don't hesitate to ask."

If possible, Maxwell turned grayer.

"But this is not the place to discuss the fine points of bedding your bride," Ben continued, slapping the poor fellow on the back. "Come to my house after. We'll open a few bottles of bubbly and celebrate with a wedding breakfast." Severson and his cook might want to kill him, but Ben had every confidence that his staff could throw together an impromptu meal.

"A-a-all right," Maxwell stuttered.

The ceremony was mercifully brief. Maxwell swayed just once, and it was his bride that caught him by the elbow. At her touch, he stilled and seemed to see her for the first time. Ben was relieved to see the viscount's evident interest in his new viscountess. He crossed his fingers and even added a prayer that the day and the night ahead would bring both of them joy, if getting leg-shackled could ever do such a thing. He was in absolutely no hurry to find out personally.

# CHAPTER 11

Evangeline had seen only the wide hall and the dining room of Ben's house before—and, of course, Ben's study the dreadful night she'd chucked away her good sense and lain beneath and on top of him. His double drawing room was very pretty, in shades of cream and apricot. His mother's touch, no doubt. Ben looked rather ridiculous perched on a spindly striped chair as he and Lord Maxwell were in earnest conversation on the far side of the room, their two fair heads nearly touching. Ben was by far the better looking, his shoulders broader, his dimples deeper, his hazel eyes gleamier in the waning afternoon light.

Each man balanced a gilt-edged plate on his lap with the remains of the hastily prepared wedding feast. Several empty bottles of champagne had already been removed, and Severson continued to circle the room with a fresh one. Evangeline had quite lost count at the number of glasses she'd consumed, but if Lizzie's flaming cheeks were any indication, they both had had enough.

"Are you nervous about tonight?" Evangeline whispered, even though the men were too far away to hear them.

Lizzie took a last sip and waved Severson away. "Terrified," she whispered back. "Lord B-basingstoke's touch was most unpleasant."

Evangeline's mouth dropped open. "You—he—I thought—"

Lizzie turned a more vivid shade of scarlet. "Oh! You misunderstand. He never managed to get me where he wanted me. But he took every opportunity to squeeze me somewhere when we met on the stairs. I had marks from his fingertips on my breast for *weeks*. And once"—the girl shuddered—"he kissed me. It was slobbery and disgusting."

Evangeline laid a hand over Lizzie's new ring, a plain gold band with a single small diamond at its center. "I'm sure Lord Maxwell will be gentler." Although sometimes a good squeeze was not unwelcome, she thought ruefully, though slobbery kisses were definitely *de trop*.

"What should I do to please my husband?" Lizzie asked, her brown eyes wide.

"I'm hardly an expert."

"No, of course not! But I assumed with you pretending to be a man all these months that you must know something of what gentlemen like. They gossip as much as any old tabby."

They did indeed. She had heard a hair-curling tale or two crawling through the underbelly of society to get her front-page scoops.

"I think," she said carefully, "that Lord Maxwell is not like most men. He is, as you must have noticed, extremely shy."

Lizzie nodded. "Yes. He cannot seem to talk to me."

"There needn't be much talking tonight. He'll get into his dressing gown and come into your room. Or his room. I'm not sure his bachelor apartments have a separate bedroom. They're on the shabby side, you know. But his marriage to you releases his funds, so I expect that will all change."

"He m-married me for *his* money," Lizzie giggled, then hiccupped.

"Well, you're not an heiress, but you're just as good as far as he's concerned. If you are gentle with *him,* not frightened of his body, I think you'll do very well together. Above all, show no disgust—no matter the man, they're all fragile when it comes to their manhood." She closed her eyes, seeing Ben's cock in her mind's eye, definitely not a fragile thing at all. He had every reason to be smug size-wise. But of course everything about him was large—it was the Scot in him. Evangeline had never seen him in his ancestral kilt, but admitted she wanted to.

But better yet, she wanted to see him in nothing at all.

She slapped her glass down on a piecrust table. "Now then, I assume you know the mechanics of the procedure?"

"N-not really. In the foundling home we were told to never, ever lift our skirts to a man. That's all."

Evangeline gritted her teeth. Her own experience was haphazard and nothing to rely upon. She was not about to tell the new little viscountess what she had allowed herself to do to Ben so recently, when he had definitely been more than "pleased." Trying to remember what her old nurse had told her thousands of years ago, when she was still a green girl and had not yet met Baron Benton Gray, she began, nearly tripping over her words as badly as Lord Maxwell.

"There is a secret, special place between your legs. Inside you. That is where the man's member goes. You've seen a male penis, perhaps? On one of Basingstoke's infant sons?"

Lizzie's brows knit. "That little thing?"

"They grow larger as the man does, naturally. And on no account are you to ever call Lord Maxwell's penis little. Is that understood?"

"Y-yes. So he puts his thing—his *big* thing—inside me. Then what?"

"Well," Evangeline sighed, "you move together. It might be a little uncomfortable at first, but don't just lie there like a dead fish. A man appreciates some participation. On the other hand, perhaps you *should* just lie there the first time to prove your innocence and see what Lord Maxwell does. He may be very quick." Thank goodness she would never marry and have to prepare a daughter for her wedding night and endure a similar discussion in the years ahead. She felt she was making a complete and utter hash of it.

"How long does it usually take?"

If one was lucky, quite a long, delicious time, but Evangeline was not going to divulge all that right now.

"It varies with the man and the circumstance." She glanced over to Maxwell, who was green about the gills. Whatever Ben was telling him seemed to have an alarming effect. "You should kiss him before submitting. Lots of kisses. And not just closed-mouth pecks. Open your mouth to his. That will relax both of you."

"Really?" Lizzie looked skeptical.

"Truly. A proper kiss cannot be overrated."

"Lord Basingstoke did not taste very good. He'd just eaten kippers, I believe. And I told you, it was so *wet*."

"Some moisture is delightful. And I'm sure Lord Maxwell will brush his teeth before bedtime."

Lizzie still did not look convinced, and truthfully, Evangeline was not convinced herself that Lord Maxwell would do the thing with the necessary skill. She hoped Ben's tutorial was going a bit better than hers. It was a pity he didn't have time to take the man to a brothel to give him some experience, no matter how tawdry.

It was out of her hands now. She had done the best she

could, killing two needy birds with one stone. Evangeline kept a little journal in her desk drawer with her successes, and tomorrow when she went into the office she would add the union of Lord and Lady Maxwell to *The London List*'s list.

The snow continued unabated outside, but eventually Lord Maxwell decided to brave it and bring his bride home. One last glass was raised, and it would have been rude of Evangeline to forgo it even if her head *was* spinning just a little.

She found herself alone with Ben in the gilded room. A roaring fire at each end made her feel distinctly overheated. The shadows were lengthening despite Severson's lighting the sconces and candelabrum before he disappeared, taking the tray of dishes and glasses with him. Evangeline needed to disappear, too—her father had been left alone long enough.

"If you would be so good as to have someone fetch me a cab, it's time I was leaving as well."

"I won't hear of it," Ben said, his golden eyebrows contracting. "I called for you. I shall bring you home as well."

"That's not at all necessary. You've done more than your duty today."

Ben smiled. "If you only knew. Maxwell and I had the most awkward conversation. I'd almost like to be a fly on the wall tonight when he consummates his marriage."

"I'm sure that wouldn't be the first time you observed such activity," Evangeline said sourly.

"Ah, but Evie, I'd so much rather participate than observe behind some knothole. Surely your research bears that out."

That was true. Ben's reputation may have been tarnished, but it did not seem pitted with perversion. Benton Gray was a healthy, rich young man who did not deny himself pleasure in any of its traditional forms, for why would he? To his credit, he'd never once claimed to be a saint.

"I spoke to Lizzie, too. I'm grateful to be spared such a discussion in the future."

"What do you mean? Surely you're not giving up your matchmaking."

"It's unlikely I'll ever encounter anyone so innocent again. And I'll never have to tell my daughter how to entertain her husband."

"Planning on having sons only?"

"Planning on never having any children, my lord, as I will never marry. And in case you were concerned, I'm certain there is no possibility of a child after last week's folly."

Ben turned his face quickly to the fire, but she had seen a flare of emotion there before he could hide it. For some reason she continued her too-honest dialogue.

"I am a fallen woman, Ben. Old. My father is ill, and I have no money. Who would marry me, even if I wished it? And I don't," she added with conviction.

Ben snorted. "Have you forgotten the sum I settled on your papa?"

"All right, I concede I'm not precisely poor at the moment. But what man wants another's leavings?"

"For God's sake, you sound like a bloody moral crusader. There's nothing wrong with you sleeping with me all those years ago. You were young and stupid and made a mistake." *So did I,* she heard him mutter.

"You were not the only man, Ben. I've had other lovers." Just the two, but she'd already said more than enough. Damn the champagne for her wayward tongue.

His face darkened and a muscle in his jaw leaped, but he did not speak for a very long minute. And when he did, his one word surprised her.

"Good."

"I beg your pardon?"

"I'd hate to think of you all alone these past years. You are a warm-blooded woman, Evie. You deserve happiness."

Happiness had not been the precise outcome of her two botched affairs, but the time for confession had passed. She needed to go—for many reasons. But she picked one that he would understand. "I must get home to my father, Ben."

"Of course. Forgive me for being so thoughtless. He must be missing you."

"Perhaps, if he remembers me today," she said wistfully.

Ben left her on the sofa while he went to order the coach to come round. Evangeline stared at the fire just as Ben had, looking for a hidden sign in the flames that would tell her what she should do. She was stuck with Benton Gray until Tuesday at least, after which she might tear up every outstanding letter, overturn the desk drawers, and kick the press with one of Mr. Ramsey's scuffed boots.

Being with Benton Gray was not safe. Not safe at all.

The carriage lanterns swayed as the horses made their slow, slippery way across town. Even with the hot bricks he'd ordered, the carriage was cold. Evie was buttoned up in her old cloak, her hat abandoned for the fur-lined hood. He had tucked several tartan blankets over her, but couldn't miss the fact that she was shivering.

"This is absurd. Come here."

He didn't wait for her obedience, but tugged her across the carriage to his lap.

"Brute," she said, but she snuggled up against him. He wrapped his arms around her, pulling the plaid wool up under her chin.

"Better?"

He felt her nod against his shoulder. She smelled of

roses and wine. Ben hoped he hadn't overdone the liquid celebration for the bride and groom. It wouldn't do to have Maxwell pass out in a drunken stupor before he had a chance to put Ben's advice to use. He was feeling a little light-headed himself.

"It was a lovely day," Evie murmured through a yawn.

"It's not over yet."

"It's nearly dark."

"That's not what I mean." He cupped her cheek and turned her face to him. "I think I'm going to kiss you."

"I wish you wouldn't." But she made no move to slide off his lap.

"I can't seem to help myself. You're right here, and your lips are so close." He slid a gloved finger across them. Her mouth was rosy, tempting. All of her made him want to ravish her in the carriage, snow be damned.

"Toss me back to the other seat, then," she replied when his finger reluctantly finished tracing her plump bottom lip.

"And watch you tremble with cold? What kind of a gentleman would I be?"

"You are no gentleman at all."

Her dark lashes flicked at his closeness, and he felt her warm breath against his face when she spoke. Ben shook his head. He had not quite gotten over last week's insult to his honor. As if he'd be stupid enough to risk his health and hers by consorting with indiscriminate women to bring madness and eventual death upon them. The one sure thing about Jane Street and its inhabitants were that they were clean of body if not necessarily pure of soul.

"You have such low expectations for me, Evie. I've told you I'm a reformed character."

"I have yet to see it."

"You'll see it. Tomorrow. This afternoon—tonight— will be my last exercise of wickedness."

"I told you—I must get home."

"Yes. But you will be thoroughly kissed before you get there."

He waited a beat, anticipating her scramble away from him. But if anything, she had stopped moving. Even her breathing seemed to have ceased.

"What are you waiting for?" she whispered.

"Permission." He was a fool to ask for it, especially from Evie. But no matter what she thought, he *was* a gentleman. She had told him last week that their *mesalliance* was at an end. For eternity. She'd been very specific and he'd agreed that nothing about their relationship had ever worked.

Except the bedding part. The fucking. The glorious melding of flesh and heat that had only gotten better between them with age.

"I thought we said—"

"I'm a man of my word. I promise I won't tear your clothes off like last time. It's only a kiss. A celebratory kiss on the good work we've done today."

He could feel her hesitation, as well as his own mutinous cock stirring beneath her bottom. She must feel it through the fabric and fur of her cloak, must know that no matter what pact they made between them, there was a stubborn thread of attraction that didn't seem to recognize good sense or propriety.

Her eyes glittered in the dim light, and then she shut them, as if she didn't want to face what was to come. He took that as assent, brushing his mouth against hers. She opened to him artlessly, and he tasted champagne and the undercurrent of her own sweet self. Sweet—what an odd word to impose upon her. Evangeline Ramsey was the least sweet woman he knew. But as his tongue swept in to conquer, her flavor drew him as no other ever had.

Her arms had gone around his neck while he parried

and licked, and Ben didn't think she pressed herself against him simply for warmth. She was responsive, returning each lazy twist of his tongue with one of her own, her teeth grazing and nipping in gentle assault. He opened his eyes to see hers still firmly closed, a fan of dark lashes shadowing her pink cheeks. If she saw him now, truly *saw* him, she would know how much he desired her for all her difficult, wiry ways. There had never been anyone who had touched him as she had, despite their bitter parting.

But the past was just that—so long ago and not worth considering. The present was everything, and short it would be as his well-groomed animals drew them ever closer to her house through the storm. For now, he had a beautiful woman in his lap, her breast thrusting against the palm that had slipped beneath her cloak, her legs parting in open invitation for him to move it lower.

But he had promised. Just because she was losing her head in the heat of this magical snow-kissed moment did not mean that he had to. So he concluded their encounter with grave intent, willing each silken nibble to be stored in his Evie dream-file to be examined later. Likely his hand would be on his iron-hard cock, which even now begged for the release that was impossible.

But not before he rained kisses on her throat and eyelids, her lashes tickling his skin. What harm could it do to ease her bodice down and cover her nipple with a searing kiss? She flinched in his arms as he suckled, drawing the raspberry areola deep between his teeth, careful not to bite her—*consume* her—as every instinct raged. Ben wished he had more mouths, one to remain trapped above by her satiny lips, one to taste her honeyed womanhood below simultaneously. The thought of her bursting on his tongue everywhere made him flinch himself.

He set her back on the squabs as though she were a gangly rag doll, straightening the fur-lined hood back over her cropped hair. She looked up at him with dazed incomprehension. He hoped she wondered why he'd stopped, wondered how he *could* stop. Wanting him not to.

"There," he said, his voice rough. "That should put a period to the itch between us. No more kisses."

"Indeed not," she said, breathless. "I was simply overcome by all your French champagne."

At least the French were good for something, Ben thought darkly, planning already to drown the rest of the evening in some of their brandy.

# CHAPTER 12

*December 17, 1820*

Ben had rolled up his shirtsleeves and Evangeline resolved not to look at the dusting of golden hair on his corded forearms. The baron was, as ever, a very distracting man. At this rate, the paper wouldn't come out until next year.

Her dummy on sheets of foolscap was lined neatly with a ruler, grids with every advertisement carefully printed, each page headed by its category. The front page detailed the charming private wedding of the elusive Lord M and his Cinderella bride, Miss S. For once every word was positive, dripping in romantic matrimonial honey that would set the ton's teeth on edge and make them long for the usual juicy scandal. But Ben had been firm that he did not want to subject his peers to her treatment, and Evangeline had reluctantly agreed. She had spent her Saturday night—still a little tipsy from the spontaneous reception at Ben's—mythologizing Lizzie's plain dress and her groom's strangled vows. The article was not her best, but it would have to do.

It took many hours just to set the type each week, so the Sunday church bells chimed outside as she and Ben huddled over the worktable, the job case between them. It had been some years since Evangeline had gone to church. Working on the Sabbath was just another sin to add to her portfolio.

"These are all jumbled," Ben complained over the compartmentalized wooden tray that held the metal sorts. "Why aren't the letters in alphabetical order?"

"They're arranged by frequency of use, the 'h' next to the 't,' for example. You'll get used to it." This was something she'd been very happy to let Frank do for her, though she could do it—had done it last week—all by herself. It was exacting, blinding work, each tiny rectangle set into its row, coppers and brasses tightening so they wouldn't migrate as they pressed into the paper.

"And they're not called letters, but sorts. You know the expression 'Out of sorts?' When one runs out of sorts, it's impossible to finish the print job and one becomes quite grumpy."

"Ha. You are a font of knowledge today, Evie."

"I'm trying to 'make a good first impression,' " she grinned. "Which is what we'll do once we finish setting up and print the first sheet, which hopefully will be free of error. We'll both go over it with a magnifying glass before we do the full print run. *The London List* is printed on one large piece of paper on both sides, then folded. As you've discovered, we could easily double the size of it with all our requests, but until we get a steam-driven press, we'll have to keep to our modest scale. I must tell you, one's arms get tired making almost five hundred copies an hour. A Koenig press would be a dream."

"You want me to spend more money. As if you haven't squeezed enough out of me."

Evangeline knew Ben could afford a dozen new presses. "You may decide it's well worth it when you cannot lift your arms Tuesday morning to comb your hair," she said pertly.

"Look, I know I said I wanted to see how things worked, but surely we can hire a pressman now and save ourselves all this trouble."

"Bored already?" She should have counted on him bailing out on her and the tedious work.

Ben frowned. "No, it's all quite fascinating, actually. But wouldn't you rather devote your time to settling your needy clientele? Concentrate on the people rather than the printing?"

That had never been a choice before—she'd had to do everything and like it. "Do you mean it? I've hired back the boys, but you'd employ another man?"

"I would. It's only been a few days, but I want my life back."

To continue his profligate ways, no doubt. "I'll ask around."

"And you can always advertise the position," he winked. He scribbled something on a piece of paper and passed it to her. It was a succinct employment ad for one skilled pressman. He was getting very good at this business already.

"Speaking of which." She picked up the blackened tiles and began to pack the form for the first ad. She remembered the original letter, written in a halting, spidery hand. A country gentleman was in need of a housekeeper/nurse. He offered very little in the way of pay, and Evangeline was not optimistic that his wish could be granted. She pictured the man, wizened and infirm, toasting his piece of stale bread over a sputtering fire, his clothes in need of laundering. Really, if she had money she'd be the softest touch imaginable, supporting as many indigent, lonely old people as she could.

Her fingers flew with practiced speed, her eye used to viewing everything backward. Ben stood next to her, too close, following her every movement. Today it was he who was wearing sandalwood cologne—her favorite scent. She felt like she was under a magnifying glass herself.

She had his complete attention.

And wasn't sure she wanted it.

"You're a marvel, Evie."

The breath of his words at her ear made her shiver.

"Not really. I'm just accustomed to it. Here. You try."

Ben squinted at the mockup. "Are you sure you want to run this advertisement? It seems—indecent."

"There is nothing exceptional about a woman seeking employment as a wet-nurse. She needs to feed herself to feed her child and, according to her letter, has plenty of milk for another." She stared at Ben. "Don't tell me you're a prude, Lord Gray. That's what women's breasts are for, you know—they're not merely playthings for men of your ilk." Like yesterday, when he'd nearly undone her with his tender dedication to her left breast. Her right one was still pouting at being neglected.

"My ilk? You make me sound unnatural for admiring the female form." His eyes drifted down to her indifferently endowed chest, covered by stock and linen and waistcoat. She felt the peculiar tug to her nipples but tried to ignore her shamelessness.

"We haven't got time for you to ogle me, Ben." She slid the leading in after the last advertisement. "Your turn. Start on the right."

Ben's large fingers were clumsy picking up and packing in the type, and Evangeline bit back her impatience. If Ben was true to his word, they would be hiring an experienced pressman for next week's edition and he would not have to labor over this chore again. His hands were altogether too big for the delicate job, although his brawn would come in handy as he operated the machinery tomorrow.

The room was snug with heat. Now that Lord Gray was

the publisher of *The London List,* he'd had plenty of coal delivered to the office, but standing so close to supervise the vexing man made her even warmer. Evangeline brushed the moisture off her upper lip and forced herself to not imagine removing her neckcloth to bare her neck and what Ben might do if she did.

He had kissed her neck—and other places—yesterday in the carriage, whether from too much celebratory champagne or simply because he could. But they had both agreed that such a thing must not happen again.

Particularly not before the newspaper was put to bed. They didn't have time to dally.

But Tuesday? Evangeline could kiss Ben on Tuesday. Evangeline wanted to kiss Ben on Tuesday.

Evangeline wanted to kiss him *now.*

He looked so earnest as he slipped the type in, his brow furrowed. But as adorable as he was, if she permitted him to continue at this pace they would never finish in time. She decided to give him—and herself—a reprieve. If she had to spend all day with him, she might not be able to keep her inconvenient emotions in check.

She was not going to find herself on the floor of the storeroom, legs wrapped around Ben as he effortlessly brought her to orgasm. And truly, it wouldn't take much. Evangeline felt fairly starved for affection. Beneath her gentleman's clothing, she was a woman awakened to the undeniable, unwelcome attractiveness of Lord Benton Gray.

She should know better. She *did* know better.

She was a hopeless case.

Ten years of tying up her heart against him, and he'd unraveled it all in less than two weeks.

She reminded herself that they fought as hard as they fucked. One didn't want constant upheaval in one's life. One wanted peace and quiet. Comfort. Security.

Which would never happen with Ben unless he was struck by lightning and forgot he was the ton's favorite rakehell.

He was not one of those dark, mysterious brooding types, which made him all the more welcome in ballrooms and bedrooms. His sunny disposition worked its magic even with her most of the time.

"That's enough. I'll take over now."

"Damn it. I'm just getting the hang of it, Evie."

"You've misspelled 'butler.' One wouldn't want 'an experienced butter.' It would be rancid." She took the frame away from him and filled in the rest of the sorts.

"What else can I do to help?"

There were hours of work ahead, fewer if she just worked alone. "You can fetch me some lunch. Something simple."

"Done! You'll be all right if I leave you?"

"Perfectly. It's Sunday, and I don't expect any interruptions. Come back in a couple of hours."

Ben looked vastly relieved as he shrugged himself into his coat, but nowhere as relieved as she was. His physical presence was both delicious and disconcerting. Best to have him go off for ale and meat pies before she forgot herself and fell into his arms once again.

Mrs. Hargreaves, the cook, had grumbled. Two days running and he'd surprised her with unexpected guests and requests for picnic baskets. But she knew which side her bread was buttered on—or butlered on, as he might have substituted. Perhaps his vision really was going—setting type was a painstaking task. Poor Evie would be blind before today was out.

He'd chosen to walk back with the basket bouncing against his hip. He needed the exercise after spending the past few days cooped up in the office and in church. But as he rounded the corner, he wondered if he should not have come by carriage so he could make a speedy escape. There were several people standing in front of *The London List*'s plate glass window, or what was left of it. Ben spotted Evie's dark head in the middle of the little mob and stepped livelier. The fool woman didn't have the sense not to confront the disenfranchised readers and advertisers who had obviously taken matters into their own rough hands.

"What's all this?" he shouted. "Back away from Mr. Ramsey if you know what's good for you."

Faces turned to him in confusion. They didn't look like the sort of ragtag people who had visited his house earlier in the week. In fact, he recognized the tobacconist he'd bought cheroots from.

"We've alerted the watch. Someone should be here soon," Evie said, her voice not pitched quite as low as it needed to be to maintain the fiction of masculine gender.

"My brother and nephews and I were just passing by this afternoon to pick up a few extra Spanish cigarillos, my lord. We heard the crash, but didn't see the blackguard who did this. Such a shame. This is a respectable district. All this fuss about closing the paper has been bad for business."

"We aren't closing," Ben said tersely. "What happened, Ev—Mr. Ramsey? Are you all right?"

She nodded, looking far too pale. And cold. She had come out into the street without her jacket. Instinctively Ben set the basket down among the shattered glass, tore his own coat off, and covered her shoulders.

"I was behind the press when it happened. I didn't see anything either."

"Why would someone do this?" the tobacconist asked. "Apart from Lord Gray before he bought the paper, that is." The man had the grace to color at his heedless words.

"I don't know. The people who were here before were upset that the paper was not going to remain in business. There's no reason to be angry now. Most everyone knows that Lord Gray has changed his mind," Evie said.

"It was even in the other newspapers," Ben added. Evie had granted the bloody interviews without him. At least the articles had not dredged up his sordid history with *The List,* just announced him as the new owner of record who intended a new direction for the paper.

"Well, gentlemen, you must have an unknown enemy. Unless it was simply a Sunday prank. Ah, here's my nephew Clarence with a member of the watch. Well done, lad."

The young man's cheeks were red from the blistering cold. Ben was freezing himself. "Let's step inside where it's warmer." Even with the broken window, the stove would be going at a merry coal-fueled clip.

The tobacconist and his family excused themselves as they were witnesses only to the aftermath. The officer of the watch did not appear overly concerned or meticulous in his taking down information for his report, and did not stay long. Ben resolved at once to hire a guard for the building and keep Evie away as much as possible. It would take some persuading, but surely she could go over all her correspondence at home and delegate the actual operation of the printing press to the employee he would also hire. Today, if he could, but it was Sunday. He explained his plans in a few soothing sentences, careful not to mention it was unseemly that she still be here in trousers pretending to be a man.

"I'm s-sure all that's not necessary," Evie chattered.

Ben added more coal to the stove. "I don't suppose I could convince you to go home."

"I'm not quite finished. We'll do the printing tomorrow, but there are still a few things left to do."

"Lunch first," Ben said firmly, pushing her down in a

chair near the stove. "Mrs. Hargreaves would never forgive me if we wasted the food."

"I'm not hungry."

"Nonsense." He rummaged in the basket he'd brought in from the street. At one time the crock of soup had been piping hot, but lukewarm was better than nothing. He ladled some into a mug and brought it to Evie's lips, his fingers on the back of her marble-cold neck. "I'll get the window boarded up this afternoon after I see you home. We'll get a glazier in tomorrow. Take a sip, love."

For a change, Evie obeyed. He broke a roll apart and placed it in her upturned grubby hand. "Eat. There's wine, too. Some cold chicken. Apple tart." He spread the feast on the desk, taking care to neatly stack Evie's papers off to one corner. "Warm enough?"

"Yes, thank you."

When Ben thought of Evie, she was like a blaze in a stove, crackling with energy, unpredictable. This afternoon, she was drained of her light.

"You were frightened, weren't you? There's no shame to it." He passed her a tumbler of Madeira, which she gulped.

"Silly of me. I was startled, but I've been in worse spots. Last winter I was nearby when they arrested Thistlewood and his friends."

Ben choked on a mouthful of chicken. "Jesus Christ, Evie! You could have been killed or arrested for high treason!" Thistlewood had stabbed a Bow Street runner during the arrest, and had wanted to kill all the king's cabinet ministers in a fantastical scheme to overthrow the government.

"I didn't organize the conspiracy, Ben. I was perfectly safe."

"Damn me. Are you a Radical, Evie?"

"Of course not. But you must admit society isn't fair.

The government has a lot to answer for, and every now and again I write about it."

Privately Ben agreed. He supposed he ought to take his seat in the House of Lords more seriously and show up now and then. "Promise me you will undertake no more foolish endeavors just to fill up the front page of my newspaper."

"My subscribers aren't really interested in politics anyway," she sighed. "They'd much rather read about you climbing down a drain pipe to escape a cuckolded husband."

"I've never done such a thing!"

Evie fixed him with a gimlet eye.

"Well, just the once. And it was the lady's overbearing brother I was escaping from and she was a widow. I was only offering her comfort in her time of loss."

"*That* makes it all right."

Hell. He was tired of Evangeline Ramsey being his judge, jury, and executioner.

"In any event, my life has changed, as has your reporting. There will be no more embarrassing disclosures." He bit savagely into a tart.

"People will be bored. They've come to expect a little titillation every Tuesday."

"Well, they won't get it from us! There's a challenge for you—use that pointed poison pen for good for a change."

Evie batted her lashes. "May I go to riots then or hang out in the halls of Parliament?"

"No, you may not! There must be something innocuous you can write about without putting yourself at risk. It's time you stayed home. In your *skirts*."

Evie stood, hands fisted, her linen napkin floating to the floor. "Are you telling me you don't want my help here?"

"Yes! No! Of course I need you until I can sell the paper. But I won't have you in danger. People are throwing bricks through the window, for heaven's sake! Who else have you targeted?"

"Maybe someone holds a grudge against *you*, my lord. They know you own *The London List* now."

"I haven't got an enemy in the world. Everyone likes me. Except you, as you tell me day after day."

"Perhaps one of your many discarded mistresses doesn't."

Ben rose, too. "I am not going to discuss my private life with you. You are my employee. And if you do not leave the premises within the next quarter of an hour, I shall carry you bodily out the door." He began to shove the remains of their lunch back into the basket while Evie stalked over to the press, fiddling with something or other. Blast the woman. She was going to give him an apoplexy yet.

Mayhap the act of vandalism was a meaningless prank, but he wasn't going to take any chances. Once he got her home safely, he'd come back with Callum and see to fixing the window, then get someone to guard the place while they worked tomorrow. He didn't much care what happened to the building tonight as long as Evie was unharmed tomorrow.

*Riots.* Mother of God. The woman was incorrigible. She might think her trousers and top hat and vicious tongue protected her, but Ben knew better. He couldn't help but stare at her shapely bum as she bent over the equipment, banging something with a spanner.

"I'm done," she said mulishly. She wiped her hands on a rag and tossed it aside. "I'll meet you here tomorrow at nine."

"No, you will not. I'll see you home now and pick you up tomorrow."

Evie rolled her eyes but got dressed and followed him out into the deserted street. They had to walk a bit before they found a jarvey. His dilapidated hackney smelled of too many unwashed passengers, but it boasted warm bricks.

This time there was no lap-sitting and no extraordinary kisses. But tomorrow was another day.

# CHAPTER 13

*December 18, 1820*

His arm was going to fall off if it didn't wash away with sweat first, but Ben was too proud to utter one word of protest as he cranked out this week's edition of *The London List*. Evie was his able printer's assistant, providing fresh sheets of paper and changes of type. Outside, one of his footmen was supervising the installation of a new window. The tobacconist Mr. Kemble had recommended a man to paint new signage on the glass with a tin of gold leaf, and he sat patiently waiting on an extra chair by Evie's desk. Anyone who chose to make mischief on *The London List* today would be wise to think twice with all the manpower on the premises.

Ben eyed the tower of finished newspapers. Everyone in London must read the wretched thing judging from the number of copies and the state of his wobbly arm. Beads of perspiration clung to his eyelashes—he must smell like a resident of the vilest slum by now. Or a pig farmer who'd thrown his lot in with the animals and rolled in muck. Or a syphilitic blind man without a nose who'd mistaken an open sewer for a bathing pool. When he got home, he would take the hottest bath he could stand and scrub every filthy inch.

Evie looked slightly the worse for wear, too. Her dark curls were damp and clinging to her well-shaped head. Her face was flushed well beyond a maiden's blush. Her neck-cloth was wilted and perspiration stained her linen shirt.

Maybe she could take a bath with him.

Ben imagined her long white body slipping into the copper tub in his dressing room. He would soap her up personally, paying special attention to her dark cleft and the ruby within. He would raise her hips and settle her on his shaft and fuck her speechless with his last ounce of strength. He'd die a happy man.

"What are you smiling at?" Evie asked, placing a sheet of paper on the press.

Ben rubbed his arm, trying to regenerate some sort of feeling. "I was thinking how I would celebrate this work-day's ending."

"*I* plan to fall into bed."

Ben's lips twitched. "My thoughts exactly."

"Well, you should never have to do this again. We will be inundated with applicants after the ad in tomorrow's paper. The pay you offered is outrageous."

"I certainly hope so. And I can afford an investment in our business."

Evie's brow lifted. "*Our* business?"

"Figure of speech. You must admit we make an excellent team."

"I'll grant that you're not as stupid as I thought you were."

"Oh, please. Your excessive compliments will go to my head."

"We wouldn't want that. You're already too self-satisfied," Evie said crisply.

If she only knew how he'd been self-satisfying last night, picturing her bent over the press as he entered her from behind. In his fantasy, she'd been strapped in place so she couldn't escape him again, a silk scarf covering her mouth so she could not object to her predicament. Ben was not generally into that sort of thing, but he had to admit the image was inordinately vivid and intriguing. To have independent and inconvenient Evangeline Ramsey subdued and at his mercy probably would never happen, but a man could dream.

The door to the street opened, and a windblown band of urchins tumbled in like a litter of rowdy puppies. Evie's paperboys. Without even being spoken to, they attacked the pile of papers, folding and bundling them for their delivery routes and mail delivery. Ben noted they took every chance they could get to stare at him as he muscled his way through his task. Likely they had never seen a lord engaged in sweat-inducing work before. Most of Ben's peers would be appalled if they wandered through the door and caught him. It was one thing to exert oneself riding or fencing in Town, but physical labor was reserved for the countryside and a brief appearance in solidarity with one's tenants during haying season.

Of course, there was no hay at Castle Gray. The sheep saw to that. The rocky soil was nibbled right down to the ground. Ben had not been to his ancestral home in several years, but was assured by his steward that all was well. The Gray fortunes had profited by the war and its need for wool for uniforms and mutton for rations, but Ben had made sure his money was not tied to one industry or investment.

"I think," Evie said, interrupting his thoughts, "that we just might be finished."

Ben did not need to hear that twice. He stepped back from the press and mopped his brow with a soiled handkerchief. His valet would recommend burning it.

Evie huddled with the boys, dropping coins into their palms for tomorrow's work. It was to Evie's credit that they all would show up before dawn—paying them in advance was unheard of, but they had proven themselves to be loyal. She had a motherly way with them, which on the face of it was ridiculous—they thought her to be a fashionable young gentleman.

"Let's celebrate. I'll stand you to a pint and pasty at The Witch and Anchor."

"What about the window?"

"My footman John is still here. He can lock up with my key when the painter's finished."

Evie hesitated. "All right. Though we're both in a rather disreputable state."

"I won't sniff your armpits if you don't sniff mine. And the pub's not a grand place. Surely you've been there, as it's just down the street."

"I've never been, actually. I'm usually too busy, and I go home to my father for lunch."

"How is he?"

A shadow crossed her face. "About the same. He'll never get better, only worse."

"I'm sorry, Evie. He was great fun when I knew him."

Robert Ramsey had been a legend, a gambler who risked all and kept his good humor even when he lost. Which was probably more often than Evie would have liked, poor girl. As a fellow Scot, Ramsey had taken Ben under his wing when he came down from university, introduced him to the highest and lowest hells.

And his daughter. Few in London even knew she existed. Ramsey kept her away from his cronies, but must have seen some good in Ben to allow them to meet. Evie had dazzled him, then dumped him on his arse.

He spoke to John while she instructed the sign painter, and they were off. The December wind was brisk, and by the time they got to the pub, Evie's cheeks had lost their pallor. To Ben's eyes, she looked even less like a young man with roses on her cheeks, so he tucked her into a booth in a dark corner to avoid discovery and ordered dinner.

Her appetite was as great as any man's, however. Ben sat back in wordless amusement as she made considerable inroads on her meal and his besides. After three tankards of ale, she leaned back on the wooden bench, her long limbs relaxed for the first time in days. The burden of the paper had been a heavy one, and Ben was glad he could share it in some small way, even if his muscles were currently in agony.

"Next week at this time I expect you will not be swilling ale but a proper cup of tea at home by the fire."

"That's if we find someone suitable."

"We will. *You* wrote the ad."

"*Your* writing skill has improved. Your original ad was good—I just embellished it a little," Evie said, returning the compliment.

Ben had exercised his brain muscles as well this past week. He'd found his role of publisher surprisingly stimulating.

And that wasn't all he'd enjoyed. Spending time with Evie, whether she was sour or sweet, had been—what? Pleasant? Far too innocuous a word. She stirred his blood, annoyed him, and challenged him. The sight of her now with her beaver hat rakishly dipping over one dark eye made him want to toss her on top of the table and have his wicked way with her. That would alarm the patrons of this relatively respectable establishment, and alarm her, too.

"I'll take you home if you're done."

"Really, Ben, I'm perfectly safe." She brushed a few crumbs from her waistcoat. It must be freeing for her to break out of the boundaries set for a woman, but she was still vulnerable. Whoever had thrown the brick through the window might be lurking on the dusk-dimmed street right now, waiting to club Evie's beaver hat off her head.

"I insist."

"Damn it. You cannot tell me what to do or how to do it, Ben."

"Someone should take you in hand." From the moment he spoke the words, he knew they were a mistake.

"As if I'll allow you or any man dominion over me!"

"Quiet. People will think we're having a lovers' quarrel."

Evie sputtered but shut her lovely mouth.

"Come. I'll hail a cab."

"You're not the bloody boss of me."

"Tsk. Language, Mr. Ramsey. There might be a lady present. Somewhere underneath all that." He gave her what he hoped to be a scorching look, mentally peeling off the man's attire that flattered her so outrageously.

But Evie naked on a night like this, so tempting, would never do. The temperature had dropped considerably since their earlier stroll down the street. Ben could see Evie's breath in the air as she stomped in irritation at the curb. She reminded him a little of an unbroken Thoroughbred, all lean lines and attitude. But according to her, she'd never be broken to bridle.

Ben wouldn't even bother trying.

Evie was a shrew. A confirmed spinster. True, she could be softhearted with all her cases of people to place and protect. He'd now seen the drawers full of begging letters for which she took no coin. What kind of businesswoman was she? She was more like some demented fairy god-mother.

Anyone looking less fairy-like would be hard to find. Although perhaps his mother's tales of sweet, inoffensive winged creatures dancing at the bottom of the garden were at odds with some of the older legends. Some fairies were spiteful—clever and capricious, quick to trick the unsuspecting innocent into giving up their best chance for happiness. Or even their babies. Ben drew the line at thinking Evie would kidnap a child, but he could see her meting out her own brand of justice from her Fairy Court in solemn pronouncements and punishing seduction.

Right now she wasn't speaking to him, not even thanking him as he helped her into the hack. Which he shouldn't have done, as she was still in her trousered disguise. The merchants on the street would think it very odd.

The streetlights had been turned on, and Ben saw people locking up and scurrying home to their suppers. *The List*'s office was dark, the new window glimmering in the gaslight. A raggedy girl selling roasted chestnuts tended the flames on her brazier at the corner, and if Ben weren't so full he would have asked the driver to stop. The carriage lurched through the thick evening traffic, the familiar sounds and smells of London Ben's only stimulation. Evie seemed determined to ignore him despite their working so seamlessly together just hours before. How was it that the glow of their mutual accomplishment had dimmed so suddenly? One minute they'd been chuckling over their ale, and the next Evie looked ready to chuck him out in the street.

He'd insulted her independence, he supposed, but really, she *was* just a lady beneath her clothes, even if she chose not to act like one. She might have a walking stick and be taller than the average man, but it wasn't as if she fenced and boxed and built up her slender limbs. Anything could happen to her as she walked the chill streets of London. Anything at all.

Yesterday it was the shattered window, when she wasn't even out in the elements. What if she'd been cut by flying glass, or worse yet, conked on the head with the brick?

Perhaps some sense might have been knocked into her, but Ben doubted it. She was the most stubborn, most vexing creature he'd ever met. His usual tricks to charm women were proving useless, but damn him if he was going to sit across from her like a lump as she shot daggers at him the whole way home. So he took a time-tested, easy route.

"I'm sorry."

"What for?" she asked, suspicious.

Ben grinned. "I don't really know. It seemed like the right thing to say."

She did not grin back. "If you don't know, then your words are meaningless. Like your life."

Ben fought his own flare of temper. "Give it a rest, Evie. I've worked like a slave all week."

"One paltry week in a lifetime of indolence. And it's only been about four days anyway. You can't count the wedding."

"Spending four days with *you* seems like a lifetime. Damn it. I suppose you'd like to roll out your personal guillotine and deprive me of my head for being a useless aristocrat."

"It is tempting. But likely to be messy." Evie's mocking lips twitched. But apparently she didn't want his blood quite yet.

"I thought we were friends again." He leaned forward and clasped her hand. She didn't withdraw her clenched fist or try to kick him. That was a good sign, no matter what horrible thing she was going to say next.

"Friends!" She said the word as if she spat worms from her mouth. "I cannot be your friend."

"And why not?" Ben asked softly. "My company is not a total anathema to you, is it?"

"You are my employer. It's unseemly for us to fraternize beyond the workplace."

Ben slid across the seat. "Dinner must have been diabolical for you. All that fraternizing. I suppose it's unseemly for me to kiss you now as well."

"Very." But she didn't dart away, and Ben took that as an invitation to continue. He was a bloody fool for her—he'd already lost his head without the assistance of Mme. Guillotine or a brick aimed at it.

Ben traced her pout with a gloved fingertip. "It might even be construed as a master taking advantage of his servant."

"I am no one's servant! And yes, it would. There should be laws against such things in the workplace. Women should not have to put up with—" She paused, her eyes dark.

"Harassment." Ben's hand glided down her caped greatcoat to where he estimated her breasts to be. It was devilish difficult to tell beneath all the layers of wool and linen.

"Exactly so. Like poor Lizzie and Lord Basingstoke. You are harassing me right now."

"I am, aren't I?" He slipped under the clasp of her coat. More fabric, but he was an expert at getting what he wanted.

"You must stop," she whispered.

"Must I?" He nuzzled her neck, nearly cutting his nose on her starched collar points.

"I'll scream."

"Yes, I believe you will. Sit back, Evie. We've a ways to go before I get you home. I pledge to be efficient. You'll enjoy your harassment, I promise."

"Ben—"

He kissed her to shut her up, covering up her insincere objections with his boldness. He met no resistance; she opened her mouth to him with greedy generosity. Her falls were unbuttoned with ease after years of his own experience undressing in dark places, and wetness drenched

his suede-gloved fingers. Too late to think about removing his gloves. Perhaps the friction of the leather was apt
to give her a new sensation he could only envy, as she
made no move to relieve him of his agony.

He'd promised to be efficient, and he was a man of his
word. Evie heaved against him, her moans swallowed up
in their unbroken kiss. He ruthlessly brought her over
twice more as she clutched his shoulders in what could be
described only as a death grip.

The hackney slowed. With all the traffic, they would
have gotten home faster on foot, but then Evie would not
have been so thoroughly harassed. From her dazed di-
shevelment, Ben wondered if he would have to carry her
to her front door.

"Take tomorrow off." He kissed her forehead. Somewhere along the way, her hat had been knocked off, and
his hand swept down to find it on the floor.

"I cannot. The boys will come for their bundles," she
said, breathless.

"What time?"

"Around five. And no," she said, pushing him away,
"you do not have to be there. I can handle it myself as I
always do." She scrambled out the door, holding her hat
over her misbuttoned breeches.

"All right," he called after her. Ben was grateful he
wouldn't have to crawl out of bed before dawn again to
try to impress Evangeline Ramsey.

Although he had a feeling his impression, like the first
fresh sheet of newsprint, was improving ever so slightly.

# CHAPTER 14

**December 19, 1820**

Thank God Ben had not shown his bloody handsome phiz at the office this morning. Sleeping his sins away—who knew what he'd been up to after he'd so shamelessly taken advantage of her in the cab? Evangeline was probably just the innocent hors d'oeuvre before his banquet of debauchery.

The boys were long gone, and there was nothing for her to do but lock up the office. She'd come back later to check the post—there was bound to be the usual slew of letters, and sometimes people came in person to check their boxes or place an ad. But right now she wanted nothing more than to crawl in Lady Pennington's well-padded lap and have a morning cup of chocolate. She and Lady Pennington had a standing date every Tuesday morning to discuss what was in the paper. And out of it.

Evangeline was nothing if not methodical, and she made one last round to inspect the premises to see that everything had been put away properly yesterday. When she got to the box of sorts, she frowned. And sniffed. A glop of something had been poured on all the letter Es. Gingerly she picked up a sticky lead tile and brought it closer. Honey, if her prominent nose was doing its work.

How very odd. She did not keep any honey with her tea things in her cupboard, and in any event, no one had drunk or eaten over the sorts as far as she knew. Unless the sign painter or John the footman had done so yesterday when Ben dragged her down the street for their dinner.

Damn. What a nuisance. One could not put out a news-paper without the letter *E,* or even spell the word *spell.* Grumbling, she scooped up the sorts and put them in a bag. She'd have to take them all home and wash them.

Suspicious now, she made another sweep of the office, but nothing else seemed out of place or damaged in any way. Maybe she was the victim of sweet-toothed mice, or perhaps one of the boys had played a prank when her back had been turned this morning. She didn't like to think that she'd been taken advantage of by a member of the male species yet again—her young employees might be a wild bunch, but she'd been good to them and they to her.

Evangeline left the bag on her desk. She was not going to burden herself by the weight of the lead letters as she visited Lady Pennington. She tied her muffler right up to her nose. People had been predicting a white Christmas this year—the brief taste of snow the other day had whet the appetites of those who would like to see London's gray winter gloom frosted with white icing. She didn't care one way or the other, but at least there was money now to replace her old fur-lined cloak with something more stylish.

Evangeline sighed. She loved gentlemen's clothes—they were warm and practical, and her movement in them was unrestricted. Unfettered. If she had to chase a footpad down the street, she could do so and had.

Deciding to walk—though she hoped not to encounter any footpads in broad daylight—Evangeline locked up and left the office.

A grubby little chestnut seller held a battered tray up on

the corner. "Mornin', guv! Some hot chestnuts for your missus?"

"No, thank you," Evangeline said, feeling for a coin in her pocket anyway. The poor girl looked half frozen. Evangeline would bring her old cloak to her once she bought a new one.

"Come from the newspaper, 'ave ye? Wot's ever 'appened to that Lady Im-Imaculata wot gets 'erself in all that tr-trouble regular like? I d-do likes to read about 'er, I do," the girl stuttered, her teeth chattering.

"I'll keep that under advisement," Evangeline said, dropping the coin on the tray. "Try to keep warm, my dear."

"Oi'll d-do that, guv."

The chestnut seller would be doomed to disappointment to read of Lady Imaculata any time soon, and probably frostbite if she stayed on the street today. Evangeline picked up her pace, really looking forward to that hot chocolate now. Scraps of paper skittered down the street in the wind, and she hoped the boys had safely delivered today's edition into the hands of customers instead of leaving it on their stoops. She preferred not to field complaints from any more readers about missing papers after last week's debacle.

Evangeline skipped up the steps of Lady Pennington's handsome house and rapped the lion's head knocker. Everything looked just as it should in this proper Mayfair neighborhood—it appeared to be the home of a conventional aristocrat, its rigidly geometric clipped boxwood bushes behind an iron fence, front door painted an unexceptional black like most of its neighbors. Lady Pennington shattered that image when she opened the door herself, a capacious apron covering a dove-gray silk dress. Her fading blond curls were covered by a cap whose lace she had probably made herself. She took Evangeline's gloved hands in her work-roughened ones and pulled her into the marble foyer.

"Mr. Ramsey!" she cried in a speaking tone in case any of her servants were nearby. "How good of you to call."

"Good day to you, Lady Pennington. You must know how much I look forward to our Tuesdays."

"You must be frozen! Come upstairs to my sitting room. Garwood has a nice wood fire going—none of that nasty coal for us. I'll tell him to fetch us some tea."

"Chocolate for me if you please, Lady Pennington. I confess I've thought of nothing else since I left my bed in the middle of the night."

"Of course, of course. Garwood, dear!" Lady Pennington called as they climbed the stairs. The butler appeared instantly, looking pained by the blandishment. His employer was not one's typical society matron. "A tray for Mr. Ramsey, with hot chocolate." She turned on the stairs and squeezed Evangeline's frozen fingers. "Perhaps a dram of brandy to go in it, too? To get your blood moving again. Your nose is quite pink."

Evangeline must have looked a sight, but she knew Lady Pennington wouldn't mind. The woman had been the only one in two years besides Ben to see through her disguise, and had never judged her for it.

"We're both of us tricksters, aren't we?" Lady Pennington had said on one occasion. "You posing as a gentleman, me pretending to be a viscountess."

"But you *are* a viscountess," Evangeline had protested.

"Thanks to you. But I'm not sure I'll ever get used to it."

Her marriage and nearly instant widowhood had scandalized the ton. Many assumed that Amy Pennington would go back to the country and obscurity, but Evangeline was delighted that her friend was still here.

When Viscount James Pennington first came to enlist her help, Evangeline had been touched by his reminiscences of his boyhood love. Amy Burton had been the daughter of his father's gamekeeper, entirely unsuitable in terms of marriage, but that had not stopped them both at sixteen from sealing their bond with something more than a kiss. Pennington's father had sent him to his sugar plantation in Jamaica, and Amy was hastily married off to a second cousin, a local farmer, and she bore Pennington's daughter and four living sons besides. This much Pennington knew from the discreet inquiries he made once he returned to England, but he'd not worked up the courage to contact Amy himself. He was ill, suffering from some malady he'd picked up in the tropics, his wife dead, his legitimate daughter settled in New Orleans with her own family. His regret was palpable.

Evangeline had known that the usual sort of ad would not do, and volunteered to be Lord Pennington's personal emissary to the Kentish countryside. Mrs. Burton's grown children had been horrified when Evangeline found her and presented Pennington's proposition. He hoped to see Amy again, and marry her if she'd have him. He intended to leave her a goodly chunk of his fortune in any case to make up for her youthful suffering.

In truth, Amy had not suffered much, except for the first few months of her marriage. But the morning sickness and disappointment did not last forever. Her late husband had been patient with her and kind to her daughter, treating the child like his own. Amy's gratitude had grown if not to love, then affection, and they had almost forty years together before he died. She had been comfortably settled among her children and grandchildren on the farm, a prosperous venture achieved through the hard work of all concerned. But the chance to do more for her family was too tempting to pass up, so she agreed to go back to London with Evangeline.

Evangeline had hosted the reunion in the freshly swept room above *The London List*'s office. Amy Burton had told her that after one look at James Pennington, she knew she'd be widowed too soon again if she married him. He was not the boy of her occasional dreams, but then she was no longer the girl of his. James had stared at her as if she was, though, and that and the prospect of financial security had overcome any reservations she might have had.

They had been married a mere week before Amy's premonition came true. She'd left off her black mourning clothes a month ago and was planning to sponsor her only granddaughter—James's daughter's child—in the spring with Evangeline's help. Not that she had proper social contacts, but Evangeline had snuck into enough events to know how things were done. There would of course be no Presentation Drawing Room, but there was no reason why Lady Pennington could not have a modest party to launch the girl. Susan was very pretty and now well-dowered. Evangeline had promised to mention the event on the front page of the paper several weeks running to ensure the girl's success.

If she still had access to the front page. It was difficult picturing herself working with Ben for the next four months. Working seemed to lead to kissing. And more. Evangeline slumped down in a chair and sighed.

"What is it, dear?" Lady Pennington unpinned her apron and folded it on the settee.

"It's nothing. I'm only a bit tired. Did I interrupt you from a domestic chore?"

"You could never interrupt, Evangeline. You know how much I look forward to your visits. But lest you think I've been dipping into the brandy myself so early in the morning, I want to assure you if you smell something untoward I was only pouring some on my Christmas fruitcakes. I do so love a drunken fruitcake, and the recipe has been handed down in my family for generations. Cook has tried to quit twice already this week because I wouldn't use hers."

"Some women are very territorial in their kitchens." Not that *she* was. Evangeline could prepare basic things—had to when her father had a losing streak and there were no servants—but was grateful someone else was cooking for her household.

The household she felt she was neglecting. Since Ben was back in her life, she'd spent even more time at the office than usual. Her father might not even notice, but Evangeline felt guilty anyway.

Garwood entered with the tray, and the next few minutes were taken up with pouring and passing. The nip of brandy in Evangeline's chocolate was delicious, and she felt the knot of tension at the back of her neck relax a fraction.

"So, tell me about your baron."

"He's not *my* baron! I can barely stand the man."

"Yes, you have painted him to be a thorough blackguard in your stories."

"He's not a blackguard—to me that implies intentional cruelty and cunning, and Ben never thinks or plans. He's just so—heedless."

"Drifting about, is he? Perhaps the ownership of the newspaper will be the making of him."

"It's probably too late." No matter what he'd said or how hard he'd worked this week, there was little chance Benton Gray would give up his degenerate behavior. How was it that men were admired for their casual morals and women were pilloried? Society was so unjust.

Lady Pennington waggled a plump finger at her. "It's

never too late, Evangeline. People can change. Especially if they have reason to."

"Do you honestly feel a rake can be reformed? I confess I have not seen it except within the pages of a novel. It's rather ludicrous to presume a sinner will suddenly prefer virtue to vice. Vice is much more fun."

"Ah, but vice becomes tiresome, don't you think? How long can one gorge on sweets before one gets sick?" Lady Pennington patted her stomach ruefully. "Do have one of those tarts before I eat them all."

Evangeline picked up the tart and studied the ruby-jeweled fruit at its center. She could remember days when she was so hungry she would have sold her soul for a bite of it. Her father's vice—gambling—had never abated, not even when she'd begged him to stop. His face would shutter and he'd tell her she didn't understand, that of course he'd win again, and win big. The odds were in his favor. In the meantime, there were no foodstuffs in the larder and bill collectors pounded at the door. How Robert Ramsey escaped debtors' prison all the years of her girlhood was a wonder.

To his credit, he'd never tried to bargain her away to settle his markers. Few of his associates knew he even *had* a daughter. They would not have been interested in a gangly, big-nosed fright anyway—she'd had a most unspectacular development into womanhood. Her feet had grown, but not her breasts. It had been such a relief to borrow men's clothing and hide her lack of feminine charms under them.

What had Ben said? That next week she'd be sipping tea in skirts. Insipid. She took a chunk off the tart and popped it into her mouth.

"Aren't they delicious? I put up the cherries myself." Lady Pennington beamed and helped herself to one from the plate. "So, how are you and the baron-who's-not-yours getting on?"

"He's a fast learner." And a fabulous kisser. "But we'll have a proper pressman by this time next week. I've advertised."

"Well! That will relieve an enormous burden from your shoulders. What will you do with your extra time?"

Evangeline thought of the stacks of letters in her drawers. She'd need to invent an extra day of the week to deal with them all. "I have some pet projects. And there is my father, of course. Now that we have a bit of money from the sale of the paper, I thought we might move house into a better neighborhood. Find something with a patch of garden so he can get some fresh air."

"An excellent idea! I do enjoy my garden here, but it's nothing like the farm. I'm going home for Christmas tomorrow, hence the fruitcakes. There's nothing like being surrounded by all the ones you love and who love you just as much at this time of year."

Evangeline nodded in agreement, although she didn't have the faintest idea what that would feel like. No one had ever really loved her or cared enough to make her fruitcake.

Botheration, but she was in a funk. Usually Lady Pennington cheered her up, but today Evangeline found no comfort in the cozy clutter of the viscountess's house. She decided she might as well go back and try to get some work done before Ben turned up to harass her, so she swallowed her brandied chocolate with some haste and excused herself as soon as it was polite to do so.

With Lady Pennington off to the country, Evangeline would not have anyone to celebrate the season with. Her father could not be depended on to know Christmas from Easter, so there was no point to hanging mistletoe or filling stockings. It would just be another lonely day.

"Stop it this instant, Evangeline Ramsey!" she chided herself as she walked down the street. She was young, had her health and a focus to her energies. There were all those people's lives to sort.

How unfortunate that she didn't have someone to sort her own.

# $\mathscr{C}$HAPTER 15

$\mathbf{B}$en had been disappointed to find *The London List*'s door locked when he finally dragged himself out of his house. He used his own finally found key and stepped into the hushed space. Hard to believe it was the site of so much frenzy yesterday. He felt a little guilty for following Evie's instructions to stay away this morning, though he'd needed the sleep. Every muscle in his arms and back still ached, but he had a far greater ache to see Evie. She had turned up like clockwork in his dreams, her coltish body bare and beautiful, her tongue mercifully tamed as she sweetly invited him to do all manner of things to her in nocturnal bliss.

What would convince her to make his dreams come true? She was unimpressed with his standing in society, his fortune, his pretty face. It was only when he was able to steal a kiss that she had melted somewhat. If he asked her to become his mistress, he imagined inkpots flying and withering invective as they did so.

To think of Evie living in his little house on Jane Street . . . Ben would dress her in scarlet to show off her pearl-white skin and insist she grow her hair back, although she looked very fetching with her cropped curls. They could have a few good years together before he finally succumbed to a loveless society marriage. That's probably all they could manage together without driving each other insane.

What was he thinking? She had her own funds now, and the care of her father. Evie didn't need Ben for anything—in fact it was rather the reverse. He still knew next to nothing about *The List*'s operations, despite his tremoring tendons and a week at Evie's feet.

He glanced around the office. What might he do to be useful and ingratiate himself to her? Everything seemed to be in place, save for a small canvas bag on the center of the desk. He picked it up, marveling at its heft. Curious, he pulled the drawstring and peered inside to find it filled with lead tiles stuck together by something sticky. How odd.

His own fingers were ink-stained now, so he thought nothing of examining the contents of the bag. *Honey?* Perhaps this was a secret cleaning solution—there were a great many strange remedies that Ben was aware of. Champagne to polish one's boots, for example—a dreadful waste of good libation, in his opinion. He licked his finger and returned the sorts to the bag.

Where could Evie be? He missed her. He paced the perimeter of the office, finally coming to a stop at the door on the back wall. He'd yet to thoroughly inspect his property—he'd been far too busy trying to publish the infernal paper—so he opened the door and climbed the dusty stair to the floor above. Motes swirled in the gray December light in what was a mostly empty space. Drums of paper rested near the stairwell, and back issues of the paper were stacked in chronological order on shelves under the eaves, going back further than the Ramsey family had owned *The London List*. Idly Ben picked up an issue from five years ago—there was no salacious headline to draw the reader in, just a deadly dull article about keeping one's tenants content in the country now that Napoleon had been defeated. An old gate-leg table stood in the center of the room, flanked by two plain chairs.

Ben sat and traced his name in the thin layer of dust on the table. If he'd had hopes to rent out the space above the office, they were dashed now. He'd have to spend money to convert the room into an apartment, and even then he couldn't imagine who would be satisfied with one grimy window that overlooked a back alley. Add the deafening sound of the press all day Monday, and the amenities were bleak indeed.

But if they needed to offer housing to a pressman and his family to sweeten the offer, Ben supposed the room might do. Having someone on the premises twenty-four hours a day might discourage brick-throwers, too.

He walked across the scuffed wood floor from wall to wall, estimating how large a carpet he'd need for the parlor space. There might even be something rolled up in his attic, as his mother was forever redecorating his townhouse. He probably had a bed or two that would make them comfortable. A small cookstove, properly vented, could heat the space as well as help in meal preparations. Ben felt a flutter of interest in this project, and sat down on one of the chairs, drawing a floor plan in the dust on the table. He rose again and walked the perimeter of imaginary walls.

Ben was so lost in his sudden architectural thoughts that he never heard Evie creep up the stairs until she was directly behind him. He was fairly sure he grinned at her like a loony when he turned, so happy was he to see her at last.

She shook her cane at him. "I heard footsteps and thought you were an intruder. You scared me half to death!"

"And you came up here expecting to brain me with that?"

"If necessary. I've a knife in the knob as well." She

twisted the silver bird that topped her cane and drew out a deadly-looking blade.

"How reassuring. You could gut me as I lay witless on the floor."

"Don't tempt me. What are you doing up here?"

"I was thinking about turning the place into suitable lodging for our new employee. To sweeten the deal, and also be on the spot to watch for any further trouble."

"I'm sure the throwing of that brick was a random event."

"I don't want to take any chances with your safety."

"Oh, for goodness' sake, Ben! I am not made of spun sugar and feathers."

Ben studied Evie, who was wiry as a spring and just as sharp. "No, I can see you are a formidable foe, what with your killer bird. How many times have you used that thing?"

Evie's thick black lashes dropped to pink-stained cheeks. "You never know what will be necessary in my line of work."

"Another reason why I'm glad you're not sneaking about looking for dirt in the dark. Running off to riots. It's a wonder you've escaped ruin these last two years."

"I didn't escape *you*," Evie muttered.

"Aye, but I bought you out with a generous offer, not bludgeoned you. It's a good thing you mostly picked on me and not some other idiot. I'm famous for my good temper."

"Hmm."

Ben expanded his arms. "What, have I not demonstrated I'm the soul of equanimity?"

"You are the soul of annoyance."

"You're impossible to please. Come see what I've planned for this space." He led her over to the dust-coated table. "See, if we put up a wall here, we can separate sleeping quarters from a kitchen cum sitting room."

Evie bent to study the straight lines he'd drawn, exposing a shell-pink ear from the outrageously high shirt points she wore to conceal her femininity. A curl at the base of her skull also captured his attention, and his dusty finger itched to touch it. Her top lip had the faintest trace of chocolate. He took a breath. Had she also been drinking brandy so early in the day? He could kiss her to find out, taste the chocolate and the liquor and lose them both to whatever was between them.

Foolishly brave, she'd come up here armed, though, so perhaps he shouldn't. Could he be satisfied just breathing a whiff of sandalwood and brandy and Evie?

The answer was no.

Her face was still cold from being out-of-doors but so soft as he touched her cheek. Her mouth opened in objection but he silenced her swiftly with his own. Definitely brandy, the wicked girl. Cherries, too. Ben's hunger ripped through him, but it was not for food.

Her hesitation did not last long—it never did when they came together. Ben was proud of himself that he could overcome her good sense so swiftly. This really was a form of madness. Evangeline Ramsey was the most vexing woman. A vexing woman who was wearing far too many layers of clothes against this frigid winter day and who had knotted her damn neckcloth so tightly he was afraid he might strangle her in the undoing of it.

She was far more fleet of finger than he, her hands already upon the portion of his chest exposed by suddenly undone buttons. Thank God she soon moved lower.

He should probably throw those old newspapers on the floor to make a bed for them, but then he'd have to stop kissing and touching her. Unthinkable. In fact, thinking was highly overrated, so he simply stopped doing it.

Evie was thinking enough for both of them. Somehow she'd clambered up on the table—there went his conversion plans—and had shimmied out of her trousers. He cupped her sex, twining his fingers in her luscious dark curls. Her dew was on them, proving to him that she wanted him as badly as he wanted her.

This wanting . . . its intensity was unnatural, but Ben didn't seem to have much choice about it. She stroked his manhood in her cool hand, but instead of dampening his ardor, the chilly friction drove him to deepen his kiss. He sought the warmth of her tongue, the heat of her folds, the silk of her skin.

She shifted her arse on the gate-leg table and spread her thighs so she was furled open to him. It was almost too easy to enter her, as if they'd been temporarily separated but now back in their rightful place. As they were meant to be. No impediments. No cross words. Just one smooth slow dance to their own orchestra, Ben's hand on Evie's supple back, the other placed between them to bring her to ecstasy. She pulsed beneath his fingertips, crying through his kiss.

Christ. If only this could last forever. The chill and dust of the attic room had disappeared, leaving nothing but Evie's wet heat surrounding his cock. Primal. Perfect.

Until he heard a sharp crack and the table toppled downward, taking them both with it. Their noses bumped, and they wound up in a tangle of wood and wool. The absurdity of it all should have stopped them, but they were still connected where it counted, and Ben was not quite done. Evie smiled and shifted, forcing his denouement, which was only slightly uncomfortable as he found himself kneeling on a turned walnut leg. She held him tight and laughed, but he knew it was not because she felt his efforts were in any way paltry. There was pure joy between them, as though ten years had been erased and they were in their first flush of love.

For it *had* been love, at least on his part, even if he'd been so very young.

Sometimes, first was best.

He came with a profound sense of peace, a beautiful, laughing woman in his arms, just where she was supposed to be.

But of course, she had other ideas. Full of ideas, was his Evie.

"I think I've got a splinter. Let me up."

Ben sighed. "Not just yet."

"You are finished, aren't you?"

Couldn't she tell? He felt as if they were absolutely one being there at the end. Their hearts were thumping together right now, chest to chest, although she seemed to still be wearing her bindings.

"Someone might be downstairs right now wanting to pick up their mail or pay for an ad."

"Let them wait." He nibbled on her ear, the very appendage that had started all this.

"Ben."

She spoke his name softly, but there was no mistaking her determination to buck him off her.

"Don't ask me to apologize. I can't."

It was her turn to sigh. "We cannot keep doing this. It's not right."

No, it wasn't right. It was beyond right. There really was no word for it in Ben's vocabulary, and he considered himself a fairly well-read man.

But if these indiscretions continued, there might be consequences. Evie might be exposed as a woman, which would not be a half-bad thing, but she also could fall pregnant. Just because she had not all those years ago did not mean she would not now. Ben was ordinarily far too careful when it came to intimate relations—had been since he was spurned by Evie. As far as he knew, there were no little Grays littering London. But he'd taken no precautions each time he and Evie combusted together.

That was irresponsible. While Evie thought the worst of him—that he was a thoughtless, useless blight on society—he didn't want to prove her right.

Of course he would provide for a child—the problem would be providing for Evie. She wouldn't permit it, he was sure. She was damnably independent, thinking the damn bird-knife on her cane would protect her from harm.

He rolled until she was on top, still embedded in her. "There. Better? I'm a human cushion. No more discomfort."

She stared down at him, her dark hair as fluffed as a chick's. "I mean it. You are my employer now. It's not proper that you take advantage of me like this." But she made no move to leap off.

"I think we took advantage of each other, Evie. We're more partners than employer-employee. I don't know my way around here yet—what would I do without you?"

"You certainly know your way around *me*. I—I don't want to be hurt."

"I'll pick out the splinters." He cupped her bottom and gave it a squeeze.

"It's not the splinters, you bloody man! I know I'm not a virgin. You saw to that long ago. But I have been relatively chaste. I'm happy as I am. I don't need—this."

Every recent moan and shiver indicated that she had in fact needed and *wanted* "this." But Ben was not going to argue with her now. Arguing with Evie, while occasionally quite stimulating, was not on his agenda at the moment. She had a point about the broken table being splintery. And hard. But having the length of her draped over him was a soft delight, even though her waistcoat button was piercing his stomach.

One day they would be fully unclothed, and have time for "this" in all its glorious manifestations. To have Evie in a feather bed, with candles flickering and celebratory wine at hand, would be a cozy alternative to the grimy floor above a print shop.

"I have a proposition for you."

She twisted off him and drew her trousers up from under a fallen chair. "Whatever it is, the answer is no."

"Aren't you curious to find out what it is? I thought you were a famous reporter, proud of your sleuthing and your scoops."

"Nothing you could say holds any interest for me." With the same efficient speed she used to get them partially undressed, she was soon mostly covered up. "I'm going downstairs to get some work done. You can lie up here all day if you wish—you're the boss, after all."

She flounced out, her substantial nose in the air. Ben would have another opportunity later to present his new plan. There were still a few weeks left to the year. After January first, he would make a resolution to swear off Evangeline Ramsey, but until then, he would make every effort to brighten the holidays by bedding the one woman he couldn't seem to forget.

# CHAPTER 16

Evangeline gripped the banister before she pitched headlong down the stairway. Benton Gray turned her into an idiot. Her heart had been beating so wildly when she went upstairs that her brain must have been deprived of whatever it needed to think straight. That brick had spooked her more than she had let on, and when she heard the floors creak above, she had been sure she was about to be murdered.

Damn. She'd left her walking stick somewhere in the mess they'd made.

Fornicating on a table—*what* had come over her? She couldn't blame her euphoria at seeing Ben solely on relief that she was not confronting a dangerous blackguard. For *he* was a dangerous blackguard, every inch of him. One minute she was looking at a drawing in the dust, and the next she was opening her legs to the dangerous blackguard himself.

Evangeline brushed her hair back from her forehead. She simply couldn't lose herself to lust. Evangeline had worked too hard over the years to beat those feminine urges down. Her brief experimentation with the two other gentlemen had been an abysmal failure.

She hadn't lied to Ben—she was happy as she was. Busy.

Solving problems. But Benton Gray was a problem she couldn't seem to solve.

She ambled over to her desk and frowned. The bag of honeyed tiles was now on her chair, and beneath it was a torn scrap of paper. She glanced around the office quickly, but no one was lurking in the corner. As she had told Ben, anyone could have visited the office, and apparently someone had while they were upstairs breaking furniture.

Evangeline picked up the note, then dropped it to the floor as if it singed her fingers.

"Ben!" she screamed. "Come down here at once!"

He took her at her word and flew down the stairs. Benton Gray was wearing his pants, just. He clutched them in front of him, bare-chested and barefoot. "What's wrong?"

"You are not dressed!"

"Of course I'm not! You were screaming! Are you all right?"

"Yes, of course. Please go back and put your clothes on."

"Not until you tell me why you sounded like a banshee."

Evie flushed. It was not like her to act missish, to call on the big strong man for help. Perhaps she was overreacting, but the crudely spelled letter had shaken her.

"What's this?" Ben bent to the floor, picked up the dirty paper and read aloud the same words she had:

*This waz a warning. U better do as I tell U or U will B sorry.*

"What the hell? A warning? What are we supposed to do?"

"Someone must have come in while we were—uh, upstairs. First the brick, then the Es. Someone wants to stop us."

"From doing what? *The Times* interview you gave on our own front page today explained the change of direction of *The London List*. We'll not be like the man holding the muck-rake in *Pilgrim's Progress* looking down at the filth any longer. That was a very nice literary allusion, by the way."

"Th-thank you," Evangeline said faintly. She wished he'd at least put on his shirt or she'd never get a crack at a celestial crown. Could one still feel sexual longing after being so thoroughly pleasured?

The answer was, regrettably, yes.

Ben's chest was broad, with a faint fuzz of golden hair strategically placed to show off his muscles to best advantage, his arms corded. Strong arms, that held her as if she would break when they weren't trying to break down her disillusions. She didn't need him, she didn't *want* him in her life.

She scooped up the bag of letters and sat down in her chair. Ben went to the front door and locked it against the next intruder.

"I'll be right back. Don't move. Don't answer the door to anyone."

Evangeline nodded, shivering. The little stove hadn't been fed since early this morning. She supposed it might be all right if she got up off her chair for that. She tossed a few shovelfuls of coal in, wishing the odor of coal wasn't so noxious. A giant gray cloud hung over parts of London in the winter. It almost made her long for the frigid fresh air of Scotland.

She'd been happy to come to London when her father won the newspaper though. Ramsey Hall was collapsing into its own corners. The house in Argyll had seemed like a prison for all her nervous energy. While her father still roamed the tables, she was stuck like the spinster she was, with a handful of servants and a quiverful of cats. No amount of judicious housekeeping could help stabilize the walls or put enough food on the table.

Evangeline wondered what the cats were doing now. There certainly had been enough mice to keep *them* fed.

Ben returned, covered and concerned. "Let me see the letter again."

She pushed it across the desk.

"Someone got in today to despoil the sorts with honey. I thought at first it might have been a mishap. Either you or the glassworker or the boys. But this note says otherwise."

"Mischief. All the better to hire someone immediately and have them live upstairs. I'll have to draw new plans." He winked at her.

She refused to be charmed. "The ad says we'll begin to see applicants tonight, but I think we'll have some men come much sooner. It would be helpful to show them prospective housing."

"I'll tidy up the remains of the table. I know we've got some furnishings in my attic that can be used. You can come home with me and pick some things out and we can hire a wagon to deliver them."

"I can't leave the office!" Even though the paper had gone out just this morning, the workweek never really ended.

"You'll not stay here by yourself waiting to be terrorized by some illiterate candidate for Bedlam. We'll leave a note on the door."

"But the advertisers—"

"Can wait. Everything can wait, Evie. We'll be back here before six, when the interviews were scheduled. I think you need to put your feet up and have a cup of tea. A proper lunch. And if we find the building burned down when we get back, there will be one less thing for you to worry about."

"Don't joke, Ben! People depend on me."

"But who do you depend on, Evie?"

His question rang in the empty air, although he had asked it softly. "Myself."

"Today you are off the hook. We'll send a note to your house, let Mrs. Spencer know that you aren't coming home."

Evangeline bit a lip. Her father expected her.

But did he? He might not even know midday from midnight.

More hours spent with Ben in the privacy of his town-house would do nothing for her resolve to keep away from him. "Will your mother be home?"

"Alas, my mother is still with her sick friend. But that's probably just as well. She was rather intrigued with you after she met you last week. Peppered me with some sharp questions. The old girl sometimes forgets I'm all grown up."

The "old girl" hadn't seemed so old to Evangeline. Ben must have been a sore trial to her over the years, always getting into one scandalous scrape or another. It was a wonder she wasn't white-haired and wizened.

So, no chaperone. Evangeline shook her head. "I don't think going to your house is a good idea."

"Well, I'm not leaving you here alone, and that's a fact. Put on your coat."

There was no point to arguing, and Evangeline discovered she didn't have the heart for it anyway. Benton Gray was wreaking havoc with her well-ordered life, and there didn't seem to be a thing she could do about it.

He fiddled with the damper of the stove while she took her coat off its peg. In a minute they had locked up and nodded to the little chestnut-seller on the corner. Impulsively, Ben bought some of the hot treats, shoving them into Evangeline's pockets to keep her warm. He flagged down a cab and they were off.

Today there was no flirtation in the seats—he sat opposite her, looking worried.

"What's wrong?"

"Do you need to ask? Ever since I bought *The List,* there's been trouble of one kind or another. I wonder if I should increase the staff at my residence. If someone is threatening the office, they may target my home as well. I'll tell my mother to stay at Lady Applegate's until we get this straightened out."

"Oh." He must be concerned for his mother. Despite his gentle teasing about her, she knew they were close.

"You look tired, Evie. Even the circles under your eyes have circles."

"Thank you," she said dryly. "You didn't seem to notice them a little while ago."

"I was overcome by gratitude that you didn't slay me on the spot with your deadly cane. Where is it, by the way?"

"I left it upstairs." She examined her left-hand glove, which needed a stitch or two. "We cannot do what we did again, Ben. You know it as well as I do."

"So you've already told me. I've a good memory. I'll try to control my animal urges if you try to control yours. Now, don't glare at me like that—you don't frighten me. Much. Let's talk about what it takes to outfit a suitable lodging for a pressman."

Evangeline had set up many a home for herself and her father over the years, and despite her general disinterest in domestic arrangements, began to rattle off a sizeable list. To her surprise, Ben had pulled out a silver pencil and notepad and jotted everything down with unexpected organization.

When they reached his house, he forgot himself and extended a hand to help her out of the carriage. "Ben," she growled, "your butler is watching."

"Severson needs a good shock. The man thinks he knows everything about me. To see me being helpful to a frail colleague who's forgotten his walking stick—"

"Do stubble it and put your damn hand down."

Ben grinned and obeyed. Of course Evangeline's boot touched a patch of ice on the pavement and she wobbled for a perilous moment before she righted herself.

"See? I could have saved you there."

"I don't need saving!"

"That's what you think. Come on." Ben jogged up the steps. "Severson, tell Mrs. Hargreaves I've brought Mr. Ramsey home for lunch. His sister was just here Saturday and raved about the refreshments she whipped up for that wedding. Striking family resemblance, what? Although I do think *Miss* Ramsey is prettier." Ben clapped her on the back in manly camaraderie and practically threw her up against the console in the hallway.

Callum appeared to take their outer-clothes. "Good afternoon, Mr. Rams-Montague."

Severson lifted a silver eyebrow. "That's Mr. Ramsey to you, boy."

Evangeline realized the lad remembered her from that night two weeks ago when she'd turned up foxed. "Th-that's all right. He's my c-cousin. We look a great deal alike."

"Yes. Mr. Ramsey comes from a large family, and it's getting larger by the hour. Have lunch sent up to us in the attics, Severson. We shall be working on a special project. Call around for a carter for later this afternoon—say, around three. We should be done by then, eh, Ramsey?" He whacked her on the back again. This time she was prepared and stopped herself before she hit the stair railing.

Another silver eyebrow was raised, but the butler merely nodded regally.

"You are a terrible liar," Ben said as they climbed the stairs. "How did you manage to go underground to get all your exclusive stories?"

"I can so lie! But I'm better with a prepared script."

"I've always found it's important to think on one's feet. To be ready for anything."

"Bully for you." The stairs were endless, but they finally reached uncarpeted pine at the upper reaches of the house. "Is your poor old butler going to have to trot up here?"

"He'll probably send Callum or John. Right this way—duck your head, there's a good fellow."

The doorway was low, but the room Evangeline entered was high-ceilinged and lit by a pair of exquisite oriel windows complete with window seats. To think that such a lovely architectural detail was wasted on furniture under Holland covers and neatly stacked trunks. If Evangeline lived here, she'd make this a garret and write to her heart's content in the hush from the street noise. The attic was warm, swept, and smelled of the bags of lavender hanging from the rafters, a far cry from the space above *The London List.*

But they were here to transform it. She lifted a corner of glazed cloth to discover a tufted brocade chaise in perfectly good repair. "This is much too grand, Ben."

"I'm sure we'll find something that will do." He stripped the linen from a club chair and sat down. No cloud of dust followed. This was the cleanest attic Evangeline had ever seen.

"There's so much up here. Where should we begin?"

"First we'll have lunch. It shouldn't be long. Cook—Mrs. Hargreaves, that is—always has something going—

she must get rid of three times as much as I ever could eat in a day."

"What a wicked waste. People are starving, Ben."

"Don't lecture me again, Evie. By get rid of, I mean give away to the poor. I've asked Mrs. H. to make extra for just that purpose. We Grays know our Christian duty, even if you think me a layabout."

"Oh." This charitable side of Ben was new to her.

But she *should* have known. She considered herself an expert on Lord Benton Gray. She'd wasted two years of her life on him.

Evangeline felt a brief twinge of shame. Perhaps she'd been foolishly vindictive. After all, it was *she* who had rejected *him,* not the other way around. How he spent the rest of his life should have meant nothing to her.

But his antics had sold a lot of papers, and helped her with her own charities, even if he was not a complicit participant.

The scuffle on the stairs told her lunch was about to be served. She sat on the chaise and tried to keep a straight face when Callum entered. He bore a huge silver tray loaded with bowls of stew that smelled divine, bread, cheese, wine, and more of the cook's apple tart. Between Lady Pennington's breakfast and Ben's lunch, Evangeline would not have to eat another morsel again tonight.

Ben leaped up and moved some boxes off a scarred drop-leaf table whose leg was wobbly and tied with twine. Evangeline vowed not to climb up on *it*—one disaster a day was enough. She supposed she should appear sufficiently manly before Callum, so she went to a corner, took down some up-ended chairs and carried them to their makeshift dining table.

Ben eyed the loose rush on the seat. "I hope I don't fall through that."

"I can bring up a proper chair for you, my lord," Callum said.

"Nonsense. Don't bother. If worse comes to worst we can picnic on the floor. Right, Ramsey?"

Sitting on the floor would lead to lying on the floor. And lying on the floor—perhaps she was only projecting her own unleashed desires. Evangeline sat on her own spindly chair and buttered a piece of bread. "I'm sure we'll be fine," she said gruffly.

"Thank you, Callum. Thank Cook, too."

"Is there anything else I can get you and Mr. Rams-Ramsey?"

Evangeline stifled her giggle.

"No, that will be all. We may need your help—and John's, too—when the carters come. We'll shift what will be going to the front of the room."

"Very good, my lord. Enjoy your luncheon, my lord. And Mr. R-Ramsey."

It was very easy to enjoy. This was the third meal Evangeline had eaten prepared from Ben's kitchen and his cook was a treasure. From what she had seen of his household, it was very well run. Ben's mother was probably responsible for that. A pity she had not been able to exert such discipline over her only son.

Ben wolfed down the food as if he were starving, but Evangeline's nerves prevented her from truly enjoying the meal. She was more worried than she let on about the goings-on at the newspaper office. If she could understand *why* they were under attack, inept as it was, she'd feel much better. Well, she investigated things. She'd just have to investigate this.

"Aren't you going to eat your apple tart?"

"Lord, no. I'm too full to think about it."

"You're much too skinny, you know," Ben said, helping himself to her plate.

She couldn't retort that he was much too fat. He was perfect. "Imagine if I looked like your mistress Veronique. No one would believe I was a man," she said lightly.

"Veronique is not my mistress anymore. I've given her up."

Evangeline sat up a little straighter. This was news of the front-page variety. "Really?"

"Yes." He filled his mouth with apples.

A one-word answer was insufficient, especially when he wouldn't meet her eyes. "Did you tire of her?"

"No."

Blast him anyhow. She watched him swallow and thought about stabbing him with a silver fork. She picked up her wineglass instead, staring into its ruby depths. She had no head for spirits lately—every time she indulged she wound up beneath or on top of Benton Gray.

"So, who is her replacement?"

"I haven't had time to interview mistresses, my dear. You've been keeping me far too busy."

Did he mean the newspaper or . . . Double blast him.

Before she could say something scathing, he crumpled his napkin and stood up. "We'd best get busy now. You take the left side of the attic; I'll take the right. I've got your list to help me." Their conversation seemed to be at an end.

Evangeline poked under more Holland covers. She found a small dresser with one knob missing and a handsome trunk that was big enough to hold a dead body. It was oddly empty—she had been hoping to find love letters or eighteenth-century gowns. No traces of Ben's boyhood, either—no toy soldiers or stuffed rabbits. Between the bureau and the trunk, there would be enough storage for an ordinary laborer's clothes. She slid the trunk forward a foot before Ben crossed the room.

"That's too heavy for you. Let me." He'd removed his

jacket and waistcoat, and his shirt was streaked faintly with dirt, which Evangeline found comforting—the attic was eerily pristine. He dragged it to the door, a strange expression on his face.

She wanted to ask him what he'd found in the boxes he'd pried open, but could see for herself. Ironstone dishes, a few pots, a rolled mattress and a faded quilt. Ben was quiet as he returned to his side of the room, his sunny demeanor absent.

Was he annoyed with her for asking about his mistress? She'd tried not to let her jealousy show. Evangeline knew she was nothing like Veronique, could never hope to be, and that was a good thing, wasn't it?

It didn't really matter. Soon whatever was between them would be relegated to an attic of its own. Ben would find a new mistress, and Evangeline would . . .

For a woman who was good with words, she could not finish her sentence.

# CHAPTER 17

Ben forced himself to breathe deeply. He'd had no idea the damned trunk was here. If he thought about it at all, which he refused to let himself do very often, he'd supposed it was in some room at Castle Gray.

Once it had held his toys when he was a boy. It had also held him for an uncomfortable number of hours after his father locked him into it. He couldn't imagine why his mother had it shipped down to the London townhouse—it was hardly a souvenir of their troubles either one of them would want. Maybe it had been filled with linens or china when they packed up and fled Scotland all those years ago.

He was glad to be getting rid of it, even if it was moving where it still would be over his head. But he might not be involved with *The London List* forever—he would eventually find a buyer, even if he had to take a financial loss. Evie could rob some other man of his sanity.

He stacked up a few ugly brown landscapes. Bare walls would be preferable to these pictures. Whoever they hired might have plenty of belongings of their own anyway. He emptied a carton and shoved mended sheets and chipped china haphazardly into it. The pile by the door was growing with basic household requirements.

He was a damned generous employer, wasn't he? Ironic,

when all he'd wanted to do was close down the gossip factory that Evie started. Those back issues he'd seen this morning had none of the sensational stories she was so good at writing. Of course, they were so dull they were only good to line a cat box.

There must be a happy medium. Ben had made compromising a fine art, and so he would reform the paper, one edition at a time.

He was so lost in thought that he startled when Evie put on hand on his shoulder. "I think I'm finished on my side. We should get back in case we have men show up early. What have you got there? You've been staring at it forever."

"A teapot. The lid is missing."

"It's pretty."

It was hand-painted, patterned with vines and roses and purple violets, an ultra-feminine object. "You can have it if you like it. I can't see a strong, strapping pressman putting his leaves into it."

"It's far too fancy for Mr. Ramsey, too."

"Save it for when you're your sister." The absurdity made Ben laugh, and the knot in his chest loosened. "Do you ever miss corsets and petticoats?"

"Not often. The usual state of our finances made my options somewhat limited when it came to fripperies. And I was always at least a season or three behind in my gowns. Pantaloons liberate me from all that silliness."

"You've enough money now to indulge yourself. How long are you going to continue this masquerade?"

"It depends, doesn't it? When you're ready to give up the paper, perhaps I'll return to my former life."

Then Ben had best get cracking finding a buyer. As charming as Evie looked in her trousers, it simply wasn't right to bury her female self under superfine and Hessians.

It wasn't right for her to bury herself under anything

that covered her translucent skin. Ben realized in their several recent encounters she had been more or less dressed. Even ten years ago, their coupling had been so quick and clandestine there had been little opportunity for total nudity.

A totally nude Evie was just what he wanted to see at the moment, something to take his mind away from his maudlin memories. There was a chaise over in the corner whose carved mahogany legs looked like they could support their weight—she *was* too skinny by half. Of course it had been a mere few hours since the other attic, but this one was much nicer. The first encounter of the day should always be followed soon after by a second. It was Ben's Law.

How to maneuver her to the chaise?

He was a much better liar than Evie.

He rose from his haunches slowly, then stumbled.

"What's the matter?" Evie asked, concern in her voice.

"Dizzy," Ben mumbled. "Don't feel well all of a sudden."

She leaped up. "I'll go get Callum or John."

That would never do. "No! Don't want to be a bother. Just get me over there so I can lie down for a minute. Clear my head."

"You should never have drunk all that wine in the daytime," Evie scolded.

"You're one to talk. Brandy for breakfast." He'd better stop talking before she brained him with some attic artifact. It was true he'd had most of the wine that had been sent up—Evie had been guarding herself against him without even knowing his diabolical plans. Of course, he hadn't known of his diabolical plans himself an hour ago.

His cock was fully aware now of those plans as Evie hovered at his elbow, guiding him to the chaise. She smelled of sandalwood and was as pale as the frost on the windows. She looked worried. Good.

"My neckcloth," Ben said weakly. "I'm about to strangle. Do I feel hot?"

Evie laid one cool hand on his forehead while she worked the knot of his necktie with the other. "I don't think you have a fever."

There she was wrong. He was burning up for her as she bent over him, her lips a little chapped from the cold and all their morning kissing. She looked tired, too—he had not meant to insult her earlier, but she worked and worried too hard and the bruising under her dark eyes was evidence. Wouldn't it be heaven if they could curl up here and take a nice long nap?

After he fucked her.

Ben frowned. The term "fucking" was so crude. There should be a better word invented for what happened between them. He'd think of one later when he had more time to give it the attention it deserved. Right now, he had other things on his plate.

He shuddered violently. "I'm so cold."

"I thought you said you were hot!"

"Hot . . . cold . . . just not right . . ." Did he seem sufficiently delirious? Perhaps he was overdoing it.

Evie straightened. "I'm going to get one of your servants."

"Don't leave me!" he grabbed her hand and pulled her down. "Just keep me warm with your body. I'm sure I'll be fine . . . soon." He gave a few more dramatic shivers for good measure and saw the misgiving on Evie's face through his own slitted eyes. Groaning might be a good strategy at this point, so he did.

"This is ridiculous," Evie mumbled as she settled like velvet over him.

"Don't ever go . . . can't live without you."

*Christ.* Where did *that* come from? He *was* sick—losing his mind. He closed his eyes so he couldn't see Evie's reaction to that tall tale. He'd been getting along just fine without Evangeline Ramsey for a decade.

She squirmed at his words, then stilled. Surely she must feel his erection fair to bursting from his falls. His mind might be going—had in fact tumbled over an abyss—but his body knew exactly what it was supposed to be doing. His arms locked around Evie—she felt so good, her slender body pressed against him. How much better it would be if he were a magician and could remove her clothes by some judicious prestidigitation.

"You are not sick at all," she said, her lips buzzing against his bare throat.

"I am. Sick with desire. Please don't try to get up."

She ignored his wishes, lifting herself as high as his embrace would allow. "Benton Gray, you *dastard.*" She hissed like an angry snake.

"Thank you. I consider that a step up from calling me bastard. I know you don't think you want to do this again, but perhaps I can persuade you." He grinned up at her, not one bit afraid, although he probably should be.

"You just—we just—not three hours ago—you cannot possibly—"she sputtered.

"Oh, yes, I can. I really, really want to. Can't you tell?" He gave a little thrust from his comfortable position. "And for once, I don't want all these damn clothes in the way. Humor me, Evie. I want to see all of you. Just this once, and then I won't bother you again. Unless you want me to."

If she agreed, she'd be making a much more deliberate decision than their recent hasty couplings. True, she'd been just as aggressive as he, a full participant in this . . . whatever it was, even if afterward she tried to push him away.

What harm could befall them? They were two adults, long past the first blush of youth.

"I promise I'll give you up by Christmas," Ben added, trying to sweeten his offer. "We'll go back to—"

Evie elbowed him. "*What*? You cannot expect me to bed you again and again for days on end!"

"Why not? It feels so good. So *right*. And Christmas will be here before you know it. Think of this as an early present to yourself." He watched her eyes sparkle and cheeks flush. She was almost beautiful when she was angry, and so easy to provoke.

"A—a—a *present*! You insufferable lunatic! It's a wonder you can find a hat for that swollen head of yours."

"It's not my head that's swollen, sweetheart. You have to admit it would be much more fun without the impediment of clothing. I can't remember the last time I saw you completely naked."

"That's because you never did. And you never will! Let me go this instant."

It had been a dream too good to be true. He should have play-acted his role a few minutes longer. Why, he'd not even had the chance to kiss her again.

Ben sighed and relaxed his arms. She flew off the chaise and stamped about the room, muttering various imprecations concerning his immortal soul.

"I'm sure you are lovely underneath everything. I wonder, are your nipples more rose-pink than apricot? I should have liked the opportunity to judge them in the daylight. I suppose I'll just have to use my imagination."

"You are not to imagine anything! If I think for one moment that you are sitting across the desk undressing me in your demented mind, I shall have no choice but to quit working for you immediately!" She was almost screaming, sounding most unlike a Mr. Ramsey.

Ben sat up and retied his neckcloth, really feeling a bit fuzzy and headachy now. Evie usually had that effect upon him. "Hush now. You'll attract the attention of the servants."

"Good! Let them know the debauched criminal they work for!" She picked up the teapot and smashed it against a wall.

"Criminal? It is not I destroying property that does not belong to me. In a country where one can be transported for stealing a handkerchief, one should be more careful with teapots."

"It was ruined anyway." She stopped her pacing, looking woefully sober. "I cannot, will not, be your mistress, Ben. I'm sorry if my actions have led you to believe otherwise."

He shrugged, attempting to resurrect his devil-may-care persona. " 'Hope springs eternal in the human breast.' "

"There will be no more talk of breasts," Evie said darkly. "Or any other part of me. Are we clear?"

"Indeed we are." He hauled himself off the chaise, feeling unusually dispirited. Someone forgot to tell his cock however, and he adjusted his breeches accordingly.

"I'm going back to the office. You make the arrangements for all this." She waved her hand at the neat pile. Presumably Severson had already gotten hold of people to deliver it and they were on their way.

"Let me get the carriage brought round."

She shook her head, stubborn to the end. She really was a little fool. Well, not little. She was taller than most gentlemen of his acquaintance. "No. I'll walk."

"Have you forgotten someone might be after you?"

"I'll not live my life in fear of silly threats. From anyone, even you."

"I don't want you to be afraid of me, damn it!"

"Then leave me alone, Ben. We have a professional relationship. Nothing more."

She opened the attic door and bounded down the stairs. It was a superb exit.

And a total lie.

Ben had time before Christmas. He'd make good use of it to bring her to his bed if it was the last thing he did this year.

# CHAPTER 18

Somehow Evangeline managed to get through all the interviews with Ben without further embarrassment. The nerve of him—playacting the invalid in the conceited belief that she would somehow fall on top of him again in his own house with all his servants spying. Ben was mad, as mad as the Mad Marquess of Conover she'd written about a time or two. There must be something in the air lately that made privileged men lose their minds and inhibitions and think they could do anything they damn well pleased.

She *must* stick to her principles.

If she could find them.

Evangeline had gotten along perfectly well without any dependable man in her life longer than she could remember. Gentlemen of the ton were disappointing creatures, ruthless and feckless by turns, with no respect for anything but their own pleasures. Gaming, whoring, doing whatever suited them to fill a few hours of idleness. She had no time for Ben's games—she had a business to run, even if it wasn't really hers any longer.

As she had suspected, a short line had already formed when she got back to the newspaper building, the applicants hours ahead of the posted time. Unemployment and unrest since the war ended were a dangerous combination, and many men were out of work. Times were changing, and not always for the better. Evangeline was very interested in politics, but had chosen mostly to report softer, more sensational stories on the front page, because that's what sold. Education took a distant second to titillation—why, most of her readers probably knew more details about Lady Imaculata Egremont's aborted elopement to France last winter than they did about the Cato Street Conspiracy.

But the men waiting did not look like dangerous revolutionaries, just cold and hungry. There was no ruthlessness or fecklessness to be seen in this ragtag lot. Half-a-dozen huddled up against the bricks, stamping their feet against the frigid temperature, so of course she had to let them in early. Most of them knew each other through their guild—London could be a small world. They spoke quietly in the far corner while she tried to go about her business, sorting letters and greeting a few people who came to check their postboxes and taking two ads. But the image of Ben on the chaise, disheveled and delicious, kept intruding.

Damn him.

An hour after her return, the devil himself arrived with the furnishings and hired all the prospective employees on the spot to help move things upstairs. Even if all of them save one was to be disappointed, they had earned something for simply showing up early, and Ben had burnished his reputation as an all-around fine fellow. She looked on as he effortlessly organized them, hefting boxes himself on his broad shoulders and racing up the stairs as if he were carrying air. Along the way, he had enough breath to joke with his impromptu crew. Democracy in action, and Evangeline felt the slightest twinge of jealousy.

Ben was friendly when others of his class would not be, and almost too open-handed with his money. She knew he was rich, but at this rate he wouldn't be for long. She and her newspaper were costing him a great deal.

No—it was his newspaper now. And she really had to find a way to continue her work and avoid his embraces. She was *not* going to be his mistress until Christmas or New Year's or St. Valentine's Day. She would have to be more successful at keeping her distance. This morning was a mistake. This afternoon had not been much better. Lying on top of Ben's hard body with its particularly hard member had turned her mind to mistressy mush. She could so easily have leaned in and kissed him into "good health" again until her instincts somehow alerted her to his ruse.

Why did he want her? For he had. The jutting evidence of his arousal was unmistakable. Because he'd been without Veronique for too long? Was Evangeline simply a convenient substitute? She knew his appetite for female flesh approached legendary status—she'd trailed after him long enough to see him at play.

How pathetic of her, really. Like a puppy in a shop window, forlornly watching everyone else's freedom outside on the pavement. She'd been little better than a Peeping Tom. But, she reminded herself, Ben had been the reason her sales had expanded—he was always good for a lark.

By the time Ben came downstairs, she was thoroughly blue-deviled and kept mostly silent. Ben asked surprisingly pertinent questions during the interviews, as if he hired pressmen every day of the week. He encouraged the applicants to keep scouring the pages of *The List* for other opportunities and pledged to find an older man less strenuous work, reminding Evangeline a little of herself. She always tried to find a silver lining among the clouds.

After promising to post the name of the new employee on the storefront window tomorrow, he overpaid each of them for aiding in the move. Then they were alone, the gas lamp lit against the gloom of the deserted office. Evangeline felt the weariness she'd kept at bay for days wash over her. Ben stretched back in the chair, his hands behind his golden head. She hoped he wasn't getting too comfortable. She was ready to agree to any decision he made concerning the new employee so she could go home to her father. True, she had her preferences—two of them, in fact. A pair of young brothers had turned up together— Joseph and Matthew Corrigan. But hiring two men when really only one was needed was a foolish extravagance, so she waited for Ben to speak.

"I liked those boys," he said, getting right to the point.

"The Corrigans?" she asked in surprise. They had come from the north to seek their fortunes, and thus far hadn't found a ha'penny.

"Yes. They seem steady. Quiet. They learned their trade at their grandfather's knee at his print shop in Carlisle, and I gather he was a hard taskmaster before he died. And they need a place to live. I think they'll work hard for us. Be grateful. And they're unmarried, so there will be no pitter-patter of little feet above our heads and no wife shouting when her man has drunk up his pay."

"You've given this some thought in a short period of time."

"You should have seen the reverence with which they handled my old castoffs upstairs. I believe they would have even liked the teapot you so fiendishly threw at the wall."

Evangeline found herself smiling at the thought of the two muscular young men sipping from flowered teacups. "I liked them, too."

"Perhaps with two men we might think about publishing the paper two or three times a week."

Evangeline's jaw dropped.

"Well, it's either that or expand the number of pages. We can't fit everything in as it is, even if you're settling the affairs of so many needy people yourself privately. We might charge the nobs more for their subscriptions, too. We'll have to work out a business plan."

Ben was absolutely full of surprises. If she had thought that he would remain an amateur publisher, it seemed she was mistaken.

"If we can increase the value and scope of the paper, it might be easier to sell. I'm not sure that's what I want to do, but it doesn't hurt to keep one's options open."

Evangeline nodded. She had thought about producing more than one edition a week, but she and Frank had not been equal to the task. It would be fair to say that Ben was taking her breath away, and not for the usual reasons.

"So, it's settled then. You put the sign up—your hand-writing's better than mine. If anyone comes in tomorrow disgruntled that they didn't get hired, let's see if we can't find them something else. Come on—you look fagged to death. I'll see you home."

Evangeline didn't argue, didn't assert her independence, didn't object to being escorted through London's dark streets by its most infamous rake. Tonight she was simply too exhausted and miserable to say a word. She climbed into the hackney, smelling sweat and an undercurrent of onions from previous passengers, and didn't even wrinkle her nose. Settling back into the squabs, she even allowed Ben to pull her scarf up and wrap it securely around her throat.

"You need a holiday," he said gruffly.

"I haven't time for one. Even with the new hires, you can't run the paper by yourself yet."

She saw a flash of white teeth in the swinging lantern light. "I bet I could."

"It is a bet you would lose, my lord."

"Let's put it to the test. Take tomorrow off. Come in Thursday and see how badly I've mucked everything up."

It would be heaven to lie abed—alone—and spend the day darning her father's socks and drinking tea. She couldn't do it.

"I've got to break in the boys. And you know we publish two days early because of Christmas next week."

Ben rubbed his chin. "The paper will go out on Sunday?"

"It's the only way. And then there will be no new edition until after Twelfth night."

"Then take Thursday off, especially since we'll be working all day Saturday."

"How can I?"

"You can. Promise."

A day away from Ben might be just what she needed. She could not seem to resist him with sufficient fervor. "All right. I promise."

"Good." He leaned back, arms folded in repose. She wished she could relax herself, but felt coiled as tightly as a spring.

He made no effort to seduce her on the way home, just whistled tunelessly as the hackney maneuvered through the icy streets. She should be grateful. She *was* grateful. When they stopped at her door, he didn't even try to act the gentleman and help her get out.

The house was dark and quiet. Her father was keeping country hours, although his days could have been spent anywhere, so little did he notice his surroundings now. In the two short weeks since he'd negotiated the gold from Ben, he'd gone into a steep decline. It was as if his last fully aware act was to secure her future.

Evangeline exchanged a few words with the night nurse and had the impish maid Patsy bring her a bowl of oatmeal. It was all Evangeline thought she had the strength to chew, and since it was her housekeeper-cook's night off, all Patsy was capable of making.

Patsy was another rescue, a former prostitute who had made her living on the street since she was eleven. She was a terrible maid but she did try hard, and had never batted an eye when Mr. Ramsey who hired her turned out to be Miss Ramsey. Patsy had seen too much in her young life to be surprised by anything.

Without being asked, Patsy brought up hot water for Evangeline's makeshift bath. Ben's scent was still on her body, and the sweet ache between her legs a reminder of their coupling. She scrubbed away, too exhausted to work up regret for this morning and even sharper regret for what didn't happen this afternoon.

She was in trouble, plain and simple. A day off was more than necessary. She'd have time to think and plan and somehow guard her heart again.

Evangeline sank into her bed after getting into the fresh nightgown that Patsy put out, and said her prayers.

*Come, blessed barrier between day and day.*

She fell asleep almost instantly. Sleep of the wicked, she thought, before the dark came.

# CHAPTER 19

*December 20, 1820*

It had been pure torture not to touch her in the cab last night. It was pure torture not to touch her today in the office, but they were now chaperoned by the two eager Corrigan brothers. Evie and the young men were discussing how to set the type in stages, so everything would not be left to one long workday. It had already been decided that they would not work on Sundays—the Corrigans were strict Methodists who took their commandments seriously. What would the boys say if they divined that one of their bosses was a female in trousers?

Evie had broken any number of rules, and Ben had helped her.

There would be no rule-breaking or drinking or carousing upstairs, which was positive in the business sense, but Ben felt a twinge for the young men who would not be sowing any wild oats. But perhaps he'd sown enough for all of them anyway.

Last night as he'd lain in bed struggling not to take himself in hand and give in to his desire for an imaginary Evie, he'd turned his mind to *The London List*. They could increase their revenue by selling more ad space. More pages, more issues—the horizons were expanding just as his need

for Evangeline Ramsey was. He'd been a newspaper publisher for only a week and already he was putting his mark
upon it.

Where he'd really like to put his mark was Evie's neat
bottom, which was upturned as she bent over the press explaining its idiosyncrasies to Joseph and Matthew in her
gruff voice. It must be a chore for her to always be per-
forming, to go against her very nature. Not that she'd ever
been one of those fluffy, frivolous girls who'd simpered
behind a lacy fan. Evie was more likely to smack him with
one.

But ah, how they'd enjoyed themselves ten years ago.
Both of them had been innocent as babes. Somehow Ben
had avoided the willing tavern maids in Cambridge, and
his first sight of Evie knocked him right on his arse when
her father brought him home one night. Not literally, of
course. She would do that only after they had known each
other a little better; as he recalled, she'd once been impressive with her fists when he'd teased her too hard. But with
her height and proud nose and wavy raven hair, she'd
seemed like a goddess to a gormless boy such as himself.

The years had been kind to her, although the weariness
and worry over her father were taking their toll. Which
was why he hadn't pressed his attentions on her again last
night when he'd very much wanted to.

Evie had too many responsibilities, he thought, and until recently he'd had none. True, he was good with his
money—rather brilliant even if he did say so himself—and
provided a handsome life for his mother when she wasn't
berating him to walk a more righteous path. But if he was
honest, he'd been something of a wastrel, almost deserving
Evie's censure on the pages of the paper.

Things had changed since he'd discovered her in her
breeches. He'd given up his mistress even if she was still
living in his Jane Street house for the winter, and he had

taken on a taxing job. To society, working for a living would be more scandalous than any wild carousing he'd done. His friends were bound to be shocked to see him with his sleeves rolled up and ink stains on his fingers.

He was enjoying himself, however. And thinking a little more clearly than he had in a while. Apart from the Christmas ball his mother had dragged him to, he'd not been out in the evenings, not been drinking brandy and playing cards until dawn. Ben had little inclination to do anything but fall into bed at the end of the day, closing his eyes to whirling black postbox numbers and ears to whispered words for help. *The List* was a clearinghouse for many desperate people; no wonder Evie's shoulders were sagging beneath the weight of so many demands.

Well, he was helping her now, and those two young fellows he'd hired for her looked likely. They'd learn the ropes fast enough. Evie was a good teacher—she'd taught him a great deal in only a short period of time, and he *could* run the office alone, at least for tomorrow. He was adamant that she take some time off, and he was the boss, wasn't he?

It was a simple pleasure to watch her stride around the office, though, tall and lean and forceful. Her bottle-green jacket was perfectly tailored, her buff trousers tight and topboots shiny. She'd perfected her manly swagger and commanded the Corrigans' attention completely.

"Ramsey," Ben barked when there was a lull in their instruction, "let's lock up for lunch and let these lads get settled upstairs. You can spare an hour for me before you go home, can you not?"

"My father—"

"Is in the good hands of his nurse. I'll bring you round to check up on him after we share a hot meal at the Witch and Anchor. I have some business to discuss with you."

He watched Evie war with herself. At length she nodded. "Very well, my lord. You two will be all right?"

"As rain, sir. We be that grateful for the job and the roof over our head. We won't disappoint, I promise." Ben was not sure whether it was Joseph or Matthew who spoke—he'd have to learn to tell them apart.

After bundling up, he and Evie were on the street, passing the poor little chestnut seller. Ben dropped coins into her bucket without pausing to buy anything, and heard her call out, "Thankee, guv! A very happy Christmas to you and yours!" That reminded him he'd not gotten his mother a gift yet. She'd been absent from home now for quite some time, taking care of Lady Applegate with her usual warmth and efficiency. Ben doubted she'd leave the dying woman alone on Christmas. He wondered if he'd be eating his flaming plum pudding quite alone this year.

He might ask Evie to join him. She must long for a bit of brightness in her drab life. They could share one of Mrs. Hargreaves's magnificent meals and then . . .

He pictured Evie with a paper crown on her cropped curls, otherwise entirely naked. What a fine present she would make.

"What do you want to talk to me about?" Puffs of white air burst from her lips, and Ben was struck by her stark wintry beauty.

"I just wanted to get you out of the office. You'll scare the Corrigans with so many lessons at once, no matter how smart they are. And I was hungry. Aren't you?"

Evie stopped still on the street outside the public house. "I don't have time to waste, Ben. I should be home with my father if I'm not at work."

"Evie." He touched her sleeve and she skittered backward. "It's just lunch. Some mulled wine if they have it. And then I want you to go home for good."

"You're firing me?"

She looked so outraged he had the sense not to laugh. "No, no. We talked about you having the day off tomorrow. Well, tomorrow starts this afternoon. You're tired. Give in."

He shoved her through the pub's swinging door before she could run down the sidewalk and raised a hand at the barkeep. "Two bowls of your best stew, ale for me and hot wine punch for the l-lad here." He'd caught himself just in time before he said "lady." Ladies were not welcome here. The taproom was crowded, but he herded her to what had become their usual table in the back. "Sit. Before you fall."

"I am perfectly fine! Why do you insist on treating me like I'm some spun-sugar fairy?"

"Evangeline," he said, his voice quiet but steady, "you are the strongest woman besides my mother I've ever met. But you've had a hard week. Weddings to arrange. Bricks. Odd threatening letters. And then there's me—your arch nemesis—you've had to contend with. You've had too much on your plate for too long. I'm not even sure going home is the best place for you—you'll worry too much about your father there."

"I *have* to worry about him."

He rested a hand over hers. "I know. It does you great credit when he was not always the father he should have been."

Ben wondered if he'd gone too far in criticizing—Robert Ramsey had been the best of fellows and a great mentor to him in his inexperienced youth, but he'd been a hardened gambler. Evie had suffered a disrupted childhood, and her young womanhood had not been much better. If she'd been brought up properly, she never would have let him take advantage of her ten years ago. She would not be slumped in an ale house opposite him now, a beaver hat tilted over her scalped head.

It was unthinkable that any lady of his acquaintance would pretend to be a man for two years in order to keep a roof over her head. But what else could she have done? She couldn't have sought a position as a governess—who would take care of her ailing father while she took care of others' children? The life of a courtesan was definitely not for her. He tried to picture Evie in one of Veronique's transparent chiffon robes and failed. Evie would snort over such excess frippery and strip down much more honestly.

And be even more seductive. Ben had always liked her bold frankness.

A serving girl brought their tray. Evie lifted her spoon but stared into it instead of dipping it into the steaming bowl.

"I do look a fright."

Good. She was coming to her senses. "No, you don't. But anyone can see you're knackered. No one expects a gentleman's skin to glow with dewy freshness, but sometimes you do yourself a disservice ignoring your feminine side. Go home. Put your feet up. Smear some warm honey on your face and slices of cucumber on your eyes."

Evie's lips turned up a fraction. "How do you know such things?"

"My mistresses, of course. I've dropped in unannounced on occasion and they've been very cross with me. I pierced the veil of mystery, you see. Caught them in their pin curls painting their nails. And here I thought they were naturally pink," he said lightly. She'd seemed interested in his mistresses yesterday, although they were a topic he'd prefer not to discuss with her. Compared to Evie—

Well, Evie had no comparison.

She was studying her own work-roughened hands. She really could do with some pampering. Ben wished he could spirit her away to some exotic location where she'd be fed sweetmeats and given milk baths. Rubbed with lotions and massaged from top to toe. A spa of some kind, minus the vile sulfuric waters. Someone could make a mint owning such a place, and he filed the idea away to run it by his man of business.

Of course, the people who really needed such an establishment couldn't afford it. Workingmen whose backs ached from ferrying ale barrels. Schoolmasters subject to one too many spitballs. Half-pay soldiers unable to sleep at night hearing imaginary cannons. Chambermaids run off their feet after a house party catering to the whims of the upper classes such as Lord Benton Gray.

He'd have to worry about the lot of them later. Right now he had Evie's comfort to see to. Ben pushed the plate of bread toward her. "Please eat. You need your strength to keep us men in line. You've got three of us now to badger and bully. That should perk you up."

"I do not badger." She bit into the bread, flicking a crumb from her lip with her tongue. Dear God, he was in a bad way if the sight of watching her eat a humble slice of bread caused his manhood to swell.

"Well, whatever it is you do, you don't need to resume it until Friday. The Corrigans and I will soldier on without you."

"I'll bring some work home with me. Letters to be considered and such."

"That rather goes against the point of relaxation, don't you think?"

"Relaxing does not make me relax," Evie said, smiling ruefully at the silliness of her statement. "I prefer to be busy. But it might be nice to work from the quiet of my own home for a change. Thank you, Ben. You're being very kind."

"It must be the Christmas season."

But it was more. Much more. Evangeline Ramsey

badgered him even when she didn't say a word, rooting around in his conscience. He could not decide if she was a good or bad influence. He only knew that the damn woman was insidious.

And irresistible.

# CHAPTER 20

*December 21, 1820*

Evangeline lay in bed as the snow floated past the windowpanes. How delightful that she didn't have to spring out of bed this morning and walk to the office. And she truly had no reason to feel guilty, as she had brought a case home yesterday crammed with folders of letters to settle. She would write letters of her own back to some of them, explaining she'd found a way to answer their advertisements without publishing them in the newspaper, or clarifying their terms. She truly did not think that Lady Paulette Veryan meant to seek *"a fat footman to see to my every need." Fit* was so much more usual, but perhaps the marchioness had eclectic tastes.

Evangeline stretched, then rang for Patsy. After an interminable wait, the girl shuffled up the stairs with a jug of lukewarm water and a copy of a rival newspaper.

Evangeline shook it out, skimming the headlines. How novel to know she had time to read every word if she chose to. In bed! Such luxury, although her Spartan room was hardly a haven of indulgence. "How is my father this morning?"

"The night nurse told the day one he had a restless

night. Mrs. Spencer's given him some laudanum to help him sleep a little."

Evangeline frowned. Laudanum could give one bad dreams—she hoped her father wouldn't suffer as his nurse had tried to give him some respite.

"Ain't you going in to work this morning? I got your clothes all laid out. The fancy red waistcoat I stitched up for you myself."

Evangeline had been avoiding the haphazard pile on the chair ever since she opened her eyes. Patsy was always trying to make Evangeline more "fashionable," although her tastes were diametrically opposed to Mr. Ramsey's, a gentleman who wished to remain unremarkable in every way. But today Evangeline could don the red waistcoat, not that she wanted to wear the garish thing—it looked like it had been made out of some whore's cast-off dress that Patsy cadged from a former colleague.

However, no one except Patsy and the rest of her little staff would see her. Evangeline had already decided to lounge about the house in trousers and shirtsleeves—far more comfortable than trying to pinch herself into a corset. Her female clothes were seasons out of date and dispiriting to get into. She'd not time yet to improve her wardrobe by spending some of the money Ben had given the household. It was quietly earning interest in her father's bank, waiting for the rainy day that would inevitably come.

But today it was snowing, coating grubby London with a dusting of deceptive purity.

"I'm working from home today, Patsy. Isn't it lucky I don't have to traipse through this wretched weather? I might as well still be in Scotland. When you get a chance, I'd love some breakfast brought to the parlor. I'll be there if Father needs me today."

Patsy held up the offensive waistcoat with a look of

pride on her face. Damn, Evangeline really would have to wear the dratted thing.

"Poor old soul needs his sleep, he does. Mrs. Spencer's that worried about him. He tried to go walking last night again. Mrs. Mendenhall doesn't think she can keep stopping him."

Evangeline's heart sank. Mrs. Mendenhall, the night nurse, was a strong, strapping woman nearly as tall as Evangeline, and much broader. Between the nurse and her father's old valet Wilfred, Evangeline had counted on them to keep Robert Ramsey comfortable and contained. But if she had to hire another minder—several, if necessary—at least she had the funds to do so, thanks to Ben. She might even find the perfect candidate in one of the letters in her case.

"Please tell Mrs. Spencer I'll speak to her once I'm dressed. It shouldn't take me long."

So much for lolling about in bed. Evangeline washed and quickly pulled on the clothes Patsy had selected. Blinking against the scarlet glare, she shrugged into the waistcoat and forced a button through a mangled buttonhole.

After looking in on her sleeping father, she had a depressing interview with Mrs. Spencer, who relayed Mrs. Mendenhall's travails at great and alarming length. Then she shut herself in the little front parlor, sat down in a worn chair before a welcome fire, and opened her case. Patsy brought in a pot of coffee, a boiled egg, and some toast, and for a few blissful minutes there was no sound but the hiss of the coals and Evangeline's unladylike chewing of her breakfast. Even the bad news about her father could not stave off her hunger—she was starving. She'd been too nervous to enjoy her lunch yesterday with Ben—rubbing knees with him under the plank table was disconcerting, and her light supper, however virtuous, had worn off.

She brushed crumbs off the ghastly waistcoat and set to work, organizing her papers into Truly Desperate, Possibly Desperate, and Not Quite Desperate Enough to Merit Extraordinary Action. Thankfully the latter pile was larger, and would fill several future editions with paid advertisement. The prospect of publishing more frequently in the new year cheered her, even if she might not be around to see it.

For Ben was too tempting, too male, too *something*.

Satisfied with her progress, she spent several minutes staring into the fire imagining Ben's something until Patsy poked her head around the door.

"There's a grand young lady downstairs in the hall to see you, miss. I mean Mr. She's looking for Mr. Ramsey, see. Good thing you're rigged out in your fine gentleman's clothes. You do look a treat today. And she *is* a lady, even though she didn't bring no maid with her. Quite sniffy, she is."

A caller here? Evangeline had never been sussed out at home, no matter how Truly Desperate the circumstances had ever been. She doubted Ben would have sent a supplicant to the house after going on and on about giving her a day off. Uneasy, she rose and put on her jacket.

"Did she tell you who she was?"

"Imogen Eggman. No, that ain't right. Ima—Ima—"

"Imaculata Egremont?"

"That's it! Said you would know her as you've been spying on her for years."

Oh dear lord. Evangeline considered picking up the poker from the fireplace to fend off the earl's mad little daughter. No doubt she was just as furious with her as Ben had been, but *The London List* had not featured Imaculata's antics for more than two months. Perhaps the anger had festered over time, so Evangeline girded herself for a tongue-lashing.

Or something else. Imaculata was visiting a gentleman's residence alone. Definitely not the done thing.

"Send her in. And don't go too far afield."

"But I got to go to the market for Cook else your poor da won't have nuffink for luncheon when he wakes up."

"Where's Wilfred?"

"Asleep. Your da kept him up all night."

"Damn. Leave the door open after you bring her up. I might have to make a quick getaway."

Patsy winked and was off. Evangeline arranged herself in front of the fire, trying to look severe at the interruption.

Lady Imaculata sailed in, chin high. And then she said something that surprised Evangeline to her toes.

*"Thankee, guv! A happy Christmas to you and yours!"*

Where had she heard those very words? And in that cockney accent, which so jangled with Lady Imaculata's appearance? The girl wore a hat with so many feathers it looked like it could fly, and an exquisite fur-lined pelisse and muff. Russian sable, if Evangeline was not mistaken. She'd had to bone up on fashion for her articles even if she owned nothing comparable herself.

"I—I beg your pardon?"

"Don't you remember the last time you saw me, Mr. Ramsey? You've passed me on the street lately often enough. I thought for sure someone with your nose for news—and it is rather an enormous nose, is it not?—would recognize me."

Evangeline tried not to let her voice betray her. "You were the chestnut seller? What sort of game have you been playing, Lady Imaculata?"

"No game. No game at all."

And she pulled a tiny pistol out of her muff and aimed it squarely at Evangeline's erratic heart.

Evangeline told herself she wasn't really frightened. It

was hard to believe that Lady Imaculata Egremont was vicious enough to pull the trigger. Violence had never been part of Lady Imaculata's notoriety, although it was said she punched the private investigator her father had hired to fetch her home from France. When Evangeline had hunted Mulgrew down for an interview, he was still sporting a black eye but had kept mum on the method of Lady Imaculata's return. Evangeline could almost sympathize with fisticuffs—Lady Imaculata had finally escaped her strict father's household only to be brought back in shackles and disgrace and locked in her room for weeks with gruel, if her servants were to be believed.

Nevertheless, she was out of her room now and Evangeline didn't like the way Lady Imaculata's unshackled hand was trembling.

"I don't suppose I could persuade you to put that gun away so we can talk like civilized human beings."

The earl's daughter shook her head. "You know I find civilization vastly overrated. I'm a free spirit, unfettered by society's conventions. You've written about me and my little adventures often enough. Thirty-two articles, I believe."

So she was out for vengeance as Ben had been.

"But I haven't written about you for months!" Evangeline protested.

"Why did you stop?"

Evangeline didn't want to insult the girl by telling her that her exploits had looked increasingly pathetic. Her rebellions had a sad, desperate quality to them. Lady Imaculata needed to rehabilitate herself in some constructive way before she did something truly stupid.

Or deadly.

"You must know Lord Gray became the focus of my investigations. Won't you sit down?" she asked hopefully.

"I'll stand, thank you. Benny is such a dear, although I

fear I was much mistaken in him. Did you know I once fancied myself quite, quite in love with him?"

*Benny?* Evangeline doubted Ben would approve of the nickname or Lady Imaculata Egremont's affections. If he was really turning over a new leaf, it would not do to be linked to a lunatic.

"You won't mind if *I* sit while we chat about Lord Gray?" If Evangeline was murdered in it, the chair needed replacing anyway.

Imaculata nodded regally, the feathers on her hat shaking as much as Evangeline's knees.

"I *did* notice that it was Lord G grabbing the headlines week after week. That's why I chose to dance with him in my altogether that night in my garden. He tried to give me his jacket, but I refused."

"Yes, he's a true gentleman," Evangeline said wryly. "The epitome of respectability." She'd been lurking in the bushes herself in order to get her exclusive. Lady Imaculata had more freckles than sense. Everywhere. Evangeline remembered that Ben and his friends were jug-bitten and disheveled, but only Lady Imaculata had removed all her clothes and plunged into the fountain.

"That was the last time you printed anything about me." Lady Imaculata sounded nearly wistful.

Evangeline's mouth dropped open. "Wait. You mean you *want* me to write about you?"

"Of course! It annoys Papa so. I kept hoping he would finally wash his hands of me and give me access to the trust Mama set up. I'd go back to France and take a lover. Or two! I have every single clipping from *The London List* pasted in an album, you know."

Good grief. "Well, if you don't shoot my head off, I can promise you next week's front page." *Benny* wouldn't like it, but Evangeline had a strong sense of self-preservation. She would happily succumb to the blackmail of a gun pointed in her direction and write *anything,* even if she had to make up the details of the incident herself.

Lady Imaculata shook her head again, her feathers in flight. "It's too late now. I can't think of anything else to do that I haven't already done. I've become quite jaded." The girl looked as if she might cry.

"What about this kidnapping and assault?" Evangeline asked, ever helpful.

"Oh, pooh. You're in your own front parlor, sitting down comfy as you please in that ratty old chair. I haven't assaulted you. Yet."

"What a relief," Evangeline murmured.

"I was going to seduce you to get you to write about me again, if you must know. But now that I know—" Imaculata's freckled cheeks turned fiery.

Evangeline was afraid she knew what was coming. Apparently Lady Imaculata had been skulking around the office in disguise for days now, exactly as Evangeline had when she was on the hunt for a story. And just the day before yesterday she had foolishly been in Ben's arms over the office, where anyone might have heard them.

Like Lady Imaculata Egremont in her chestnut seller's disguise. Dripping honey into the sorts. Writing idiotic letters.

"Know what?"

"That you and Benny are more than employer and employee. I heard you upstairs going at it like rabid dogs Tuesday when I left that threatening note. You should lock your doors, you know. Not everyone is as modern as I. It's quite all right, I won't judge you. Love is love. But if you want your secret kept, you'll come up with some juicy bit of gossip about me, something so outrageous my father will have no choice but to let me go."

Evangeline hid her smile. What would established cocksman Lord Benton Gray have to say if he knew someone thought he was a molly? Not that there was anything wrong with that.

Just the possibility of hanging.

"I have a bit of juicy gossip for you myself. I'm not a man, Lady Imaculata. Lord Gray has done nothing he can be blackmailed over, nor have I. We are two consenting adults. If we kissed, it was because we could." And very much wanted to. In fact, Evangeline could think of little else but kissing Ben right now, even if a gun was currently directed at her left shoulder. Which was why she had to retire from her business, no matter how much it pained her or her clientele.

Lady Imaculata's confusion was comical. "Not a man? But you're wearing trousers!"

"And you were dressed as a street vendor. Just because the cat has kittens in the oven, it doesn't make them biscuits. Look." She unwound her neckcloth and moved into the light from the window. "No Adam's apple. No beard." Though there was one vexing black hair on her chin she plucked ruthlessly each month. "It's suited me to be in disguise for the newspaper business. A gentleman has much greater freedom. A woman can only get about so far in society without someone drawing a line over which she cannot step."

"By Jove!" The girl's face lit up. "I could wear trousers, too! It would *slay* Papa. It goes against that Bible verse—he's always quoting Bible verses at me—what is it? 'The woman shall not wear that which pertaineth unto a man, neither shall a man put on a woman's garment: for all that do so are an abomination unto the Lord thy God.' "

Despite the impressive biblical recitation, Imaculata Egremont would never pass as a boy. She was deliciously curvy, and had masses of beautiful red hair that would have to be cut, and so Evangeline told her.

"I suppose you're right. Damn and blast. It seemed like

a fiendishly simple solution to drive Papa mad, too." She began to pace, and Evangeline was happy to see that the gun was now pointed at a china lamp.

"Why do you want to drive him mad? Be patient a little while longer. Surely you're almost old enough to get your inheritance."

"I'd get it if I marry, but who will have me? It's two more years before I turn twenty-one. By then I'll be too old to enjoy myself."

Evangeline flared in irritation. "What rot. I'm two and thirty and still 'enjoy myself,' as you put it, and I expect to for decades to come." Although a life without Ben would be less than enjoyable. "Age is just a number. It's your attitude that determines your level of enjoyment."

"You don't understand."

"I understand you're a spoiled heiress who has gone out of your way to be provoking since you emerged from the schoolroom. Two years of courting scandal! The world is bored with you by now."

Lady Imaculata stopped and spun, aiming the gun back at Evangeline's red waistcoat. "You needn't be so rude."

"Rude! You're holding a gun on me in my own house, my girl. Pardon me if my manners leave something to be desired. You're lucky your father hasn't clapped you into an asylum."

Lady Imaculata's big green eyes began to fill with tears. "Do you think so? I almost wish he would. Then he couldn't make me—" Her lips closed.

Evangeline felt a sudden dread, and it had nothing to do with the mother-of-pearl-handled pistol pointed at her. "Make you what?"

"He does things to me," Lady Imaculata said, her voice barely above a whisper.

Evangeline forgot about the gun and walked across the floor. "What things?"

"Unspeakable things. Oh, if I were to marry, my husband will still find me to be a virgin. Technically. But Papa will never let me marry. He turned down the six proposals I had the first Season I came out. I would have gladly married any of them, even Lord Hastings who was about a hundred and smelled of camphor. I knew then I had to do something to break away. But it didn't matter what scheme I came upon—my father locked me up and beat me and kept turning away my suitors. Now, of course, I don't have any. Hoisted on my own petard." Imaculata laughed bitterly, and Evangeline was struck by how often what one thought one knew proved to be entirely incorrect. Lord Egremont had a sterling reputation, and was pitied by the ton for the tarnished behavior of his only child. If what Imaculata said was true, their pity was misplaced.

"Surely you have a relative you can turn to."

"I don't. No one would believe me now anyway. My father is a *saint*. And I—well, I've sinned too often to be taken seriously. You probably don't even think I'm telling the truth."

"I—I think I do. How long has your father—" Evangeline found words failed her. She'd seen a lot of unsavory things as a reporter, but this was pure evil.

"Since my mother died. I was fifteen. At first, he just held me because he said he was lonely. Then he went further. If I didn't cooperate, he beat me. Told me it was my lustful nature that drove him to it. I really don't think I can stand two more years of it, Mr. Ramsey. Miss Ramsey. What *is* your name?"

"Evangeline." Her mind was whirling with possibilities. How to get Imaculata Egremont away from her father for the next two years? Her reputation was ruined—no young lordling was apt to saddle himself with her as a wife despite her lush curves and winsome freckles. Evangeline felt a twinge of guilt. *The London List* articles had played their part in that. In her well-publicized attempts to liberate herself from her father's domination, Imaculata had only narrowed her opportunities for freedom.

Not that marriage was at all freeing. The girl would be exchanging one heavy hand for another. But a husband's touch would not be *unnatural*. Evangeline shuddered.

"Is your inheritance large?"

"It's respectable. More than enough to get me settled somewhere out of the way. Eventually when I'm old like you I might have to find a job. Or become a courtesan." Imaculata brightened a bit at that prospect.

"Nonsense! Let me think." Evangeline paced, oblivious to the wavering pistol trained on her back. "Would you object to employment now? I know of a country gentleman who needs a housekeeper/nurse. He can't pay much but lives quietly outside some vowel-free village in Wales. That's *miles* from London. Your father would never think to look for you there. Can you cook?"

"Of course not!"

"You must be able to boil an egg at least. Feed him roasted chestnuts. The man"—Evie rifled through the Truly Desperate pile—"a Major Ripton-Jones, seems rather needy. He's an invalid and probably exists on porridge and well water. You could take care of him for two years and then return to Town for your inheritance."

"Unless the old man dies. My food would probably poison him."

"I'll buy you a cookery book. And if you should need another position, I'll find you one."

Lady Imaculata sat down in a chair and slipped the gun back into her muff. "It wasn't loaded, you know."

"That was very sensible of you. I wonder that you have not turned it on your father."

"I've thought about it, but I'm not a total fool despite

what you've written about me." She swallowed. "I'm not sure this idea of yours is a good one. Me, a housekeeper to an old bachelor gentleman? Have you got anything, *anything* else?"

Evangeline had an excellent memory, and there was nothing that suited Lady Imaculata's predicament so much as Major Ripton-Jones's. It would provide her with a roof over her head far from the abuse of her father, and give the girl something to focus on besides nonsensical pleasure and pointless rebellion. "As you've said, nothing you've done so far, no matter how outrageous, has moved your father to release your funds. I doubt anything could. There is something quite wrong with him."

"Indeed. Thank you for taking my side, Evangeline." Lady Imaculata reached into her muff again and blew her nose into an embroidered handkerchief.

"Now, we'll have to disguise you and give you a new name."

"My middle name is Anne. I've always liked it."

"Excellent. Anne Mont. Close enough to your real name for you to recognize it. Of course, you'll be *Mrs*. Mont."

The newly named Mrs. Mont trumpeted into the handkerchief once more. "What's happened to my husband?"

"Killed at Waterloo. You must have been a child bride."

"Fourteen?" The girl giggled. "How shocking, even for me."

"I'll write your references myself. Lady Pennington won't mind if I sign her name to one. But I think you should dye your hair at least until you get to where you're going—it's much too flashy and you might be recognized. No doubt your father will set Mr. Mulgrew back on your trail. Come upstairs to my room. I can cook up something, I think, or you can borrow one of my wigs. We'll send you off to Wales tomorrow."

Lady Imaculata's eyes shone. "Now *this* is a true adventure! How can I ever thank you, Evangeline?"

"Just don't kill off poor Major Ripton-Jones. It will wreck havoc with my success stories."

# CHAPTER 21

*December 22, 1820*

Evangeline resolved not to speak of Imaculata's situation to Ben. There was no telling what he might do when he discovered why the girl had vandalized the newspaper office and held Evangeline at gunpoint. For all she knew he could have her arrested, or worse, challenge Egremont to a duel for despoiling his only child. Ben had a surprisingly honorable streak now that he'd stopped being so selfish. So when she returned to work a little late on Friday morning due to sending the girl off to Wales, she sat quietly on her side of the desk trying very hard not to stare at Ben through her lashes.

"You look much better," Ben said. He hadn't noticed the nut-brown dye beneath her fingernails adding to the usual black ink stains on her hands. When Evangeline left *The List,* she might even become a hairdresser. Of course ladies of the ton seemed to prefer Frenchmen in that role, so it would mean continuing her masculine masquerade and rivaling Ben's former mistress in fracturing French.

"I feel better." And she did. It was always thrilling to solve a problem for one of her readers. A pity she had such difficulty with her own life.

She realized suddenly that the office was missing two

large young bodies and there was no thumping overhead. "Where are the boys?"

"I've sent the Corrigans home for Christmas at my expense."

"But you just hired them the day before yesterday!"

"They've a widowed mother, you know, and they worry about her." Ben frowned. "I hope they get there on time—winter travel is so undependable. I've sent them north with my man of business—he was going to Scotland anyway for me and can deposit them on their doorstep. We won't need them if we're shuttering the paper for two weeks."

"That's generous of you." And annoying as well. Evangeline acknowledged to herself she'd been vastly relieved at the extra help, and now it had vanished.

"When they return, we'll talk about getting the paper out twice a week. They seemed most eager to earn their bread."

"I suppose we can manage alone again if we must." She pictured Ben's damp shirt clinging to the contours of his back, his arse snug in his buff trousers as he mastered the machine. Sometimes an active imagination was not a good thing.

"We've only got next week's issue to put out, and the type is all set for everything you left behind."

Evangeline had followed her predecessor's tradition of closing the paper until after Twelfth Night, although last year she'd weathered her share of complaints about denying good gossip to the ton for such a length of time. Lots of naughtiness ensued with the Lords of Misrule, but London would have to remain ignorant of it this year.

"The boys are good workers. We had a very productive day yesterday," Ben continued, closing up a ledger.

"As did I."

"Slept well, did you?"

"Like a baby," Evangeline lied. Imaculata had shared her bed and kicked like a mule all night long. They had decided they would not risk her returning home to get any keepsakes for her journey lest her father find a way to prevent her from leaving. There might already be investigators all over London this morning searching for her.

"It's Christmas Eve Sunday. I wonder if you've given any thought to the front-page article. We should have something uplifting in honor of the season."

"I do have something in mind." Another lie. She'd been far too busy yesterday arranging Imaculata's disappearance to do anything but organize her letters. "I'm going to write it right now. Would you mind setting these ads? They seemed most important to me."

"Certainly."

With Ben far across the room, Evangeline felt his inevitable physical influence over her reduce a fraction. She tried very hard not to look at him as he slid the sorts into their frames, but each clack of a lead tile against another reminded her he was there.

What on earth was she to write about? The only scoop she had was so sensational and so un-uplifting that she didn't dare to print it. Lord Egremont was no one to antagonize. He had influence in the highest reaches of government, and could shut down *The London List* on some pretext or other if he suspected Evangeline knew what he'd done to his daughter.

She grinned. The perfect subject was right in front of her. He kept touting his attributes, and perhaps he was telling the truth. There was nothing more heartwarming and romantic than reading about a reformed rake.

Those faithful readers will recognize Lord G, who has oft appeared in this very spot of prominence. Though he now may be the owner of record of the paper you are holding in your hands, he has no editorial say or sway over this reporter except to request that *The London List* refrain from the revelation of negative or salacious personal details of its newsworthy subjects. One may hear regretful sighs throughout London and perhaps across the land, but upon this decision Lord G cannot be moved. So you, loyal readers, may look for news of an uplifting nature on this page in the future. Tips from the readership are welcome as usual, as it is sometimes difficult for this humble reporter to find the sparkling diamonds within the rough stones.

It is with some pleasure I can verify that Lord G himself appears to have turned over a shiny emerald-green leaf himself. No longer is he to be found ensconced in the demimondaine every evening, orchestrating amusements sure to shock the most sober-minded reader and his long-suffering widowed mama. He is, in fact, concerned with other widowed mamas, providing transportation so that two hardworking sons may join their mother for Christmas. Lord G suffers from hitherto unknown charitable impulses, offering heartfelt marital advice and providing a lavish wedding reception to total strangers, generously ensuring that an elderly gentleman is comfortable in his retirement, even handing money to chestnut sellers with no expectations of chestnuts. These not-insignificant acts of kindness indicate to this reporter that there may be hope of a reformation to his character. Who knows what wonders the new year will bring?

*The London List* wishes you a Happy Christmas and much joy, peace, health, and prosperity in the Year of Our Lord, One Thousand Eight-hundred Twenty-one.

The story wasn't very long, but that left more room for ads and a frame of holly and ivy. She'd set the front page herself once she got rid of Ben. She'd worry about him noticing the article later.

He couldn't object—he'd promised her he wouldn't interfere in the paper if she stopped exposing his peccadilloes and the foibles of society's other wastrels. Ben never said anything about never appearing in print again, and one should never say never anyhow—it was an invitation to certain ruin. Evangeline capped the inkpot and leaned back in her chair.

Yes indeed, her day had been well-spent and it was not yet noon.

She got up and strode across the office to the bank of mailboxes, tucking replies and end-of-year rental fee notices into them. There were a good number of people who preferred to receive their letters here instead of their homes. Evangeline was certain she was supporting several illicit affairs, but the box rates were exorbitant and just another way for her to fund her own charity cases. Some good should come from those doing bad, or so she told herself whenever her conscience troubled her.

Which was not often. Who was she to sit as judge and jury?

Except she had. With Ben. But look how that had turned out—he was serious about something that wasn't his own pleasure for the first time in years. She had done him a favor by persecuting him weekly, had she not? Here he was, newly responsible, sweating over honest labor.

She jumped as the object of her thoughts placed a hand on her shoulder. "I'm done, my lady. What other tasks do you have for me?"

His warm breath buffeted the back of her head. Evangeline could fairly feel her hair curling in response. Oh, she was hopeless. Hopeless. What was she to do about the dreadfully inconvenient longing deep in the pit of her stomach?

"Get your hand off me!" She didn't sound nearly as off-putting as she wanted.

"I thought we were better friends than that. But whatever my lady desires." Ben stepped back, and she could feel the loss between them.

She spun on one booted heel. "We are not friends!"

"Are we not? I thought we were dealing together rather well."

"By 'rather well,' I suppose you mean that we are lovers once more. Well, we are not. That must stop and so I told you."

"Yes. You tell me over and over again. And yet—" He lifted an annoying brow.

"Stop being so damn smug! We have scratched that itch for once and all." Evangeline turned to stuff a crumpled bill into a letter box.

"Have we? I confess I don't feel properly soothed. You do something to me, Evie."

"I'd like to do something to you—you—you man!"

"What, no adjective? Did you use up all the good words in your story? What did you write about, by the way?"

He was safely at his side of the desk now, a sunny smile on his wretchedly handsome face. She clenched a fist, balling up the last of the bills.

"You told me I'd have full authorial authority when you took over the paper."

"Somehow that doesn't make me feel very confident at the moment. What have you done, Evie?"

"Nothing that need concern you," she said airily. She was glad she'd locked up the article in her desk drawer. "Since we seem to have accomplished everything we set out to do today already, I suggest you take the rest of the afternoon off. You'll need to conserve your strength to crank out the paper tomorrow."

"I've plenty of strength. I'd like to show you how much."

She could see he was not about to give up. Well, why

would he? He was at the pinnacle of his manly prowess. It was almost a shame, really, for her to waste this opportunity with him, no matter how irritating she found him otherwise. She was not likely to get a better offer at her advanced age.

But she might live decades yet. Decades with . . . nothing to look forward to.

No companionship. No physical touch save a cat twisting about her ankles or a dog's head in her lap. She couldn't be bothered to try to break in another lover—Ben had ruined her.

What had he suggested? An affair until Christmas. That was just a few days away.

Could she do it and remain unscathed? Could she disrobe totally to weather his scrutiny? They had always been in too much of a rush when they were young, and afraid of discovery. And lately—she could not feel shame for the overwhelming need and heedless haste to join with him. She may as well have tried to swim against the strongest tide.

More important, if she gave in and floated in dangerously deep waters with him, could she steer herself back on Boxing Day to the odd friendship that was between them now? She guessed he liked their verbal sparring as well as she did.

He was right—she was as itchy for him as if she'd stepped into a patch of poison ivy.

"All right."

Both eyebrows raised. "All right what?"

"The other day you proposed to conduct a *liaison* with me until Christmas. I accept."

To his credit, he didn't gasp like a dying carp, nor did he look particularly triumphant at her sudden change of heart. His hazel eyes widened slightly, but remained steady on her. She could almost feel the heat of his focus, could almost hear the gears whirring in his beautiful blond head as he debated what he should say next. She solved that problem for him.

"You are perfectly correct in assuming our attraction is a mutual if very inconvenient thing. I believe a few days of intercourse may blunt whatever need there is, and we will go back to being employer-employee. I think I should tell you, though, that I'll stay on only for a short time thereafter. I expect you to sell the paper, or find a replacement for me as soon as possible."

"You're irreplaceable," Ben murmured.

"No one is irreplaceable, not even I," Evangeline said briskly. Best to look upon this as a quasi-business arrangement, not a romantic interlude. Romance had very little to do with the way she was feeling. She was, quite simply, in lust. Burning up with it. Had been ever since the night in Ben's little library. There was no point in trying to delude herself further. She was a grown woman, nearly *old,* and while her years should have taught her something, her wisdom was out the window where Baron Benton Gray was concerned. She would lose herself if she tried to stay on.

A few days. No more. New Year's Day at the very latest. And then—

Then her new life would begin as her father's ebbed.

# CHAPTER 22

Never look a gift horse in the mouth. *Life is short, art long, opportunity fleeting, experience misleading, judgment diffi-cult.* A few other half-baked quotations rattled around Ben's head as he stared at Evie, who stood proud and tall by the desk. It would be hard to find anyone looking less seductive and willing for all her brazen words. She may as well have been discussing the weather or what to eat for supper.

Why had she changed her mind? He'd done nothing particularly charming this morning as far as he could re-call.

Ben felt the slightest apprehension. When he'd sug-gested a brief affair with her up in the attics, he'd not been entirely serious. Putting a time limit on his frankly raging desire for Evangeline Ramsey was an exercise in futility. God knows he'd resisted thinking about her for years in anything but the grumpiest way—she'd broken his heart as thoroughly as she had smashed that teapot. He'd been re-sentful and hurt, but trying to convince himself he'd made a lucky escape had never truly taken root.

He was a fool for her. He was a fool, period.

And now she would break his heart all over again, be-cause a few days with Evie were just not enough.

He would take what he could get, though—he was no hair-shirted monk. And if he could parlay days into weeks, he'd make his best effort. He'd made a career of being irresistible to the fairer sex, although up till now he'd thought Evie imperially impervious to his winning ways.

"Until Christmas."

Evie nodded.

"Today is Friday. Christmas Day is Monday. That's not even a full week."

"Beggars can't be choosers."

She thought him a beggar, did she? Was his sapheadedness so very obvious? She did tend to reduce him into an unmanly puddle, but he thought he'd concealed his want a bit better.

"I'm not sure your proposal is worth pursuing," he said, trying to muster up what dignity he could. He was *not* some damn beggar.

She stiffened. "It was your idea. Are you so inconstant in your thoughts you have forgotten?"

"Perhaps you bewitched me." There was no perhaps about it.

"I'm hardly the bewitching type." She shrugged, aiming for dismissiveness. "Never mind then."

"I didn't say I wouldn't do it. I thought we might negotiate a little."

"There is nothing to negotiate! Either you're interested or you're not."

He stood and leaned over the desk, still tall enough to look down on her. "I didn't say I wasn't interested. But two and a half days seems like a rather paltry amount, considering we'll be working like madmen here all Saturday and have no time for anything but the damned paper. One cannot in good conscience even count Saturday, so we're down to one and a half days. I have an engagement this evening, which gives us even less time even if I were to take you back into the storage closet right this minute. I wouldn't feel right intruding in the Corrigans' new lodgings, would you?"

"The—the storage closet?"

Her shock was amusing, but he'd fuck her on top of the desk if he had to.

"I agree it might not be entirely comfortable. Brooms and whatnot. You did say we could consider ourselves done for the day, though, in which case we can return to my home for a short afternoon of delight. Which leaves us Sunday." Ben shook his head in regret. "No. It won't do. Unless—"

"What?" she snapped.

"Let's extend our idyll until the first of the new year. I'll agree not to hold you to every single day if you find you have other obligations. But a few additional days will give us the flexibility we need to put this—whatever it is—behind us. We can make a resolution to that effect. Hell, I'll even put it in writing."

Ben expected her to argue, but instead she pulled out her chair and reached for the inkpot. In a furious few seconds she had scrawled out the basic terms of their bargain. Ben was pleased to read upside down that she'd put down January 1, 1821, as the end date, and he planned to hold her right until midnight. His heart kicked, his cock twitched, and the desk looked more inviting than ever.

But that was no way to begin what he hoped would be an affair that neither of them would want to end. Why couldn't they continue to work and play together? Why couldn't they m—

Good God, what was he thinking? He must be hungry. Light-headed. He'd almost allowed himself to contemplate a future with the most—

Clearly, he couldn't think at all. For one part of his brain wanted to call her disastrous, the other desirable. Perhaps Evie was both, but one thing Ben knew—she was giving him a headache right now to match the pain in his unattended erection.

He covered her inky hand with his. "Let's lock up. Now."

She gazed up at him, her eyes so dark the pupils were indistinguishable from the ebony surrounding them. "You are my employer. Whatever you say."

"Don't play meek miss with me, Evie. I value you for your spirit." And he wanted that spirit above him and below him as soon as he could flag down a jarvey.

She looked down at the paper. "Are we making a mistake?"

"Don't renege, my darling. But if you should change your mind, I'll burn it." He snatched it from the desk and jammed it into his pocket. He'd rather set himself on fire first than miss this opportunity.

"I'll get my coat then."

"Allow me." In a trice, Ben had bundled her up and shut the door firmly behind him. The frigid air should have dampened his ardor, but instead he just wanted to wrap himself around Evie in the cab.

Which he did, heedless of shocking anyone who might see two gentlemen engaged in a frantic kiss. He could kiss Evie forever—they fit together so perfectly, their tongues in such harmony and with only the slightest bump of their noses at the very beginning before Ben angled himself properly. She tasted of peppermint and smelled like sandalwood. He dropped his gloves to the floor so he could cup her smooth, flushed cheek and the rough curls at the nape of her neck.

Once he'd tangled himself in midnight hair that fell

down to her waist, imagining her clad in nothing else. Ben had seen only bits of her white skin then and bits of her now, but this afternoon would be a revelation. He longed to see the curve of her hip, the shadow of her navel, the wiry hair at her apex. He would brush it aside with his fingertips first thing when he finally got her into his bed and plunge his tongue into her folds, where she would not taste of peppermint but something darker and more elemental. He'd have her at his mercy, writhing and pleading, shattering for him and him alone. No other man should ever be blessed to see her as he would in fifteen or so minutes, damn the traffic on the busy thoroughfare.

But he'd make good use of the time, drugging her into acquiescence. She wasn't objecting to anything now, was she? There was no hesitation as she clutched his shoulders and returned his kiss with anxious fervor. She was alive and eager, brushing against him, stroking his damnably thick greatcoat with animation. Evie was a fully participatory partner in this delicious bargain they'd made, wrapping her long limbs around him as best she could in the confines of the carriage.

Minutes now. He couldn't carry her straight upstairs. Severson would have an apoplexy. Couldn't bring her to his bedroom really, despite the fact that the bed was big enough for several energetic lovers—he didn't entertain gentlemen in his sleeping quarters. The attic, while having a certain sentimental value, was ultimately uncomfortable. His small study, the site of their renewed acquaintance, would have to serve, at least for today. He'd have to think of somewhere better tomorrow, but right now he really couldn't think at all.

How many couch cushions were there? They were both too tall to manage if they had to lie upon the short sofa—the study was too small to accommodate a larger piece of furniture. Just as his trousers were becoming too small to accommodate his manhood, Evie's hand caressed his stones. He shuddered and deepened his kiss, wanting to swallow her up in all her frenzied splendor. If the driver didn't get them home soon—

They both lurched forward as the vehicle came to an abrupt stop. The ever-efficient Callum would open the carriage door any second, and Evie was still half on Ben's lap. He set her aside swiftly and straightened her cravat. Her lips were bruised, her cheeks scarlet, her eyes unfocused. There could be no surer proof of his seductive ability, or anything more damning before his observant servants.

"Pull yourself together," he whispered. "And stop looking at me like that. Think of me at my most irritating. Or picture me kicking a puppy or an orphan."

Evie opened her reddened lips, then snapped them shut. She reached down to pick up his gloves, and when she faced him again, he could feel the distance between them. Necessary to get through the gauntlet at Gray House, but disappointing all the same.

Callum's earnest freckled face peered through the smudged window. He held the door while Evie stumbled out and Ben paid the driver, who gave him a smirk. Perhaps the man had eyes in the back of his head, or a hidden mirror, for Ben was certain he was aware of what had just transpired in his humble conveyance.

"It isn't what you think," Ben growled at him, overtipping.

"It's none of my business what you and the young gentleman do, my lord, but not everyone is as understanding as I am. I've a boy in the navy, y'see. He's told me a tale or two."

"I'm not—he isn't—" Why was he trying to explain

himself on the street to a stranger? It really wasn't much better that he was taking a gently bred woman into his house so he could thoroughly ravish her. He was a cur.

A cur with a wrinkled written agreement in his pocket whose terms he was anxious to fulfill.

"Good afternoon to you, then. Good luck to your son."

"And to you, my lord. You'd best be more careful in the future."

"Thank you for your concern." He stepped onto the curb, where Callum was waiting with Evie. Severson stood sentry at the door, letting all the cold air of London in. "Mr. Ramsey and I will be working in my study all afternoon and are not to be disturbed for any reason save the house burning down."

"Will you not be wanting a luncheon, my lord?" Severson asked as he divested Evie of her coat and hat while Callum tended to him.

Evie shook her head almost imperceptibly. Good. He could not wait either to wade through a cutlet and a glass of wine. To be sure he was hungry, but for nothing but Evangeline Ramsey.

"No, thank you. We've too much to get settled today."

"May I remind your lordship you have an early dinner with your mother at Lady Applegate's?"

"Yes, I'm aware, which is why I cannot waste any more time talking. No interruptions. None."

"Very good, my lord."

Ben frogmarched Evie to the back of his house and into the little private library. His hand shook as he turned the key in the lock, and not from the cold. Evie was as far away as she could be, standing in front of the green velvet-curtained window that looked out into the small back garden, her back rigid. Gone was the supple, wild woman from the carriage, and Ben mourned the loss.

"Evie." His voice was rough with longing.

She turned and lifted an eyebrow. "What's your pleasure, my lord?"

"You. You are my pleasure." And he walked across the room to make it true.

# CHAPTER 23

Evie's jacket fell to the floor. His hands were still shaking as he slipped the cufflinks from her narrow wrists and dropped them to the desk. She stood resolutely still, her dark eyes searching his face as he removed each article of clothing. Her neckcloth was child's play to unknot—he should teach her a more elaborate design to ensure she remain a fashionable young sprig. Odd that she would be considered old for a woman, but as a male, she appeared quite youthful.

He'd best not think of her as old. Somehow he had no doubt she could divine his thoughts and she'd have his head before he got her out of her smalls.

If Evie did know what he was thinking, she would know that he was as nervous as an untried lad fearful of being caught on the landing with the chambermaid. This was not their first time alone together, but it was the first time Ben would see her in her smooth, marble-white entirety—not just a thin slice of skin here and there as they fell upon each other in haste. He could be deliberate. Slow. Make her ache for him as much as he ached for her.

A muscle jumped at her throat, and he bent to nip it. She swallowed a cry and put a tentative hand on his shoulder. He captured that next for a quick kiss, then placed her arm at her side so he could continue to unwrap the present he'd lusted after for so long.

He toyed with a tarnished button on her waistcoat and watched the rise and fall of her chest. Evie was making an obvious effort to remain calm, but her breaths betrayed her. Slipping the button from its prison, he tugged up the linen shirt from her trousers. Her skin was warm, soft, womanly despite her attempt to deceive. No man would be fooled at this point—she felt as tender as an angel. He moved up her torso to the strips of fabric she used to bind her exquisite breasts—those gentle raspberry-tipped swells that suited her so perfectly. Suited him, too. Other women might have more up top, but she needed not an extra inch to compel completely.

He'd best stop thinking of other women, not that anyone compared to his Evie. She was the love of his youth. She was the l—

*Dear God.* What sort of spell had she cast over him? This was Evie. Difficult. Demanding. Ink-stained.

And so very dear to him.

Ben had to kiss her to prove it, and so he did. She melted into his chest, and he was once again reminded that they were both still wearing too many clothes. If he lost sight of his objective, he'd find himself tangled in wool on the carpet once again and today's chance would be lost. They didn't have many days in their bargain to begin with—he couldn't waste an hour being precipitous and deprive himself of everything he'd dreamed of for much of the past decade. So he stole his lips from hers and set her back. She looked dreamy herself—her eyes unfocused, her cheeks pale, her mouth stained. If he tapped her with a finger, he had no doubt she'd sway to the floor where he could have his wicked way with her.

But no. Concentrate. There was the waistcoat to shrug

from her shoulders, the shirt to unfasten and pull over her head. The bandages covering her breasts needed to be untied and unwound, her nipples awakened by his kisses. Her sandalwood scent filled his senses. Never would he be satisfied with insipid violets or rosewater again. He worshipped her with his mouth until she swayed in fact and he caught her just in time.

"Ben—"

Her voice was husky with need, deeper than the one she used to pretend to be Mr. Ramsey. Honeyed with an edge of desperation. He'd never heard anything sweeter.

"Hush. Let me love you."

She nodded, her lashes tipped with tears. By God he was good at this—he'd honed his skills for just this moment, to bring Evie with him to a place that belonged only to them. His tongue circled the hardened tip of her breast, then he suckled, drawing her deep inside. Ben wanted to devour her one fragrant, delicious inch at a time.

She was no longer still, but swept her fingers through his hair, holding him close. He couldn't get close enough, couldn't taste enough, could not ever be limited to mere days of this. He'd have to find a way to—

"Ah! *Please.*"

Yes. He wanted to please her in every way imaginable. The first step would be to rid her of those buff breeches and lick into her heaven. She was helping even now by clumsily dealing with her falls. His hand cupped her mons as he continued to kiss her perfect breasts—she hadn't been wearing smalls after all, the naughty wench. One finger told him she was already hot and wet for what was to come even as she shivered.

"Are you cold?" His servants always fed a modest fire in the grate in his study. It was wasteful but damn welcome.

She nodded again. Of course she was. Her bare skin was

pebbled beneath his palms. Without thinking he lifted her to the couch before the fire and regretfully covered her with the soft old Scottish plaid that had been draped on the arm. He turned his attention to the fire, tossing a heaping shovelful of coal onto the hearth and stirring it all to brighter life. In the meantime, Evie kicked off her boots and slid off her pants and stockings, all the while keeping the blanket tucked under her chin and robbing him of the sight of her.

"I promise you'll be warm in a minute." He was blazing with heat himself, burning. It was time to get rid of his own clothes, which he did with alacrity. Evie's eyes flashed wide from her perch on the sofa, and she slowly dropped the plaid from her shoulders.

My God but she was lovely, her chin lifted to expose her long neck. The breasts he'd kissed to berry-ripeness peaked invitingly. Her curls were as disordered as his thoughts, black tufts satin-soft between his fingers as he bent to kiss her again. Her lips parted, and he was lost.

Somehow he managed to scoop her to the floor, arranging the sofa cushions and blanket into a haphazard pallet before the fire. She nestled into the pile rather brazenly as though she knew he wanted to see her every angle. She was lithe, too lean, really—how he'd like to feed her sugared dates or some rare delicacy to sweeten her from the inside out. The ivory of her thighs contrasted with the ebony of her nether hair, but he sought yet another color—the ruby-pink of her womanly folds. He parted her limbs, watching her face as he did so, waiting for permission to satisfy his craving. Evie blinked once in surprise, then gave a tentative smile. How could she not know she possessed him utterly? He would show her the only way he knew.

She jolted as his tongue swept along her seam, his hands covering her dense curls. She opened to him, her long legs relaxing on the pillows. Ben buried himself as deep as he could go, all the while pressing his thumb against the jewel of flesh at her apex. He was patient, diligent, and was soon rewarded by her helpless shudders and too-quiet cries. She was afraid of discovery.

One day he'd see to it that she could scream the roof down.

But today he would move up her exquisite body and cover her mouth gratefully for one quick kiss, sink himself into her sublime femininity, surround himself with her hot liquid glory, rise above her as their eyes met in elemental understanding. There was no shyness or pretense between them now, just the mutual agreement that she was his woman and he was her man. This was what they were made for, what was meant to be after the years of self-denial and bickering. Their bargain might be of finite duration, but by God, Ben would use every moment of time with her to change her mind.

He could spill himself inside her and trap her, but he wanted Evie on her own terms. No coercion. No compromise. He was close now to doing the wrong thing for them both, and with an agonizing stab of conscience, pulled himself from her and spent onto her belly, gripping her tight, kissing away the silver tear coursing down her cheek.

He remembered their first time, when she'd cried after he'd taken her innocence. Ben had been stricken with guilt as only a virginal lummox could be, but she'd assured him the tears were happy ones, that she'd discovered a pleasure she hadn't known existed. Had she just been flattering him? It was practically unheard of for a female virgin to enjoy her first time, although Lord knows he had. Ben had never felt so powerful. Yet he'd been vulnerable too, anxious to please her.

He hoped she was pleased today—he had considerably more finesse now, and knew enough to bring her to orgasm again with his hand as he cradled her to him, their bodies slick with heat. Wave after wave took her, and he didn't stop until he thought she couldn't bear anymore. Eyes closed now, her black lashes fluttered against flushed cheeks. Her lips were plump and strawberry-hued, her tongue darting out to capture the last of his kiss. If Ben were to be struck blind in the next minute, his last sight on earth would be absolute perfection.

There was no need to say anything. They lay before the fire, awash in delicious exhaustion. Evie's body thrummed against his, her pulse racing, her hips bucking with aftershocks as his fingers remained firmly at her center. She made no effort to brush him away, and in truth he could barely move a muscle.

When he was a little boy, he'd ventured out into a winter storm in Scotland. He'd been flattened by the wind into a snowbank and couldn't stand upright until he thought he'd freeze to death. He'd been outdoors probably only for a few minutes, but his helplessness seemed to last forever. Severson had found him and returned him to his safe bed before his arguing parents had even noticed he was missing, and he'd lain immobile until morning, his limbs leaden. The lassitude Ben experienced now was similar, if the reason for it much more pleasant. He was warm and eminently comfortable curled up with Evie, the thin winter sunlight dappling her fair skin. She sighed and stretched into him, her short curls tickling his neck.

"I wish—" *Shut up, you fool.* Her elfin hair was lovely as it was. What woman welcomed criticism of her appearance? But how beautiful she'd be with black silken hair to her waist.

She stirred. "Wish what?"

"Nothing. For more time today. I'm a dutiful son, you know. My mother remains at Lady Applegate's and I promised to look in on them."

"I should go home to my father as well."

He cupped her chin. "Not yet, Evie. I want to look at you. Do you realize for all our encounters this is the first time I've seen all of you?"

She bit a lip. "And what do you think, my lord?"

"I think you are magnificent. In or out of breeches."

The flash of her dark eyes told him she didn't quite believe it. True, she was not his usual buxom fare, although he'd long preferred brunettes. Something about opposites attracting, he supposed. A man's mistress should conform to certain society standards, but a man's wife—

She'd ensorcelled him. His brain was pudding. He wasn't going to marry Evangeline Ramsey unless he wanted to be at the brink of murder or suicide on a daily basis.

But to fuck her—

He frowned. What they had just done wasn't quite so cold or crude.

Or simple. Ben had a feeling he'd just complicated his dedicatedly uncomplicated life.

"What's the matter?"

"Nothing. Nothing at all. I can die happy now."

"Don't be silly, Ben."

"Are you telling me you didn't enjoy yourself?" His hand moved up her slender body to cover one diamond-hard nipple. "Your body tells me otherwise."

"Arrogant ass."

"I'll not argue with you now. I'm too happy."

"And I'm too hot." She made a weak attempt to push him away, but he only gathered her closer.

"What time shall I call for you tomorrow?"

"The paper—"

"We'll run off the damn paper. Starting at the crack of dawn if you wish. But afterward, you're mine."

"You said we weren't counting Saturday."

"I'm sure we can squeeze in a couple of hours." To prove it, he squeezed her bottom, the shameless man.

"Then I should go home to my father. I've neglected him frightfully of late."

"Fine. Invite me for tea."

"What?"

"Tea. You know. Hot water. Leaves. Toss the two in a pot and hope for the best. I'm not particular about my sandwiches, although I loathe fish paste. Shall we say four o'clock? I shall have washed off the sweat by then."

"You can't come to my house!" she hissed. "My servants will know what's going on."

"I'll bribe that wretched little maid of yours again. I have no doubt she's got a price. And the nurse likes me. I could tell."

Evie smacked his chest. "You are impossible."

"Frequently," he agreed. "But we might have a moment or two of privacy among the teacups. I promise I won't take too long."

"That does not sound propitious."

"I promise *you* won't take too long either. I know what I'm about now."

"Insufferable, pompous—"

He ended her diatribe with a gentle yet demanding kiss. She had no choice but to succumb, for as he'd said, he knew what he was about. And he had just enough time to show her how thorough he could be in a limited amount of time before he needed to present himself to his mother and her invalid friend.

Ben was learning each of Evie's pleasure points, welcome lessons indeed, for they gave him so much satisfaction in return. To see her shake, to hear her ragged breaths, to feel her satin skin beneath him was worth every second he spent kneeling into the carpet. When he was done, she wouldn't have the strength to utter one dismissive word.

In the end, she had whispered "Ben" as if it were a benediction. He couldn't help but revel in smug success as he dressed her and bundled her into his carriage. A few scattered stars broke through the gloom of the winter dusk, obvious symbols to him of the brighter days ahead.

# CHAPTER 24

*December 23, 1820*

She was weak. Physically *and* mentally. Last night she'd barely been able to climb into Ben's well-appointed carriage her wobbly legs had betrayed her so, and her mind was swirling like the densest London fog.

What had she agreed to? No, she hadn't agreed—she'd actually proposed this hell-born bargain with Lord Benton Gray. The words had come out of her own now well-kissed mouth.

And *such* kisses. Evangeline wondered that she had any morsel of herself left after Ben had devoured her everywhere,

She felt a flush of what should be regret, but honestly— how could one have resisted what he'd done to her? She was only human.

She waited for him to fetch her, although she was impatient to get started. They had a long day ahead of them, and the thought of him across the tea table later made her especially nervous. The room looked even shabbier than usual to after the glimmer and sheen of Ben's study. She had no leather sofa cushions to toss upon the floor, no colorful Ankara carpet to recline upon.

The clock chimed eight. It was soon ten after. Where was he?

Evangeline paced, her long strides making short work of the parlor floor. They had a thousand things to do—she still had to set the front page and her paean to Ben's quasi-reformation. Maybe she could send him off to a coffee-house while she did so and blindfold him when he came back.

The door burst open and banged against the peeling wallpaper. Patsy entered, bristling with uncontained excitement, Ben on her heels. "His lordship, Baron Benton Gray to see you, miss. Right this way, my lord. Is there anything I can get you, my lord?"

"How much will it cost me?" Ben asked.

"Not a farthing, my lord. I'd do anything for you for free, I would."

"Patsy Morgan! That is quite enough. Go away. Far away. We shan't need you for anything. What kept you?" she asked, wanting to kick herself for letting Ben know she'd been aware of his lateness.

"I actually was doing newspaper business, Evie. I went down to the office—in the dark, mind you, so give me some points. I couldn't sleep, so I thought I'd make good use of my wakefulness to surprise you by getting the front page ready. What the hell is the meaning of this?" He reached into a pocket and shook a folded sheet of paper at her.

Oh dear. He'd found her flattering article, with all its lovely holly berries sketched around it. To her dismay, he tore it into tiny pieces and tossed them onto the cold hearth.

"Every word of it was true, wasn't it? And positive."

"I'll be a laughingstock, Evie! I want no more attention brought to my life—it's no one's business what I do or don't do. And quite frankly I've always had a charitable bent, even if *you've* never noticed. But I prefer to stay anonymous. Printing this rubbish will set every lad who wants to go home to his mother on my doorstep. Thanks to you, I've had quite enough of that kind of interruption to my household already. You cannot publish it. I won't allow it."

"But you said I could write anything—"

"Not about me!" he snapped.

Ben's color was high, his eyes the shade of a storm at sea. He did not look at all like a man who wanted to get under her skirts any time soon, so she sat down. "Would you like some tea or perhaps something stronger?"

"I don't want any bloody tea! I want you to promise me that you will never, ever write anything about me again." To her relief, he stopped looming over her and sat down, too.

"Not even when you marry?"

"I'm not getting married! What poor girl would have me after you've vilified me in print for two years?"

"Well, the article you object so to went a little way to make up for that."

It was Ben's turn to snort. The china clock ticked as they sat opposite each other, both too stubborn to speak further. Evangeline wondered what she would write now. There wasn't much time, and Ben's presence had driven out all cogent thought from her head.

"If that's all then." She waved a hand toward the door. "We really need to be going."

"Oh, no, my girl. You'll not get rid of me so easily."

"I can't sit here all day with you glowering at me. I've got too much work to do."

Ben stood up. "Very well. But you haven't heard the end of it."

"Oh, I believe I have! Somehow I've wounded your feelings because I was nice to you. Don't worry. I'll never make *that* mistake again."

"Nice! Save me from your nice. I'd rather you hurl teapots at my head."

"That can also be arranged."

"Four o'clock was the designated time, correct?"

Evangeline's mouth dropped open. "You don't mean to keep our appointment!"

"Why wouldn't I?"

"Because—because we are fighting."

"I imagine a few hours of hard labor will help me work out my frustrations. And then we'll continue our discussion."

"I have nothing more to say."

"We'll see about that."

Evangeline had spent the longest short day of her life working at Ben's furious, silent pace. She had never prepared the paper in such a paltry amount of time, or written a more banal front-page story. Even her newsboys had worked like little fiends with Ben's offer of a Christmas bonus to motivate them, and the paper would be delivered well before her patrons spoke their Sunday morning prayers on Christmas Eve.

And now she was home, with serious misgivings and a curious Patsy tripping over her feet with a wooden tray loaded with relative delicacies for their grand visitor. Evangeline could only be relieved that her father had a slight cold and had not left his bed today—Mrs. Spencer was sitting with him, reading a volume of Sir Walter Scott's. Evangeline had looked in on him when she came home and had weathered the vacant stare he gave her as she squeezed his hand. She was unknown to him today.

She was unknown to herself. What had happened to the crusading reporter of vice? She was wallowing in vice herself.

But just for a few days. Until the new year and all that it would bring.

She had financial independence now. She would leave

*The London List* and live quietly somewhere with her father. Evangeline would just have to trust that Ben would see it was imperative to continue her labor on behalf of those in need.

And even if he didn't do things in quite her style, she would have to give up control. She certainly could not go on working for the man who made her feel so—

Decadent.

Depraved.

Delicious.

"Are you sure you want to be wearin' *that*?" Patsy sniffed.

Evangeline glanced down at the perfectly serviceable dark blue dress. It was a decade out of style with not a ruffle or ribbon in sight, the wool soft from long years of wear. "What's wrong with it?"

"You look like a nun, you do. Baron Gray is top o'the trees, he is. You might make more of an effort."

Evangeline had definitely allowed Patsy to become too familiar, and familiarity bred contempt, as was clear from the look of disgust on her maid's face. "We work together, Patsy. I'm not trying to impress him."

" 'Work together'? Is that what they're calling it now? La, in my day, I would've made quick 'work' of a tempting toff like that. Looks like a lion and roars like one between the sheets too, I'll bet."

"That is more than enough, Patsy. You are dismissed."

This is what came of giving in to a bleeding heart—hiring an impertinent, incompetent maid who got right to the crux of the matter. Did Patsy see something on her face that revealed what she and Ben had been up to yesterday? Evangeline had donned her nun-like dress just to dispel such speculation, apparently to no avail.

The little china clock on the mantel chimed four. Evangeline picked at a lace-edged napkin, wondering how long it would take Ben to swallow his tea and then swallow her up again.

If he wanted to. It was not at all clear after today that he did.

She'd have to lock the room. And they'd both have to take a vow of silence. She could easily imagine Patsy with her ear at the door, a smirk on her face and an "I told you so" as she helped Evangeline get out of her damned corset later.

Oh, today was all wrong, had started badly and could get worse. Her house was the most inappropriate spot in which to conduct a liaison, if in fact Ben intended to keep their bargain. But where *could* they go? His house was little better. He had an army of attentive servants who wouldn't be fooled forever.

What would it be like to run off somewhere? Evangeline pictured a snug wattle-and-daub cottage. Thatch roof. Roses winding their way around a window. Silly. It was the wrong time of year for roses, but perhaps pansies could survive in a pot at the door. She could practically smell the peat smoke in the crisp country air and taste the snowflakes on her tongue. There would be a huge feather bed in a nook off the kitchen—

How perfectly ridiculous she was being. A visit to Jane Street was much more likely, with all its trappings of gilded sin. Ben was not a man for humble cottages and coziness. He'd grown up in a castle, for heaven's sake, and his townhouse had every luxury.

A swift glance at the clock told her it was now quarter past the hour, and still her exalted guest had not arrived. After some reflection, he might not be as anxious as she was to resume their carnal relationship—he'd been very angry—and a feeling of foolishness crept into her heart and took hold. She poured herself a cup of steadying tea, willing herself to stay away from the window as daylight faded.

She was a too-skinny spinster, with a shocking lack of hair and a big nose. Somehow these facts were not so problematic when she dressed as a man, and Evangeline had an urge to go to her room and take off the nun-dress and don a pair of inexpressible trousers. Hang it if it kept him waiting—he'd made her wait, and damned irritating it was. She gulped a mouthful of hot tea and burned the roof of her mouth. Maybe he wouldn't kiss her.

There.

When she heard the bell ring downstairs, she exhaled the breath she didn't know she was holding. For the second time today Patsy announced Lord Gray. He had bathed and changed into beautifully tailored clothes, as though he was taking tea with a duchess. Patsy may have been right that she was dowdy in comparison.

"Thank you, Patsy. That will be all. If you wish to take the rest of the afternoon off, I'm sure I can manage. Go visit a friend."

"Why, that's right generous of you, miss. But it will be dark soon. The streets of London are not safe for an innocent girl."

Evangeline stifled a snort. "Then go up to the attic and make me a new waistcoat or something."

"I reckon I could do that. I found the most fetching purple velvet shot all through with silver in the market last week."

Evangeline supposed she'd have to wear the thing, hopefully on a dark London street where no one would see it. "Very well. Keep to your room. Please tell everyone that this is a working tea for us and we are not to be disturbed. We have some unanticipated newspaper business."

Patsy winked broadly. "Aye, miss. Anything you say,

miss. Work away." She nodded to Ben, then slammed the door behind her.

Evangeline was sure she heard the maid laugh out loud all the way down the hallway.

"I'm going to lock the door."

"Surely you don't mean to stay and . . ." Her voice trailed away. It was clear he was still furious with her—he didn't intend to still provide her with pleasure, did he?

"You have some apologizing to do."

She set her cup down with an audible clink. "Well, I am not sorry I tried to rehabilitate your reputation."

"Your written words would have been unnecessary if you hadn't defamed me in the first place."

Oh, really, what nonsense. *The London List* was not the only newspaper that published blind items about the hijinx of the aristocracy—she just did it better. Evangeline was not going to pretend to feel guilty over what every other self-respecting and ambitious reporter tried to do. "Good grief, Ben, had it not been *The List,* you would have come to the attention of some other journal, and have. Everyone enjoys gossip about the ton. You were hardly a pattern card of virtue."

"I've done nothing that any other unmarried man of means in my class has not done. So I kept mistresses. I gambled. I drank. Notify Satan. He'll laugh in your face." He broke a biscuit somewhat violently in half between his ink-stained fingers but did not eat it.

He was right. He could have been much worse. Been like Imaculata's father, for example, a secret deviant. Anything Ben had done had been out in the open with a wicked smile on his handsome face.

"All right. I'm sorry. Happy now?"

"Not even close. Words are cheap, written or spoken. I believe I prefer action."

A muscle twitched in his cheek. Why, he was finding all

this *amusing*. His anger had dissipated, like a summer thunderstorm that moved over the landscape. It had been quite a long thunderstorm, however.

"And how will you act, my lord?"

"It is not I who has to atone for my transgressions, Miss Ramsey. Pass me a sandwich, please. I'm suddenly very . . . hungry."

He was wrong. Satan would welcome him with open arms, like recognizing like. She was sorry now there was no fish paste, just butter and parsley rounds and a few muffins filled with thinly sliced ham. Evangeline put several sandwiches on a plate and added an unbroken biscuit and a mince tartlet. "How do you take your tea?"

"With a healthy dose of whiskey. You do have some?"

"My father sometimes remembers he'd like a tot before bedtime." And there were days when she needed to drink a little to forget. She rose and went to the drinks cupboard, bypassing the teacup for a tumbler. "Here you are."

"You won't join me?"

"If I'm to be atoning, I wish to be clearheaded."

Ben grinned. "Wise girl." He drank half the contents, then ate all his food in record time while she choked down a single slice of buttered bread.

"Is your father resting? I was looking forward to seeing him today."

Well, that was a comedown. "You came here to take tea with my father?"

"No, Evie, don't be naïve. I came to keep you to our agreement in every way I can manage within the limited confines of your parlor. But if you think a visit from me after would do him good—"

Evie shook her head. "He's got a cold at the moment. You wouldn't want to be sneezed on."

"Very probably not. I expect the Ramsey proboscis is a force to be reckoned with."

"Some might consider it deadly."

He leaned over and put a fingertip to her nose. "Not deadly. Just determined. I wouldn't have your nose any other way, Evie. It suits you." His green eyes were intent, his voice laced with drugging sincerity. Evangeline felt a blush coming on. He really was a consummate rake who should be put in his place, but right now the only place she wanted him was between her legs.

Stupid, stupid.

Well, she'd been indifferently educated as a girl. Anything she knew now was the result of hard work and punishing experience gleaned from the gambling capitals of Europe.

His broad hand went back to wrap itself around his glass, whereupon he drained it. "Finish your tea," he said with authority. Ordered her to do so, really. Evangeline didn't like taking orders, and her tea must be quite cold by now. She shook her head, not that she wished to indicate she was all that anxious to resume what they'd started in his private library. Not at all.

"All right then. I suppose I've forgiven you. We'll proceed."

*We'll proceed?* He spoke of their encounter as if they were following a list of some kind. First, disrobe. Second, fornicate. Third, button up and leave. Fourth, forget her after January 1.

She wanted to be forgotten, did she not? They could not go on working together, not after *this,* whatever it was.

"I'm honored I've earned your forgiveness, my lord. I'll sleep so much better tonight, I'm sure. What would you have me do? I must remind you, we are in my home and the walls have ears."

"That maid of yours does at any rate. Cheeky little baggage. Why do you put up with her?"

Evangeline did not wish to gossip, and besides, Ben

would think her mad for hiring the girl after finding her half-dressed and shivering on a street corner last winter. "She *is* a bit of a trial sometimes. But she's had a hard life."

"You're too softhearted by half. It's a wonder I'm not stepping over blind kittens and mangy puppies."

There had been no money left in her household budget for pets until Ben had purchased the newspaper. She'd always wanted a dog, something that had been denied her as a girl since she and her father had no fixed address most of her childhood years. When she retired from the paper, she'd get a dog for company—something large and shaggy and loyal. She might speak to it instead of talking to herself as she was wont to do, and Patsy wouldn't have cause to tease her.

But she was not going to waste one more minute conjuring up an imaginary dog. "Are we *proceeding* or not?"

"By all means. It's just that I can't decide where to start."

Evangeline lifted a brow. "Oh?"

"I seem to remember you on your knees a few weeks ago. You know, the night you tried to kill me. I confess I've been unable to get that image out of my mind, not that I've tried very hard. It's a comforting memory, especially when you turn vicious on me. I remind myself you can be so much more accommodating and thus am able to ignore your insults somewhat more easily. But were I to ask you to *proceed* in that fashion, I might be considered selfish. We wouldn't want that now, would we?"

Evangeline tried to keep her composure. "We would not."

Ben leaned back in his chair and steepled his inky fingers, fingers that Evangeline was anxious to have sweep across her body. "I suppose we might take turns."

"We might."

"Or perhaps we could coordinate our efforts to provide mutual satisfaction."

Evangeline's high-necked, long-sleeved dress suddenly became much too restrictive. If he was proposing what she thought, the logistics would be tricky but certainly worth exploring.

Ben extended a hand. "Ready, Evie? Let's see if we can't make some new memories."

"You must promise to be quiet," she whispered, rising from her chair.

"Believe me, my mouth will be much too busy to utter one word." He brought her hand to his lips, kissed each knuckle, then brushed over her palm with the tip of his tongue. As if that were not bad enough, he chose to suckle her forefinger, releasing it only after she gave an involuntary groan. "As will yours. Hush, beginning right now."

Tight. The dress was much too tight. Hot. Itchy. But Ben was relieving her of it in his efficient way, and then *proceeded* to efficiently spoil her for any other man.

Somehow he shed his clothes in an instant and guided her into a position that should provoke laughter or discomfort, but resulted in neither. Evangeline had never felt so wanton in her life, nor so very connected with Ben in the most primitive and private way. She returned every attention she received with newfound skill of her own, and it was not long before the tension built, then erupted in a torrent of sensation that swept through their circle and over their edge of control. Evangeline had no breath left, and certainly no shame. For how could something this amazing be wrong?

Ben rolled away on her worn carpet and reversed himself, taking her in his arms. His body was hot and hard, still pulsing from the volcanic fury between them.

"See?" he whispered. "I told you we'd be quiet."

Evangeline was fairly sure she might have groaned in agonized ecstasy sometime during this extraordinary event, but she was too tired to argue. She wished she could re-

main right where she was for the remainder of the day, safe
and cosseted in Ben's embrace, but duty would call to her
soon. The night nurse Mrs. Mendenhall was going to be
late, and it fell to Evangeline to sit with her father for a few
hours tonight.

"You should go."

Ben kissed her damp brow. "I don't want to."

"I have to attend to my father."

"I can sit with you."

Evangeline searched his face. "You would do that?
Why? It will be boring, watching him sleep."

"I'll watch you then. Perhaps the old boy will wake up
and we can play a hand of cards for old times' sake."

How comforting it would be to share her burden with
Ben, but Evangeline shook her head. "One never knows
what will set him off. He might not recognize you, and
think you've come to murder him."

"He's that bad off? He seemed fine when I met with
him—what was it, three weeks ago?"

Was that all the time it was? So much had happened it
made Evangeline's head spin.

But she mustn't get used to *this*—to be lying in boneless
delight with her lover. In eight days their experiment
would be over and the cold new year would be here.

# *C*HAPTER 25

*December 24, 1820*

Lady Pennington had gone to Kent for Christmas, so Evangeline had no excuse to refuse Ben's offer to take her home once the papers had been delivered and the office tidied for the holiday hiatus. Evangeline planned to still come in to work during the time the office was shuttered—there would be letters to prioritize and stories to research and lives to lighten, but the printing press would be idle and her hours would not be so arduous.

She might even accept Ben's offer to join him for Christmas lunch tomorrow. Her father would not know the meaning of the day, and he was much too ill for Christmas goose—his cold had worsened and settled in his chest, resulting in an alarming cough. The doctor had visited yesterday and was optimistic about his recovery if he was kept quiet and fed a diet of tea and broth. Robert Ramsey's body was still fit for a man of his age, but his mind would never be what it was.

The mercy of it was that her father didn't seem to know the severity of his circumstances. Most of the time he was cheerful, if vague. His demons came out at night though, when he rose from his bed in search of the nearest gaming hell. His old valet Wilfred had long been overdue for a raise, and now that Ben enlarged their coffers, Evangeline had seen to it.

The sky was overcast, dark clouds heavy with the portent of snow. All of London was grumbling about this winter's weather, but Evangeline had been buried in too many of Scotland's storms to object to a snowflake or two. She was buttoned up now to her nose in her brown plaid greatcoat, its flaps snapping smartly in the wind, but could have done with hot chestnuts in her pockets to keep her warm. She wondered if Lady Imaculata had arrived on the old major's Welsh doorstep yet. There had been no news from that quarter, but Evangeline didn't expect any. The less that connected her to the girl's disappearance, the better.

The Sunday streets seemed even more deserted than usual. No doubt everyone was getting snug by the fire, readying themselves for their family festivities tomorrow. Evangeline had Christmas envelopes for her small staff, knowing that in these hard times money was preferable to a badly knitted sock. Thanks to Ben, the envelopes were thicker than they might have been.

A donkey cart a quarter-filled with kissing boughs and branches of holly rumbled by them, then stopped. "Oi, gents! Some fresh greenery for your ladies?" the driver asked. From the looks of his limited wares, he'd had a successful day so far.

Ben looked at Evangeline and nodded. "We'll take what we can carry. Deliver the rest to this address." He pulled out a silver case and handed his card and an obscene number of notes to the man.

"Ben! Are you mad?"

"It's Christmas, Evie, or near to. I reckon this fellow wants to go home before the snow flies, and I haven't so much as a leaf on the mantel at home. My mama usually takes care of all that, but she's been busy with Lady

Applegate. I expect you're in a similar fix. What harm can a bit of mistletoe do you? Here, stretch out your arms." He heaped a mixture of branches onto her coat sleeves, then took twice as much for himself.

"Mistletoe is poisonous, is it not?"

"Hazardous, but not deadly, I believe. We're not going to eat it, Evie, just kiss under it."

"We are, are we?"

"Oh, yes. There are just seven days left to our bargain. We are going to decorate your parlor, and then your bedroom."

"You can't come into my bedroom!" Evie gasped.

"Oh? And why not? Afraid of your servants? They work for you, not the other way around. One mustn't worry what the lower classes think."

"Ben, I *am* one of the lower classes."

"Nonsense. Your father comes from a perfectly respectable family. Isn't he cousin to some marquess or other? And your mother was the daughter of a baronet."

"He's never laid eyes on the Marquess of Sandiford. And my mother was disowned when she married. The only reason my father still has Ramsey House is that it is entailed and he couldn't gamble it away."

"No matter," Ben said airily. "Do you inherit it or is it all to go to some chinless nephew thrice removed?"

"It goes to the first-born Ramsey child regardless of gender." Not that it would do her any good. The house was missing some strategic amenities, like the greater part of the west-wing roof.

"See? Then you are an heiress."

She snorted and tripped over a curb that she couldn't see because of the prickly bundle in her arms.

"Steady. We'll make up some sort of excuse for your servants. Perhaps I've come to measure the windows for new drapes as a Christmas present."

She could use some household refurbishment, but Ben was a very unlikely interior decorator. "I'll have to live with them after you and I are finished," she reminded him.

"Well, that puts us in a pickle, then. Where are we to go?" Ben sighed. "I suppose it will have to be tea in your parlor again, then."

"That would be best," she agreed. They had managed extraordinarily well on the floor doing that extraordinary thing. Seven more days of it, and she'd be dead of pleasure.

They trudged on, dropping the odd berry onto the frosty pavement. Patsy opened the door at once, something else that was extraordinary. The maid relieved them of their twigs and boughs and dumped them on the floor, where more berries scattered. Perhaps the greenery was not quite as fresh as the seller had promised.

"What do you want me to do with all this mess then?" she asked, looking at the mess she herself had made.

"Don't worry, Patsy," Ben said as he handed her his coat. "I'll take care of it. Your mistress and I are going to decorate the parlor and don't wish to be disturbed. It might take us a while to get everything just so. You'll all have a lovely surprise when we're done."

Evangeline watched as the maid struggled to keep a straight face. Lord, the girl *knew*, probably had known from the first time Ben had taken her on his study floor.

"Certainly, my lord. Will you be wanting any refreshments to keep your strength up as you deck the halls?" Patsy winked right at him, removing any vestigial doubt Evangeline might have harbored about fooling her maid for one blasted instant.

"That would be delightful, Patsy. Some tea and whatever Cook has handy. I'm not fussy." Ben gave her one of his never-fail smiles.

"Aye, you've got your mind on other things, I expect.

Indulge me, my lord." Patsy bent to retrieve a sprig of mistletoe and held it over her evil little head. "I haven't been properly kissed in an age, not since Miss Evangeline rescued me from the streets, and then there weren't really much proper about those kisses. Give a girl something to dream over, do."

Ben's mouth had dropped open, whether from Patsy's bold flirtation or the realization that Evangeline had a prostitute for a maid. But then he laughed and gave her a kiss, not quite quick enough to suit Evangeline, but longer than Patsy expected or deserved.

Patsy looked stunned, as well she might. Evangeline sympathized entirely—Ben's kisses were explosive.

"Tea, Patsy," Evangeline reminded her, snapping fingers in front of the girl's love-struck face.

"Yes, sir. I mean miss. I'll be right up with it." She scurried down to the kitchen and Evangeline gave Ben her dirtiest look.

"That was not sporting of you."

"It was just an innocent kiss," Ben shrugged. "Not her first, I take it."

Evangeline grabbed some branches from the hall floor. "Not her first. The poor girl has been kissing since she was eleven. I hope she doesn't murder me in my bed tonight to clear a path to you."

"If you let me sleep over, I could protect you."

Evangeline swatted him with holly. "Be serious."

"I am. I'm told I don't snore much."

"*I'm* told I do. Get the rest of this, will you?"

She climbed the stairs, clutching the boughs to her breast. The house was tall and narrow, with a mostly unused dining room on the ground floor and the parlor directly over it. The bedrooms were on the floor above and the servants slept in a rabbit warren of rooms in the attic. When they had returned to London, Evangeline had

rented the house because it was close to the newspaper office and cheap, but every time Ben crossed her threshold
she was aware of just how very modest her dwelling was.

There was no fire laid in the grate, but Ben set about to
remedy that while Evangeline tucked the wilting greenery
around the room. It was not enough to improve the surroundings by much, but it did help.

After a bit, during which Ben and Evangeline stared at
everything in the room but each other, Patsy came up
with a tray and a pot of tea. Ben remembered where the
liquor was kept and poured them both a drink, and they
picked through Cook's offerings so as not to offend her.
The door was locked again, and Evangeline found herself
on the floor with mistletoe hovering over her nether re-
gions.

"Yes, please," she said, and she bit her thumb to keep
from screaming.

# $\mathscr{C}$HAPTER 26

*January 1, 1821*

Their week was over. Well, *almost* over. Each day had brought them closer together. One evening, Ben had surprised Evie by taking her for a private supper at a discreet hotel. Their suite had been lovely and every one of her desires had been fulfilled, once she had gotten over her nervousness at the opulence. It was the first time they had actually shared a bed—and the bed had been magnificent, with silk hangings, a deep feather mattress and an array of tasseled pillows that had cushioned them sublimely as they varied their positions. Evangeline said she had felt as if she was posing for one of those naughty gentlemen's books, the kind usually titled *One Hundred and One Ways to Heaven* or something like it.

Heaven had certainly been at hand, and she'd been able to make as much noise as she deemed necessary, which was quite a lot.

At the stroke of midnight on New Year's Eve, Ben had solemnly kissed Evie and helped her back into her clothes. She had been in her mannish disguise this evening, as he'd taken her to a party first before they'd returned to his house to privately ring in the New Year. The party was not his choice, but Evie had been curious when she'd picked up the invitation on his desk and had badgered him until he gave in. The revels felt forced and flat to him, and he wondered how he could have spent so many similar nights in such company, but Evie had claimed she needed *something* to write about to keep her readers amused. She'd promised not to be too harsh on the lords and ladies who'd tippled too much, and would not print one word about finding Lady Farrington fucking a man who was not Lord Farrington against the music room wall.

They had ridden almost all the way to her house when he remembered to tell her. How could he have forgotten? He'd realized it the first moment she'd put pen to paper, but had been lulled by her every wistful sigh and fleeting look of regret as they spent their last night together he didn't make his case.

It was not their last night.

"Wait."

Her head was on his shoulder, though he assumed that in her mind they were no longer officially having an affair. She might claim that she was sleepy—that he had worn her out—but he hoped it was something more.

"Our agreement. I've got it right here." He'd carried it next to his heart every day since he'd signed it.

"Mm."

"Let me check something." He unfolded the paper and held it under the flickering carriage light.

"Just as I thought. January First."

"Yes. Today is the first. Just."

"Well, it says here we are to terminate our arrangement on the first day of January."

She yawned. "Didn't we just say that?"

"Yes, but it's still the first day of January, and will be until it's the second day of January."

"You are giving me a headache."

"Too much champagne for you. You are mine until midnight."

Evie seemed to wake up suddenly. "What kind of trick is this?"

"No trick. Look, you signed it. You have lovely handwriting, by the way. You know the old superstition. I was wondering how to get a well-favored dark-haired lad to cross my threshold for luck on New Year's Day, and here you are in those tight evening breeches! I'll just get my driver to turn around."

"You can't do that! I've got to get home! And we're *finished*, Ben. You promised."

"I did. And we're *finished* tomorrow. Tonight—today you will sleep in my bed in my house. We've never done that."

"And we're not going to do that! I'm expected home."

"I'll get you there by daylight. No one will think it odd you're out celebrating on New Year's Eve. It's not as if you have a proper chaperone to convince. You're a grown woman. Independent. And as good as your word, absolutely reeking with honor."

She couldn't argue with that, although she did like to argue about most everything. Ben couldn't see her face very well in the shadows, but he thought if he did he might consider ducking right about—

Now.

"How long have you been planning to pull the rug out from under me, you miserable worm?"

"I like you on the rug, Evie. And, we've discovered, on beds, too."

"Oh! You let me go on and on all night long about the last night we'd spend together, you, you—"

Ben grabbed her hand. "You never said one word, Evie, not one. Now you may have been thinking it—even I have no idea what's going on in your frighteningly fertile mind. I imagine it's pretty harrowing in there some of the time. I meant to remind you of the exact terms of our bargain, but the opportunity never came up." But other things had. Something was coming up right now and he settled her hand in his lap.

"You are a wretched, wretched man."

But she did seem pleased by the evidence of her influence on him. He'd make their last day as memorable as possible if it was the very last thing he did.

If she was the very last woman he ever took to bed.

Somehow that thought did not bother him as much as it should. Perhaps he was destined for holy orders.

Or a lunatic asylum.

He tapped the roof of the carriage and changed his instructions.

Evie tsked. "Your poor coachman. Staying up late to take me home and then going right back on your whim."

"I pay him well enough, believe me. And let's agree to let him sleep in. Never mind about you returning by dawn."

"Ben—"

"I'll send a footman with a message so that no one worries about you. Let's spend the whole of the day together and make the most of it."

"I haven't any clothes!"

"Evie, darling, you will not need any clothes."

She grumbled but Ben couldn't hear the invective over the clip of the horses' hooves. This was turning out even better than he'd planned. For once they'd spend the day in quiet domestic bliss, no newspaper to print, no ads to compose, nothing to argue over. As was his New Year's Day tradition, he'd given his servants the day off, so Ben would take care of her himself. Bring up her bathwater. Feed her—

Hm. Something. He was no cook but sure Mrs. Hargreaves's larder was full. It was a tradition to begin the year as you meant to go on, and Mrs. Hargreaves was nothing if not traditional. An empty cupboard signaled a hungry year ahead, and she'd have none of that.

They'd spend the day in dressing gowns when they weren't out of them. This was one New Year's Day when he didn't have a sore head or a need to lie in a silent dark room, eschewing all human contact. He wanted plenty of human contact—Evie's, to be specific.

The entire day. The horizon was limitless. He might even be able to steal a few hours of sleep for himself knowing that Evie was lying next to him.

Evie entered the darkened house just ahead of him, and Ben gave her a quick kiss on the forehead. "First across the threshold. For luck."

"You won't have any. I'm not really a man, you idiot. Female first footers are supposed to bring disaster, you know." She stomped up the stairs as though he was sending her to her doom. He wondered where these traditions came from. Superstitions, really. Technically as the "lucky bird," Evie should have coal or silver or salt in her pocket, too, which he doubted. And if he were to be absolutely technical, she was right—she was no tall, dark-haired man, even if she had fooled a roomful of drunken partygoers tonight.

His bed was as wrecked as they had left it. Evie, looking glum, chose to sit on a chair by the fireplace.

"Why so blue-deviled?" Ben asked.

"I was ready for all this to be over."

"Were you?"

She didn't meet his eyes, but nodded.

"I imagine I cannot get you to extend our contract," he said softly.

"No! Nothing good can come of this, Ben. We're different as chalk and cheese."

"What does that mean, anyway? And which of us is the cheese?"

"You know what it means! We have nothing in common."

"Don't we?" He begged to differ, but there was no point in reminding her of their mutual purpose among the crumpled sheets just an hour ago.

"No, we don't. This is folly."

She was right. To prolong their affair even for a day was the purest folly. He had been vastly better off before he had found her bending over the printing press the first full week of December. Now he was—

What, exactly? Close to being lovelorn.

He couldn't be *in love*, could he? Love was rubbish, meant only for silly novels and stage plays where everyone inevitably died in Act III. Blood and bodies everywhere with some narrator reflecting philosophically on the futility of life. Ben didn't feel for Evie now what he had felt when he was twenty and was sure what love was. So sure that he'd proposed marriage and had his love thrown back in his face. He had not allowed himself to feel anything like that again.

But he was feeling *something*. And dash it, it felt like honor. He could not force Evie to stay here with him all day no matter how much he wanted her to.

He gave the fire a vicious poke. "My coachman is not going to be happy with me."

She straightened from her slump. "What do you mean?"

"We don't seem to understand each other at all this evening, do we? Maybe we never have. I'm taking you home, Evangeline, just as you wish. I'll not press my point on our agreement—we're not before a court of law, are we? But I'll want one last kiss before I give you up."

Even asking for that was a mistake. He was not sure he could stop at a single kiss.

"Here or there?"

"Pardon?"

"Here in this room, or on my doorstep? Perhaps in the carriage would be better. There are too many people abroad tonight who might see us and come to the wrong conclusion."

That was Evie, always thinking, looking around the corner for calamity.

"Here would be best, then, although you know my carriage is comfortable."

"Much *too* comfortable. I'll want to go home alone to keep you to your word about the 'last kiss' business. I don't trust you for a minute. Shall I remain seated or stand? I don't think we should even consider the bed."

He couldn't help himself—he grinned at the absurdity of the conversation. "Quite right. That might lead to all sorts of complications. But I'm hurt you don't trust me, Evie. I don't know what more I can do to prove my worth to you."

Her lashes dropped, casting long shadows on her cheeks. He'd only been trustworthy for less than a month, and only because he'd been working so hard to get into her breeches. Perhaps she was correct in doubting him.

"I trust you, Ben. It's me I don't trust."

His heart soared briefly, but in the end it was still the same—this was their last night. Soon she would leave his employ altogether. But the last few days had been very worth it.

"Stand up, sweetheart. I don't want to get a crick in my back."

She faced him, lifting her proud chin. "Good-bye, then."

"Good-bye. Thank you for everything."

Lord, what a lummox he was. She hadn't done him any ordinary favor, but gifted him with her body and loaned him her soul.

Stolen his heart.

She touched his cheek and pressed her lips against his. Soft, familiar now, yielding. He was afraid to touch her, certain his resolve would unravel and he'd be unwrapping her from her linen and wool in a trice. He concentrated on their connection—smooth lips and tongue, sweet moisture, artful sweep. His breath hitched when Evie moaned into his mouth but he refused to step further into the kiss.

Control.

Common sense.

Confound it, he was not a saint. He carried her to the bed. She made no objection he was aware of, and he was aware of *everything*. Her hands tore at his trousers and her own, grabbing his cock almost painfully. She assuaged his discomfort immediately by guiding him inside her. So much for his sensual fantasy of candlelit skin on skin. Once again they were scratched and smothered by clothing.

It was still perfect.

And over too soon. There were a few tears to wipe again—only Evie's he was sure. He was merely perspiring from exertions, wasn't he? Clothes to straighten, the coachman to summon, the quiet of his bedroom to endure as the carriage carried her away. It was a new year, but not precisely a happy one.

# CHAPTER 27

*January 5, 1821*

Ben was hungry enough to eat roasted chestnuts for lunch, but the little urchin who'd lingered on their corner for days had disappeared some time before Christmas. Evie had already gone home to her father, so the Witch and Anchor it was. He was in the process of rolling down his sleeves when the door opened and a gust of cold wind hurtled a slender woman into the office. She wore a sable tippet over a dark gray walking dress and was heavily veiled. Even with the fur at her throat, she must be freezing. Ben's instincts went on alert.

"May I help you, madam?" he asked smoothly, as if he knew what to do with one of Evie's strays. But he had dealt with Lord Egremont professionally just a little while ago, when the man came to him in desperation. His impetuous daughter Imaculata was missing again, and despite hiring the best in the business to find her, the poor man had spent a lonely Christmas without her. Ben had taken the particulars down and pledged to run the advertisement for the next month. He'd felt so sorry for the earl he was tempted to offer to do it for nothing, but Evangeline would give him hell. Egremont could afford whatever rates they charged, and the paper was a business, after all.

"M–Mr. Ramsey?"

"I am his associate. Mr. Ramsey has gone to lunch but should return shortly. Would you care to wait?"

He thought he could see the woman's misery right through the veil. "But I'm sure I can be of as much service as Mr. Ramsey," he added quickly. "Do you wish to place an ad?"

"What? No, no. Never mind. I was foolish to come." She turned to the door, but Ben knew he couldn't let her leave.

"I promise to help you, no matter what it is you need," he said in all earnestness.

"What I need . . . would be illegal. And immoral."

A cultivated voice expressing unconventional sentiments. This was no lady's maid seeking a new position.

"Then you've come to just the right place. I'm Benton Gray. Perhaps you've read about me on the pages of this very paper. I'm known for my immorality." Though not lately. He was biting his tongue clean through trying not to lick Evie in some sensitive spot as she brusquely went about their newspaper business. The past four days had been nearly unbearable.

She promised to be gone soon, and then licking would be out of the question. But he had made a promise, too, hellish as it was to keep it, and his tongue stayed firmly where God put it.

"*You* are Lord Gray? You look so . . . normal."

"Yes, no horns to speak of, as you can see. And I *have* reformed, no matter what everyone else thinks. Please sit down. May I get you a cup of tea?"

"No, thank you. I came to give Mr. Ramsey a . . . tip. For the front page."

Ben frowned. "Since taking over the ownership of *The London List,* I am no longer publishing scurrilous news."

"I noticed. But I thought—forget I ever came." Her gloved hand touched the doorknob.

"Please don't go! Perhaps it would help if you talked to me about what is troubling you. I—*we* might be able to do something about it without putting anything in black and white."

The woman hesitated. Ben worked up his usual charming smile to reassure her.

Her reluctance was evident, but then Ben noted a definitive dip of the gray bonnet on her head. "Very well. I don't have much time. He doesn't know I've gone out. And when he discovers I'm not in my room—" She shivered.

"Are you in danger?" Ben thought of the days and nights of his father's rages and his fist clenched.

"No. *I* am not. But he will take his displeasure out on the servants. And my son." The lady wilted into the chair Ben pushed toward her.

"Is it your husband you speak of? You don't have to tell me his name if you are uncomfortable."

The woman laughed weakly. "I came to give his name. To expose him. But you won't."

"I might change my mind. Are you sure about the tea?"

"Perfectly." She took a deep breath. "I am Lady Dustin. Do you know my husband?"

Ben recalled a rather nondescript earl, brown eyes, receding hairline—the type of man you might pass a thousand times without noticing. "I believe so. He belongs to my club, lunches there nearly daily, correct? Then is good for a few hands of whist to while away the afternoon."

Lady Dustin nodded. "When he comes home, he brutalizes the staff. Bullies the men. F-fornicates with the women and sometimes makes me watch. He beats our son. 'To make a man out of him,' he says. I cannot do a thing about any of it. When I've tried to intercede, I only made the situation worse. He . . . enjoys my humiliation, and is ruthless to those who try to stand by me. He broke my last maid's arm, then dismissed her without a reference. I do without a maid now—I don't want to bring anyone else into the house to suffer." She lifted her veil. Ben saw a bleak exhaustion on her unpowdered face—a very young, attractive face, save for the dark circles under her eyes. "It would be better if he just hurt *me*, but he won't. Not physically at any rate. I've even thought about killing myself—or killing *him*—but that would make it too easy for him. I worry about our boy. He's only three." There were no tears during this grim recitation, just a dull, matter-of-fact delivery. Ben thought if she were not telling the truth, then she was a marvelous actress.

But it was difficult to think of Dustin as this kind of predator. Ben did not know the man well, but there had never been any whispers of impropriety. And if anyone knew improper gentlemen, it was Ben. He rubbed his ink-stained fingers together, marshaling his thoughts.

"You don't believe me," the countess said, sounding as if she hadn't really expected anything else.

"I didn't say that, did I? What about your family?"

"They tell me if anything is wrong with my marriage, it is my fault for being an undutiful wife. That if I satisfied my husband he would not be so angry."

*Dear God.* But no. Where was God when such things happened? Ben had prayed to God for years as a boy in Scotland and had come to the conclusion that Scotland must be much too far from Heaven to be heard.

But then his father had died in the middle of one of his tirades. Dropped to the stone floors of Castle Gray, blood bright from the wound to his head. Ten-year-old Ben knew then that God *had* heard, and that he'd killed his father with all those prayers and was glad of it.

A man might do as he pleased in his own home. It was

the law of the land. If Dustin beat his pretty wife as Ben's father had beaten his, no one would intercede, and his treatment of his staff wouldn't merit even a flick of an eyelash. In these days of high unemployment and unrest, there were plenty of servants who would put up with most anything to keep food in their bellies.

"I am sympathetic to your plight, Lady Dustin. More than you know. But even if Ev—Mr. Ramsey were here, I could not agree to publish your accusations without corroboration. No one should be pilloried in the press—I have reason to know. And have you thought of the repercussions if this degenerate behavior is known to society? Your husband would suspect you provided the information and might turn his designs upon you."

Her words were determined. "I—I want to run away. With my son. I have some money put by."

Children belonged to their father, or their father's family. It was almost unheard of for an estranged wife to be permitted to raise a child, and the heir to an earldom would definitely be under the purview of his father.

What would Evie say to all this? He didn't have to ask her—he knew. Ben made up his own mind, feeling a kind of thrill he'd never experienced before. No wonder Evie had been so insistent to keep *The London List* going. This do-gooding was exhilarating. No doubt she would be dealing with this domestic dilemma in a far more creative fashion, but Ben was a simple man. A rich man. He had the necessary means to resolve Lady Dustin's problems, at least temporarily. He hoped she liked Scotland.

"I will help you, if you swear not to breathe a word of your whereabouts to anyone."

Her lips flattened. "That won't be hard. There is no one in my family who cares enough about me to care where I've gone."

"You and your son may stay at my estate in Scotland for

the time being, until we can get this business sorted out with your husband. It's winter, though, and it will be damned cold—snowdrifts above your head and everyone goes to bed when it's dark at three o'clock in the afternoon. Are you sure you want to leave society?"

"Society means nothing to me. Because of its expectations, at seventeen I married a man who has made my life a misery. But why would you do this, Lord Gray? If Horace discovers what you've done, he will ruin you."

"I'd like to see him try. Can you get your boy away without notice? You would of course take nothing with you, just the clothes on your backs to attract no attention. I'll provide you with whatever's necessary—I'm a regular Croesus, you know."

"You are serious? Truly, truly serious?"

"I believe I am. Give me a week to work out the particulars."

Her face fell. A week would seem like an eternity to her. Anything could happen to her child in the next seven days.

"Forget that. Come back here tomorrow—whenever you can. I'll spirit you and the boy away somehow. You may have to do without everything you're used to for a bit."

"I'd be willing to go naked if it meant my son was safe, Lord Gray." Her blush was fierce but her chin was high.

Ben almost wished the child was with her now, so he could make them disappear immediately. A man like Dustin, who liked to make people squirm and suffer, would be a dangerous, unpredictable enemy. Odd, because he looked so innocuous. Unremarkable. Ben had never heard anything much about the man, had never seen him in his usual low company haunts. Apparently Dustin kept his vices close to home, terrorizing his wife by proxy.

Whatever faults Ben had, they had been on full view in

the sunshine and in the moonlight. Perhaps it was time to shine a light on the Earl of Dustin and make sure he never had power over anyone again.

Lady Dustin fidgeted in her chair. Ben could appreciate her anxiety—he wanted to set his non-plan in motion. Evie would be back soon, and two heads were better than one.

Wouldn't she be surprised? Perhaps even proud of him. Of course he was not acting the knight for Evangeline Ramsey's benefit, but it wouldn't hurt to have a mite of Evie's admiration.

"You are sure you weren't followed here?"

"Reasonably. I walked a few blocks from Dustin House and hailed a hackney. No one would have reason to suspect I'd come here."

"Take no one in your household in confidence, not even if they may have a grievance almost as great as yours. Perhaps you shouldn't try to get back here with your boy—it may be too difficult."

"I can dose Peter's nurse with my laudanum—at least that's what I planned to do. She is one of my husband's more willing victims, and I don't care a jot if she wakes with a headache and he chooses to punish her for misplacing his son. I take breakfast in the nursery with them nearly every morning. No one would think it strange if I went up there early."

"Excellent. I'll have a carriage around the western corner—that's the left—of Margaret Street for you at six o'clock. Can you manage that, do you think? It will be dark yet."

"I'm not afraid of the dark. Will you be there?"

Ben did not relish the prospect of a flight to Scotland in January with Lady Dustin and her toddler. They would require stout protection, but he was too well-known— thanks to Evie and her clever little drawings that sometimes accompanied her articles. And Lord Dustin must be diverted before he realized his wife and son were missing, much more up his alley. Ben could be quite a diverting figure.

He'd have to hire Veronique back, and probably bribe her to boot, even though he was still providing for her. She was unmolested in his Jane Street house, tapping her toes until spring, when Ben had indicated he'd probably sell the house. No doubt she was examining a slew of offers from other gentlemen, biding her time to pick the perfect one. She was a luscious morsel, Ben thought ruefully, always agreeable, as far from being anything like Evangeline Ramsey as possible. He'd warn all the Jane Street servants to be especially vigilant for the next few days while he temporarily fell back into his wicked ways.

Ben reached across the desk and patted her gloved hand. "I'm afraid that's impossible. I'll send some reliable servants with you. I have plans for your husband, Lady Dustin. By the time he turns up at home, you will be long gone. Have courage. This will all come to rights, I promise."

He'd better make sure of it to earn the look of gratitude on Lady Dustin's face. After escorting her to the door, he scribbled a note to Evie. He couldn't wait for her to come back, and besides, he was rather proud of all the ideas he was coming up with on his own. There wasn't much time—he had a great many details to attend to, one of which was lunch at his club. His appetite may have disappeared, but there was something oddly tasty on the menu.

# CHAPTER 28

*January 10, 1821*

Evangeline had kept Ben's cryptic note on the corner of her desk for five days now. Whatever was "vitally important" remained a complete mystery, as was the whereabouts of the author of those words.

It was hardly a love note. Barely legible. What it was was annoying. He had left her in the lurch to put the paper to bed by herself, after all his protestations of newfound responsibility and reform. Thank goodness Joseph and Matthew were back and knew what they were doing. They had made themselves useful in any number of ways, so that Evangeline could tell herself she barely missed Ben.

She'd gotten used to seeing him hunched over her desk, his shaggy blond hair tumbling over a bronze eyebrow. He was getting lines from squinting at the endless round of letters, and his fingertips were just as black as hers. His recent work had been particularly satisfactory, especially in composing the advertisements. He was economical with his words and had devised the most cunning abbreviations, which saved space so they were able to include more ads. There was now a key box at the top of the page which explained some of the more arcane shorthand, so that one would not mistake "hus" for housekeeper. A great many women seemed to be wanting husbands this month—perhaps it was the January cold or the boredom of the winter darkness. Evangeline could not imagine the extenuating circumstances under which she'd advertise for a man in *The London List*. She was more than happy as she was.

Wasn't she?

She smacked the doubtful voice back. After all, she had gainful employment—no matter how brief it would be, and really, she *did* have to leave soon. Ben's disappearance was most inconvenient—she couldn't just disappear, too. But while she was stuck here, she did society good and earned more than enough money to see to her father's comfort.

But days went by without him seeming to *see* her. There was a blankness behind his eyes and his wit and sparkle with his nurses had completely disappeared. She went home to him for lunch out of habit, though Evangeline was certain he didn't recognize her most of the time. She didn't bother changing into a dress any more when she was with him, and had stopped talking about moving their household to more gracious accommodations. Robert Ramsey wouldn't appreciate the difference and it might only send him further into confusion.

She was doing her duty. As she always had, through good and bad times. His time was short, all the more reason to leave *The List* in Ben's surprisingly competent hands. There would come a day when she didn't have to worry about her father, and she would regret his passing. For all his flaws, he had loved her and had done the best he could.

Evangeline felt a tear course down her cheek, and batted it away impatiently. There was no time for self-pity—she wouldn't be here much longer and there was so much work to do. Which was why she looked up in annoyance several minutes later as the door to the street opened and banged with some force against the wall as the wind took it.

The man who entered was nondescript, neither handsome nor ugly, but dressed beautifully in the finest stare of fashion, although his clothing was unfortunately rumpled and stained. He looked as if he'd arrived directly from a bender of mythic proportions. Even from across the room, she detected the lingering aroma of hashish and wine, a debilitating combination. Sensing his agitation, she rose respectfully from the desk and made a deliberate effort to lower the timbre of her voice.

"May I help you, my lord?" It didn't take a genius to recognize him as a member of the ton for all his current scruffiness.

"Where's Gray?"

"I'm afraid Lord Gray is not here at present," she replied smoothly. "I'm certain *I* can help you."

"And I am certain you cannot," the man snapped. "There's something havey-cavey about all this. I should have known better, but that damned fellow can be most persuasive."

"You are talking in riddles, Lord . . . ?" She pitched her voice in question.

"I am the Earl of Dustin, not that it means anything to the likes of you. And you may tell your employer if he had anything to do with my wife's disappearance, he won't live long enough to regret it! She is not at home—hasn't been for four damn days! And she's taken my son, the bitch. When I get my hands on her—" He stopped suddenly, apparently realizing what he was about to reveal. He stalked forward and pointed a trembling finger in the direction of Evangeline's nose. "If I read one word of this—just one— in this rag of yours, I'll see you jailed for libel and anything else I can think of. And you can tell Gray that his little Jane Street whore isn't worth the money he pays her either. I've had kitchen maids do better at servicing me. I want to see him as soon as he comes in. He's probably still stuffing his cock down some woman's throat."

Evangeline recoiled from Lord Dustin's sour breath and spittle. And his words. From what she could gather, Ben had eloped with Lady Dustin, or he had led Lord Dustin astray on Jane Street. Either possibility was dismaying and not precisely "vitally important."

But Ben owed her nothing. Even though they had ended their impetuous affair, she felt her heart splinter just a bit before she drew her spine straight, spitefully smug that she topped the vile Lord Dustin by a few inches. "I shall tell him of your visit when he returns. Are you sure you don't wish to place an ad in the Lost and Found column for your wife? Or perhaps an employment ad for a new kitchen maid? Although one would have to be awfully desperate to get down on her knees for the likes of *you*."

Lord Dustin's face mottled in fury. "You young whelp! I'll see you ruined."

"You can try. Be careful of whom you threaten, Lord Dustin. I may not be an earl, but I have my resources."

Lord Dustin turned his glare to the mammoth printing press at the back of the shop. "A few well-placed strikes from a hammer and your resources would be rubbish."

Evangeline knew a threat from this man was likely to be far more substantial than the petty vandalism of Lady Imaculata Egremont. But the Corrigan brothers lived upstairs now, and could be counted on to keep watch over the building. When Ben came back—*if* Ben came back— she'd apprise him of this latest difficulty and determine what their future was.

"*The London List* belongs to Lord Gray now. It would not be wise of you to act against a fellow peer of the realm or his property."

"We'll see about that. You tell him what I said, you hear? And I won't pay a nickel for his house—I've no need of a mistress, especially his leavings."

The door slammed again, this time in closing. Evangeline realized she was literally shaking in her topboots. She collapsed into her chair and picked up Ben's note. How many times had she read it already? There was indeed something havey-cavey going on, and it was time for her to put on her hat and find out what it was.

Somehow her wobbly legs now felt leaden. Did she really want to know where Ben had been since he scribbled that note to her?

True to his word, he had not touched her since New Year's Day. A random smoldering look or two did not count. They'd made their pact to tamp down their lust for each other. Evangeline was careful not to meet his eyes over their shared desk or brush against him when they went to the crowded pub after work or admire the curve of his broad back as he bent over the press. His hands were becoming as skilled on the iron gears as they had been on her skin. They'd had their weeks of madness, and now had settled into a routine, sticking strictly to business.

She couldn't expect him to remain celibate. There was no reason for him to do so—there was no understanding between them now, no vow, no promise. He may have partnered well with her in the office, but she was not his true partner in life.

Still, a shard of disappointment pierced her. It had not taken him very long to revert to his rakish ways.

Half an hour later, she was standing in the little cul-de-sac that everyone who was anyone spoke of in hushed awe—Jane Street, home to the most exotic, erotic women in London. Just a dozen houses, identical save for their painted doors. There was a gate and sentry box at the end, guarded by night watchmen who prevented the uninvited from staring into the long narrow windows for a peek of sin. Evangeline had managed to slip by them before, but it was still daylight, so no subterfuge was necessary.

She knew which house was Ben's; knew in fact which prominent man owned each property and essentially the poor girl housed within. The women had been purchased as willing slaves. She supposed becoming a cosseted mistress was a giant step up from street prostitution, but neither position appealed to her in the least. To be utterly dependent on a man could lead to nothing but heartbreak.

The door to Number Two Jane Street was painted a vibrant yellow, a beacon of sunshine on this bleak winter day. Evangeline had seen the matching jonquils in the little front garden last spring and yellow marigolds in the fall when she had been spying on Ben, but there was nothing now save a crusting of silver-gray ice on the ground. She took a deep breath and mounted the steps.

The rap of the knocker echoed on the deserted street. It was early afternoon, but more than likely the inhabitants were still asleep after their night of debauchery. Jane Street was legendary for its nighttime revels, many of which had been organized by Lord Benton Gray. But Evangeline knew that the courtesans arranged their own daytime amusements—there were card parties and teas to kill the time as the ladies waited to be poked and prodded by their keepers. No matter how exquisite the surroundings or the jewels or the furs, the life of a Jane Street mistress must be boring beyond belief. A girl needed to dedicate her life to the peculiar needs of her master, hoping that the effort would see her into comfortable old age, stockpiling enough trinkets to barter away the inevitable loneliness. There was no job security when a woman lost her youthful looks and a man lost interest.

Evangeline had seen Ben's mistress Veronique at a distance, but never expected the woman to open the door herself. She was in ravishing dishabille, a pale peach robe slipping from a creamy shoulder, her long dark hair disarranged in the most provocative way. Evangeline towered over the woman by a good foot, and this time did not relish her size advantage.

"*Bonjour, monsieur.* 'ow may I 'elp you?"

It was Evangeline's opinion that Veronique had probably been born Veronica far from the shores of France, but she was too distracted to dust off her schoolgirl French to prove it. "My name is Ramsey. I am looking for my employer, Lord Gray. Is he here?"

"*Mais, oui,* but 'e is—'ow you say—under the 'atches. My Ben was a very naughty boy last night, very naughty indeed. He and that *cochon* Dustin were at me all the night long." Veronique wrinkled her powdered nose, but she still was stupifyingly beautiful, with nary a dark circle or wrinkle or smudged bit of paint to lend credence to her words. She looked dew-kissed—and man-kissed, judging by the bright pink bruises on her slender neck. Evangeline's stomach knotted in revulsion and something very much like jealousy.

"I must see him. It's—it's *vitally important,*" she said, using Ben's own words. A five-day sexual escapade hardly qualified, but some small part of her heart was relieved that Ben had not run away with Lady Dustin.

Veronique slowly eyed her up and down, and Evangeline felt herself flaming at the examination. For one mad instant, Evangeline longed to rip open her shirt and reveal her bound breasts, not that there was much to bind. To be flirted with by Ben's mistress was absolutely insupportable. The woman was a sublimely sensual creature—no wonder Ben had gone back to Veronique. Evangeline couldn't hope to compete with such artful beauty.

Not that she wanted to.

No, not at all.

"Let me take your 'at, and you must come into my salon, *n'est pas*? To make yourself so *comfortable* while I rouse milord. *Je suis désolée* that I cannot offer you a little something, but my staff, they are enjoying a 'oliday after what they 'ave been through these past days. Such a nasty man, that Dustin. If I did not 'old Ben in such 'igh regard, I would never 'ave agreed to such things as we 'ave done. Though of course, Ben was *tres généreux*, as always. 'e is such a gentleman, but then you must know that now that you work so closely with 'im. You are sorry, yes, for writing all those bad things? I think 'e 'as forgiven you, 'owever. 'e has mentioned you quite often, worrying that his little *vacance* 'ere would be a problem for you."

Problem was not quite the correct word, but Evangeline refused to let her temper loose until she could direct it at the man who was responsible for provoking it. She sank into a plush sofa while Veronique fluttered out of the room in a waft of scented chiffon.

The parlor was precisely what one would expect in a notorious love nest. The furniture was dark red velvet, the carpets thick, the paintings naughty. Evangeline was disappointed that Ben apparently had so little originality, but maybe Veronique had done the decorating.

So this is where he'd spent the past few days. Well, not in *this* room, but above in his mistress's bed in a *ménage à trois*. But for all she knew, here, too. Ben was not afraid of a little rugburn. The fact that the third party was male puzzled her, for Ben had never shown an inclination in that direction as far as she knew. Although maybe that's why he admired her in trousers, she thought grimly.

A little ormolu clock ticked on the mantel. Evangeline imagined the fluffy Veronique counting the hours until Ben came to her. She had to admit to herself he was worth the wait—December's indiscretions had been beyond satisfying. But January had come, and Evangeline had not kept him sufficiently intrigued to prevent him from going back to his old ways, not that she had tried. If anything, she had probably pushed him right back into Veronique's arms.

She straightened her shoulders and stood as she heard Ben thump down the stairs. He had the grace to look shamefaced as he entered, his ruddy cheeks matching the scarlet tassels on the sofa cushions, his magnificent body clad only in a black-and-gold striped dressing gown. His feet, Evangeline noted, were bare, and she stifled the urge to stomp his toes into the Persian rug.

"This isn't what you think," Ben began.

"Don't bother trying to explain. I had a visit from the Earl of Dustin this morning. He deputized me to tell you he plans to kill us both if news of his wife gets out, and that he won't buy this house or your whore from you. He wants to see you as soon as you . . . finish up here. And you'll be happy to know the paper went out without a hitch this week, although I cannot guarantee next week's issue. I quit."

"What? No, wait, Evie!" Ben caught her coat sleeve as she tried to get past him.

The last thing she wanted was a scene within hearing of his exquisite little mistress, who must be lurking somewhere about, ready for action as she was well-paid to be. "Let go of me at once," she hissed.

"I won't." He had on his earnest puppy-dog face, the one she hadn't seen in ten years. "Please sit down and I'll tell you everything."

"Your words will mean nothing. You know I planned to leave *The List* anyway. I'll just leave sooner than expected."

"Give me a minute to tell you—"

"I'm sure I don't want to know, though it doesn't take any intellect to figure it out. But really, it's none of my business. Why should I care what you do and who you do it with?" Her nose was as high in the air as she could make it. Pray let him believe she didn't feel a shred of anything but contempt.

"I haven't done anything! Well, not much, at any rate."

"I'm not stupid, Ben. I admit I was naïve in thinking you had changed—"

"I have, I swear! I've stayed here for a very good reason. You say Dustin knows his wife has left him?" His hand remained on her elbow, its warm pressure seeping through the fabric and heating her skin.

"Don't tell me you've had her, too. Wherever do you find the time?"

"Enough, Evangeline." Suddenly the puppy barked. Ben no longer looked so anxious to please her. In fact, he looked like he might even be growing irritated.

Lord Benton Gray's lack of anger was legendary. When faced with anything that would cause an ordinary mortal to snap, he presented an unruffled, calm demeanor. When Evangeline had broken with him all those years ago, she'd had to push—and push hard—to get him to go away. He'd been amusing company these past weeks, quick with a quip and untroubled by many of the things that caused her concern. It was nearly a relief to see the spark in his eye and hear the growl in his words. She much preferred a worthy opponent, was in fact fairly itching for a fight.

If only the delicate, delicious Veronique was not within shouting distance.

Ben shoved her back down into the cushions. "Be quiet now, if you can. Yes, I have been more or less here since I left the office. I'm sorry I abdicated my responsibilities, but I did it for you."

"For *me*? Am I to be pleased you've been drinking and drugging and fornicating for days?"

"I'll admit to the first two. Veronique will tell you my part in the other was minimal at best."

"How very comforting," Evangeline sneered.

"Oh, Christ, do shut up. You are so damned self-righteous it's sickening."

"How dare you criticize me, you—you libertine!"

"If you continue to interrupt me I'm going to have to kiss you, and right now I find I do not especially want to."

Evangeline found no words to respond to that, so she crossed her arms and waited. Whatever lies he would say were bound to be ridiculous. She watched as he fiddled with the fringe on a curtain. The weak sunlight was enough to halo his golden head, although anyone less like an angel would be hard to find.

"On Friday, a woman came to the office looking for you. Lady Dustin. I don't even know what her first name is," Ben mused. "She wanted you to write one of your character assassination pieces on her husband. I believe you said you've had the dubious pleasure of meeting him this morning. He's a bully and a tyrant. I told her I'd help her get away from him, and have done so. With any luck, she's over the border by now—that is, if she and her little boy and Callum and my second housemaid aren't stuck in a snowdrift."

"What?"

"Is your hearing deficient? I've just confessed to being a White Knight, fighting off a dragon of a husband, just the sort of thing you've been doing for two years. It hasn't been a picnic distracting the bastard, either, but between Veronique and some of the other Janes, we managed."

*The Janes*? It was the ton's nickname for the dozen women who lived on the street. None of them had such a commonplace name, however. Evangeline knew there had once been a Carmela, and there was now a Victorina and a Mignon and a Persephone, goddesses all. Ben had spent four days with more than one mistress, but according to him it had been for a good cause.

He had helped Lady Dustin—whatever her Christian name was—flee her husband? Why would he do such a thing? A man might exercise his husbandly rights any way he chose, and his wife had to endure whatever choice he made. If the earl had beaten the countess, no one would be expected to step forward.

But Ben had.

"I don't understand."

"I've probably done a stupid thing—if Dustin finds out I'm complicit in the disappearance of his wife, he'll kill me and then you can go back to running *The List* alone. Quite frankly, I feel half-dead now. A bullet might be a welcome thing." Ben moved toward a decanter of brandy and poured some into a tumbler. He swirled it about for a few seconds, then tossed it back. "Hair of the dog. What we need to do now is neutralize the man, convince him to go abroad or, if we're lucky, shoot himself. I can't keep his wife at Castle Gray forever."

Evangeline's mouth dropped open. "You've hidden her in your *home*?"

"What else was I to do? The poor girl was desperate. Dustin punishes his son to torment her. He breaks people's arms. You'd never know it to look at him, would you?"

Evangeline thought of Lady Imaculata's father, equally innocent-looking. One never knew what went on within a man's mind and behind closed doors.

"How do you know she was telling the truth?"

Ben gave her a sharp look. "Give me some credit. At first I was wary, but after I spent a few minutes with her, I just *knew*. She reminded me of—of people I've known who are living in terror of some man's fist. Only in this case, Dustin doesn't lay a hand on her, only the people close to her. That's almost more vicious." He moved away from the window and sat down opposite, his bulk looking somewhat comical in a dainty tufted chair. "I didn't want to involve the paper in any more scandalous stories, but now I'm not so sure. Perhaps we should fix it so Dustin never has the power to hurt anyone again."

"What can we do?"

"I was rather hoping you'd think of something. I've done all I can here, keeping him chained to Veronique's bed while his wife got away. I was hoping he'd stay a full week—that way, traces of his wife's journey would be harder to discover. If he hires that chap Mulgrew, we're sunk."

"The private investigator? Why don't you hire him first? Pay him to mislead Dustin," Evangeline suggested.

"By God, I knew I liked you for a reason. That's a brilliant idea. Mulgrew's got a sterling reputation as a family man. I don't think he'd want to bring a wife back to such a husband."

Evangeline remembered he'd brought back Lady Imaculata from France, but then no one had told him about Lord Egremont's peculiar attentions to his daughter first. She felt the headache she'd been harboring since she crossed the threshold of Number Two Jane Street fade ever so slightly. "And you really want to write about Dustin on the front page?"

"Let me think about that when I've got a clearer head. We'd have to witness his bad behavior and make sure others do, too. Maybe I should throw a party."

"All that liquor had gone to your head. You are not making the slightest bit of sense."

Ben grinned. "Oh, yes I am. I've been thinking about selling this house. What could be more entertaining than to invite a bunch of proper gentlemen to view it and Veronique? We could have an orgy, with Lord Dustin smack in the center."

"He doesn't seem to be inclined to be your friend at the

moment," Evangeline reminded him. "And was most unimpressed with Veronique."

Ben snapped his fingers. "Words said to save his pride. Believe me, he's been a happy man these past few days. He's throttled enough throats and twisted enough arms to slake his depravity. He's a brutal bugger."

"And the Janes permitted this?" Evangeline wondered. No amount of remuneration would persuade her to subjugate herself to such things.

"They like me," Ben shrugged. "I promised no real harm would come to them, and it didn't. Arabella's protector is at the Congress of Vienna so she had free time, and Mignon's gentleman is laid up with the gout. They were at loose ends and a little bored, I think."

*Unbelievable.* But it really was not for her to judge. If she had been beautiful, she might just as easily found herself as someone's mistress during the very lean years with her gambling father.

"You'll have your work cut out for you to get Dustin back here."

"Leave it to me. In the meantime, discover all you can about Dustin's fortune. His habits and haunts and so on. You excel at that sort of thing. He'll never know what hit him." Ben beamed and it was hard not to be carried along by his optimism.

The day had been full of surprises so far. Who knew what would be next?

# *C*HAPTER 29

*January 12, 1821*

Evangeline was feeling the thrill of the chase. Her blood had not sung quite in tune since Ben forbade her from trolling society's underbelly for scandal. Her last stories had been of an uplifting nature, and thus unbearably boring. While she was still undecided as to the wisdom of exposing Lord Dustin's sins in print, she at least was enjoying rummaging through the complicated network of his financial interests and friendships.

She had gone to her usual sources yesterday—the neighborhood servants and tradesmen who knew everything worth knowing. It seemed Dustin's fortune was in steep decline. His young wife's settlement—Allison was her name—had pretty much been run through, and he owed a great deal of money to his tailor. Though he dined at his club nearly every day, he had formed no warm relationships with his peers, although it was clear he wanted to impress them somehow. The gossip belowstairs was that he was a very hard man to work for. Evangeline was surprised she had not been asked to rescue one of his servants from cruel treatment already.

Lady Dustin's family, while financially comfortable, was undistinguished. It had been quite a step up for Allison

Barry to marry an earl, and they were now set on finding similarly situated husbands for their other daughters. A runaway wife would significantly compromise their ambitions, and Evangeline filed that away for future use as a bargaining chip if the Barrys could be made to sympathize with their oldest child.

Sifting through the details, she could not for the life of her see how they might shame Dustin enough to give up his bad behavior. He didn't have close friends to shock or living family—apart from his wife and child—to embarrass. There were some men, Dustin probably among them, who could get sexually excited only when making others suffer. It might not even be possible for Dustin to change his nature.

Change . . . according to Ben, he had left his own wicked ways behind, even if Evangeline had thought otherwise at first. And it seemed he'd taken on a fair amount of personal risk, hiding Lady Dustin at his Scottish estate. If discovered, he might be accused by Dustin of alienating the affections of his wife in a criminal conversation suit. If Dustin chose to divorce his wife, she'd lose her son and that action would blacken Ben's name far more thoroughly than Evangeline had ever done in *The London List*. Ben might consider all this a lark, with talks of orgies and subterfuge, but Evangeline knew there were serious consequences to his impulsive actions.

Even worse, Allison Barry, Countess of Dustin, would be destroyed.

Evangeline frowned over her bits of paper, and was so lost in thought she barely registered Ben's arrival.

"Beautiful morning, isn't it?"

Evangeline looked up. Sleet was pinging at the window. "What have you done now?"

"Sent out invitations. The party for Dustin's demise is tomorrow night."

"Tomorrow! But I haven't come up with a strategy yet."

"All taken care of. Or it will be, with your help."

"You know I'll help you."

Ben hung his hat and coat on a hook. "I hope you won't mind playacting a part again."

"I thought you said I didn't lie well," Evangeline reminded him.

"Oh, you've got experience in this role. I want you to just be yourself, your Mr. Ramsey self. A young man out on the town. You are going to seduce Lord Dustin."

Evangeline choked. "I beg your pardon?"

"You have noticed, haven't you, that a certain kind of man finds you very attractive?"

"I can assure you Dustin did *not* find me attractive!" The man had been repelled by her and her station, thinking himself far above her.

"But he will, when he thinks you are Miss Ramsey. But then he's going to discover that you're Mr. Ramsey."

"You have been in the brandy and it's not even ten o'-clock," Evangeline accused.

"No, my angel. I am perfectly sober. Our aim is to expose Dustin's perversity."

"But he isn't a molly, is he? And anyway, calling that *perversity* seems vastly unfair to the men who are made that way." Evangeline had met several gentlemen of that persuasion over the years, and always felt the bias against them was most unfair, not to mention fatal.

"I agree absolutely. Dustin is about as masculine as they come, a bully who thinks his vicious behavior proves his manhood. Imagine his disgrace when he realizes the courtesan he's been making up to in front of all his cronies is, in fact, a man. He'll be shattered, and so mortified that he'll happily accept my generous offer of passage to India to make his fortune."

"*I* can't be a courtesan," Evangeline sputtered. "Look at me!"

"I am looking at you," Ben said softly. "And you are lovely as you are, but with Veronique's help, you will be dazzling."

He was mad. Utterly deranged. And India! The whole scheme was—

Rather tidy. Dustin's reputation would be ruined, and his financial position was already very shaky. He might just jump at the chance to absent himself from England's shores and agree to leave his wife and child unharmed. With any luck, he might die of some dreadful Indian disease, too.

"I don't know, Ben. I cannot see myself as a *femme fatale*." She was mercilessly realistic about her shortcomings.

"You managed to snag me, Evie."

"You're an idiot."

"There should be none of that with Dustin. No sharp words, no disparagement. Just all honeyed sweetness and seduction. Come, we haven't a minute to waste. We're going to Jane Street."

It had taken most of two days before Veronique and the other Janes were satisfied with Evangeline's appearance. Evangeline had been pinched, plumped, and powdered so that she was unrecognizable even to herself. Veronique had done something rather magical with stage make-up so Evangeline's nose was just a shadow of its former self. Her eyes were ringed with kohl, her long lashes blackened, her lips and cheeks rouged. Her ice-blue spangled dress, left behind by someone named Lucy who had run off and married her protector, fit her angular body like a dream, and revealed assets Evangeline didn't really have. Her wig was a glorious mass of golden curls, which was the most difficult thing to get used to.

"There. Feckin' perfect." Veronique had dispensed with

her French accent sometime around teatime yesterday afternoon, for which Evangeline was grateful. "'e'll not be able to resist you or my name's not Veronica O'Brien. 'e likes blondes—gave Arabella a spanking she'll not forget anytime soon. The man is a feckin' pig."

Evangeline nodded. She could endure a spanking for a good cause.

"Now, this is what you must do—no, don't sit down, you'll tear the dress. We want to save that for when you're in the gent's lap."

Evangeline listened to her instructions until she thought her ears would bleed. Her heart hammered and her throat dried. She could hear the guests downstairs. The other girls were already down there, tickling chins and pouring Ben's liquor with a heavy hand.

Every eye was on her as Veronique pushed her into the parlor. Ben grinned and winked at her, and she had to look away. The men outnumbered the ladies by far, and Evangeline noted they were all avowed cocksmen—Ben had gathered up the ton's most notorious womanizers and promised them entertainment. But there were a few unfamiliar faces. One of them must be Dustin's banker, and she knew some of his other creditors had also been invited this evening because she had written the invitations herself.

" 'ere she is, messieurs, our latest *edition* to Jane Street's *jeune filles*. May I present Evelyn? She is as yet without the protection of a suitable gentleman. Perhaps one of you will be *tres* lucky tonight, *hein*? What do you t'ink, Mademoiselle? Which of these so *gentil* gentlemen catches your eye?"

"I'm sure I couldn't say," Evangeline said, casting her eyes to her huge feet. She hastily tucked them under her diaphanous skirts.

"I'm all the man this lovely Amazon could ever want,"

someone said to ribald cheers. But Evangeline would not be tugged over like a rag doll. Ben had promised to pave the way for Dustin's attentions only.

"Bah. I should tell you, young Evelyn has, 'ow you say, special needs. *Preferences.* She likes to be under a man in every way. Under 'is t'umb, I believe you English would say. She desires a man who will keep 'er in 'er place. By whatever means *necessaire.*"

"Then I'm her man." Dustin said, stepping forward like clockwork. The man was predictable to a fault.

"You do not look so *formidable* to me, Lord Dustin," Veronique said dismissively.

"Looks are deceiving, you little bitch. I know what to do with my women. Here, I'll show you. Come."

Evangeline jumped at the command but couldn't seem to move forward. Veronique gave her a little shove in the man's direction.

"Good evening, my lord," she said, her voice husky.

Dustin grabbed her arm hard enough to leave marks. "Let's go upstairs and get this evening started. I trust you have no objections, Gray?"

"Why go upstairs? So many steps. So little time." Ben gave the earl a bland smile. "You're among sympathetic gentlemen tonight, Dustin. We like a good show. Nothing you could do will shock us. We're unshockable, wouldn't you say, my good fellows?"

There was a general roar of approval. Good Lord. There really was to be an orgy, with Evangeline at its center. Her cheeks flamed with heat, but she angled a padded hip into Dustin. "I'm game, my lord. Are you?"

"Always ready, my dear. Let me show you how ready."

Evangeline was relieved she was wearing gloves, so the contact with Dustin's erection wasn't quite so acute. But she couldn't avoid his mouth as he brought it down to slobber on her. She hoped her shudder could be taken as a frisson of desire, and she wrapped her arms around the man as though she were a delicate vine climbing a rotten trellis, rubbing gingerly up against him to the catcalls of the other guests.

How far would she need to go? The disgusting kiss was not enough. She needed to make him touch her *down there,* so he would feel the little—well, not so little—sand-stuffed replica of manhood that the girls had sewn up to tuck into her smalls. It was imperative she not give Dustin time to detect that her manhood was not real, so she was poised to rip off the blond wig and reveal her true gender. Well, her faux gender. It was all a bit of a Chinese puzzle box at this point.

The kiss seemed endless, and the blasted man seemed more interested in squeezing the batting in her bodice rather than her codpiece. It was Ben's clear voice that reminded the earl what they were here for.

"For God's sake, man, how long must we wait? The Janes are getting jealous."

"I've plenty left over for them, too," Dustin boasted as he came up for air, his lips slimy. "Are you wet for me, Evelyn?"

Evangeline batted a clumpy eyelash. "What do you think?" She drew his hand to her thighs just as he'd drawn hers to his.

It was comical to watch him turn white, then green. "What the hell?" he whispered. "What's the meaning of this?"

"Do you feel how hard I am for you, Dustin?" she purred, dropping her voice an octave but speaking quite loudly. "It's such a pity that Lord Gray wouldn't let us go upstairs so we could have our usual privacy. But, as I said, I'm game." She reached up as she had practiced, and the blond wig slithered to the floor.

"The devil! Evelyn's not a whore! She's—he's a man!"

Much like the horrible kiss, the laughter was endless. Dustin was brick-red now, his fist raised.

"Ramsey! From the bloody newspaper," he growled.

"Don't bother hitting him." Ben stepped forward, actually pulling out a quizzing glass and examining her as if she were a slug. "By all that's holy, you're right, Dustin. That's my employee, Evelyn Ramsey. So that's where you've been off to lately, having it on with old Dustin here. I'm afraid I'm going to have to fire you, my boy. I can't have this kind of scandal associated with *The London List*. It's bad for business. Whatever will your poor twin sister say? My heart breaks for her."

Well, she had been looking to make an exit from the paper, and this was as spectacular a one as she was likely to get.

"That's all right. Dusty will take care of me, won't you, darling?"

"I never—you lying bastard! I've never touched him before, not once!" Dustin turned desperately to his audience. "You must believe me. I only fuck women."

"And beat them, too, don't forget," Evangeline chimed in. "And your little boy when he gets in the way. But I like to be hit. So we should get on quite nicely."

"Ev-*Evelyn*," Ben warned. "Don't press your luck." He stepped in front of her. "Surely we can come to some amenable arrangement. My friends won't gossip about this, will you?"

There were snorts and more laughter. "At least Ramsey here won't be writing about it on the front page unless he wants to hang," someone chuckled.

"Oh, dear. I'm afraid you're about to be judged somewhat harshly, Lord Dustin."

"And that's not all." The director of Dustin's bank stepped forward. "You owe us a great deal of money. I've decided, sir, that you are a risk we simply cannot afford.

I'll expect payment in full by Monday morning or we'll see you in the Fleet." The other creditors added to his demand.

Dustin gulped and gasped. Everything he said was met with ridicule, and Evangeline could almost feel sorry for him except for his vile taste on her tongue.

"I'm afraid the party's over. Veronique, would you see these gentlemen to the door? Perhaps I can be of some help to Lord Dustin. I do feel responsible somehow. Ramsey, I am disappointed in you, but we'll discuss it later. Now, Dustin—"

Ben threw an arm around Dustin and led the man into a corner of Veronique's red parlor. Evangeline grabbed the wig and her fur-lined cloak by the door and stepped onto the pavement before the other guests could corner *her*. Ben's coachman was waiting at the end of the street, chatting with the sentry that was posted in the evening to keep Jane Street's secrets. Tonight was one scandal that was bound to escape.

"His lordship said to take you straight to his house, Mr. Ramsey. But it really is Miss Ramsey, ain't it? You're wearing a dress and all even if your hair's funny."

Evangeline wasn't really sure who she was supposed to be at the moment, so she just nodded and climbed into the carriage.

She hadn't expected to be deposited at Ben's house, but was greeted formally by Severson, who received her as if she didn't resemble a confused courtesan.

"My lord has arranged for a bath here for you, Mr.— Miss Ramsey. Really," he said, sounding almost hurt, "if he had confided in me earlier about your subterfuge it would have saved all of us concern. The staff was wondering, you know. Lord Gray has not been himself lately."

"And that's a good thing, is it not?"

"Well, I suppose it is. This way—but you do know where his lordship's bedroom is, don't you?"

Evangeline blushed. She certainly did.

It was heaven to sink into hot water and scrub off the paint and perfume that Veronique and the girls had insisted upon. Being a courtesan was time-consuming work, even out of bed.

When she had washed away all traces of Lord Dustin, she put the glimmering blue dress back on for lack of any other proper attire. It did not fit half so well since her padding was now wound up on a chair. Severson had left wine by the fireside, so she took a glass, wondering how long it would take Ben to convince Dustin to run away.

Not long. She heard him whistling up the stairs and swallowed the last of the glass.

"Well done, Evangeline!" Ben was windblown and grinning from ear to ear.

"There was no trouble?"

"Lord, no. The man is leaving London at first light. How convenient I had a ticket in my pocket for passage on *The Star of the East*." He poured himself a glass and sat down on the chair opposite.

"And he didn't suspect?"

"He might have, but what could he do about it? They'll be talking about him for years. He knows he can't show himself in society. And I promised to pay his debts in full."

It was Evangeline's turn to whistle. "What about Lady Dustin?"

"Ah." Ben took a sip and set the glass down. "I had to pretend I knew absolutely nothing about Lady Dustin. He never even mentioned her. It was up to me to ask if he had anyone I needed to notify for him. He remembered her and his son as an afterthought."

"The beast."

"Aye, he is that. But by spring Lady Dustin can return to London. I'll clear out the house of her troublesome servants. I expect you can find me a fresh batch?"

"You can find them yourself, Ben. I have to leave the newspaper—on your orders."

"Evelyn does. But not Evangeline."

"What?" She'd had only the one glass of wine.

"You can't leave yet, Evie. If you put on a wig you can come into the office in skirts, looking for your brother. I'm going to take pity on you and hire you for a while. Take pity on *me*. I'm not ready to run the paper by myself yet."

"Oh, Ben—"

"Not a word. Not tonight. You were magnificent, Evie, and I want to celebrate." His eyes went to the tangle of blond hair that lay across her rolls of padding.

She could pretend to be Evelyn—a *female* Evelyn. She'd better slap the wig on her head before her good sense caught up to her.

# CHAPTER 30

*January 14, 1821*

His plan was brilliant. Bound to succeed. And so he told himself every step of the way to *The London List* office as distant church bells chimed.

Ben walked at a brisk pace, both out of the need to escape the cold and to get this declaration over with. He was not ordinarily a coward—any of his friends would vouch for him as being the staunchest of fellows, heedless of risks and reputation. He had climbed buildings to enter bedrooms and chased runaway carriages before they toppled down cliffs. Well, just one carriage, but the effort had been intense and the carriage's owner had been grateful enough to him to let him enter her bedroom without climbing. He has assisted an abused wife and child by offering them shelter under his very own roof, risking the wrath of not only her husband but all of society. He had engineered the destruction of her husband and celebrated that fact with a few hours of unsurpassed sexual pleasure with Evangeline in his very own bedroom, servants be damned.

How hard could a proposal be? True, he'd done it once before, but the humiliation of rejection had blotted out his memory more or less over the years. Ben wasn't going to get down on one knee as before, so Evie could glare at him down her long nose, or even kick him away. She was capable of anything. He wasn't going to try to flatter her with romantic muck, for a woman like Evie didn't have an ounce of romance when it came to him.

But she was softhearted toward all the poor unfortunates who implored her daily to solve their problems. That was one of the reasons she hadn't left his employ yet. Those warmer feelings were the key to getting her locked up into his arms for eternity—or for as long as he could keep her abed. He wasn't entirely convinced she would agree to all his terms, but surely she wouldn't expect him to be celibate in their marriage. She might not like him, but she did seem to like fucking him, and that was a start of some sort, wasn't it?

Gad, but he was an idiot. Why did he want her? He really couldn't say, except he'd wanted no one else but her ever since he was a boy, despite cutting a wide swath through the demimonde. He wouldn't lie and say he'd never enjoyed himself, but sex with Evie was singular. If anything, the intensity had quadrupled as they moved into their middle age. Perhaps it was Ben's last gasp of virility. Whatever it was, his mouth dried and his cock stiffened at the sight of her in her outrageous breeches.

People had made marriages built on lesser foundations. And he was prepared to sweeten the deal—to make her an offer she couldn't possibly refuse.

The office was still dark. Ben felt some triumph for dragging himself out of bed before Evie. She must be every bit as exhausted as he from their night of passion. This undercover work added a dash of danger to their relationship, which acted like an aphrodisiac. Ben could only thank Lord Dustin for being such a scoundrel.

But first things first. He pulled his mother's ring out of his pocket. The emerald was obscenely large, and the diamonds surrounding it were not insignificant. He tried to picture it on Evie's grubby hand—even though Joseph and Matthew did most of the work now, Evie still managed to get into the thick of everything. She'd never be a conventional wife, and that was fine, for Ben found most conventions rather strangling.

His mother would be happy. She'd liked *Mr.* Ramsey, so it shouldn't be a stretch to get her to like Miss Ramsey as well. She always asked about his "colleague," approving of the change wrought over Ben now that he'd gotten serious about business. It was nearly annoying—Ben had been serious about his investments for years, but hadn't dived into ditches or descended into mines personally before. Apparently all it took was a little dirt under his fingernails to get his mother's respect.

He was perfectly clean now. His cravat was crisp, his tawny leonine hair tamed. If Evie didn't interrupt him, Ben had every hope of reciting his lines with dignity.

He didn't have long to wait. Evie was nothing if not punctual. Responsible. That was what he was counting on.

She blushed when she entered the door and saw him, probably remembering what she'd done with him a scant few hours ago. Their New Year's deal seemed definitively broken. She had come in her gentleman's garb, out of habit, no doubt.

"You're here early," she said gruffly, shrugging out of her greatcoat.

"I've told you time and again that I'm a reformed man."

"Words are cheap, as you once said."

"Not yours, Evie. They've cost me a pretty penny now, haven't they? Your salary is astronomical. But surely my actions speak for themselves. An observant reporter such as yourself must note the dramatic change in my character."

"Hm," she said, damnably noncommittal. Perhaps if he

rescued orphans from a burning building she might see him with new eyes, but setting fire to property was a criminal offense, not to mention causing worry to the poor children was not at all cricket.

She sat at her desk—he still thought of it as hers although he'd propped his feet up often enough on it—and rifled through a stack of correspondence. He rounded the corner and put his hand down firmly on hers.

"The letters can wait."

"Are you mad? There are not enough hours in the day to sort all these out, and we have a deadline. I've yet to write something up about the Dustin affair. It will be discreet, don't worry, just that he's off to India for a change of scenery. And I—I must leave soon. You've fired me."

"I've hired Evangeline."

"You know I cannot stay on after—" She blushed. She remembered as well as he did. It had been hell keeping his hands off her since New Year's, but last night had been worth the drought. She had been exquisite, flush with triumph and very brazen in the blond wig. "You've taken me from my business far too much this week."

"*Our* business. Besides, it's Sunday. A day of rest."

"Not for me! Joseph and Matthew may not work today, but they'll expect the dummy to be ready and I haven't even written the lead."

She was her usually prickly hedgehog self. How to soothe her without feeling the sting of her bristles?

"I have a proposition for you—one that will eliminate your constant fear that some need will go unmet."

"Oh? And what is that? I grant you've been adequate in your assistance, but do you have a secret twin like I apparently do to share the load?"

"Better than a twin. And I'd never willingly share you with anyone, Evie."

She turned scarlet. "Oh! You are a devil."

"I suppose, but as I've said, I'm working on my wings. Can't you spare me a moment?" He squeezed her hand, which he was surprised to realize was still in his.

"Oh, very well. Make it quick."

"Now, Evie," he chided, "many things can be said about me, but I'm never quick."

He heard her say the words *impossible* and *arrogant* but he chose to ignore them.

"I want to talk to you about your father's house in Scotland."

Her dark brows knit. "The house in Argyll? It's virtually uninhabitable. I won't go back there—you can't make me!"

"No one said anything about you leaving London. The paper would fold without your expertise, especially now that we plan more issues per week. But I was thinking that the house might make a satisfactory accommodation for your strays once it was fixed up."

She stared up at him blankly.

"You know, all those people there in that pile who have no proper home or livelihood." He gestured to the letters on her desk. "Like that old gent in Wales who needed a housekeeper or nurse but couldn't pay much. Imagine if he was in a home with other old fellows and there were plenty of housekeepers and nurses to keep track of everyone."

"I—I found him someone suitable."

"Did you? Jolly good. But there must be others whose ads go answered."

She nodded. "Yes, lots. I'm not a miracle worker."

He cupped her cheek. "Ah, but you are. Look at the changes you've wrought in me."

Her lashes fluttered and at first he thought he'd gotten through to her. But then she spoke.

"Really, Ben, get to the point. I don't have all day for your flummery."

"I am prepared to make the necessary modifications to the house in Scotland to accommodate a whole host of needy people, including your father. Orphans, too. We could establish a school. An all-purpose charity home, if you will. As I recall the house is as big as a palace, and there were endless outbuildings, weren't there? There will be round-the-clock staff gleaned from the employment files—you would pick only the most experienced, competent people. And the neediest potential residents. I'd pay the salaries and of course collect no rent from the guests. There would always be a place for those who needed one. Lady Dustin's dilemma has inspired me—I can't stash people in Castle Gray indefinitely. There's just one caveat."

Evie was looking at him as if he'd grown two heads—his secret twin must be somewhere about. Her lovely mouth was open but she did not speak.

"Don't you want to know my price?"

She rose from the desk, toppling the chair in her fury. "Just because I forgot myself last night in the thrill of our success—I have told you time and time again I will not be your Jane Street mistress, you horrible man!"

Ben took a step backward. "I don't want you to be my mistress, you irritating woman! I want you to be my wife!"

Not the most tactful proposal, but there it was. The words hung in the air. Evie sank slowly down, forgetting the chair was no longer beneath her. She landed in an indelicate heap, saved from total exposure by her trousers. Damn it.

Ben rounded the desk and hauled her to her feet. She was as supple as a willow branch, swaying on unsteady legs.

"Pardon me?" she croaked.

He set her on the edge of the desk. "I'm asking you to marry me. I realize this is not the most romantic proposal in the world, but you are a practical woman. I'm not going to waste my time trying to turn your head with pretty words and flummery, as you call it. I know you are not totally averse to me—you were crying my name in the middle of the night, after all. Shrieking, really. Loud enough to wake the dead. There is a bond between us, odd and annoying as it may seem to you. And to me, for that matter. I can't seem to keep my hands off you. I need a wife and you might as well be it. I will be faithful, if you are worried. You are more than enough woman for me." She always had been.

Evie closed her black eyes. "Explain this to me again."

"It's a sop to my conscience, really. I can make a contribution to society after my years of negligence. Kill all the birds that worry you so with one stone. You'll have a safe place for your father, although if you want him to live with us, I would of course accede to your wishes. I think you might be happier, though, if you didn't have to watch him decline. I know that he doesn't recognize you now. Or anyone. Mrs. Spencer told me. If you agree to marry me, I'll have an army of carpenters in Argyll before the week is out. I think we could open up the home by late spring. My man of business says half the roof is sound, which is one small mercy."

"Your man of business?" Evie asked faintly.

"I sent him to Scotland right before Christmas, remember? There was some trifling matter to be settled on my estate and it seemed convenient for him to inquire after your father's property while he was there. He was not particularly pleased with me, I can tell you. Snow. Ice. The usual winter inconvenience. Even the Hogmanay celebration was a disappointment to him. He broke a tooth on a black bun, poor devil. I had to increase his wages. But I'm blessed with more money than I know what to do with. There's enough to repair Ramsey Hall and keep quite a crowd fed and comfortable and cared for there for years."

"You really want to marry me?" Evie still sounded dazed, which was a good sign, wasn't it?

"I do. We've gotten along well enough as we've put out the paper, wouldn't you say? I mean, apart from the fighting. I don't suppose we'll ever stop our endless bickering, but I can live with it. And if you're amenable, a child or two would make my mother happy."

Evie picked up an inkpot and rolled it between her hands. Ben hoped she was not going to aim it at his head. If he recalled the incident with the smashed teapot, she had an excellent arm. "Let me see if I understand you. You call me a harpy, and want children to please your *mother.* You think I can be bribed by appealing to my sense of social justice to spend the rest of my life at your beck and call."

"Just so. Except I wouldn't expect you to be much good at the becking and the calling. I know you too well. And please put that down. You're making me nervous."

Evie dropped the pot to the floor, where it shattered. Ben stepped away from the glass slivers and spreading puddle. Good for the floorboards that it had been almost empty. "There's no need for destruction of property, Evie. Let's be sensible adults about this thing. You'll have whatever you need to make you happy. Be a baroness. Just say yes."

Ben's heart squeezed in the silence. He was not going to beg. In his opinion, he'd made a generous offer and the fact that he was prepared to withstand Evie's bullying for the foreseeable future surely was in his favor. It was not as though she had other offers. No doubt she would make him an uncomfortable wife, but perhaps with time he could tame her.

He didn't pull the ring from his pocket. Perhaps he should—it was a rather convincing expression of affection, but she hadn't thought much of it the last time. He did not want to look desperate. He was *not* desperate.

"I—I'll have to think about it." Evie slid off the desk and righted the chair. "Give me your handkerchief."

Ben expelled the breath he'd been holding. "Fine," he said, passing her a square of white linen, which she dropped over the ink mess. His valet Timms would have no hope of ever getting it white again. "But I'll need an answer soon if I'm to get your father's house renovated."

"I can't think right now—I need to write up the Lord Dustin article while the events are still fresh in my mind. You can pick the rest of the ads this week. I'll inform you of my decision Tuesday afternoon."

So brisk. So efficient. Well, what had he expected? For her to weep gratefully in his arms and tell him she'd loved him forever? He pulled a chair to the other side of the desk and looked through the batch of letters, words scrambling together. Every now and again he looked through his lashes to see Evie staring at the blank sheet of foolscap, a pencil stub between her fingers.

He went to a cabinet for a new pot of ink and set it between them. She traded her pencil for her pen and began to write with vigor, her print clear although slanting somewhat crookedly across the page.

She had not asked about his plans for the newspaper. Would he and Evie be sitting across from each other twenty years from now, scratching out other peoples' wants and wantonness? Ben saw Evie, a lacy matron's cap tied beneath her stubborn chin and spectacles on her formidable nose, still zealous in her pursuit of truth. It might be difficult to dangle from balconies in their old age, but the

prospect of growing old with Evie was surprisingly comforting.

Tuesday was two days away. He could wait. He'd waited
ten years already.

# CHAPTER 31

Evangeline took her frustration out on the foolscap, tearing it in spots and blunting two pen nibs. She skewered Lord Dustin with as many double entendres as she could recall without resorting to a dictionary. Ben appeared placid across the way, stacking the letters in piles as she'd taught him, oblivious to the fact that she wanted to jump over the desk and pummel him for delivering the worst proposal in all Christendom.

And the rest of the world besides. Whatever religion one practiced, there could be no more inept, unromantic intentions to marry uttered than what had just fallen from Lord Benton Gray's well-formed lips.

When he had proposed ten years ago, there had been kisses from those lips, a bouquet of snowdrops and smuggled French champagne. He'd fed her oysters from their silvery shells by candlelight. He'd produced a spectacular emerald, which had been extremely difficult to turn down. Evangeline was not avaricious, but that ring had been sublime. For a moment she'd almost put it on her finger, but then she remembered why marriage to Ben would be a bad idea. He might have money for all those luxuries at the moment, but if he continued to gamble so recklessly, he would lose everything. She couldn't bear to find herself in the same position as a wife as she had as a daughter. All the years of scraping by and making do, alternating with brief periods of semi-security. She was worn down by the uncertainty of it all.

And he had been too young for her—for anyone, really. Ben was like a big shaggy yellow puppy, all big paws and wagging tail, so good-natured it was unnatural. So she had hurled all his optimistic romantic drivel back at him, sparing them both later disappointment.

A smidgeon of romantic drivel would have been nice this morning, but apparently she'd cured Ben of that. His offer was extraordinary, though—she had no doubt she could fill up every inch of space at Ramsey Hall, including the broom closet. A tremendous weight would be removed from her, for her conscience prickled constantly. She was turning into one of those women who could not find happiness if anything at all was awry.

Evangeline knew what she'd said earlier was true—she was no miracle worker. But by damn, she tried, and tried hard. If she were a man, she'd run for the House of Commons and take her case to government, but she was thwarted by her sex—just another inequity that needed correction. Women had no votes, no legal claim to their own children, for heaven's sake. Look at Lord Dustin, the cur. Beating his child and then fornicating with the governess as his heir huddled hungry and alone. Something had to be done.

She looked up at Ben, his golden curls lit by the necessary lamplight in the gloom of the winter morning.

"Will you take your seat in the House of Lords if we marry?"

Ben folded a letter into the "no" pile. "Do you want me to? I confess it has already occurred to me to do so. Without your prompting. It was one of my New Year's resolutions, although I thought to get the newspaper business under my belt first."

Evangeline was struck by his calm tone. It was clear he'd already given it some thought. He *was* serious about turning over a new leaf. Although if he gave up everything, there would be enough leaves for an entire tree, if not a forest.

A man like Benton Gray would be bored to bits by the usual minutiae of government, but perhaps she could make him shake it up.

"Would you vote as I asked, since the country has not seen fit to allow me my own voice?"

Ben's genial expression remained in place, but his words were measured. "I am my own man, Evie, and would vote as I see fit after examining all sides of the issues. However, you could attempt to persuade me to your point of view. You have any number of attributes in your arsenal that might change a man's mind."

Flattery yet self-assuredness. Her respect for him rose a notch. Maybe he wasn't such a careless hedonist after all.

"Is that one of your requirements? For me to become political? I must tell you, I cannot see myself as Prime Minister for at least another twenty years."

Evangeline suppressed a grin. Ben was as far from being like the swarthy, repressive Lord Liverpool as was possible. She supposed the man had presided over such draconian laws in the war's aftermath thinking he was holding British society together, and perhaps he had.

"I don't know what my requirements are as yet," Evangeline answered. "I told you I am not ready to give the matter of your proposal my full attention."

"I shall wait on tenterhooks." He got back to reading the correspondence, and Evangeline had to admit that his outward composure miffed her. She herself was still seething with contrary emotions, not the least of which was an urgent desire to kiss the wretched man. The pen slipped from her fingers, leaving a spatter of ink across the torn paper.

"I need to go for a walk."

"Now? I thought you wanted to finish your article."

"I won't be gone long." Evangeline stumbled up and began getting into her outerwear.

Ben rose, too. "Do you want me to walk with you?"

"No! That is to say, I've remembered something I must do. Lock up when you leave."

Ben looked down at his piles. "I'll be at these for some time yet."

"I don't know when I'll be back. If worse turns to worst, we can deliver the paper a day late."

"Good heavens! That's not a bit like you, Evie. Riots might result if there's a delay. I don't want to risk that."

"Then *you* write about that evil bastard Dustin. You'll make more sense than I do at present."

Ben made no move to stop her as she moved toward the door. Part of her yearned to be encapsulated in his arms, but she was not about to confuse herself any further by throwing herself at him.

Bloody, bloody hell. Why had he chosen this morning to propose, and propose in such a ham-handed, horrible way? She hated him intensely.

In her haste to leave, she forgot her hat. A blast of cold air ruffled her hair and snaked beneath her upturned collar. It wasn't Tuesday, but she turned in the direction of Lady Pennington's townhouse, praying she would find her friend home on a Sunday morning and not in church. Or worse, still in the country in the bosom of her happy farming family.

She wiped a stray tear from her cheek with a gloved finger before it froze to her skin. It was unconscionable to be crying when she had the offer she'd never allowed herself to dream of. For how could she marry Ben when they were always at such odds? It was one thing to throw caution to the wind and have sexual congress with him. But to turn him from lover to husband? To speak to him over the breakfast table without wanting to tear his head off? Evangeline knew she was outspoken and difficult. A man like Ben would tire of her, no matter his profession of faithfulness. He must have been tempted back on Jane Street when he was luring Lord Dustin to his doom. His former mistress Veronique was the most delightful little thing, really. How long would it take him to go back to her or find someone just like her?

By the time she reached Lady Pennington's, she was awash with misery. One glance in the mirror in the foyer told her she now resembled a vampire with her tear-reddened eyes. Even Lady Pennington's butler Garwood was prompted to offer a handkerchief after he helped her with his greatcoat.

"Something's in my eye," Evangeline said gruffly as she mopped her face. "A cinder or something. Frightful wind out there." Gentlemen did not walk around London crying.

"I'm sorry to hear that, sir. Is there anything I can provide that may assist you?"

"Thank you, Garwood, but no." No butler would have what she needed at the moment.

"I'll just announce you to Lady Pennington then. I believe she is awake but still abed."

Evangeline felt a bit stricken for intruding at such an early hour—she often forgot that normal people did not rise at the crack of dawn to put out a newspaper. She and Ben had been in the office forever, or so it seemed.

Garwood returned quickly and escorted her upstairs. Amy Pennington was with her cinnamon toast and tea amid a mound of lacy pillows and a patchwork counterpane. She wore a soft pink bed jacket and a frilly cap that covered her silver-blond hair, and was quite the most adorable thing Evangeline had seen in days.

Lady Pennington took one look at Evangeline and said, "Whiskey, Garwood. Bring up a bottle." She thrust her tray at him.

"Certainly, ma'am," Garwood said smoothly as if it were routine to drink before ten o'clock in the morning with a young gentleman in one's boudoir. He disappeared through the door and Evangeline swayed, suddenly feeling exhausted.

Lady Pennington patted the bed. "Sit before you fall down. What is wrong?"

"Everything!" Evangeline burst into tears, still clutching Garwood's handkerchief.

"Has that dreadful man left you then? More fool he for not recognizing what a jewel you are! I've half a mind to go to him and give him a piece of my mind, the bounder."

Evangeline's sob turned to a hiccupping laugh. "No need. He's asked me to marry him, Amy."

Lady Pennington broke out into a radiant smile. For an older woman, she still had most of her teeth and used them to her advantage. "But that's excellent news! Why are you so upset? You did say yes, didn't you?"

Evangeline blew her nose. "I couldn't."

"But why not? He won't keep asking you, you know. If you wait another ten years, you'll waste what's left of your youth."

"He presented it all as a business proposition. If I agree to marry him, he'll found a kind of home hospital for my father and others like him—children, too—it seems like the most unlikely place, but we could hire lots of staff to solve their unemployment problems and provide a safe haven for those in need."

"How extraordinary. And how kind of him. I know how much you take these burdens to heart. Think how different your life would be if you could get your people settled comfortably."

"There isn't a house big enough in the world, Amy."

"But such a place would be a start, wouldn't it? He must be very rich."

"I suppose." Evangeline knew he'd had the blunt for every frivolous amusement under the sun—she'd watched him spend it from the shadows.

"And he must love you very much," Lady Pennington said, thoughtful.

"If he does, he never said one word. Not one," Evangeline said bitterly. "He thinks he's of an age to finally settle down, and I'm handy. His *mother* wants grandchildren, and he says I might manage it."

"Ah." Lady Pennington was prevented from saying more by the arrival of Garwood, who did not blink to find young Mr. Ramsey on his mistress's bed. He deftly poured two tots of whiskey into crystal tumblers and left them, closing the door behind him.

"Oh, bother. Does he think I'm here for an assignation?" Evangeline asked, almost laughing at the absurdity.

"Garwood is very old-fashioned. I believe it is a trial for him to serve a gamekeeper's daughter and farmer's wife, but he had great loyalty to my late husband. He chose to come with me when James's cousin inherited Pennington House and I bought this one. Sometimes I think I should go back to Kent permanently so he can find a more suitable employer."

"Oh, I hope you don't move back to the farm. I'd miss you dreadfully. You're my only friend."

Lady Pennington raised her glass. "To friendship. Although, my dear, you need to have friends your own age."

"That's rather difficult at present. I'm neither fish nor fowl."

"I have never asked, but how did you decide on this

subterfuge? I do admire your figure in trousers, though—
I could never pull it off, even when I was the girl James
loved. Nature gave me panniers, I'm afraid."

Evangeline took a sip of whiskey, feeling warmer already. "When my father won the newspaper, we came
back to London. It was clear to me even then that his wits
were failing. I told him I'd hire someone to take over, but
after several disastrous interviews, I decided to do it myself. I've never been a beauty, or especially graceful, and
after the sneers I received from those I tried to hire—they
treated me like a brainless featherhead, Amy. As if a
woman couldn't know how things should be done. It
seemed the simplest solution—to become a man—far
fewer impediments to moving about society. No chaperone necessary. No ridiculous rules of propriety. As a girl
I'd sometimes larked about in boys' clothing, but now I
had reason to be serious. It's the rare woman who is permitted to be successful in business, and I wasn't interested
in being unsuccessful—we needed every penny of revenue. It's been an adventure, most of the time. Frank Hallett knew because I told him, but no one has recognized
my ruse, save you and Ben."

"More fools they. But I imagine if you didn't have a
woman's tender heart, *The London List* would not be the
force for good it is now. You should be proud. What does
Lord Gray plan to do about the paper if you marry him?"

"He didn't say. He hasn't spoken much of selling it
lately. I think he's enjoying himself."

"No doubt because he can gaze at you across the desk.
But would he want his wife involved in trade?"

"I'm not going to sit at home and tat and bake biscuits,"
Evangeline replied, feeling herself flush at her impolitic
words. "I mean, your lace is exquisite, and you're a marvelous cook, but I'm hopelessly undomesticated. When

forced to—and I was, often, as a girl—I can do the basics, but I'd much rather not."

Lady Pennington patted her hand. "No, you're a crusader. Which is why your Ben is so clever to hit upon a scheme that you cannot refuse."

"But I can't marry him!" Evangeline cried. "He'll break my heart."

"Pish. You're made of stronger stuff. Even if he disappoints, as all men are wont to do—women, too—you'll have your charity."

"I cannot promise to obey him."

"Well, you can say the words and keep your fingers crossed beneath your bridal bouquet. I did so twice."

"Amy! You lied in church?"

"I'm sure I'm not the first. The point of marriage is not obedience—not for either wife or husband. A good marriage provides congenial companionship. Give and take and compromise for a common cause. You don't want to be a lonely old woman like me."

"Oh! You shame me. How selfish I am to go on—"

"Stop. I'm honored you chose to come here. But I admit I've been thinking of looking for a man again. Perhaps after Susan has found a husband this spring. I can put an ad in your paper." Her china blue eyes twinkled.

Evangeline managed to keep her mouth from gaping open. "I shall be happy to oblige to see you married again."

"You foolish girl! As if I want to spoil my golden years catering to some peevish man. I am surprisingly content living in Town with all this luxury. But it wouldn't go amiss if every now and then I had someone to warm my bed."

Now Evangeline couldn't help but show her shock.

"Close your mouth dear. You'll catch flies if any are brave enough to live through this nasty winter. Do you suppose because I am nearly sixty that I've lost all desire? However, most men my age are not appealing. And they, despite their handicaps, are looking for a silly young thing to produce heirs, not a plump country grandmama. No, no more husbands. If Garwood were not so very stiff-necked, I'd make him an offer, though he'd probably drop dead. He's quite a fine looking fellow, don't you think?"

Evangeline choked, then threw her head back and laughed so hard she began to cry again. Lady Pennington took her to her capacious bosom, heedless of the damp to her bed jacket. "There, there. Let it all out. And you know you must accept Lord Gray's proposal. Your marriage may start off as a convenience for the both of you, but I bet one of my lemon scones that it will turn into a love match. Wait and see."

Evangeline knew already that she loved Benton Gray, damn his glorious hazel green eyes. But she would lose her hard-won independence unless she kept him at arm's length. All the security in the world was not worth subjugating herself to the whims of a notorious rakehell.

"I'll think about it," Evangeline sniffed, even though her mind was nearly made up.

# CHAPTER 32

Evangeline had insisted that the banns be called, which was damned aggravating. Ben had been perfectly willing to pony up for another special license—if he could do it for that stuttering fool Maxwell, he could do it for himself.

He was as much a fool; he might not stutter, but the sight of Evie waltzing around the office in skirts had been enough to break his concentration. She had allowed him to furnish her with a new wardrobe as an early bride-gift, and wore fashionably elegant wigs which completely transformed her.

Mr. Ramsey was long-gone, rumored to be off to India with his lover. In his place was his sister, who had come to Ben brokenhearted at her brother's scandal. What could he do but hire the poor girl in his place? She also had a way with words, as anyone could see from reading the past few weeks' editions. And yes, wasn't he a generous-hearted soul for hiring the sister of the very scoundrel who'd blackened his name for so long? True, he'd kept Evelyn Ramsey on at first because the lad knew all the ins and outs of *The List,* but Evangeline was surprisingly smart for a woman. And they would not be caught in their own scandal, because Ben had done the right, practical thing and proposed almost immediately. It was time he settled down—one would have to in all honesty agree he'd sown enough wild oats to provide a kingdom's worth of porridge.

Evangeline Ramsey might have a bad brother, but she was a virginal spinster, caring singlehandedly for her father—not a beauty, to be sure, but anyone might admire her great height and bearing. One didn't dare to speak against her in any case, for it was obvious Ben was protective of his future wife, keeping her to himself rather than dragging her off to ton parties. All the head-scratching and whispering didn't seem to affect him at all, and it was reluctantly acknowledged that Lord Benton Alexander Dunbarton Gray was not the amusing man he used to be.

Ben hadn't much to laugh about lately—Evie's father had been too ill to leave his bed to attend their wedding, and she would not hear of marrying without his presence. It was not his deteriorating mind that was the problem, but a common cold that had laid him low now for over a month. If anything, the news of his daughter's impending marriage seemed to break through his fog, and he was nearly as impatient as Ben to see the matter accomplished. So it was enormous relief on all sides when he improved enough so they could finally set the wedding date for the first of March, a scant three months from the time Ben had stormed into the offices of *The London List* and ogled Evie's backside.

He was ogling it right now. Ben had eschewed any sort of bachelor celebration and was spending the night before his wedding—the scandalous whole of it—with his beloved in his bed. He couldn't believe he had talked her into staying, but of course it hadn't been painless. He'd been forced to add Patsy to his household staff despite her glaring unsuitability as a lady's maid. Severson was not happy, but Callum and John and the rest of the younger men were tripping over themselves to impress the girl. There was bound to be trouble belowstairs, and Ben was steeling himself for a lifetime of it on all the floors of his house.

However, at the moment trouble was far from his mind. Evie reclined on his bed, reading a book. Yes, damn it, reading. The fact that she did it naked was some consolation, but he couldn't help but want her to toss the bloody thing on the floor and pay him some attention. If she looked up, she would see his robe tenting into the next street. He cleared his throat.

"Did you say something?"

"Would it matter if I did? What is that you're reading, anyway?" He sounded petulant even to himself.

"Don't be a bore, Ben. I was just making good use of my time while you bathed." She shut the book and smiled up at him like a damn Delilah.

"It would have been better if you had joined me," he grumbled, untying his robe and sinking into the mattress.

"Are you saying I'm dirty? I took a bath before your coachman picked me up."

She looked clean. She looked *delicious*. Downright lickable. "I can't tell." He took an experimental sniff. "Still the sandalwood? What about all that fancy French perfume I gave you?"

"You really have to stop giving me things, you know. All those fripperies are a dreadful waste of money when so many of our countrymen are going hungry."

"Evie, I'm giving away my money to strangers as fast as I can make it. At least let me spend a little of it on you. It pleases me."

Her lips turned up. "And you must be pleased as often as possible."

"I must. I must be pleased fairly soon or I'll go mad."

"Oh, you men are always complaining—you're *in pain* from your lustful nature, or some such, trying to wheedle your way up some poor girl's skirts."

"You're not wearing any."

Evie looked down at herself. "Why, I'm not. How shocking. Are you in pain, my lord?"

"I'm dying, Evie. Only you can save me."

She laughed. "What rubbish. I suppose that line has worked for you a time or two."

He'd never said anything like it before, but she didn't need to know. Theirs was, after all, a business arrangement. "Is it working now?"

"It might be. You might have to do some more persuading."

He could do that, and did. His first attempt at persuasion was to place his tongue into her feminine core, which she obligingly opened to him. Worshipping her with his mouth was not difficult, and she seemed vested in the outcome, which was not long in coming. He glided up her body, still using his tongue as a disarming weapon, teasing her skin as she shivered, using his fingers to touch what his mouth didn't. He was as persuasive as he could be, limited as he was by only two hands and one wicked tongue. But there was something left in his arsenal, which Evie to her credit had found as she came out of her sensual stupor.

Her grip was velvet, her intentions clear. Turnabout was fair play, and she wriggled on the bed until she was able to take him into the lush heaven of her mouth. Ben forgot who was persuading who—whom? Correct grammar was equally distant at this moment. He lay flat on his back, utterly captivated and happy to be at her sweetest mercy.

But he wanted to finish this round of their evening deep inside her body, his own covering hers in primal possession. Some might call him old-fashioned. He simply called himself lucky that tonight would be repeated for the rest of his life until he drew his last breath. Ben was optimistic that Evie would keep him entranced until he didn't have a tooth in his head. She'd had an unaccountably strong hold on him so far without really trying. What would she be like if he could make her love him?

For he would. He had years to practice and a fortune to fritter away on her pet causes. She couldn't deny him forever.

If they had a child together, their bond would grow even stronger. He might plant his seed in her tonight, now that their marriage was on the morrow. There was no need to be careful, no scandal to skirt. He could lose himself and find himself, all at the same time.

"Evie." Stark need was upon him. She raised her black eyes, looking much as the first temptress Evie must have to poor Adam. "I want to come inside you."

She gave his cock one more agonizing kiss, then settled back for him to have his way. He hoped it was her way as well, this union of their bodies. Tomorrow he would parrot words in church that had been written centuries ago, but tonight was his true, wordless pledge. He would be the man she needed for as long as they were blessed to live.

Ben looked into her eyes through each twist and thrust, until his crisis was near. He had to kiss her, taste her, consume her as he emptied himself into her perfection. They were one, though two hearts beat frantically. She had his, and he would make it his life's work to earn hers.

# $\mathscr{C}$HAPTER 33

*March 1, 1821*

There was a tentative tap at the bedroom door.

"Bloody hell. This is our wedding night! Now what?"

"Hush, Ben. It's not as if you have waited months to take my virginity. You bedded me just this morning, and very satisfactorily, too. Come!"

Severson poked his head in, keeping his eyes firmly fixed on the ground. Evangeline was still covered from head to toe in Ben's robe, which she preferred to the useless lacy confections he'd bought for her. She had pulled up the covers to her chin besides, so the poor man didn't need to look so embarrassed.

"Lord Gray, Lady Gray, I hesitate to intrude. But there is a couple downstairs who are most anxious to see you. They say they were bound for your wedding when the axle of their carriage broke."

Ben had relented and agreed to appear in print one last time. He'd allowed her to put notice of their engagement and future wedding on the front page when she had been stumped for a story last month, but the exact details had been private. Who could these well-wishers be?

"We didn't invite anyone besides our parents and Lady

Pennington to the wedding," Ben grumped. To his mind the wedding this morning had been a poky affair, with old Severson of all people serving as his best man, but Evangeline had been adamant. No bridal veil and brace of bridesmaids for her. When she was ready, she'd step into society on Ben's arm. Until then, she wanted him all to herself, just to make sure he really was sufficiently reformed—she planned to make sure of it every single evening and mornings besides.

In a month or two she might dispense with those itchy wigs and go about in public in her own fashionably shorn locks. Ben wanted her to grow out her hair again, but she rather liked the freedom of short hair. If she had to give up her trousers, she could at least have something of Mr. Ramsey left.

"Who are they?"

"A Major and Mrs. Ripton-Jones, my lady. Perfectly respectable people, if I'm any judge of character."

"Imaculata!" Evangeline gasped.

"No, my lady. The gentleman called her Anne."

"Severson, offer Major and Mrs. Ripton-Jones some refreshment. We'll be down shortly." Evangeline jumped out of bed. "Oh, good lord, she's married the old gent. When she said she would have taken ancient Lord Hastings as a husband, I didn't believe her."

"What the devil are you talking about?" Ben asked.

"Surely you remember Lady Imaculata Egremont."

Ben lost the ruddy color on his cheeks. "I swear I never touched her, Evie. I admit I did *see* her. It was hard not to. And I suppose she pursued me a bit. But she was a wild little thing, too wild even for me. I love only you and will always be true."

"Oh, shut up and get dressed, Ben. I never told you, but she came to me before Christmas. With a gun, actually. She was behind all those strange events at the office. The broken window and the honey in the box of sorts, etcetera. I thought it best to place Lady Imaculata far out of reach in a position in a gentleman's household."

Ben's response was comical. "What? Are you all right? Of course you are—here you stand with that lunatic grin on your face. You found that scatterbrained—and apparently dangerous—girl a job? As what? Mischief maker-in-chief? Evie, what have you done? Think of all the ads her father's placed in the paper! Lord Egremont will come after you. He's been crazed to get her back since she disappeared."

"I imagine so. I'll explain later.

"But it's our wedding night," Ben grumbled, picking up his breeches from a chair.

"And we have many more nights ahead, my darling. Especially if you love only me and will always be true."

Ben paused, one foot tangled in his pants leg. "My God. I just said that, didn't I?"

"Yes, and without a priest's suggestion. For the record, I love you, too."

Ben's breeches dropped to the floor. "Ah, Evie, what fools we've been. I thought you married me for the money for your charity projects." He shuffled toward her, somewhat hampered by the fabric at his ankles, and took her in his arms.

"Don't be absurd. I married you for you. How could I not? I've loved you since you were twenty years old. I must say I like how you've grown up."

"I can show you just how much I've grown—"

"Yes, yes. I have eyes. Put that thing away for half an hour. I am just dying of curiosity. And just maybe we'll have an exclusive for the paper next week!"

"The paper. Always the paper." Ben brushed his lips at the back of her neck and her every hair stood on end.

"Printers' ink is in my blood, I'm afraid. Be a lamb and do up these buttons."

Reluctantly Ben got them both dressed and they found their uninvited guests in the double parlor. Evangeline managed to not gape too obviously at the darkly hand-some man who held a sandwich to the lips of Lady Imac-ulata Egremont with his right hand, the left sleeve of his coat pinned neatly to his side. The couple both hastily rose from the little table, Imaculata blushing in competition with her back-to-its-original color red hair, which was also neatly pinned in place.

"Evangeline! I wish you happy! Gareth and I read about the impending wedding in *The London List* and wanted to come to thank you in person. I'm so sorry we've disturbed you at this late hour."

Evangeline smiled. "Nonsense. It's not even eight o'clock."

"But it's our *wedding night*," Ben continued to complain.

"I say, I am sorry. My wife insisted we see you as soon as we got to Town, Lord Gray. When my Annie wants something, it's hard to deny her. I'm sure you know the feeling."

"I'm afraid I do, Major. Please be seated. Well, *Annie,* I see congratulations are due all the way around." Ben looked at the new Mrs. Ripton-Jones expectantly.

"Gareth and I have come to town to get my money," Lady Imaculata said. "Now that I'm married, Papa will have to turn it over to me."

"But I asked her to marry me without knowing she was an heiress," Major Ripton-Jones was quick to add. "And I *did* know her history, once she told me who she really was. *The List* reached even my distant corner of Wales, as you know from my letter. And when she told me what had happened to her—my poor love." Major Ripton-Jones squeezed Imaculata's hand. "I've promised her not to kill the bastard with my one bare hand, but I don't mind telling you I'll enjoy making the old goat squirm tomorrow."

Ben was naturally puzzled, and Evangeline could see she had some explaining to do later. "What can we do to help?"

"Just write a story about us. Gareth is a genuine war hero, a fine man. I want to surprise those people who doubted I had a lick of sense in me. Explain I'm completely reformed. When our children come up to London, I don't want them to be ashamed."

"And find us a housekeeper. My Annie has many talents, but cooking and cleaning are not among them," Major Ripton-Jones said in his delightful Welsh burr.

"Done, on both counts," Evangeline said, rising from the settee. "Come see us tomorrow to give us the particulars of your courtship. I imagine it was very romantic."

Lady Imaculata—Annie, now—nodded. "Gareth saved my life when I burned his house down."

"Not the whole house, mind you, just the kitchen wing. And it was a mercy, if you know what I mean. We've been taking all our meals in the village inn since, but that's becoming somewhat inconvenient now that we think Annie is increasing." Major Ripton-Jones beamed at his wife, and her blushes intensified.

That was quick work. Ah. True love. Evangeline could see she needed to alter Major Ripton-Jones's entry in her notebook. What a perfectly delightful way to end the day.

Well, it wasn't ended yet. It was her wedding night, and many more delights were to come if she had anything to say about it.

Arrangements were made for the following day and good-byes were said. She and Ben stood alone in the parlor.

"I believe you have something more to tell me," Ben said, with an edge to his voice.

"And the particulars are too unpleasant to divulge on our wedding night. Let's just say I helped Lady Imaculata Egremont escape from an ogre. Ha! Lord Ogremont! Sometimes my wit positively astounds me."

"You are much too easily astounded." He was close now, his green eyes glittering. She put a few blackened fingers on his cheek.

"Don't be mulish, dearest. I didn't tell you everything because I wasn't looking for a knight in shining armor to save the world. I'd quite given up that such a man existed. Until you."

Ben fiddled with her buttons. "Don't try to sweet-talk me."

Evangeline lifted a winged dark brow. "I don't want to *talk* to you at all."

With a growl, Ben pounced. Evangeline prayed Severson would forget to collect the Ripton-Jones's supper tray until much later, for it seemed the baron was not going to formally consummate their marriage in the baroness's suite but on the parlor floor.

And she had no objection. How could she? Evangeline had her exclusive for next week's edition and a handsome new husband. Joined together, they'd give readers satisfaction as long as *The London List* landed on doorsteps and dining room tables.

But tonight was dedicated to a different sort of joining and a much more satisfying satisfaction than Evangeline's usual solution to a problem. She didn't need clever words or concise descriptions, for frankly Ben blasted all rational thought out of her head when he—

Oh. Yes. When he did that. And *that.*

"Did you say something, Evie?"

"No," she sighed happily. "I'm speechless."

Have you tried Maggie's Courtesan Court series?

*Mistress by Mistake*

### Scandal Is Only the Beginning . . .

Charlotte Fallon let her guarded virtue fall once—and she's paid dearly for it ever since. She swore she'd never succumb to men's desires again. But even a village spinster's life miles from temptation can't save her from a sister with no shame whatsoever. Or a heart that longs for more, whatever the cost . . .

Sir Michael Bayard found more than he expected in his bed when he finally joined his new mistress. He'd fantasized about her dewy skin and luscious curves, assured her understanding that what passed between them was mere dalliance. But he didn't expect the innocence and heat of her response in his arms. Nor her surprisingly sharp tongue once she was out of them . . .

A few days of abandon cannot undo the hard-learned lessons of a lifetime. Nor can an honest passion burn away the restraints of society's judgments. Unless, of course, one believes in nonsense like true love . . .

*Mistress by Midnight*

### First Comes Seduction . . .

As children, Desmond Ryland, Marquess of Conover, and Laurette Vincent were inseparable. As young adults, their friendship blossomed into love. But then fate intervened, sending them down different paths. Years later, Con still can't forget his beautiful Laurette. Now he's determined to make her his forever. There's just one problem. Laurette keeps refusing his marriage proposals. Throwing honor to the wind, Con decides that the only way Laurette will wed him is if he thoroughly seduces her. . . .

### Then Comes Marriage . . .

Laurette's pulse still quickens every time she thinks of Con and the scorching passion they once shared. She aches to taste the pleasure Con offers her. But she knows she can't. For so much has happened since they were last lovers. But how long can she resist the consuming desire that demands to be obeyed . . . ?

*Mistress by Marriage*

## Too Late for Cold Feet

Baron Edward Christie prided himself on his reputation for even temperament and reserve. That was before he met Caroline Parker. Wedding a scandalous beauty by special license days after they met did not inspire respect for his sangfroid. Moving her to a notorious lovebirds' nest as punishment for her flighty nature was perhaps also a blow. And of course talk has gotten out of his irresistible clandestine visits. Christie must put his wife aside—if only he can get her out of his blood first.

## Too Hot to Refuse

Caroline Parker was prepared to hear the worst: that her husband had determined to divorce her, spare them both the torture of passion they can neither tame nor escape. But his plan is wickeder than any she's ever heard. Life as his wife is suffocating. But she cannot resist becoming her own husband's mistress . . .

*Master of Sin*

### Flying from Sin . . .

Andrew Rossiter has used his gorgeous body and angelic face for all they're worth—shocking the proper, seducing the willing, and pleasuring the wealthy. But with a tiny son depending on him for rescue, suddenly discretion is far more important than desire. He'll have to bury his past and quench his desires—fast. And he'll have to find somewhere his deliciously filthy reputation hasn't yet reached. . . .

### . . . Into Seduction

Miss Gemma Peartree seems like a plain, virginal governess. True, she has a sharp wit and a sharper tongue, but handsome Mr. Ross wouldn't notice Gemma herself. Or so she hopes. No matter how many sparks fly between them, she has too much to hide to catch his eye. But with the storms of a Scottish winter driving them together, it will be hard enough to keep her secrets. Keeping her hands to herself might prove entirely impossible. . . .

Printed in the United States
by Baker & Taylor Publisher Services